YOU MAY RENEW YOUR
BOOKS BY PHONE 415215

SUBJECT TO RECALL
Item on Loan From
QL/P-3 Lancashire

1 4 APR 2010

Our Ref: 1617005
Your Ref: 1605147

1 7 MAY 2021

LL 60

AUTHOR
HUNTER, E

CLASS
F

23. JAN 97

17. AUG

TITLE   Criminal conversation

Lancashire
County
Council
THE LANCASHIRE LIBR
Library Headquarters,
143, Corporation St.,
PRESTON PR1 2UQ
100% recycled paper

D1342863

CRIMINAL CONVERSATION

Also by EVAN HUNTER

NOVELS

1954: The Blackboard Jungle
1956: Second Ending
1958: Strangers When We Meet
1959: A Matter of Conviction
1961: Mothers and Daughters
1964: Buddwing
1966: The Paper Dragon
1967: A Horse's Head
1968: Last Summer
1969: Sons
1971: Nobody Knew They Were There
1972: Every Little Crook and Nanny
1973: Come Winter
1974: Streets of Gold
1976: The Chisholms
1981: Love, Dad
1983: Far from the Sea
1984: Lizzie

SHORT STORY COLLECTIONS

1963: Happy New Year, Herbie
1972: The Easter Man

CHILDREN'S BOOKS

1952: Find the Feathered Serpent
1959: The Remarkable Harry
1961: The Wonderful Button
1976: Me and Mr. Stenner

SCREENPLAYS

1959: Strangers When We Meet
1962: The Birds
1972: Fuzz
1979: Walk Proud

TELEPLAYS

1979: The Chisholms
1980: The Legend of Walks Far Woman
1986: Dream West

CRIMINAL CONVERSATION

Evan Hunter

Hodder & Stoughton
LONDON SYDNEY AUCKLAND

Copyright © 1994 by Hui Corporation. All rights reserved

First published in Great Britain in 1994
by Hodder and Stoughton
A Division of Hodder Headline PLC
Published in the United States of America by Warner Books, Inc.

The right of Evan Hunter to be identified as the Author of
the Work has been asserted by him in accordance with the
Copyright, Designs and Patents Act 1988.

10 9 8 7 6 5 4 3 2 1

All rights reserved. No part of this publication may be
reproduced, stored in a retrieval system, or transmitted,
in any form or by any means without the prior written
permission of the publisher, nor be otherwise circulated
in any form of binding or cover other than that in which
it is published and without a similar condition being
imposed on the subsequent purchaser.

A CIP catalogue record for this title is available from
The British Library

ISBN 0 340 59885 9

Printed and bound in Great Britain by
Mackays of Chatham PLC, Chatham, Kent

Hodder and Stoughton Ltd
A Division of Hodder Headline PLC
338 Euston Road
London NW1 3BH

06137240

This is for my daughter,
AMANDA FINLEY

LANCASHIRE LIBRARY			
LL		LM	6FLt
LK		LH	
LA		LC	
LW		LB	
LS		LF	
LZ		ML	

Although several real places, organizations, institutions, and agencies are mentioned by name in these pages, all of the characters and events portrayed are fictitious.

—And so the conversation slips
Among velleities and carefully caught regrets
Through attenuated tones of violins
Mingled with remote cornets
And begins.

T. S. Eliot
Portrait of a Lady

CRIMINAL CONVERSATION

1: DECEMBER 21–DECEMBER 30

Luretta Barnes was the smartest girl Sarah taught. Rap as poetry, poetry as rap was a good concept. Luretta disagreed with it.

"Ice-T ain't Allen Ginsberg," she told Sarah. "No way you gonna compare *Soul on Ice* to *Howl*. No way, Mrs. Welles."

A scholarship student, Luretta was the only black girl in the entire sophomore class. The only one now taking a stand *against* rap as poetry.

"You want to call it doggerel," she said, "that's fine by me. But poetry? Come on, Mrs. Welles. Callin rap *poetry* is like callin Michael Jackson *Pavarotti*."

The other girls all laughed.

Luretta soaked it up.

Gorgeous fourteen-year-old with a smile like starshine, hair done up in ten thousand braids, little colored glass beads strung in them, could have been a model in an instant, wanted to be a lawyer. She'd somehow learned from one of the other girls that Mrs. Welles's husband was a lawyer in the DA's Office. One day, she stopped Sarah in the halls, asked if her husband could use a good assistant. Sharpen pencils, empty trash baskets, whatever, it'd beat her after-school job at McDonald's. Sarah said she was pretty sure all such jobs were civil service, which meant taking an exam and so on. She said she'd ask her husband, though. Michael had confirmed it.

"He's missin out on a future *star*," Luretta had said, grinning her celestial smile.

Sarah was now qualifying the comparison, hedging the lesson so that rap could be considered *protest* poetry, or perhaps poetic *commentary*, in much the same way that Lennon's or McCartney's lyrics for the Beatles could rightfully be considered such.

" 'Eleanor Rigby,' for example," she said, "is really a poem of protest, wouldn't you say? An elegy for the lonely? A cry for pity? And it's social commentary as well, isn't it? Eleanor keeping her face in a jar by the door? Father MacKenzie giving his sermon and no one showing up for it?"

Most of these fifteen-year-olds knew "Eleanor Rigby," but just barely. To many of them, the Beatles might have been a quartet of strolling Elizabethan minstrels. McCartney was in his fifties, after all, an old man in the eyes of these precocious adolescents. Sarah plunged ahead regardless. She'd have brought in some of her own tapes if she'd known she'd be taking this tack—which by the way wasn't a bad one. Instead, she was winging it now only because Luretta had taken her unexpected position.

"Or what's 'I Am the Walrus,' " she said, gathering steam, "if not a protest against England's tax laws? All the graphic references to death and dying? You've all heard the expression 'Nothing's sure but death and taxes,' haven't you?"

No one had heard the expression. Smartest kids in the city of New York here at Greer, none of them had ever heard about death and taxes or, for that matter, "I Am the Walrus."

Except Luretta.

"Lennon *was* a poet," she said. "You're comparing pigs and pork chops, they're not the same at all."

"Excuse me, but who's *Lennon*?" one of the girls asked.

"Spare me," Luretta said, and rolled her lovely brown eyes.

"John Lennon," Sarah said.

"Wasn't he the man some nut shot outside the Dakota?" another girl asked.

Good lesson to teach sometime, Sarah thought. The way people are remembered. Would Woody Allen be remembered as a child molester or as the preeminent director of his time? Would Oliver North be remembered as a hero to his country or a traitor to the sacred precepts of democracy? And would John Lennon, after all was said and done, be remembered solely as the man some nut shot outside an apartment building on New York's Upper West Side?

The bell rang.

"Nuts," Sarah said, and smiled.

She said this every day at the end of each and every one of her classes. It was an absolutely genuine expression of regret; she really did hate the sound of the bell that signaled the end of a class. But it had become nonetheless something of a signature trademark.

Luretta came up to her.

"That might've been condescending," she said. "Calling them poets just cause they're black."

"Good point," Sarah said. "We'll discuss it next time."

Michael always sided with their daughter. No matter what the issue, he always came down hard on Mollie's side. He was doing the same thing now. Sarah thought she'd made her point clearly enough at the dinner table. There was no sense putting up a Christmas tree when they'd be leaving for St. Bart's on the twenty-sixth. Today was the twenty-first. Even if they managed to get it up and decorated by tomorrow night . . .

"And by the way," she said. "Anything taller than six feet is out of the question."

"Six feet! That's a *shrub*, Mom!"

This from Mollie.

Twelve years old, secure in the knowledge that her father was defending her case and the verdict was already in. They had just come down from their apartment. It was close to seven-thirty, and snow was falling; it made Sarah feel even more like Scrooge attacking the Cratchits.

"Even if it's decorated by tomorrow night," she said, picking up her earlier thought, "we'll be gone on Saturday and we won't be back . . ."

"We can enjoy it while we're here," Michael said, grinning like a bribed judge, and looking brawny and woodsy in an olive-green loden coat with toggle fasteners, the hood pulled up over his head.

"Sure, for four whole days," Sarah said. "We won't be home till the third. By that time, with no one here to water it . . ."

"We can leave a key with the super."

"I don't like him going into the apartment when we're not here."

"I'll give him ten bucks."

"Give *me* the ten bucks, Dad," Mollie said. "*I'll* stay home and water it."

"Sure you will," Michael said, and Mollie giggled.

"Who'll put up the lights?" Sarah asked.

Last-ditch stand. Plea bargaining.

"I will," Michael said.

"No taller than eight feet," she said.

"Deal," he said, and took her hand, and winked at Mollie.

They walked through the gently drifting flakes, scanning the trees lining the sidewalk, holding hands and deliberately matching strides as if they were still in college together, strolling across campus. At five-eleven, Michael was three inches taller than she was, but her legs were long and she had no trouble keeping up. She had dressed tonight in jeans and boots and a navy peacoat, a red woolen hat pulled down over her short blond hair. Mollie rushed ahead of them, eager to find a suitable tree, gushing over every huge one that caught her eye.

"Mom!"

Her voice rising on a triumphant note of discovery.

Warily, Sarah went to her.

She was standing beside a stubbled, potbellied man wearing brown woolen gloves with the fingers and thumbs cut off, a green hat with earflaps, baggy brown corduroy trousers, and soggy high-topped workmen's boots. His row of trees, strung with tiny lights from one end to the other and flanked by a Chinese restaurant on the left and a dry-cleaning shop on the right, leaned against the brick side of the building behind them. One of his gloved hands was buried in a sheaf of branches and wrapped around the slim upper trunk of the tree Mollie had selected. Chewing on the stub of a dead cigar, he raised his eyebrows expectantly, awaiting Sarah's verdict.

Her daughter stood before the casual cascade of strung lights, proud that she had found such a perfectly formed tree, no taller than the eight feet Sarah had prescribed, full and thick and dense with the bluest green needles. Touched by the faint glow of the lights, Mollie's hair—cut straight to the shoulders and brushed in casual bangs on her forehead—took on the momentary look of soft beaten gold. Snowflakes fluttered past her face. Her eyes were wide in anticipation. A sudden gust of wind sent tendrils of blond hair drifting across her face, passing over her pale blue eyes like a silken curtain. All the innocence of Christmas seemed to glow in those suddenly revealed eyes, luminous and hopeful, as Mollie stood beside her cherished prize, her ferreted and coveted treasure, her eyes begging approval and acceptance. For one evanescent moment, Sarah felt this would be the last time she ever saw such innocence on the face of her child.

"It's lovely," she said, and went to her and held her close.

★　★　★

The message was on the answering machine when they got back to the apartment. The machine's red message light blinked like a monster's eye.

"Michael," the woman's voice said, "this is Jackie Diaz. Can you get back to me right away? I'm still at the office."

They both looked up at the clock.

Six forty-seven.

Seconds later, the machine's metallic voice announced the date and time of the call.

"Monday, December twenty-first, six thirty-one P.M."

"Who's Jackie Diaz?" Sarah asked.

"Narcotics, Manhattan South."

"It can wait till after dinner," Sarah said.

"Might be important," Michael said.

He was already reaching for the phone.

"Michael, please," she said. "I'm about to start . . ."

"This'll just take a sec," he said, and looked through his personal directory for Jackie's number. Frowning, Sarah went to the freezer. Michael dialed. On the other end, the phone rang and rang and . . .

"Narcotics."

"Detective Diaz, please."

"Who's calling?"

"ADA Welles."

"Hold, please."

Michael waited. Across the room, Sarah was noisily tossing plastic dishes into the microwave. In the television den, Mollie was tuned in to MTV.

"Michael, hi, sorry, I was down the hall. Can you get here right away?"

"What is it?"

"I just ran a routine buy-bust, six ounces of coke from a turd named Dominick Di Nobili. I've been questioning him for the past two hours. He's ready to squeal like a pig."

"About what?"

"Mob shit, Michael."
"Be in my office in half an hour."

The light snow had turned into a full-fledged blizzard.

If no one had mentioned the mob, no one would have been here on a night like tonight; the meeting would have been postponed at least till the snow stopped. But someone *had* mentioned the mob, and so Detective/Second Grade Jacqueline Diaz and Deputy Unit Chief Michael Welles were here in room 667 at One Hogan Place to hear what Dominick Di Nobili had to say for himself.

Jackie was twenty-three or -four, Michael guessed, a diminutive redhead of Puerto Rican ancestry, born and raised in Brooklyn, and educated at John Jay. She was still wearing the blue jeans and hooded sweatshirt she'd been wearing when the routine buy went down. Michael had worked with her before, when she was an undercover with Street Crime and he was a prosecutor in the Career Criminal program. She liked working with him, and she'd called him now because it looked like she'd stumbled onto real meat in his new bailiwick, which happened to be organized crime.

Di Nobili had begun shaking in his boots the minute she flashed the tin and clapped the cuffs on him and her informant, who'd been taken off in another car, never to be heard from since; good snitches were hard to come by, and she didn't want to burn him. Di Nobili, on the other hand, was looking at fifteen to life on an A-1 felony, which was the sale of the six ounces of cocaine. Even before she read him his rights, he was begging for mercy, telling her they'd kill him, telling her she had to let him go, this was the first time he'd done anything like this . . .

"A virgin, huh?"

"No, I mean it, please, you got to listen to me, they'll kill me, I mean it."

"Who's that?"

"*All* of them!"

"Which narrowed the field a bit," she told Michael now.
"What it turned out . . ."

What it turned out was that Di Nobili, although a waiter
by profession, happened to be an inveterate horseplayer by
avocation. Worse than that, he was a gambler who invariably
lost, and it seemed he was now into a Manhattan loan shark
for some fifteen thousand bucks, and had failed to meet last
week's minimum payment of $750. This oversight had
earned him a severe beating, witness his two black eyes and
his swollen lip. Moreover, the shy had threatened to kill him
if he didn't come up with the *full* fifteen K plus *two* weeks'
interest by Christmas Day, which was arbitrarily chosen as
settlement date, little coal in Dom's stocking this year.

"Now this is where it gets really interesting," Jackie
said. "Di Nobili takes his case to a lady friend of his who's
very well connected, hmm? Her connection, according to Di
Nobili, is a capo in Queens, where Di Nobili lives. The
Colotti family, do you know the people?"

"I know the people," Michael said.

"I go Uh-huh, because now I'm beginning to smell roses
here, even though I know he may be full of shit because he
got caught selling six fuckin ounces of coke. The capo he's
talking about is the lady friend's cousin, and he owns a restaurant in Forest Hills. His name is Jimmy Angelli, also known
as Jimmy Angels, ring a bell?"

"Vaguely."

"So the lady friend takes Dom to her cousin, and Dom
explains that he can't *possibly* come up with fifteen K plus
interest before Christmas, at which time this loan shark'll kill
him. He really believes this. Now *you* know and *I* know that
nobody ever kills anybody who owes him money because
then he'll *never* get the money back. But *Dom* doesn't know
this, so he's wetting his pants because he thinks he's going
to hell for Christmas. Jimmy Angels listens patiently because
Dom's lady friend *is* his cousin, after all, and he owes at least

this much respect to his father's brother. He asks Dom who this loan shark might be, and Dom tells him it's a person named Salvatore Bonifacio, also known as Sal the . . ."

"Sal the Barber," Michael said. "The Faviola family in Manhattan."

"The Faviola family," Jackie said, and nodded. "Who so far, since Anthony went bye-bye, is still on good terms with the Colotti family."

"That's what we think, anyway," Michael said.

"That's what we think, too. Territories nicely divided, nobody killing anybody for stupid reasons. So *far*."

"So far," Michael agreed.

"Anyway . . . because of his cousin, Jimmy Angels agrees to go see a capo he knows in the Faviola family, to ask if he, the capo, could maybe ask Sal the Barber to take the pressure off this very good friend of Jimmy's dear cousin. The capo tells Jimmy he'll see what he can do . . . this all took place yesterday, by the way. Dom's latest payment was due Friday, which is when they ran him through the wringer. Saturday he didn't show up for work because he looked like a steam roller ran over him, and Sunday he went to see his lady friend, who took him to Jimmy Angels and so on."

"Got it."

"This morning the Faviola capo . . ."

"What's *his* name?"

"Di Nobili doesn't know."

"Okay."

". . . calls Jimmy Angels with a proposition. He goes through all the respect bullshit first—this is a matter of respect, you owe someone money, you don't pay him it shows a lack of respect, ta-da ta-da ta-da—and then he tells him if his cousin's friend is willing to work off the debt, they might have an errand he can run for them. And if he does okay the first time, maybe there'll be *other* errands in the future, till he works off the debt completely, how does *that* sound? You understand, this is strictly a *favor* the Faviola family is doing for the Colotti family, respect, honor, all that bullshit all over again."

"Let me guess what the errand was," Michael said.

"You're ahead of me."

"Dom is the courier who delivers six ounces of cocaine for them . . ."

". . . and innocently walks into a sting we've been setting up for weeks. Neither family *knew* what Dom was walking into, of course, they *still* don't know, for that matter. Which is why this is so sweet, huh? Before, he only owed the Faviola loan shark. But now he *also* has to worry about the Colottis cause they went to bat for him. He's in terror, Michael, believe me," Jackie said, and grinned. "He's ready to sell his mother."

"You done good," Michael said, and returned the grin. "Let's go get him."

There was neither a video camera nor a tape recorder in the room, no one taking shorthand, no one scribbling notes, no one watching through a one-way mirror. The conversation would be strictly off the record.

Di Nobili was a bear of a man wearing a sports jacket and gray flannel slacks over a blue turtleneck sweater. Brown loafers. Hair thinning a bit. Clean-shaven. Except for the shiners and the fat lip, he looked to Michael like a suburban husband who'd once played college football. According to Jackie, though, the only athletic activity Di Nobili had ever performed—aside from rumored assaults hither and yon— was bodybuilding during the six years he'd spent at Ossining on a B-felony conviction. His record indicated that he was thirty-nine years old, three years older than Michael. Even if he took the minimum fall on the pending charges, he'd be fifty-four when he got out of jail. He wasn't worried about jail, though; he was worried about getting killed.

"You understand, don't you," Michael said, "that you belong to us?"

"I understand that."

"We'll relocate you, and keep you safe from these people, but that means you'll do exactly what we tell you to do. Otherwise, you can roll the dice and take your chances with *us* in court or *them* on the street."

"I want to cooperate here," Di Nobili said.

"Good. I want you to read this and sign it."

"What is it?"

"A waiver of arraignment," Michael said, and handed it to him. The paper read:

WAIVER OF SPEEDY ARRAIGNMENT

I, <u>Dominick Di Nobili</u>, understand that I have been arrested for violation of <u>Section 220.43</u> of the New York Penal Law [criminal sale of a controlled substance in the first degree].

I have been read my constitutional rights by Detective <u>Second Grade Jacqueline Diaz</u> of the New York City Police Department, and understand those rights.

I have also been informed of my right to a speedy arraignment . . .

"Nobody informed me of this," Di Nobili said.

"You're being informed now," Michael said.

. . . my right to a speedy arraignment and understand this right.

Fully aware of my rights, I am desirous of cooperating with the authorities. However, no promises whatsoever have been made to me regarding . . .

"I thought you said you were gonna relocate me."

"*If* you're not shitting us," Jackie said. "If you *are* shitting us, we've still got the flash as evidence, and all bets . . ."

"The what?"

"The *flash* money. The twenty-three grand you accepted for the dope."

"Oh."

"If you're shitting us, all bets are off."

"I'm not shitting you."

"Fine. Then sign the fuckin waiver," Jackie said.

"I want to read it all first."

. . . whatsoever have been made to me regarding my cooperation.

In order to fully cooperate with the authorities, I consent to the delay of my arraignment. I do this knowing that I have the right to be speedily arraigned but desire not to be immediately arraigned because of the impact such arraignment might have on my ability to cooperate.

"What does that mean?" Di Nobili asked.

"It means if we arraign you, they'll know you were busted."

"Oh."

"And you'll be worthless to us."

"Oh."

"So?" Michael said. "You want to sign it?"

"Yeah, okay," Di Nobili said.

He signed the waiver and dated it. Jackie witnessed it.

"Okay," Michael said, "where'd you pick up the dope?"

"A butcher shop in Brooklyn."

"Who gave it to you there?"

"Guy named Artie. I never saw him before in my life. I was supposed to go in and tell him I was Dominick here for the pork chops. He gave me a package wrapped like meat. In like that white paper, you know?"

"Who told you what to say?"

"Sal the Barber. He's the only one I know in this whole thing."

"How about Jimmy Angels? You know him, too, don't you?"

"I never met him. He's my friend's cousin."

"What's your friend's name?"

"I want to leave her out of this."

"Listen," Jackie said sharply. "Maybe you didn't understand the man. You want to play golf here or you want to fuck around?"

"Huh?" Di Nobili said.

"Tell him your girlfriend's name. The man's deputy chief of the Organized Crime Unit, we're wasting his fucking time here."

"Her name is Lucy."

"Lucy what?"

"Angelli. She's Jimmy's cousin."

"Sal told you where to pick up the stuff, is that right?"

"Yeah."

"And where to deliver it."

"Yeah, he gave me the name Anna Garcia, I was supposed to meet her outside this takee-outee joint in Chinatown."

"That's the name I was going by," Jackie said, and smiled. "I went with another undercover, guy weighs two hundred pounds, case old Dom here decided to hit me on the head and *steal* the dope."

"Yeah," Di Nobili said glumly.

"What else?" Michael asked.

"He said I should expect twenty-three grand in exchange for the coke."

"Sal did?"

"Yeah."

"Who were you supposed to deliver the money to?"

"Sal."

"Where?"

"A restaurant named La Luna."

"Where's that?"

"Fifty-eighth Street."

"You've met him there before?"

"Yeah. To make payments on the loan."

"What was he charging you?"

"Five points a week."

"Not exactly Chase Manhattan," Jackie said.

"When were you supposed to meet him?"

"You mean today?"

"Today, yes."

"Right after it went down."

"That was six o'clock," Jackie said. "That makes you a little late, Dom."

"Yeah, it makes me a little late," Di Nobili said, and started looking very worried again.

"I want you to call him," Michael said. "Have you got a number for him?"

"Yeah."

Michael went to a file cabinet across the room, opened a drawer, and took from it a wrapped telephone pickup the Tech Unit had bought at Radio Shack. Attaching the suction cup to the earpiece of his phone, he said, "This is what I want you to say to him. Tell him everything went down the way it was supposed to, but you had a flat tire, and you had to have it fixed, which the garage just finished doing. You got that so far?"

"No, I'm a fucking moron," Di Nobili said.

Michael looked at him.

"Mister," he said, "you want me to go home, is that it?"

"I'm sorry," Di Nobili said.

"Just keep on being an asshole," Michael said, "and I'm out of here in a minute. Capeesh?"

"Yeah, yeah."

"Good," he said, and plugged the cable into his taping and monitoring deck. "If he asks you what took so long to get a flat fixed, you tell him it's the holidays and the weather is bad."

"Will he buy that?" Jackie asked.

"I think so," Di Nobili said.

"Make *sure* he does," Michael said. "Tell him you'll bring the money to him now, but it might take a while, the streets haven't been plowed yet, traffic's backed up, whatever you want to say. I want to buy a few hours," Michael said, turning to Jackie, "give us time to wire him, set up the excuse for . . ."

"What do you mean?" Di Nobili said. "You're gonna *wire* me?"

"He still doesn't understand," Jackie said, shaking her head.

"You'll be going in wired, yes," Michael said. "Any problems with that?"

"No, sir."

"Good. Call him."

Di Nobili fished a slip of paper from his wallet, consulted it, and then, holding it in his left hand, punched out the number with his right hand. The equipment was set up so that everything being taped could be monitored simultaneously; Michael and Jackie both put on earphones. The phone rang once, twice, three times . . .

"La Luna," a man's voice said.

"Let me talk to Sal," Di Nobili said.

"Who's this?"

"Dominick Di Nobili."

"He knows you?"

"He knows me."

"Hold on."

Michael nodded approval. He noticed that Di Nobili had broken out in a cold sweat.

"Hello?"

A man's voice. Gruff.

"Sal?"

"Yeah."

"This is Dom."

"Where the fuck are you, Dom?"

"I'm in a garage on Canal Street. I just had a flat tire fixed."

"You know what time it is?"

"Yeah, it's late, I know."

"I been waitin for your call since six o'clock."

"I was lookin for a phone booth when I got the flat."

"How'd it go?"

"Fine."

"Any problems?"

"No problems."

"And you're where now?"

"The garage that fixed the flat. I got to pay my bill, and then I'm out of here."

"What took you all this time to get a flat fixed?"

"It's the holidays. Also the traffic's terrible. And I don't know this fuckin part of the city," he said, improvising. "Time I found an open garage . . ."

"So is it fixed now?"

"Yeah, I told you."

"So when can you get here? I been waitin here two fuckin hours for you."

"I can come there right now, you want me to."

"Yeah, do it."

"But I got to warn you, the roads are really terrible, Sal, it's a fuckin blizzard out there. It might take me a while t'get uptown, I mean it."

"You're on Canal, what the fuck's gonna take you so long to get to Fifty-eighth?"

"You should see it out there, Sal. There's cars stuck all over the place . . ."

"I don't give . . ."

". . . slippin and slidin, I never seen anything like this in my life."

"So get a dogsled. I don't give a shit it takes you till midnight, I'll be here waitin for you."

"Okay, but it might be a long wait, is all I'm sayin."

"I got nothin else planned," Sal said, and hung up.

Di Nobili looked at Michael.

"Good," Michael said.

It was close to ten o'clock when Di Nobili walked into La Luna Restaurant on Fifty-eighth Street and Eighth Avenue. Di Nobili was wearing under his clothing two pieces of equipment: a JBird digital disc recorder and a KEL transmitter. An empty car had been parked across the street from the restaurant. It was equipped with a repeater that would receive the signal from Di Nobili's transmitter and send it out again, at a much higher frequency, to the unmarked sedan in which Jackie and Michael were parked three blocks away. There would be *two* recordings made, one on the JBird's microchips, the other on the monitoring tape. They had warned Di Nobili not to sit too close to the clatter of silverware or china, or anywhere near a jukebox or a speaker. He had told them Sal usually conducted business in a quiet corner booth near the kitchen. Also, at this hour on a Monday night, there shouldn't be too many customers in the restaurant. They were hoping there wouldn't be.

Jackie had previously signed out for the twenty-three thousand they'd used in the buy-bust, but this was a whole new operation, and if Di Nobili's information proved useless, they would need the flash as evidence when they brought him to trial on the Section 220. Michael personally signed out for a fresh wad of cash—which happened to be five grand short. The shortage was what Dom would attempt to explain to Sal the Barber in the next ten minutes. This was why they'd needed to buy the extra time, so that Dom could reasonably account for how he'd happened to come up with eighteen thousand dollars instead of the twenty-three he'd got for the dope. They were hoping the cash discrepancy, and Dom's explanation for it, would lead to the next step in the escalation.

Neither of them was wearing earphones, which would have been noticeable from the sidewalk. Instead, the monitoring and recording equipment sat on the floor of the car, the volume control turned up. They waited expectantly now, a man and a woman who looked like a loving couple with eyes only for each other, but who were instead two law enforcement officers who were all ears. Softly, silently, the snow fell relentlessly on the car, covering it in white.

"Took you long enough," Sal said.

Sal Bonifacio, he of the gruff voice, the short temper, and the quick fists. Sal the Barber.

"Yeah, well, I told you," Dom said.

"Where's the money?"

"Right here."

Silence. Dom undoubtedly taking the envelope of cash out of his pocket, handing it over to Sal.

"She test it?"

"No."

"I'm surprised. Must be she trusts us, huh?"

Sal laughing. Dom joining in. Honor among thieves. Good cause for laughter.

"What'd she look like?"

"Who?"

"The cunt. Anna Garcia."

"Good-looking redhead."

In the car, Jackie whispered, "Thanks, Dom."

"What I hear, I wouldn't mind boffin her."

"Me neither," Dom said, and both men laughed again.

"Regular fan club," Jackie whispered.

"But she didn't test it, huh?" Sal said.

"She didn't say nothin about it, so I didn't say nothin, either."

"Good thinking. Did you count this money?"

"I counted it."

"Then why's there only eighteen here?"

Michael held his breath.

"Well . . . that's what I wanted to talk to you about,"
Dom said.

"I'm listenin."

"You see . . ."

"This better be good, Dominick. Cause if you think
what happened to you *Friday* was bad, then you don't know
what can *really* happen when I'm pissed off. Where's the other
fuckin five grand?"

"You see, on the way here . . ."

"Two fuckin hours to get here, Dominick. You call me
eight o'clock, you get here ten o'clock. What are you, the
Two Hour Man, Dominick? You get the cash at six, you call
me at eight, you get here at ten, and you're five grand *short*?
Where's the rest of the fuckin money, Dominick?"

"I lost it in a crap game."

"You *what*?"

"I . . ."

"You're dead, Dominick."

"Listen, Sal, I . . ."

"No, no, you're dead."

"Please, Sal, I can ex—"

"This is how you repay a favor? I'm supposed to go to
Frankie, tell him you *bet* it?"

"Frankie who?" Michael whispered.

"You think you can just steal money from . . ."

"I didn't steal it, Sal. I borrowed it. To get in this . . ."

"You borrowed it from *who*, Dominick?"

"From you. Temporarily."

"Dominick, you *already* owe me fifteen grand plus interest. By Friday, when it comes due, that'll be sixteen thousand
five hundred fuckin *dollars* you owe me, Dominick. Are you
saying you borrowed *another* five grand from me? Without
first asking for it?"

"I was gonna tell you when I saw you. Which is what I'm doing now."

"You're telling me you borrowed another five grand from me, is that right?"

"Yes."

"You dumb fuckin shit, this ain't *me* you're jerkin around, this is Frankie *Palumbo* whose money you bet!"

"O-*kay!*" Michael said.

"Frankie does a favor for that shithead Angelli in Queens whose ugly cousin you're fuckin, you think the whole world don't know it, a married man? Does Angelli know he ast Frankie a favor for a married man fuckin his cousin? And *this* is the way you pay Frankie back? This is the respect you show for a man whose ass you should be kissing in Macy's window? You know what's going to happen to you now? First . . ."

"Sal . . ."

"First, I'm gonna *personally* beat the shit out of you for embarrassing me in front of Frankie, and then I'm gonna turn you over to *him*, and *he's* gonna make sure you never steal money from nobody in the Faviola family ever again. You think you understand that, Dominick?"

"Let me talk to Jimmy again, okay?" Dom said. "Let me explain to *him* what . . ."

"You don't have to talk to Jimmy no more, Jimmy done everything he could for you. This ain't *Colotti* business no more, this is *Faviola* business. Where's your fuckin respect?"

"Jimmy can explain it to him."

"There's nothin to explain. You stole five fuckin grand from Frankie Palumbo after he done a favor for you. What's there to explain?"

"I thought I was borrowin it from *you*, Sal."

"You mean you thought you were *stealin* it from me."

"No, no. I was gonna pay you interest, same as before."

"*What* pay me interest? You fuckin piece of *shit*, you

can't meet your payments *now*, how'd you expect to pay me on *another* five grand?"

"I figured the same arrangement as before."

"Without askin me first?"

"I figured I'd tell you later."

"You're a dumb fuck, Dominick."

"I realize that now. I shoulda ast you first. But I really thought this was your money, Sal, I didn't know . . ."

"Yeah, well it ain't."

"I'm really sorry I done this, Sal, embarrassin the two families this way, I'm really sorry, Sal."

"You shoulda thought about that *before* doin something so stupid."

"I thought I was borrowin it."

"Stupid fuck," Sal said, and Michael visualized him shaking his head. There was a long silence. Jackie looked at Michael. Michael shrugged. They waited.

"I'll tell you the truth," Sal said, "this is already out of my hands, Dom. You really stepped out of line this time. I call Frankie about this, he'll tell me to break both your fuckin legs and throw you in the river."

"Maybe when you call him, you can ask him to talk to . . ."

"I call him, I can tell you what his response is gonna be. He's gonna say don't bother me with this shit, take care of it."

"Maybe *Jimmy'd* be willing to guarantee the loan . . ."

"Why would . . . ?"

". . . while I work it off."

"Work it off *how*? You mean deliver some *more* coke and get *paid* for it and then go *lose* the money in some *other* crap game, is that what you had in mind, you stupid shit?"

"He's getting mad all over again," Jackie said.

"Could you at least *ask* him?" Dom said.

"Ask him *what*?"

"To sit down with Jimmy, talk it over."

"He'll say fuck Jimmy and fuck you, too. He already went out of his way, and this is how you show your gratitude? That's what he'll say, I'm tellin you right now."

"Just ask him, Sal. Please."

"A sitdown, huh?"

"Please."

"*If* I call Frankie . . . and I'm only sayin *if* . . . he's gonna want this on his terms and at his convenience, I can promise you that. You caused a lot of fuckin trouble here, Dom, the two families, and now you want a sitdown, which is bringing two important people together to discuss *your* fuckin fuckup. That takes balls, I gotta tell you. How do you *know* Angelli'll guarantee the loan? How do you . . . ?"

"Well, I *don't* know. My friend'll have to ask him."

"Who you're fuckin."

"Well."

"I better be *some* kind of diplomat," Sal said.

"You're gonna call him?"

"Wait right here. You move out of this booth, you better run all the way to Yugoslavia."

There was the sound of footsteps retreating. And now that the two men were no longer talking, Michael could hear other sounds in the restaurant, the muted voices of busboys and waiters as they began closing down for the night, the clink of silverware as the tables were set for tomorrow's lunch crowd, the sound of a radio being tuned to a talk show. They waited. The snow kept falling.

"Okay."

Sal's voice again.

Closer as he slid into the booth.

"You're a very lucky man, Dominick. He said Jimmy should call him, they'll set something up for after Christmas."

"Thank you," Dominick said.

"You better fuck his cousin good between now and then," Sal said.

It was still early enough in the afternoon for the beach to be unbearably hot. Even in the shade of the striped umbrella, Sarah felt uncomfortable, but she suspected this had less to do with the heat than with her sister's conversation. Heather was telling her that she'd wanted to kill her husband the moment she'd found out. The island was French, women went topless on the beaches here. Heather sat bare-breasted on the blanket under the umbrella, saying she'd wanted to smash in his face with a hatchet. Her sister sitting topless made Sarah feel yet more uncomfortable, people walking by. She herself had not yet found the courage to take off her bikini top. Probably never would.

"Like when he was sleeping," Heather said. "I wanted to pick up a hatchet and smash in his face."

"Oh come on," Sarah said.

"I mean it. Smash his face in. Then leave the house, fly somewhere out of the country, disappear from sight."

The beach was on the southern side of the island, in an isolated cove far from the many hotels clustered on St. Bart's Atlantic side. The house their parents owned was on a small verdant hill overlooking the beach, a good thousand yards from the nearest house, a twenty-minute Mini-Moke ride to the nearest good hotel in Morne Lurin. Mollie was inside the house, napping. Yolande, her mother's housekeeper, was sweeping off the wooden verandah that ran around the house on three sides. The sound of her broom swished a whispered counterpoint to their conversation, such as it was. The tide was going out. Lazy wavelets lapped the shore. All was tranquil and serene, but her sister was telling her she'd felt like doing murder. Sarah didn't want to hear any of this. She felt trapped on the sweltering beach.

"This was after I found out about his little bimbo,"

Heather said. "He used to come home late from the office,
tell me he was working after hours on this important account,
that important account, I believed him. Her name was Felicity, I wanted to kill *her*, too. I kept wishing I'd come home
and find him in bed with her, kill them both with the same
hatchet, chop up their faces, disappear from sight. Come
down here afterwards, but this'd be the first place the police
would look, am I right?"

"Probably," Sarah said.

"This was right after Halloween, when I found out. It
was a Sunday night, a woman in the building was giving a
Halloween party. I went dressed as a sexy witch. Doug went
dressed as a hairy warlock. Some guy supposed to be Dracula
kept chasing me all over the place, telling me he wanted to
bite me on the neck. Doug had the gall later to tell me it
made him jealous, the count wanting to bite me on the neck.
He's screwing little Felicity blind two, three nights a week,
he pretends to be jealous of some drunken jackass with fake
fangs."

She shook her head in wonder. A drop of sweat rolled
down between her naked breasts.

"He called her later that night," she said. "That's how I
found out."

"How?" Sarah asked.

"I got up to pee—I always pee the whole night through
when I've had too much wine, don't you? Doug wasn't in
bed. This is three in the morning, I think Where's Doug?
Reasonably, no? Three in the morning? Is Doug in the bathroom? Is Doug *also* peeing? Will I have to wait in line? Or
shall I go use the bathroom down the hall, off the study? But
no, Doug is *not* in the bathroom, the bathroom is empty. So
I relieve myself, as they say, and I go back into the bedroom,
and Doug *still* isn't in bed, so where *is* Doug? Overwhelmed
by curiosity—as who wouldn't be, my dear, it's three in the
morning—I go out in the hall, and I see a light burning in
the study, and I call out 'Doug?' and I hear a click. *Click*. Just

a tiny little *click* but I know it's somebody hanging up a phone. Three o'clock in the morning, and my husband's making a phone call down the hall. Well, he comes out of the study wearing nothing but pajama bottoms and a shit-eating grin, and he tells me he had to look up a word in the dictionary. A *word*? I say. Driving me crazy, he says. Couldn't sleep. A *word*? I say again. *What* word? I'm still believing him, you see. I'm still thinking I must be mistaken about that click, it couldn't have been him hanging up the phone, it had to be something else, maybe he was just closing the dictionary. *Eohippus*, he tells me. That's the word he was looking up, three o'clock in the morning. Eohippus. You mean like the *horse*? I say. He says Yes, exactly, but how do you *spell* it? *That's* what was driving me crazy.

"Well, that's reasonable, too, no? I mean, *that's* something a person can understand, am I right? The burning question of whether it's *i-o* or *e-o*? Three o'clock in the morning, we're standing in the hall, and he's telling me he got out of bed to go look up *eohippus* and it's *e-o*, and now he can go back to sleep, which he promptly does, snoring, with his hand tucked between my legs. The next night, when I get home from work and he's still at the office with one of his *important* accounts, the bastard, I look up *eohippus*. It's *e-o*, all right. I figure Listen, there are stranger things than a man looking up *eohippus* three o'clock in the morning. But then the phone bill comes on November seventh."

"Uh-oh," Sarah said.

"Indeed. Listed under long-distance calls for the first day of November at two forty-eight in the morning is a call to Wilton, Connecticut. Twelve-minute call, so maybe I *wasn't* wrong about that click, hmm? Gives the phone number and all, lo and behold. I call the phone company and tell them the number is unfamiliar to me, can they please let me know to whom it is listed? Very cool and very calm, to *whom*, mind you, even though my hand is shaking on the phone. The operator tells me the phone is listed to one Felicity Cooperman, who is a junior copywriter at the agency, who by the way curtsies me half to death every time I go up there. Nineteen years old if she's a day, and my husband is calling her at two forty-eight in the morning on All Saints' Day. That was when I decided to smash in his head with a hatchet the very first opportunity I got."

"I'm glad you didn't," Sarah said.

"Cooler heads prevailed," Heather said, and smiled.

She herself looked nineteen when she smiled. Big girlish grin cracking her face, blue eyes squinching shut. Thirty-two years old, still looked like a teenager, firm cupcake breasts, flat tummy, the long legs and lithe body of a team swimmer—which she'd been in high school. Well, no children. Which, considering her present situation, was a blessing, Sarah guessed.

"I called a lawyer recommended to me by the woman who threw the Halloween party who's herself been divorced three times. I told her a friend of mine was having trouble with her husband, and so on and so forth, lying in my teeth, I don't think she believed me for a minute. Anyway, the lawyer tells me I should put a tail on Mr. Douglas Rowell, which I agree to do, and it turns out I was mistaken in my surmise, he *isn't* screwing young Felicity blind two, three times a week, he's screwing her deaf, *dumb*, and blind every day on his lunch hour, *plus* the two, three times a week he has to work late on all those *important* accounts of his. You should hear the tapes, Sarah, they're . . ."

"You've got *tapes*?"

"Well, *a* tape, actually. I'll play it for you some night."

"Here? *With* you?"

"No, no. Actually, it's in the lawyer's office. Strictly X rated, not for the kiddies. *Doug's Delicious Dick*, starring nineteen-year-old Felicity Cooperman in the role she made famous, delivering the unforgettable line, 'I just *adore* sucking your gweat big dick, golly gee I can just come *heaps* sucking that big bee-*yoo*-ti-ful dick of yours,' the little *bitch*!" Heather said, and flicked angrily at a sand fly. "I could kill them both," she said. "With a *hatchet!*"

"Don't tell that to Michael when he gets here."

"When will that be, anyway?"

"As soon as he can get away. Something important came up."

This was the twenty-eighth of December. Sarah had taken Mollie down on the day after Christmas. Michael was still up north; apparently some sort of big meeting was to take place today, and the DA had insisted he stay in town for it. Heather hadn't yet told her parents that she and Doug were separated. Wait till she dropped *that* bombshell. Little Dougie? Sweet little Dougie? Yes, Mom, sweet little Dougie with the big bee-*yoo*-ti-ful dick little Felicity just *adores* sucking. They were in London at the moment, at Claridge's, where they went every year at this time. *Stay as long as you like, darlings. We won't be back till the middle of January.*

"And when he *does* get here . . ."

"Yeah?"

"Put on your top."

"Mom?"

Twelve-year-old Mollie, standing on the verandah looking as sleepy-eyed as an eight year old and wearing only white cotton panties in possible emulation of her aunt. Brown as a pudding after only two days in the Caribbean sun, she blinked into the glare and said, "Can I go in the water now?"

"Come on down, sweetie," Sarah called.

Her sister shot her a look. She wasn't yet finished with her one-sided conversation, and she didn't need a child intruding. Impatiently, silently scowling, she watched as Sarah hugged her daughter close and asked if she'd had a good nap, and why didn't she ask Yolande to give her some cookies and milk, and then she could put on her bathing suit and maybe Mommy and Aunt Heather would go in the water with her. Aunt Heather sat frowning through all of this. There were more important conversations than those with a

twelve-year-old child. Besides, why did Sarah persist on calling herself *Mommy* and talking virtual baby talk to a twelve
year old with perceptibly budding breasts? All this was on
Heather's face as Mollie walked flat-footed back into the
house.

"I wanted to go to bed with every man in sight," Heather
said. "Have you ever felt that way?"

"No," Sarah said.

"Kill him first, then go to bed with every construction
worker in New York," Heather said.

Sarah glanced toward the verandah. Her daughter had
already gone into the house.

"I mean, this was a violent need for *revenge*. This wasn't
your garden-variety urge to stray—which I never did, by the
way, fool that I was, and more's the pity. Have you ever?"

"Ever what?" Sarah asked.

"Strayed."

"Cheat on *Michael*, do you mean?"

"Well, who *else* would you cheat on? He's your husband,
isn't he?"

"I've never cheated on him, no."

"I've gone to bed with sixteen men since I found out
about Doug. That was on the day after Halloween, less than
two months ago. Sixteen men in less than two months, that
comes to a different man every four days, give or take a few
percentage points. If my lawyer knew, he'd kill me."

"I think you ought to be careful," Sarah said.

"Not with that tape in our hands."

"I'm not talking about a divorce settlement. I'm talking
about . . ."

"*Fuck* safe sex, I don't care anymore," Heather said.
"Was Michael your first one?"

"No," Sarah said.

"Who was?"

"A boy at Duke."

"You never told me."

"I feel funny telling you now."

"I was a virgin when I married Doug," Heather said, and suddenly her voice broke. "Shit!" she said, and reached for her handbag, and yanked a lace-edged handkerchief from it just as the tears welled in her eyes. "I hate that bastard," she said, "I really hate him. I can forgive *her*, she's just a dumb impressionable . . . no, goddamn it, I hate them *both*!" she said, and covered her face with the handkerchief and began sobbing uncontrollably into it.

"Did you see that?" Andrew asked.

"Very healthy girl," Willie said.

They were walking up the beach together, back toward where Andrew had parked the VW. Half an hour earlier, there hadn't been anyone on the beach here in front of the big house, just the blanket and the striped umbrella and a paperback novel lying open on a towel. Andrew noticed details like that. The paperback novel. A romance novel. He'd wondered at the time who was reading it. Now he wondered which of the two blondes the book belonged to. The topless one who was crying, or the one trying to comfort her. He wondered if they were sisters. He wondered if they lived together in the house there.

"I meant did you notice she was *crying*?" he said.

"No. Who?"

"The one without the top."

"No, I didn't notice. If you want my opinion, they're asking for it when they parade around naked like that. Even if that's the custom with the French here."

"Those two weren't French," Andrew said.

"How do you know?"

"The book was in English. I saw the title."

"What book?"

"The one on the towel."

When Andrew was a child, he'd been as blond as either of the two women they'd just passed. His hair had turned first a muddy blond and then the sort of chestnut brown it now was. His eyes, too, were a darker blue than they'd been when he was a boy, and whereas his ears were still a bit large for his face, they were not quite as prominent as they'd been then. He'd eventually grown into them, all kids with big ears do, but he still wore his hair somewhat long, perhaps as a reminder that he'd once worn it that way deliberately, to hide the big ears.

The beach ahead of them was empty now. The striped umbrella was some hundred yards behind them. It was a good half-mile to the car, perhaps a bit more than that. Their conversation turned to business again.

"How much are they asking?" Andrew said.

"You have to understand these people are amateurs," Willie said.

"Worst kind of people to deal with. Did you explain the exchange to them?"

"They understand all that. Andrew, let me tell you something," Willie said, and looked around to make sure they weren't being overheard, even though the beach ahead and behind was empty.

Andrew admired the way Willie looked. He had to be at least sixty, some thirty years older than Andrew, but he had the well-toned, tanned appearance of a man who spent a lot of time swimming and sunning in the Caribbean. Andrew figured they were about the same height and weight—six feet tall, a hundred and eighty pounds, give or take—but Willie seemed in much better shape. Both men were wearing swimming briefs. Andrew was still relatively white; he'd flown down only yesterday.

"They don't care," Willie said. "They just don't have the vision. They think what they've got going'll last forever, the demand'll never dry up. What they're saying is they don't *need* what we can provide, they're doing fine, they'll keep *on* doing fine. If nothing's broken, why fix it, you follow? So they just aren't interested. I told them we'd be doing all the work, we'd do the spadework with the Chinese, we'd provide the ships, load and unload on both ends, this doesn't matter to them. Since they don't think they need us, the swap doesn't interest them. They're dumb amateurs, they can't see the beauty of this thing."

"Who've you been talking to?" Andrew asked.

"Alonso Moreno."

"Does he know I'm here?"

"He knows you're here."

"Does he know we want an answer?"

"He knows that, too. Andrew, I told you, they don't *care*."

"Where's he staying?"

"He's got houses all over these islands. He stays where he *wants* to stay."

"Where's his house on *this* island?"

"I don't know."

"I thought you've been talking to him."

"I have."

"And you don't know where he's staying?"

"If you're Alonso Moreno, you don't send out cards with your address on them."

"How do you get in touch with him?"

"Through a waiter at the hotel. I tell him I want a meet, he phones Moreno, sets it up."

"Where have you been meeting?"

"On a boat. They pick me up on the dock in Gustavia."

"Tell your waiter friend I want to see Moreno personally."

"He'll tell you to go fuck yourself, Andrew."

"Tell him, anyway," Andrew said, and smiled.

There was something chilling about that smile. It reminded Willie of Andrew's father when he was young.

"I'll see what I can do," he said. "When do you want this?"

★ ★ ★

Because Frankie Palumbo of the Faviola family in Manhattan was out of the goodness of his heart willing to listen
to still further bullshit about this deadbeat thief who was
somehow related to Jimmy Angelli of the Colotti family
in Queens, he was the one who chose the location for the
sitdown.

Lucy Angelli got the information from her cousin and
immediately called Dom Di Nobili to tell him when and
where the meeting would take place. She also told him that
his presence was not called for; his fate would be determined
privately by the two capos. Dom immediately reported the
time and place to Michael.

It was bad news that they didn't want Dom there when
they talked; this meant they couldn't send him in wired. But
the DA's Office, the FBI, and the NYPD conducted routine,
long-standing surveillance on a day-by-day basis, and there
were bugs already in place at many wiseguy hangouts where
business was conducted. Michael made some calls to see if
the Ristorante Romano on MacDougal Street was one of
them. It was not. This meant they had to start from scratch.

Costumed as a quartet of New York's Bravest, wearing
firemen's gear and carrying hoses and axes and all the other
paraphernalia, four detectives from the DA's Office Squad
honored the place with a visit on Christmas Eve, ostensibly
to extinguish a small electrical fire that had mysteriously
started in the restaurant's basement. During all their chopping
and hacking and spritzing and shouting and swearing down
there, they incidentally managed to tap into the restaurant's
telephone lines to provide a power source for the Brady bug
they buried in the basement's ceiling—and consequently the
floor of the room above. This self-contained transmitter was
the size of a half-dollar, and it was now positioned directly
under the prestigious corner table Frankie Palumbo favored
on his visits to the place. The owner of the Ristorante Romano tipped the "firemen" four hundred dollars when they

left, this because he knew firemen were bigger thieves than anybody who came to the place, and he considered himself lucky they hadn't helped themselves to the stolen twenty-year-old Scotch stacked in cases along the wall opposite the fuse boxes and telephone panels.

At three-thirty on the afternoon of December twenty-eighth, while Sarah and Heather and Mollie splashed in the warm lucid waters off the house on St. Bart's, Michael sat in a parked car with an ADA named Georgie Giardino, the Rackets Bureau's most ardent mob-watcher.

Georgie's grandfather had been born in Italy, and lived in America for five years before he got his citizenship papers, at which time he could rightfully be called an Italian-American. In Georgie's eyes, this was the only time the hyphenate could be used properly. His parents had been born here of Italian-American parents, but this did not make them similarly *Italian*-Americans, it made them simply *Americans*. The two men meeting in the restaurant today had also been born in America, and despite their Italian-sounding names, they too were American. In fact, neither Frankie Palumbo nor Jimmy Angelli felt the slightest allegiance to a country that was as foreign to them as Saudi Arabia. Even their parents, similarly born in the good old U.S. of A., had little concern for what went on in Italy. Most of them would never visit Italy in their lifetime. Italy was a foreign country where, they'd been told, the food wasn't as good as you could get in any Italian restaurant in New York. This was not like the Irish or the Jews, whose ferocious ties to Northern Ireland and Israel would have been considered seditious in a less tolerant land. The irony was that although these hoods called themselves "Italians," they were no more Italian than Michael himself was. Or, for that matter, Georgie Giardino.

Frankie Palumbo and Jimmy Angelli were Americans, take it or leave it, like it or not. And like any other good Americans, they believed in a free society wherein someone who worked hard and played by the rules could prosper and be happy. The rules they played by were not necessarily the same rules most other Americans played by, but they did obey them. And they did prosper. Georgie despised them *and* their fucking rules. It was, in fact, his firm belief that until every last Mafioso son of a bitch was in jail, *any* American of Italian descent would suffer through association. That was why he was sitting alongside Michael today, freezing his ass off in a parked car two blocks from the Ristorante Romano, waiting to hear and record the conversation that would take place between two or more American gangsters in an Italian restaurant.

The first of them to arrive was Jimmy Angelli, one of the *caporegimi* of the Colotti family in Queens.

"Hey, Mr. Angelli, long time no see, what's the matter you don't come to the city no more."

The restaurant owner, they surmised.

The city was Manhattan.

Anyone who lived in New York knew that there was the Bronx, Queens, Brooklyn, Staten Island—and the City.

There was another man with Angelli.

They didn't get his name till Angelli said, "Danny, sit over there."

This was while the two men were still alone. Angelli was probably indicating that his goon sit with his back to the wall, where he could see anyone coming in the front door. It did not take too many restaurant rubouts before you learned where to sit.

Frank Palumbo and his goon arrived some ten minutes later, fashionably tardy as befitted the offended capo of Manhattan's Faviola family. After all, some stupid cocksucker thief guaranteed by the Colotti family had shortchanged him five grand after he'd done them a favor. He could afford to play this one like the boss himself instead of one of a hundred lieutenants in the Faviola family.

At the recent trial of Anthony Faviola, convicted and sentenced boss of the notorious Manhattan family, the U.S.

Attorney had introduced in evidence the taped conversations that were the result of a year-long wiretap surveillance. On those tapes, a man identified as Anthony Faviola had, among other things, ordered two hit men to do several murders in New Jersey. The defense called his younger brother, Rudy, as a witness and he was the first to testify that on the night his brother had allegedly made the call from his mother's house in Oyster Bay, Long Island, he was instead at his own palatial home in Stonington, Connecticut, playing poker with six legitimate businessmen. The six men were each called in turn, and each corroborated the fact that at eight twenty-seven that night—the time at which the incriminating interstate call was allegedly made—Anthony was laying a full house on the table, aces up. The jury didn't believe any of them.

Anthony was now serving five consecutive lifetime sentences in the maximum security prison at Leavenworth, Kansas. Four of these sentences were for the murders he'd ordered. The fifth had been tacked on under the federal Racketeer-Influenced and Corrupt Organizations statute—familiarly known as the RICO statute—under which murders committed in the furtherance of criminal enterprise were punishable by lifetime sentences.

Anthony was locked in his cell for twenty-three hours every day, and his visiting privileges were severely limited as well because he'd been deliberately sent to a federal prison far from family, friends, and former associates. Some die-hard followers insisted that he was still running the mob from inside, but from everything the DA's Office had been able to learn, his underboss brother, Rudy, next in line and loyal to the end, was now boss—with Anthony's blessings. Rudy was affectionately known as "The Accountant," a nickname that had nothing to do with balancing books. When both brothers were coming along as soldiers in the Tortocello family, Rudy had built a reputation as an enforcer, a man to whom you had *better* account or else.

Sitting in the parked car now, Michael and Georgie were hoping to hear something that would connect Rudy Faviola to the dope deal that had gone down outside a takee-outee restaurant in Chinatown. Six ounces of cocaine was an A-1 felony. If they could tie this to an additional felony and a misdemeanor, each committed within the past three years, then under Section 460.20—defined as the Organized Crime Control Act—they might be able to send the *new* boss out to Kansas, too, Toto. Well, not quite. Anthony Faviola was serving federal time; an OCCA offender would be sent to a state prison.

"How you doin, Jim?" Palumbo said. "You been waitin long?"

"Just a few minutes," Angelli said. "You're lookin good, Frank."

"I could stand to lose a few pounds," Palumbo said. "Over there, Joey."

Indicating a chair for *his* goon, no doubt.

The men ordered wine.

The bug recorded the ritual Mafia foreplay.

The inquiring after one's health and one's family, the show of respect, esteem, and admiration.

Ta-da ta-da ta-da, as Jackie Diaz had put it.

The men did not order lunch.

Palumbo got down to brass tacks almost immediately.

"What do you suggest we do with this asshole you sent us?" he asked.

"I never even met the stupid fuck," Angelli said.

"So that's who you recommended me? Somebody you never met?"

"I was doing a favor for my cousin."

"Some favor you done me, he fucks me out of five grand."

"You'll get the money back, Frankie."

"When? How?"

"That's what I want to work out with you."

"You work it out with me, you think it's gonna fly, huh?"

Advertising-agency talk.

"I'm hoping it will."

"I still ain't heard what you plan to do. All I know is somebody's got five thousand bucks of my money. And from what Sal tells me, there's another fifteen grand kickin around out there, plus interest. So who is this *jih-drool,* you're goin out on a limb for him? We got good relations, this asshole's gonna fuck them up, we ain't careful."

"Which is why we're here," Angelli said. "To make sure that doesn't happen."

"Anybody else, it'd already be too late for talk. The man would be gone."

"I know that."

"We go back a long way, Jim . . ."

"I know that, too. That's why I'm here today, Frank. To ask that we don't let this thing get out of hand. We don't do anything foolish could cause trouble between the families. *We* don't want that, and we're sure *you* don't want that, either."

"Who *is* this asshole, anyway, the fuckin *Pope* you're defendin him this way?"

"My cousin's in love with him, what the fuck can I do?" Angelli said.

"Does she know he's married?"

"She knows. But he's gettin a divorce."

"Yeah, divorce my ass."

"That's what he told her."

"How we gonna make this right, Jimmy?"

"How do you want it to go, Frank? You're the one got hurt here, you tell me."

"I'm glad to hear you talking this way."

"What's right is right," Angelli said.

"I don't know what to tell you. This is money that was *stolen,* you understand? I go higher with this, I know just what I'm gonna hear. Stolen *money*? Hey, come on. You know what to do, why you even *bothering* me with this? That's what I'll hear."

"I thought," Angelli said, and sighed heavily. "I thought . . . we all go back a long way. You, me . . . Rudy. Other families, there's been trouble, but us, never. That's cause there's always been the proper respect, am I right, Frank?"

"Till now."

"No. No, Frankie, don't say that, please. This isn't a matter of disrespect Colotti to Faviola, it ain't that at all. This is a jerk we're dealin with here, a man with no sense. Di Nobili's a fuckin jerk, I admit it, I told my cousin what she sees in this jerk is beyond me. Women, what can I tell you? He's a jerk, he's a loser, he's a fuckin thief, he's all these things, I agree with you. But he's also somebody not worth *botherin* with, you follow me, Frank? We can settle this without goin the whole nine yards. It don't have to be that *drastic*, you understand what I'm sayin? It ain't even worth Rudy's *time* to be thinkin of something so drastic. What I thought is if you talked to him, he might find it in his heart to give this jerk a break. That's all I'm askin. Figure out a way for this jackass to work it off. The fifteen, the additional five, take it out of his fuckin ass, work his ass off till he pays it all back."

"You gonna guarantee it, Jimmy?"

"That's askin a lot, Frank. I don't even know the man. He's a jerk my cousin's involved with, I'm pleadin this for her, not for him. She's flesh and blood, Frankie. She's my first cousin. We were kids together, we grew up together. Like you and me. And Rudy."

"Rudy, huh?"

"If you could talk to him . . ."

"Where you been, Jim?"

"What?"

"I'll see what I can do," Palumbo said, but there was a note of finality in his voice. "I'll talk it over with Le—"

There was the sound of his chair being shoved back, thunderously close to the bug.

". . . and get back to you. That's the best I can say right now. No promises."

"Who?" Michael asked.

"Shhhh!"

The men were still talking, exchanging farewells, sending regards, thanking each other for having given the time to this important matter. But the business was finished, there was really nothing more to say. Now there was the sound of more chairs being shoved back, registering like an avalanche on the bug. Then footsteps. And the distant voice of the restaurant owner calling his farewells. And the sound of a door closing. And then only the restaurant's background noises.

"Who did he say?" Michael asked.

"It sounded like 'Lena.' "

"That's what I thought."

"Who the hell is *Lena*?"

"I don't know."

"That name mean anything to you? Lena?"

"Maybe it's his wife's name. Maybe Palumbo's gonna talk it over with *her.*"

Michael looked at him.

"Well," Georgie said, and shrugged.

"This is a terrible connection," Sarah said. "Where are you?"

"At the office," Michael said. "Shall I try it again?"

"Maybe I should call you back."

"It's cheaper from here, isn't it?"

"Let me call you back, anyway."

"Okay, good," Michael said, and hung up.

She'd been dressing for dinner when he called, and she stood now in bra and panties in the largest guest room, hers

through seniority whenever she and her sister were visiting
together. There were four bedrooms in the house, all of them
on the second floor, all with glorious views of the ocean. The
master bedroom in particular, with its French doors opening
on the sea, offered a vista to the south that encompassed miles
of open water to Statia and St. Kitts. Behind the house, to
the northwest, you could see all the way up the mountain to
the houses surrounding the hotel on Morne Lurin, a spectacu-
larly twinkling view at night. Sitting at the dressing table
facing the window wall, Sarah dialed Michael's office directly. Beyond the open French doors, the sun was beginning
to dip toward the water, staining the sky in its wake.

"Organized Crime, Welles."

"How do you do, Mr. Welles," she said, "I wish to
report a crime, please."

"What *is* the crime, ma'am?" he asked, recognizing her
voice at once.

"Reckless Abandonment," Sarah said.

"No such crime, ma'am. We've got Abandonment of a
Child, that's Section Two-Six-Oh of the . . ."

"This is an *adult*," she said. "The person abandoned."

"An adult, yes, ma'am. Male or female?"

"Female, Mr. Welles. *Very*. Michael, I'm beginning to
feel *neglected*. When are you . . . ?"

"Ahhh, yes, Criminal Negligence, ma'am, Section One-
Two . . ."

"When are you coming *down* here?"

"As soon as I can, honey."

"I miss you."

"I miss you, too. But I've got to keep at this. I may be
onto something, Sarah. I won't know till I dig a little deeper.
Anyway, how*ever* this goes, I'll be down for sure on New
Year's Eve."

"That means we'll only be together a day or so before
we have to head home."

"Two full days and three nights."

"I *still* don't see what's so important about this. Did Scanlon cancel anyone *else's* vacation?"

"Georgie had to postpone till tomorrow."

"Then why don't *you* leave tomorrow?"

"Then no one'd be here working the case."

"*What* case?"

"That's a secret."

"Even from me."

"Even from you."

"Withholding Evidence from a Spouse, class E felony punishable by . . ."

"I love you," he said.

"I love you, too. *Please* hurry down here."

"As soon as I can, honey. What are your plans for tonight?"

"It's my sister's last night . . ."

"I know."

"Yolande's feeding Mollie right this minute. Heather and I are going into Gustavia for dinner, like grown-ups."

"What are you wearing?"

"Later? Or right this minute?"

"Which would I like better?"

"Right this minute. But I haven't got time."

"Tell me, anyway."

"Lacy white bra and panties."

"Mmmm. High heels?"

"Not yet. Call me later, we'll talk dirty."

"What time?"

"Everyone should be asleep by eleven or so."

"Why don't you call me?"

"Okay. You'd better be alone."

"I'll be waiting."

"Me, too."

"I love you."

"I love you, too," she said.

"Later," he said, and hung up.

★ ★ ★

There was laughter down the hall.

The place was so empty, it seemed to echo. About all
that was happening in the criminal courts this week were a
handful of arraignments in AR One and AR Two, and the
processing of new arrests in the Complaint Room. Aside
from a skeleton staff necessary to keep the wheels of justice
barely grinding, the big gray complex on Centre Street was
virtually devoid of personnel. Michael sat alone before the
computer in the sixth-floor office. The calendar on the wall
read December 28, the digital clock on his desk read 6:37 P.M.
He'd give it a few more hours and then quit for the day, take
a taxi uptown to Spark's for a good steak. He felt as if he
were the last man alive in a city demolished by the bomb.
The laughter down the hall was gone now. There was the
click of high-heeled shoes on the marble floor outside, fading.
He turned back to the screen again.

Not all of the Faviola tapes had been computerized.
There were more than eight thousand hours of conversation,
and of these only a bit more than half had been transferred
to computer disks since the trial ended this past August. The
process was somewhat lackadaisical. Before the trial, the U.S.
Attorney had incessantly sifted and resifted each and every
conversation. The accumulated evidence had been used to
send Anthony Faviola away forever, but there was nothing
more that could be done to him. In fact, when Michael made
his call to the Feds, they'd asked him what the hell he *wanted*
with all that stuff? He told them he was doing background
research, and they'd let it go at that. No one had expected
any real explanation; everyone in law enforcement was well
aware of the keen competition among agencies. Which was
one of the reasons Sarah was in the Caribbean and Michael
was here in New York looking for any reference to a person
named Lena.

I'll see what I can do, Palumbo had said. *I'll talk it over*

with Lena, and get back to you. That's the best I can say right now.
No promises.

Everyone in the DA's Office felt certain that the moment Anthony Faviola got sent west, his younger brother, Rudy, took over as the new boss of the family. But Palumbo hadn't said he'd talk it over with *Rudy.* In fact . . .

Michael switched on the tape again.

"Rudy, huh?"

"If you could talk to him . . ."

"Where you been, Jim?"

"What?"

Something derisive in Palumbo's voice.

Where you been, Jim?

And then saying he'd talk it over with *Lena.*

So who the hell was Lena?

Frankie Palumbo was married to a woman named Grace. He had two daughters, one of them named Filomena—after his mother—and the other named Firenze, after his grandfather's birthplace in Italy. Frankie was fifty-two years old and had never been to Italy, big surprise. There was no one named Lena in Anthony Faviola's family. Nor in Rudy's. Not a Lena in the carload.

So who is Lena, what is she? Michael wondered. And what the hell am I doing here in New York three days after Christmas, chasing Mafia ghosts on a computer, because *my* boss, my own *personal* boss of all bosses, thinks that if Rudy Faviola is not currently running the show, then we'd better learn damn fast who *is.*

Lena.

Michael fantasized a voluptuous dark-haired woman of indeterminate Mediterranean origin. Lena. And the swan? Oh? No kidding? In college, before he'd met Sarah, his taste had run to poetry and to dark-haired women . . . well, even though he'd known better, he'd still thought of them as *girls,* actually. He was now thirty-six, this was back during the seventies; Betty Friedan had published her *Feminine Mystique* a decade earlier, and Erica Jong had just begun telling the world about her ten thousand and one orgasms.

Michael was twenty-one when he met the first blonde he'd ever dated, the last girl—or even woman—he'd *ever* date again because that blonde happened to be a nineteen-year-old junior named Sarah Fitch whom he married a year later, after he'd graduated with his B.S. degree, and while she was still in her senior year. His parents helped him through law school—it was a matter of pride that he'd later repaid them every cent—until Sarah herself graduated with a B.A. and got a license to teach English, which she'd done here and there all over New York while *he* trudged uptown to Columbia. She still taught at the Greer Academy, where she'd settled in some eight years ago, after getting her master's from NYU. He was always surprised when a woman obviously in her late twenties stopped "Mrs. Welles" on the street and told her how much she'd enjoyed being in her class. Well, Sarah was thirty-four now. She'd started teaching when she was twenty-three; those sixteen year olds back then were now in their late twenties.

Lena.

Maybe it wasn't a woman's name at all. No woman behind the throne here, no woman whose advice was earnestly sought. Maybe it was a man's *family* name, maybe the Lena with whom Palumbo had to talk it over was a Johnny Lena or a Joey Lena or a Foonzie Lena. If so, had his name ever cropped up in the hundreds of conversations between the Brothers Faviola at all hours of the day and night? Many of these conversations were in crude code. The mob was ever alert to the marvels of electronic surveillance. When they weren't talking what sounded totally innocuous to anyone listening but which obviously had great import to the chatterers themselves, they were turning on record players or water taps or showers or television sets to obscure whatever they were saying in plain English laced with a few bastardized

Italian expressions like *boff-on-gool* and *stroon-zeh* and *mah-nedge* and *jih-drool* and *mool-een-yahn*. The U.S. Attorney had nailed Faviola on four murders because he'd been stupid enough to believe the place he was calling from was inordinately safe: his mother's house in Oyster Bay. Who would have thought those *sfasciumi* could have got into Stella Faviola's fortresslike, fenced-in gray stone mansion on the North Shore, there to install their insidious listening devices?

Lena.

Earlier this evening, Michael had kicked up **FAVIOLA, RUDY** on the computer, and then he'd typed in **LENA** and hit the SEARCH key, and lo and behold there was not a single LENA, uppercase or lower, to be found. As a lark, he'd typed in **LEDA** and hit the same search key, and got nothing there, either, small surprise. This meant that in none of Rudy's conversations with his brother had the name Lena, or for that matter Leda, been uttered—at least not on the tapes that had already been computerized.

Michael was praying there'd be something on the computer. He did not relish wading through thousands of pages of typed transcript, reading the remainder of the conversations word for word.

He decided to go straight for the jugular, do a wider search of the entire file, which was broken down into month-by-month folders starting in September of 1991, when the federal surveillance had begun in earnest. He called up each folder in turn, scanning them for the name Lena. Nothing for September or October of '91. Zilch for November. Lots of Christmas talk in December, and a few near misses when the computer gave him first *polenta*, and then *lenona*, both of which contained the letters *l-e-n-a* in succession—close but no cigar. He went back to the drawing board, clicked the little box for **Exact Match**, and typed in the name with a capital **L** followed by the letters **e**, **n**, and **a** in lowercase. **Lena**. Once more unto the breach, dear friends.

Nothing for January of 1992.

Nothing in February, either.

The computerized stuff ended with the conversations taped in March.

There was no Lena mentioned in that month, either.

With a mountain of transcripts looming before him, Michael went back to the little box he'd earlier clicked for an exact match, and canceled the command. He started again with the folder for January of '92, searching for the letters **l**, **e**, **n**, and **a** in any combination in either upper or lower case.

In January, he got Anthony talking to someone about a new calendar for the year, obviously a code. **Ca**len**dar**. Later that month, he got him asking about a dry-**clean**ing delivery, probably another code, the letters coming up in the sequence *l-e-a-n* this time. Still later in the month, Anthony inquired about the price of a Macintosh IIsi from a store called Com-put**erlan**d. In March, the last folder in the computer file, there was only a single *l-e-n-a* combination, in the name **Leon**ard, whoever the hell he might have been. Michael still didn't want to tackle those forbidding transcripts. In the possibility that he or Georgie had heard the name wrong, he widened the search so that the computer would call up anything even closely resembling the name Lena. If, for example, a transcribing typist had misspelled Lena as Lexna or even Leyna or Lina or Lema, chances are the computer would yank out the word unless it was really too preposterously distant.

He hit the SEARCH key.

In the folder for December of last year, Anthony had told his dear Rudy that he still hadn't bought Leno anything for Christmas.

Leno.

Not Lena.

Leno with an *o*.

There were no other mentions of the name Leno in any of the conversations already computerized. Michael would have to hit the transcripts, after all.

Sighing heavily, he shut down for the night and looked

at his watch. Quarter past eight—my, how the time does fly when you're having a good time. He was ravenously hungry.

Heather had chosen the spot, a hotel restaurant with a poolside piano bar and a terrific view of the harbor. When they walked in, Heather in pink, Sarah in white, the piano player was doing a medley of Cole Porter tunes. He nodded in their direction and immediately segued into "I Get a Kick out of You," which seemed a bit obvious to Sarah but which her sister seemed to appreciate nonetheless. They were shown to a table on the terrace, overlooking a wide curve of harbor with twinkling dockside lights and bobbing boats and beyond the dark water a cluster of softer yellow lights in the rolling hills. The night was soft. There was the sweet scent of frangipani on the air.

"I want something tall and dark and very strong," Heather said to the waiter, and smiled and added, "To *drink*, that is," compounding the felony. At his suggestion, she ordered a concoction called "Pirate's Flagon," which he said had seven different kinds of rum in it. Sarah ordered a Beefeater martini, on the rocks, couple of olives, what the hell. After two of those, she felt like calling Michael straight from the restaurant, tell him she'd taken off her lacy white panties in the ladies' room and was now standing in white, high-heeled, ankle-strapped sandals at the wall phone, naked under her white pleated dress, what did he intend doing about it, huh? Instead, she ordered the fish special of the day, a red snapper *papillote*. Heather was looking a bit glassy-eyed after her seven kinds of rum times two. She ordered the curried goat and avocado in Antilles sauce. The waiter suggested a dry white wine—French, of course, what else?—and they were halfway through the bottle when the two men they'd seen on the beach earlier today walked in.

"I'll take the young one," Heather said.

"I'll take Michael," Sarah said.

"Michael's ten thousand miles away."

"Then *I'll* take the young one," Sarah said, and both women giggled like schoolgirls.

"Actually, the one with the white hair is better looking," Heather said, looking over toward where the men were being seated at the other end of the curved terrace.

"*Gray* hair," Sarah said.

"Looks white to me. Handsome as sin."

"How's the curried goat?" Sarah asked.

"Much better than the shrimp fricassee I had the other night," Heather said, and glanced again toward where the men were now ordering drinks. "Do you think the white-haired one would like to fricassee *me*? I sure would like to fricassee *him*."

"*Gray*-haired," Sarah corrected again.

"The young one has big ears," Heather said.

"The better to hear you," Sarah said, lowering her voice and raising her eyebrows in warning.

"Clark Gable had big ears, you know. He was famous for his big ears," Heather said. "Did you know that men with big ears are supposed to have big dicks, too?"

Sarah almost choked on her fish.

"That's the truth," Heather said.

"Anyway, it's *noses*," Sarah whispered.

"What is?"

"If you have a big *nose*, you're supposed to have a big penis."

"Did Pinocchio have a big penis?"

"Did Dumbo?" Sarah asked, and both women burst out laughing again.

"They'll throw us out of here," Heather said, covering her mouth with her napkin, trying to stifle the laughter.

"I wouldn't blame them," Sarah said.

"I think I'll go ask him to dance."

"I don't think that's such a good idea," Sarah said.

"Why not? My last night here? Kiss me my sweet, for tomorrow I die."

"No one else is dancing."

"Break the ice, what the hell."

"Your goat'll get cold."

"Better my *goat* than something else," Heather said, and grinned mischievously. "Why is it that whenever I feel like dancing, the goddamn band is playing something Latin?"

Actually, it seemed to Sarah that the piano player was still playing Cole Porter. Something from *Kiss Me, Kate*, in fact. Something that sounded very much like "So in Love with You Am I," but maybe the beat *was* Latin, it was difficult to tell. She looked at her watch. If they got out of here by nine-thirty, ten, she could call Michael by . . .

"Taxi waiting?" Heather asked.

"No, no. Sorry, I didn't . . ."

"Am I boring you, sis?" Heather said.

"Of course not. I promised to call Michael again, that's all."

"But *do* I bore you? Tell me the truth, Sarah. I'm your sister, do you find me boring?"

"No, I find you very interesting, in fact."

"But am I a boring person, Sarah? Tell me. Please."

"No, you're a fascinating person."

"Then why did *Doug* find me boring?"

"I never got the impression he did."

"Then why'd he start up with a nineteen-year-old *twit*?"

"I have no idea."

"What do nineteen year olds *talk* about, anyway? Their trips to the record shop in the mall? Who do you think is more boring, Michael or Douglas?"

"I don't think either one of them is boring."

"I think Michael is boring."

"Don't let *him* hear you say that."

"And put on my top when he gets here, I know, I know."

"You'll be *gone* when he gets here," Sarah said. "*If* he gets here."

"Don't you find him boring?"

"No, I find him very interesting."

"Don't you find him too . . . lawyerly? I find lawyers very boring, Sarah. I'm sorry, but that's the truth. Lawyers are very boring. At least advertising isn't boring. I think Michael is attractive, but very boring. Is he any good in bed?"

"Yes, he's very good."

"I don't see how he can be. A boring person like that."

"Well . . ."

"Really, sis. How can a boring person like Michael be any good in bed? At least Douglas isn't boring. *Wasn't*."

"Well . . ."

"You don't like me talking this way, do you?"

"Well, no, I don't."

"Have you ever noticed that if we put our husbands together, we get Michael Douglas?"

"What?"

"Michael and Douglas. Put them together you get a handsome movie star who's definitely not *boring*, that's for sure. Do you remember him with his pants down in *Fatal Attraction*? Tripping all over the room with what's her name? Meryl Streep. Have you ever made passionate love like that with Michael? Where you can't wait to take off your clothes?"

"That's none of your business."

"You just answered the question, sis."

"No, I didn't. It's simply none of your business, what Michael and I do together."

"Glenn Close, it was," Heather said.

In *fact*, Sarah thought, when I get back to the house tonight, Michael and I are going to have a glorious phone phuck, how about *that*, sis?

"Why doesn't that guy play something slow and romantic?" Heather said. "I want to go dance with Whitey. See if I can talk him into a little fricas*see* or two. Curried goat makes a person horny, did you know that?"

"Stop it, he's looking this way," Sarah whispered.

"Whitey?"

"No, the young one."

"Those are the two from the beach today," Andrew said.

"Which one had her top off?" Willie asked.

"The one in pink, I think."

"The other one's better looking," Willie said.

Andrew was thinking that women sometimes looked better when they were dressed to kill than when they were naked or even half-naked. The one who'd been topless on the beach this afternoon, for example, was now wearing a short pink sort of T-shirt dress with a gold belt and gold high-heeled sandals, no bra under the dress, and somehow this was sexier than her sitting there in just her bikini bottom this afternoon, he didn't know why.

"You think they're twins?" Willie asked.

"No, the one in white looks older," Andrew said.

"What do you think? Thirty, thirty-five?"

"In there."

"Good-looking women, though. Both of them."

"Mm," Andrew said, and looked over at them again.

The one in white was definitely the older sister. Flaring white pleated skirt, white scoop-neck top, gold chain and pendant, white high-heeled sandals, all tan and white and golden. The sister was younger and fresher looking, but there was something more sophisticated about the one in white, the way she lifted her wine glass, the way she tilted her head at just the right angle. Sexier somehow. Given his choice, he'd take the one in white, too.

The waiter came with their drinks just then. Canadian on the rocks for Andrew, a planter's punch for Willie. Willie raised his glass in a toast to the two women sitting across the room. The one in the pink dress looked at him and then turned away in seeming disdain.

"Bingo," Willie said.

★ ★ ★

"So what do you think, sis?" Heather asked. "Can you find your way back alone tonight?"

"You're not serious," Sarah said.

"I seem to have caught Whitey's eye."

"You may catch more than that . . ."

"Who cares?"

". . . picking up strangers in a bar."

"A *restaurant*, please. And only *one* stranger. Unless the one with the big ears wants to join us."

"I think you *are* serious."

"You just watch me, kid."

"Your plane leaves at nine."

"Plenty of time."

"The man's in his *sixties!*"

"Good, I'll give him a heart attack."

"Whatever you do, leave me out of it," Sarah said.

"Who invited you?"

"I mean it."

"Watch him melt," Heather said, and turned toward where the two men were sitting, and leveled a long, lingering, blue-eyed gaze at the white-haired one.

"What time is the boat meeting me?" Andrew asked.

"Did you see that?"

"No. What?"

"The one in pink. She just invited me to her room."

"They're not staying here," Andrew said. "They live in that house on the beach."

"Better yet."

"The boat," Andrew reminded him.

"They'll send a dinghy to the dock at ten tomorrow morning. They're very prompt, so be on time. I told them you'd be alone, the way you wanted it. I prefer the one in white, but I'm willing to settle," Willie said. "You want the one in white?"

"No," Andrew said. "I want a good night's sleep. This meeting tomorrow is important."

"Always mix business with pleasure," Willie said. "That's a rule here in the islands."

"Whose rule?"

"Mine. You sure you don't want the one in white?"

"Positive."

"Then I'll take both of them."

"Do you plan to eat first, or are you going to jump them right here in the dining room?" Andrew asked.

"Maybe both," Willie said, and grinned like a shark.

The one with the white hair approached their table while they were having coffee and dessert.

"Good evening, ladies," he said.

Heather looked up at him.

Nothing in her eyes. No hint that she had noticed him earlier, had in fact blatantly flirted with him across the room. Sarah had to admire her sister's cool.

"My name is Willie Isetti," he said. "I was wondering if you'd like to join my friend and I for an after-dinner drink. There are some quiet tables in the bar area . . ."

"Thank you, no," Heather said, her voice only a few degrees icier than the glare in her pale blue eyes.

"Sorry to have bothered you," he said, and smiled weakly, and walked back across the room to where the young one was sitting alone at the table.

Sarah looked at her sister.

"He doesn't know grammar," Heather said, and shrugged.

"I thought *I* was the English teacher."

"Besides, my plane *is* at nine."

"Um-huh."

"And he *is* in his sixties."

"Um-huh."

"And he's not as good-looking now that I'm sober."

"Then let's go home," Sarah said.

She left Heather touching up her lipstick at the mirror in the ladies' room while she went outside to get the car from the valet. She was waiting under the hibiscus-covered trellis at the front of the hotel, the side away from the harbor and the spectacular view, when the young one with the ears came outside.

He said nothing to her.

They stood at opposite ends of the small curved entryway to the hotel, the strong heavy aroma of angel's-trumpet suffusing the night air. The silence lengthened until it became too obviously awkward.

"Nice night," she said.

"Lovely," he said.

The valet arrived just then, pulling the car up to a squealing stop, leaping out, leaving the driver-side door open for her, and then running around to open the passenger-side door. Thinking they were together, he looked surprised when Sarah and not the man tipped him four francs.

"Did you have a car, too, sir?" he asked.

"Red VW," he said, and handed him the keys.

"The license plate?"

"Sorry, I don't know."

The valet shook his head.

"They like you to remember the license plate number," Sarah told him. "These rental cars from the airport all look alike."

"I should have realized that," he said, and turned to the valet. "I parked it under the big tree there," he told him, and pointed it out.

"You should have let *me* park it, sir," the valet said, looking offended.

"Sorry about that," he said, and smiled.

"I'll get it for you, sir."

"Thank you."

Heather came out of the hotel just then.

"Well, good night," Sarah said.

"Good night," he said.

Heather looked at him briefly and then got into the car. As they pulled away from the hotel, she arched a brow and said, "Fast work, sis."

Sarah was thinking she'd be talking to Michael in less than twenty minutes.

The phone rang some ten times before he picked up.

"Hullo?"

His voice sounded sleep-sodden, almost drugged.

"Michael?"

"Mm."

"It's me."

"Uh-huh."

"Wake up, darling."

"Uh-huh," he said.

"Wake up, it's me."

"Mm."

"Wake up, Michael."

"Mm."

"Michael?"

"Uh-huh."

"It's me," she said. "Sarah."

"Okay, g'night," he said.

There was a click on the line.

"Michael?" she said.

Silence.

"Michael?"

She looked at the phone receiver, so startled that she burst out laughing. Shaking her head, the laughter subsiding, she put the receiver back on its cradle, lay back against the pillows again, and visualized Michael at home all tangled in the bedclothes, dead asleep, not knowing whether she was lying there beside him or calling from the moon, having forgotten completely the promises of long-distance sex they'd made earlier tonight.

It was too bad, actually.

She'd really been ready for him.

Looking out at the star-drenched night, she lay silent and still for a long long while before finally she fell asleep.

The computerized tapes had brought Michael current to April of 1992. From there on, it was either listening to the tapes themselves or reading the typed transcripts of them. It was simpler to read transcripts than to listen to tapes, which were often hard to understand. He decided to read.

This was now nine-thirty on Tuesday morning, the twenty-ninth. He had phoned Sarah before leaving for work, vaguely remembering a call from her in the middle of the night, and apologizing for having drunk a bit too much at Spark's, which restaurant always made him feel like a gangster himself; maybe that's why he went there. Sarah had graciously allowed that perhaps she and her sister—who'd be leaving for the airport in about twenty minutes, she informed him—had *also* drunk a bit too much, so maybe they should try it another time, like how about right *now*, she'd suggested. He'd told her he was on his way to the office, but he'd call her later.

The people who'd typed the transcripts had worked very closely with the actual investigative team. Through long association, the detectives who'd done the wiretap surveillance knew each of the voices on the tape intimately and could instantly clear up any confusion the typists may have had when a voice sounded too similar to another one. Anthony Faviola had a deep, sonorous voice, cultivated over the years to disguise a faintly lingering Brooklyn accent; someone named *Tony* might have used "deses" or "doses," but not someone named *Anthony*, if you please. Anthony had once been quoted as saying that he thought the nickname *Tony* sounded like "some kind of ignorant wop." *Anthony,* on the other hand (although he'd never said anything to that effect), must have sounded to him like a British prime minister. Michael couldn't blame him. He himself hated anyone calling him Mike, which sounded to him like a bartender. Office rumor had it that Faviola had once taken speech lessons from a teacher on Park Avenue, but this was unsubstantiated. Whatever the case, he didn't sound *quite* like a mobster, but neither did he sound like Professor Higgins.

His brother was something else again. There was no mistaking Rudy whenever he opened his mouth. His voice was rumbling and gravelly, and he mangled the English language as brutally as he'd once mangled recalcitrant debtors. Even when he was in a room with other gangsters whose disrespect for English rivaled his own, he was completely identifiable, preferring to shout every word he uttered, a habit that had caused the investigating detectives innumerable problems with their gain controls. On the typed transcripts, there was no problem with voices. Anthony was identified by the initials AF. Rudy was RF. PB was Peter Bardo. These were the three key players. At the time of the surveillance AF was still boss. RF was underboss. PB was consigliere, third in command.

Presumably, when AF went out to Kansas, RF became boss, PB became underboss, and the man presumed to have organized the mob's entire narcotics operation back when they were just beginning to dabble in dope—an elderly thug named Louis "Fat Nickie" Nicoletta—had taken over as consigliere. But back in the spring of 1992, they might have been talking about someone like Dominick Di Nobili, small world.

AF: The way I see this, Rude, it's not going to be fruitful to lean on this man. We're discussing a large sum of money, which it's clear he doesn't have.

RF: Smack him real good, he'll *find* the fuckin money in a hurry, take it from me.

AF: And if he doesn't? How does *that* make us look?

RF: It makes us look a guy doesn't pay one way he pays *another* fuckin way.

AF: But we still won't have the money, will we? What if we give him a grace period, say a week, to come up with what he owes? No interest for a week. We . . .

RF: That sets an example for every fuckin deadbeat in town.

AF: This is fifty grand we're talking, Rude, a man can't just . . .

RF: This is *also* a matter of principle we're talkin.

AF: Agreed. But if a man is broke, he can't come up with . . .

RF: He's broke cause he bets the fuckin ponies with money *we* lent him.

AF: Even so . . .

RF: Besides, it was only *twenty* when he borrowed it. It's cause he ain't payin it back, it goes through the fuckin roof.

AF: Go talk to him, okay? Tell him your brother's giving him a week free, out of the goodness of his heart. Tell him once the week's up, I won't be able to control the animals who work for me.

RF: *(Laughing)* Fuckin animals, yeah.

On and on. The daily routine of running a vast business empire, coupled with the more mundane matters confronting a busy chief executive officer . . .

AF: Petey, what do *you* think?

PB: I think a gift is appropriate. But a modest one.

AF: How modest?

PB: Three bills. No more than that.

AF: Isn't that kind of cheap for a christening? What'd we spend on Giannino when *his* kid was christened?

PB: I can check.

AF: Check, would you? And send Danielli the same. He hears we sent Giannino's kid something more expensive, he'll take offense.

RF: Fuckin hardheaded wop.

AF: What is it, anyway? A boy or a girl?

PB: A girl.

GL: Grows up lookin like Terry, she'll be a winner.

GL. Identified in the transcript's index as the capo in charge of the Gerald Lacizzare Crew, which at the time of the surveillance operated a loan-sharking business that took in thousands of dollars a week in interest, charging rates of between 156 and 312 percent a year.

Danielli was Felix Danielli, who at the time of the surveillance was running an illegal horse betting parlor that did business in excess of twenty thousand dollars a week. His wife, Teresa, was purported to be an extravagantly beautiful woman.

RF: Love to boff that broad.

Rudy Faviola again, the underboss, undoubtedly licking his lips while professing his desire, this despite strict mob rules against hitting on any family member's wife or daughter.

On and on. From the mundane to the ridiculous . . .

RF: I'm dancing, right, when all of a sudden I hear this broad cut a giant fart, it's the first time I ever heard a broad I wasn't fucking fart.

AF: *(Laughing)* This is the girl you're dancing with?

RF: Yeah, right on the dance floor. A fart like an explosion. And, oh *Jesus*, what a *stink*!

LN: People probably thought it was *you* made the fart.

LN. Louis "Fat Nickie" Nicoletta. Presumably the new consigliere, but at the time of the surveillance, the man directing much of the family's narcotics activities.

RF: That's what I was afraid of, Nick! They'd think *I'm* the one stinkin up Vinny's fuckin wedding. Big fat cunt stinkin like a New Jersey sewer.

LN: I never had a woman fart while I was fuckin her.

RF: Maybe you ain't fuckin them right.

LN: Kick her right out of the bed, she farts on me.

Conversation upon conversation, from the ridiculous to the sublime . . .

BT: This is supposed to be a realistic movie, you understand?

Bobby Triani, identified in the index as Rudy Faviola's son-in-law, and a capo overseeing the family's vast stolen-property operation, including a "theft to order" scheme that utilized the services of corrupt United Parcel Service employees.

LN: I don't go to the movies no more. I always get in trouble I go to the movies.

AF: What kind of trouble? You want some more of this, Nick?

LN: No, thanks. I'm always tellin people shut up. The ones behind me talkin.

RF: I almost *did* shoot some cocksucker talkin behind me, he was givin away the whole fuckin movie.

BT: You *shoulda* shot him.

RF: I mean it, the whole fuckin movie. Here's where he jumps out the window, here's where she catches him with the blonde, here's where the fuckin tiger gets loose, here's . . .

LN: The whole fuckin movie.

RF: I turned around and shoved the piece in his fuckin face, I told him shut up or I'll blow off your nose. He tells me he's gonna go get the usher. I tell him go ahead go get the fuckin usher, I'll blow off *his* nose, too.

BT: You shoulda shot the cocksucker.

LN: Did he shut up? I'll bet he didn't.

RF: No, he didn't, they got no fuckin manners. This is good sauce, Anth.

AF: Thank you.

RF: I mean it. This is superb sauce.

BT: You shoulda shot the cocksucker.
    And then back to business again . . .

AF: We can't relate this to what they do in Harlem. That's a whole different family there in Harlem, and they've got their own way of dealing with the spics.

PB: I'm only suggesting we discuss it with them . . .

RF: They're fuckin hardheads in Harlem. We go in there to talk there's gonna be war.

AF: Discuss *what* with them, Petey?

PB: A proper piece of the action.

RF: You're not talkin *nigger* Harlem, are you?

PB: No, no.

RF: Cause that's entirely out of the question. Fuckin niggers won't listen to *shit*.

PB: I'm talking about East Harlem.

AF: *East* Harlem, Rudy.

RF: Cause the niggers are out of the question.

AF: I still don't know what you have in mind, Petey.

PB: The Colombians run the coffee up through Mexico . . .

A transparent code word for cocaine. Never knew who might be listening. In this case, an absolutely correct assumption, but little did they *really* know . . .

PB: . . . and a lot of it ends up in East Harlem. So we're supposed to have an agreement with them, am I right? But we're not getting a piece on the coffee goes in there.

AF: I have something more important in mind down the line, Petey. I don't want to rock the boat just now.

PB: This wouldn't be boosting the *Colombians*, you understand . . .

AF: I know that. But the balance is pretty shaky right now, and I don't want anything upsetting it further.

RF: You want my opinion, the fuckin spics are gonna do away with the people in Harlem entirely. Who the fuck needs a middleman? They got their own distribution setup, the Harlem people are like a fuckin fifth wheel.

AF: I think so, yes. That's all part of it.

Michael kept reading the transcript.

On another day, in another month, there was a philosophical discussion about the very real services these noble gangsters provided. Present at this lofty seminar were Anthony Faviola and his laureate brother, Rudy, Fat Nickie Nicoletta, who never went to the movies anymore, Peter Bardo the consigliere, and Felix Danielli, who had the gorgeous wife Rudy would have loved to boff.

AF: When you think of it, what are we doing that's so terrible?

RF: What are we doing, right?

AF: Why is gambling against the law? Is it such a sin to gamble?

LN: They gambled in the Bible, even. I saw a movie, they were gambling for Jesus' robe.

PB: You're right, Anthony, gambling should be legal.

AF: It should. But meanwhile, it's against the law. So what do we do? We provide what the people want. They want to gamble, we give them the means to gamble.

LN: His robe they were shooting dice for. The robe he was wearing.

AF: What's the lottery, if not legal gambling?

RF: What's OTB?

AF: It's *all* legal gambling. But when *we* run it, it's against the law. Why? We're giving the same odds, no? We're not rigging anything, we run a fair game. We take our vig, sure, but doesn't the state take a vig?

The vigorish, or the percentage, or the house cut, the edge that made any gambling a winning proposition for the mob. Even when they lost, they won. Bet a hundred bucks on a football game, the bookie paid you the hundred if you won, but if you lost he collected a hundred and ten.

PB: How about lending money? You know what the banks are getting *legally* now? The interest rate on a *legal* loan?

RF: Through the fuckin roof, I bet.

PB: Close to what we're asking, that's for sure.

AF: But what's a man supposed to do when a bank turns him down? Is it a sin to have bad credit?

RF: Make a guy feel like a fuckin scumbag, the banks.

LN: Turn you down no reason at all.

AF: They come to us, their credit is always good.

At three to five percent a *week*, compounded, Michael thought. Put *that* on your calculator, see what the interest on a ten-thousand-dollar loan comes to after a few months of five-percent interest.

RF: It's a service, plain and simple. Like you said, Anth.

AF: Sure, but they make it illegal.

LN: A service we provide.

RF: Where else can a guy needs money go? Temporary.

LN: Who's gonna lend it to him?

RF: Also, they say we bust a guy's head he don't pay. So what does a *bank* do? A bank takes the fuckin guy's *house* away, is what the bank does.

AF: One way or another, they're out to get us.

RF: Make our fuckin lives miserable.

LN: The cocksuckers.

Michael almost missed the first mention. It came during the second week in June. It was in a monitored two-way telephone conversation between Anthony and his brother. Michael's eyes passed right over the word because it wasn't an exact match. The transcript read:

AF: What bothers me, Rude, is they may really have something this time. They're acting as if they've got something.

RF: It's the same old shit, Anth. They always come in blowin wind, they ain't got a fuckin thing on you and they know it.

AF: All those indictments.

RF: They ain't got shit.

AF: Murder, Rudy. That's heavy.

RF: You never murdered anybody your whole life.

AF: Never let up.

RF: Cocksuckers.

AF: Mick-a-lino's worried, too.

RF: I'll go talk to him.

AF: Calm him down, tell him I'll be okay. He's worried.

RF: Sure he is. But don't *you* worry, huh, Anth? Nobody's
gonna hurt you.
AF: Yeah.
RF: You hear me?
AF: Yeah, thanks, Rudy.
RF: I'll go talk t'Lino.

There it was again. *Mick*-a-lino the first time around,
just plain *Lino*, with the *L* capitalized, the second time. The
capitalization was the typist's choice, Michael guessed,
guided by the detective who'd actually listened to the conversations as they were being recorded. Listening to the sitdown
talk between Frankie Palumbo and Jimmy Angels in the Ristorante Romano, Michael and Georgie had thought they'd
heard the name *Lena*. The typist who'd transferred the Faviola tapes to the computer disk had spelled the name L-E-N-
O when the matter of the Christmas gift had been mentioned
in December of 1991. And now the typist doing the transcript
had spelled it L-I-N-O, as in Mick-a-lino and Lino. How had
this been pronounced on the original tapes? As in "wino"? If
so, this couldn't possibly be related to Lena. Michael debated
consulting the tapes themselves at this point. Instead, he kept
reading the transcript.

The next time the letters L-I-N-O came up in sequence
was during another telephone conversation, this time between Anthony Faviola and his wife, Tessie, during the
month of August, shortly before the start of Faviola's trial.
Faviola was calling from Club Sorrento, where several
bugs had been planted, and to which he referred simply as
"the club." Tessie was on the bug-free house phone in
Stonington. Before the investigating detectives tuned out
on this privileged husband-wife communication, they'd
recorded:

AF: I have a few more things to take care of here at the club,
then I'll be coming home.
TF: Be careful, the weekend traffic.

AF: Yeah, don't worry.

TF: What time do you think you'll be?

AF: Six, six-thirty. For supper, anyway.

Supper. A holdover from the Brooklyn days, when the evening meal at Stella Faviola's table was always called "supper" and never "dinner."

AF: Is Lino still coming up?

TF: He's already here.

AF: Oh? Good. Tell him I'll see him later, okay?

TF: Drive careful.

Lino again. An apparent guest in Faviola's impregnable Connecticut fortress. Lino. Short for *Mick*-a-lino? Or had this been *Michelino* on the tapes? The diminutive of Michele? Transmogrified by a tone-deaf WASP typist to some sort of bastardized English? Michele. Pronounced "Mee-*kay*-lay" in Italian. Michael knew because "Michael" just happened to be his name, and that's what he'd been called the one and only time he'd been to Italy, Michele, with a hard *ch* as opposed to the soft one in the French "Michel."

Michele.

Michael.

Michelino.

Little Michael.

Anthony Faviola had no children or grandchildren named Michael. Nor had the name figured prominently in any of the trial material, any of the volumes of transcripts the U.S. Attorney's Office had studied and restudied in its successful bid to put Faviola away forever. If anyone had noticed mention of a Michael or a Little Michael, no significance had been given to the names. Until now.

Now a Queens waiter who owed money to a Manhattan loan shark had agreed to courier some dope and had walked into a sting set up by Narcotics. And during a conversation between a pair of capos trying to save his ass, a Faviola lieutenant had said he'd talk it over with Lena—or so they'd

thought. But Lena had become Leno, and from there it was
a hop, skip, and jump to Mick-a-lino to Michelino to Little
Michael.

He checked the tapes.

The name had, in fact, been pronounced in the Italian
way, Michelino, and transcribed by the typist in phonetic
English. Which meant that Lino didn't rhyme with *wino*, it
rhymed with *clean*-o.

Michelino.

Little Michael.

Once more unto the breach, Michael thought, and
plunged into the transcript yet another time.

Alonso Moreno was known in some circles as *La Culebra*, which meant The Snake. Andrew guessed this had more
to do with his business practices than with his looks. He was,
in fact, quite a handsome man.

Sitting on the foredeck of a forty-eight-foot Grand
Banks—not particularly known for speed, but no one was
trying to outrace anyone today—Moreno offered Andrew a
cigarette, shrugged when he declined it, and then lighted his
own and turned politely away to exhale a stream of smoke.
Turning back to Andrew, his dark glasses reflecting bright
morning sunlight, he said, "I already told your people no,"
and then snapped his fingers at a man wearing knee-length
white cotton shorts and a white cotton sweater, and pointed
immediately to the pitcher of lemonade sitting on a low table
fastened to the deck with cleats. The man in white poured
their glasses full again. The cigarette in one hand, the glass
of lemonade in the other, Moreno alternately sipped and
puffed.

"So why are you here?" he asked.

Andrew figured Moreno had a good ten years on him,
thirty-eight, thirty-nine, in there. Rudolph Valentino
looks, black hair slicked back from a pronounced widow's
peak, aquiline nose a trifle too long for his face, androgynous

Mick Jagger lips, puffing and sipping, calmly waiting for a reply. Too polite to say you're wasting my fucking time here. But wise enough to realize Andrew had come all the way from New York and was not to be summarily dismissed.

"I'm here because I don't think this was explained properly to you."

"It was explained," Moreno said, and suddenly took off the sunglasses.

Eyes so brown they looked black.

Maybe that's where he'd got the Snake nickname.

Black eyes reflecting sunlight.

Out on the water, a speedboat towing a skier behind it appeared suddenly on the horizon.

"Mr. Isetti explained it to me fully."

Slight Spanish accent. Andrew had heard someplace that Moreno was college-educated, had been studying to be a doctor, in fact. He imagined Moreno with a scalpel in his hand. The thought was frightening.

"The business aspects," Andrew said.

"*Every* aspect," Moreno said. "We're not interested."

"We consider this a very rich deal."

"We're rich enough," Moreno said, and smiled.

"We're not," Andrew said, and returned the smile.

"*Qué pena,*" Moreno said.

"We figure a person can always get richer than he is."

Moreno said nothing. Bored, he puffed on his cigarette and sipped at his lemonade. Out on the water, the speedboat cut a wider arc. The skier behind it let out an exuberant yell.

"We figure that a person who doesn't want to get richer runs the risk of getting poorer," Andrew said.

"I don't see that risk."

"Do you know how Columbus happened to discover America?"

"What?" Moreno said.

"I said, 'Do you . . . ?' "

"I heard you. What does it mean?"

"He was looking for China."

"So?"

"We're bringing China right to your doorstep. You don't have to go looking for it."

"I'm *not* looking for it. *You're* the one who's looking for it."

"No, we're looking for an expanded market that'll . . ."

"Good, you go look for it. *We're* happy with America."

"I don't think you're hearing me," Andrew said.

"I'm hearing you fine, thank you very much," Moreno said. "That's just a child out there, you know? The skier."

Andrew glanced briefly over the water and then turned his attention back to Moreno.

"You supply your product," he said, "the Chinese supply theirs. Our European associates turn it over, and we distribute all over America and Europe."

"We *already* distribute in America and Europe," Moreno said.

"Not the new product."

"We don't *need* any new products."

"We think you do."

"Hey, really, who the fuck cares *what* you think?" Moreno said.

"Mr. Moreno, I think you'd better . . ."

"No, don't 'Mr. Moreno' me, and don't tell me what I better do, I do what I *want* to do, never mind what I *better* do. I told Isetti we're not interested, he says I think you owe us the courtesy of hearing what Andrew has to say, he came all the way down here from New York. Okay, I just listened to what Andrew has to say, and we're *still* not interested. I don't know who sent you . . ."

"Nobody *sent* me, Mr. Moreno."

"But whoever it was . . ."

"I came on my own."

"Fine. Go back on your own. Tell whoever sent you . . ."

"This is the last time I'll explain it," Andrew said, and sighed wearily, as if trying to instruct a particularly recalcitrant child. "We're working out a three-way deal with the Chinese. If you'd like to join us, you're more than welcome. That's why I'm here. But if you refuse to see the merits, we'll have to go ahead without you. I think you can understand how difficult we can make things . . ."

"Listen, get off my boat, okay?" Moreno said, and then, in Spanish, to the man in the white cotton shorts and sweater, *"Llevarlo de vuelta a la costa, no hay nada más que discutir aquí."* He extended his hand to Andrew, said, "Our business is finished, Alberico will take you . . ." and then stopped in midsentence and got to his feet and pointed out over the water, and said, "That child's in trouble."

From where Sarah sat at the wheel of the speedboat, her head craned over her shoulder, she knew only that Mollie had suddenly gone under. Spills were common, though, and Mollie had been water-skiing ever since she was seven, when her grandfather added a speedboat to his other Caribbean possessions. She was skilled and daring, and until this moment, Sarah had never felt the slightest qualms about allowing her daughter to rip up the ocean behind a boat doing twenty miles an hour over open water. In fact, for the past year now, Mollie had been skiing without a life vest, pleading greater freedom of movement and a thorough knowledge of what she was doing, and Sarah hadn't seen any danger to it.

She swung the boat around in a tight turn now, opened the throttle full, and headed back toward where she'd last seen Mollie. There was a moderate chop today, the boat skidded and thudded over the waves as she closed the distance, waiting for her daughter to surface, avoiding the towrope, the last thing she wanted now was to get the rope tangled in the boat's . . . *there!* Mollie's blond head popping to the surface. Mouth opening wide to suck in air, waves breaking under her chin. Some twenty yards beyond her, a man was standing at the railing of a big Grand Banks, yelling in Spanish. And then another man climbed onto the rail, hung there against the sky for just a moment, dove overboard, and began swimming toward Mollie just as she went under again.

Sarah silently willed the speedboat forward, urging it to go faster than it possibly could, pushing it against wind and chop, the towline safely behind her, aware now of the swimmer in the water, plowing against the waves in a fast crawl to where Mollie's head broke the surface again. Another mouthful of air, Sarah was close enough to see her face now, panic in those blue eyes. She clawed at the sky, and went under for the third time, and the swimmer dove down after her.

Sarah pulled back on the throttle, began circling the area where her daughter and the swimmer had gone under. There was only the sound of the idling engine now, the boat lazily circling the spot where they'd disappeared, the sky so blue overhead, the seconds lengthening, and lengthening and lengthening, and . . .

She was on the edge of screaming when first Mollie's head broke the surface of the water, and then her narrow shoulders, and then the swimmer's hands clutching her waist. His own head broke the surface at last, brown hair flattened against his skull. He sucked in a deep breath of air, pushed aside Mollie's flailing hands, and rolled her onto her back. Cupping her chin with one hand, he swam her over to where Sarah leaned over the gunwales and lifted her daughter into the boat.

Two weeks before he was arrested and charged with four counts of second-degree murder, Anthony Faviola's thoughts—and his conversation—turned to matters merely mortal. It was almost as if he knew what was coming. Knew that he'd soon be looking not only at the four counts, each of which carried lifetime sentences under the federal guidelines, but also at *another* possible lifetime sentence on a RICO charge.

The conversation had taken place at the bugged corner

table in Club Sorrento. The *boss's* table. Reserved for Faviola and his closest cronies whenever they dropped in, which was often. In the transcript, Anthony and his brother, Rudy, were identified by the now-familiar initials AF and RF. Apparently the men were drinking; perhaps Anthony might not have been so candid were he not somewhat in his cups. And whereas Michael had never held a soft spot in his heart for *anyone* who broke the law, he felt something like sympathy as he read the words of this man who did not know he was being taped and could not have known what the future held in store for him, and yet who was predicting it quite sadly and accurately:

AF: I keep thinking they're closing in on me.

RF: Come on, come on.

AF: I mean it, Rude. Everywhere I go, everything I do, they're on top of me. It's like they won't let me breathe.

RF: Fuck 'em, that's just the way they are. They got nothin better to do than break people's balls.

AF: Have some more of this.

RF: Just a little.

AF: Say when.

RF: That's enough, ay, hold it.

AF: I don't care for myself, you understand. I've had a good life.

RF: Don't let them fucks bother you, Anth. They're nothin.

AF: It's not me I care about. It's Tessie, the kids. What kind of life can it be for them, these bums coming around all the time?

RF: They're nothin, don't let them get to you.

AF: Angela and Carol, I don't think it bothers them as much as . . .

RF: They're beautiful girls, Anth. You got beautiful daughters.

AF: They love their Uncle Rudy, I can tell you that.

RF: I'd break their heads, they didn't.

(Laughter)

AF: But a son. It's different for a son. How many kids like him get to go to college? But he fucked up, right? I think because he liked Vegas too much.

RF: Well, yeah, Vegas.

AF: Tessie was so proud of him. So he gets himself kicked out for drinkin an' fightin. Have some more of this.

RF: Thanks. Watch how you're pouring, you son of a bitch, you'll get me drunk.

AF: You know how much I paid for this?

RF: How much?

AF: Six ninety-five a bottle.

RF: Come on.

AF: I'm serious. I bought six cases.

RF: Where'd you get this, six ninety-five a bottle?

AF: The guy around the corner.

RF: What is it, Spanish? They make cheap wine, the Spanish.

AF: No, no, it's Italian.

RF: Six fuckin ninety-five? I can't believe it.

AF: It's delicious, I think.

RF: It's fuckin *superb*.

AF: Six ninety-five.

RF: But, you know, Anth, when it comes to kids . . .

AF: It should *all* be as simple as wine.

RF: Nothin's simple, Anth. Forget anything bein simple, there's nothin simple.

AF: Girls are different.

RF: Also, they're both married. You got to remember that. It makes a difference.

AF: Oh, sure. Nice boys, too, they married. You like them?

RF: Oh, sure. Well, not Sam so much. He's a fuckin know-it-all. But the other one . . .

AF: Larry.

RF: Yeah, Larry.

AF: Larry, yeah. He's okay.

RF: He's very nice. A good kid. He likes me, too, I can tell. His fuckin Uncle Rudy. He calls me Uncle Rudy.

AF: You know what I wish. This is if God forbid they ever send me away, what I wish . . .

RF: Come on, stop it. Have some more wine. Come on. I don't like to hear this shit.

Back to the good cheap wine again, Michael thought. Six ninety-five a bottle from the guy around the corner. Italian wine. It should all be as simple as wine. He wished they'd mentioned the label. At six ninety-five a bottle, he'd buy six cases himself.

AF: But if they *do* put me away, Rude . . .

RF: That's never gonna happen, so don't even *think* it.

AF: But *if* they do, you know who I want to take over for me?

RF: I hope you're not gonna say me, cause I'll tell you the truth, I don't *want* the fuckin job.

AF: Listen, you'd be terrific, Rudy, but . . .

RF: Thanks, I don't want it. Anyway, you're not going no place, so forget it. Have some more wine, you jackass, stop talkin stupid.

Little more vino? Michael thought. Little more vino, bro? We'll both go home in a wheelbarrow, you push, I'll ride. Say when. Plop, plop, plink, plink, plop, plop, plop.

RF: And I hope you ain't thinkin of Petey Bardo, neither. I got nothin against him, I promise you, but he's got the personality of a fuckin rivet. *Salute!* Jesus, this is truly superb. He's excellent at what he does cause he looks like a fuckin judge, those brown suits he wears, I never met nobody likes brown the way Petey does, I swear to God. But can you imagine him sittin down with some of the people from Harlem, f'example, havin a few drinks with *that* bunch? Can you imagine him *ever* loosenin up that way? He's a fuckin stiff, Anth, even if he *is* married to Josie. It takes more than just brains to keep this thing of ours together, this thing we got.

AF: So who *do* you think? If I ever had to retire, you know.

RF: Probably who you were gonna say yourself.

AF: Who do you think I was about to say?

RF: If he *wants* it, that is.

AF: Who?

RF: He may like Vegas too much. Atlantic City too much. This is responsibility here. Girls, he likes girls too much. And gambling. He takes over for you, he's got to have his head *here*, Anth, and not up some snatch. His head and his heart got to be *here*.

AF: I think we have the same person in mind.

RF: Sure. Lino, am I right?

AF: Lino, yes.

And there it was.

It had been her own fault, allowing Mollie to go out there without a life jacket, but she'd been doing that forever, and there'd been no reason to believe . . .

No, there was no excuse.

What was she supposed to tell Michael? That she'd almost allowed their daughter to drown? That if it hadn't been for the bravery of a total stranger, Mollie might now be . . .

Well, not entirely a *total* stranger.

This was the man she'd said hello to last night outside the restaurant, the one Heather thought had big ears. Standing on the deck of the small boat, dripping wet and out of breath, hands on his hips, head bent, he watched silently as Sarah knelt over her daughter. Mollie was coughing and sputtering and spitting, but she seemed otherwise fine, if totally shaken.

"Thank you," Sarah had whispered, more to God than to the tall stranger.

He nodded, still gasping for breath after the exertion of his hard swim against the chop.

He introduced himself as Andrew Farrell.

Said he was here in St. Bart's on business, staying at the Guanahani.

She said she didn't know how to thank him.

She would later remember all this in minute detail.

He said all he asked was a ride back to the yacht so he could pick up his shoes. She realized then that he'd dived overboard fully clothed, except for the shoes. White long-sleeved shirt plastered to his arms and chest, pale pastel-blue cotton trousers soaking wet.

She thanked him again as he climbed the ladder onto the Grand Banks. In a small voice, Mollie piped, "Thank you, Mr. Farrell."

It wasn't until later that afternoon that Sarah called the Guanahani and asked for Andrew Farrell, please. When he answered the phone, she told him who she was . . .

"Sarah Welles, you saved my daughter's life . . ."

. . . as if there were a dozen Sarah Welleses whose daughters' lives he'd saved, and then said she really felt they owed him more than a boat ride back to retrieve his shoes . . .

No, don't be silly, he said, I was happy to be of assistance.

She would remember all this later.

Well, she said, my daughter and I feel we haven't truly expressed our gratitude. Mr. Farrell . . . if you have no other plans, could we possibly take you to dinner tonight? Mollie suggested that you choose anyplace you like on the island . . .

Only if it's my treat, he said.

She would remember all this.

No, no, she said, of *course* not, that's not the idea at *all*.

My treat, he said. I'll pick you up at seven-thirty. I know where the house is.

Later, she would wonder how he knew.

Seven-thirty is fine, she said, but I insist that . . .

See you later, he said, and hung up.

★ ★ ★

Michael caught Georgie at home at four that afternoon, packing for his trip to Vail.

"Few questions," he said.

"I'm on vacation," Georgie said.

"Regarding Anthony Faviola," Michael said.

"I'm *still* on vacation."

"One *quick* question, then."

"Better make it *very* quick. I'm almost out the door."

"Who's Lino?"

"You asked me yesterday, and I *still* don't know."

"Not Lena, *Lino*. Or *Mick*-a-lino."

"I haven't the foggiest."

"Never came across that name, huh?"

"Never."

"I thought if *anyone* would know . . ."

"No, I don't. Michael, I'm sorry, but my plane . . ."

"Can I come over there now?"

"No."

"I want to look at your scrapbooks."

"No. I'll be back in the office on the eleventh. We can talk then."

"Georgie . . ."

"Georgie me not. The slopes are calling."

"I need to look at your clippings on Faviola."

"Go to the library. Look up F-A-V . . ."

"Georgie, *please*. I think I'm onto something, but I have to . . ."

"Whatever it is, it can wait till the eleventh."

"How about whoever took over for him?"

"His brother did. Everybody knows that."

"Maybe not."

There was a long silence on the line.

"Then who?"

"Somebody named Lino."

"I *still* don't know him."

"Let me look at the scrapbooks."

"No."

"I can be there in twenty minutes . . ."

"I'm *leaving* here in an hour."

"I'll take them with me. I'll bring a suitcase . . ."

"You'd better bring a *trunk*."

"Can I come?"

"Come already," Georgie said, and hung up.

The place he'd chosen was on one of the island's highest mountains, an aerie that offered stunning views from the terrace and the restaurant. They had drinks first on the terrace, Mollie ordering a club soda with lime and then launching into a long discourse on how it felt to be drowning and to have your whole *life*—all twelve years of it—flashing before your eyes like a music video.

"I'll never forget the exact minute and hour," she said, sipping through a straw and batting her lashes at Andrew over the rim of her glass, obviously already madly in love with the man who'd saved her life at twenty minutes to eleven this morning . . .

"But how do you *know* what time it was?" he said.

"I asked Mom. Did I try to drown you?"

"No, no."

"If I'd tried to drown you, would you have knocked me unconscious?"

"I don't think so."

"I've seen them do that in movies."

"I didn't have to. You were very cooperative."

They sat on the terrace sipping their drinks, reliving the morning's experience, Sarah admitting she got *really* frightened the moment she saw Mollie go under for the second time . . .

"Is it true about the third time being the last one?" Mollie interrupted.

"I think so," Andrew said. "Unless you're twelve. Then you get five times."

. . . and then virtually panicking when she went under for the third time.

"What happened was I think when I hit the water the breath got knocked out of me and I was a little stunned for a few seconds, which is why I sucked in water. Then I started choking and coughing, and I sucked in even *more* water and all of a sudden I couldn't *breathe*! I was never so scared in my life. Well, once before actually. When Luis yanked me out of the way of that taxi."

"Who's Luis?" Andrew asked.

"The doorman at our building."

"Where's that?"

"East Eighty-first. I was crossing the street when this cab zoomed around the corner and almost ran me over. If it wasn't for Luis, I wouldn't have been *alive* today for you to save me."

"I think you ought to send Mr. Farrell a dozen roses every year at this time," Sarah said.

"Andrew," he corrected. "And I think the opposite would be better. This is the first time I've ever saved anyone's life."

"My *hero*!" Mollie said broadly, and rolled her eyes in a mock swoon.

"Mrs. Welles? Another drink?"

"Sarah," she corrected. "Are *you* having one?"

"*I* am," Mollie said.

"Let's all have another," Andrew said.

"Let's," Sarah said.

"Does anyone call you Sadie?" he asked.

"Sadie? Oh my God, no."

"Isn't that a nickname for Sarah?"

"I suppose so. But Sadie?" she said, and turned to Mollie. "Can you visualize me as a *Sadie*?"

"Sounds like a shopping-bag lady," Mollie said.

"How about Sassy?" Andrew asked.

"Me? *Sassy*?"

"That's Sarah Vaughan's nickname."

"Who's Sarah Vaughan?" Mollie asked.

"A singer," Andrew said.

"Sounds like a stripper," Mollie said. "Sassy."

"Does anyone ever call you Andy?" Sarah asked.

"No."

"Why not?"

"I don't know. I guess it just doesn't fit."

"Sometimes Mom calls me *Millicent*," Mollie said, and pulled a face. "When she's mad at me."

"Why?"

"Because Mollie's a nickname for Millicent."

"But is that your full name? Millicent?"

"Hell, no," Mollie said. "I know," she said at once to Sarah, "that's a dime." And then, to Andrew, "When I was little, they used to charge me a dime every time I cursed."

"Didn't work, though," Sarah said. "As you can see."

They went in to dinner at a quarter past eight. Mollie and Sarah ordered the lobster medallions with kiwi fruit and Andrew asked the waiter what the *coulommier* was, and ordered it when he learned it was cheese in puff pastry. For her main course, Mollie ordered the lamb in green pepper sauce—"Medium rare, please"—and both Sarah and Michael ordered the grouper fricassee. For no good reason, Sarah suddenly remembered her sister's running gag about wanting to fricassee the one with the white hair. Unconsciously, she looked at Andrew's ears to see if they really *were* big, and then turned away when he noticed her studying him.

As if reading her mind, he said, "I should have asked your sister to join us."

"She's gone," Sarah said. "How'd you know . . . ?"

"You look a lot . . ."

"Aunt Heather's getting a divorce," Mollie said.

"Too bad," Andrew said.

"Uncle Doug's got a bimbo."

"Mollie's had too many drinks," Sarah said, and smiled.

Andrew smiled back.

"They don't have any alcohol in them, Mom," Mollie said.

"Good thing."

"Anyway, he *knows* what a bimbo is."

"Sure," Andrew said. "It's a tropical drink."

"Mr. *Farr*-ell!"

"Cross between the limbo and the marimba."

"Maybe I'm drinking one," Mollie said, and peered into her glass, and then looked up sharply and said, "Those aren't *drinks*."

"Really?" Andrew said, and winked again.

Mollie winked back.

"So what are *you* guys doing down here?" Andrew asked. "Besides drowning."

"We're all on vacation. That's Grandma's house we're staying in. Daddy couldn't come cause he had work to do."

"That's a shame."

"He'll be down on New Year's Eve."

"Or maybe sooner," Sarah said. "I hope."

"What does he do?"

In the early days of their marriage, when Michael was a rookie ADA, she had learned quickly enough that it was frequently best not to broadcast the fact that he worked for the District Attorney's Office. As an example, they would often be at parties where pot was being passed around. This wasn't even a crime, it was a mere violation, but what was an ADA to do in such circumstances? Walk away from it? In which case, people would mutter, "*Some* District Attorney's Office *we've* got!" Make an arrest at the scene? "*Some* chickenshit jackass Michael Welles is!" When asked, she'd learned simply to say, "Michael's a lawyer." If pressed, she would say, "He works downtown." If pressed further, she would say, "He works for the city." And if forced against the wall, she would say, "He's the city's corporate counsel on civil suits," an outright lie. Later on, when Michael began investigating criminals who would as soon shoot you as blink at you, he'd cautioned her specifically against the danger of mentioning he was an ADA. Mollie knew the routine. Together, they went through the drill now.

"He's a lawyer," Sarah said.

"Works downtown," Mollie said.

"For the city," Sarah said.

"Mom's a teacher," Mollie said, changing the subject.

"Where do you teach?" Andrew asked.

"The Greer Academy," Sarah said.

"That's a preppie school for girl nerds," Mollie said.

"Where do *you* go to school?"

"Hanover."

"That's what you get if you drink too many bimbos," he said. "A hanover."

Mollie giggled.

"What subject do you teach?" he asked.

"Me?" Mollie asked.

"English," Sarah said.

"Where's that? The Greer Academy?"

"Sixtieth and Park."

"Near Christ Church," Mollie said.

"I thought you were an actress," Andrew said. "Or a model."

"Me?" Mollie asked.

"You, too," Andrew said, and smiled.

Sarah wondered if she was blushing.

"Are you here on vacation, too?" she asked.

"Business," he said. "I leave tomorrow morning."

"Oh, *nooo*," Mollie said, and grimaced.

"Shall we order some wine?" Andrew asked. "Would anyone . . . ?"

"How stupid of me," Sarah said, and signaled to the waiter. "I meant what I said, you know. You're our guest tonight."

"No way," he said.

"Please let us, Andrew."

This was the first time she'd used his name. She would remember later that the first time she used his name was when they were discussing who would pay the check.

"Well . . . okay," he said.

"Good," Sarah said, and signaled to the waiter.

"A Chardonnay might be nice," Mollie suggested, and grinned at Andrew and batted her lashes again.

The scrapbooks went back some fifteen years.

It was then that Anthony Faviola emerged as a powerful figure in the hierarchy of organized crime, and it was then that Georgie Giardino passed his bar exams and entered the Manhattan District Attorney's Office as a rookie in one of the five trial bureaus.

Michael sat in bed now with a ham sandwich and a bottle of beer, Georgie's scrapbooks spread on the covers around him, the wind howling outside, the television going in the background for company.

The first item in the scrapbooks was an article that had been printed in the *Daily News* when Faviola's only son was born. There had been two daughters before then, and now a male child, which was apparent reason for rejoicing in Staten Island. The *News* headlined the piece **A FAMILY MAN**.

The pun was not lost on Michael. He remembered a front-page headline in the *News*, announcing the fact that NASA had lost radio contact with a space rocket containing experimental white mice. The headline had read:

MISSILE MUM
MICE MISSING

So it was no surprise to him that an article purporting to be about the wife, daughters, and newborn son of a man who was a multimillionaire building contractor in New York City hinted in its headline and in the following heavily slanted story that Mr. Anthony Faviola was "a family man" of quite another sort, the family being a *Mafia* family in Manhattan, the head of which was none other than the proud papa himself. The article was liberally illustrated with photographs of Faviola and his wife, Faviola and his two daughters, aged respectively four and two, and Faviola and the newborn son, three months old at the time of publication. All of the pictures had been taken in front of a modest development house on Staten Island; apparently, Faviola had not yet moved his family to the mansion in Stonington.

There were later articles that showed the palatial estate Faviola built in Connecticut, articles in newspapers and magazines charting the rise, one might have thought, of a respectable businessman instead of a cutthroat racketeer who had bludgeoned his way to the number-one position in the mob. And because Americans were endlessly fascinated by stories about gangsters, the comings and goings of the Faviola family—but especially those of the don himself, in *and* out of court—were recorded with all the solemnity accorded to royalty of a sort.

Here was the older daughter at a lavish sixteenth birthday party her father threw for her, and here was the boychild on his first pair of skis at Stowe, and here was the younger daughter graduating from Choate-Rosemary Hall, and here was the elder daughter again, this time getting married at St. Patrick's Cathedral to a man named Samuel Caglieri, and here was the son at seventeen, wearing a Kent football uniform. Even though the infrequent pictures of Faviola's wife, Tessie, showed a good-looking blond woman with pale eyes and an attractive smile, she was obviously somewhat camera shy—perhaps because her husband's appearances in court were making bigger and bigger headlines each time he was charged with a crime and exonerated by yet another jury.

The boy and the elder daughter obviously favored the wife, with the same light eyes and fair hair. The second daughter had Faviola's dark hair and brown eyes.

The most recent mention of Faviola's son was in an article in *People* magazine, no less, some nine or ten years back. The article was headlined in typical *People* style:

Playboy Son of Mafia Don Says 'Live and Let Die!'

The subtitle beneath this read:
Andy Boy won't eat his broccoli, but his Crime Boss Papa doesn't seem to mind footing the bills in Las Vegas.

Beneath this was an almost-full-page black-and-white photograph of a rather good-looking young man in swimming trunks, standing at the edge of a Vegas swimming pool with his legs apart, his arms above his head like spread wings, and a huge grin on his tanned face. The article, like the magazine itself, was long on style and heavy on folksy content.

When the piece was published, the only son of Anthony Faviola was in attendance at UCLA, but it seemed his studies didn't deter him from popping up to Vegas every other weekend or so, where he was a favorite of the town's chorus girls and a high roller at all of the casinos. The article implied, in fact, that his frequent visits to Vegas had more to do with his father's business interests than with sheer pleasure. Described as "quick-witted and quick-fisted," young Andrew, though ostensibly a student, was—according to the magazine's innuendo—actually supervising his father's vast Las Vegas gambling operation.

A montage of photos on the second page of the piece showed the son in a variety of poses at various ages, each with an appropriate caption. The little blond boy playing with a pail and shovel on a beach someplace was captioned TWO-YEAR-OLD FUTURE CONTRACTOR. There was a picture of him at Disneyland, wearing Mickey Mouse ears and looking up gravely at his father. This was captioned **ALL EARS FOR PAPA'S ADVICE**. Another picture showed him as a darker-haired gangly twelve year old in a tuxedo, dancing with his blond sister in a ball gown. This one was captioned **AT THE COPA WITH SWEET-SIXTEEN ANGELA**. There was yet another picture, a recent one and obviously posed, of him sitting alone on a bench in Central Park, his nose buried in a book. This one was captioned **STUDYING FOR FINALS**.

The picture with the Mickey Mouse ears caught Michael's attention. The kid *did* look a bit jug-eared in some of his earlier photos, and Michael wondered whether *People* was calling attention to his aural appurtenances while supposedly commenting on the Mickey Mouse getup. Nor had Michael forgotten the tape's several references to Michelino, which was why he was here in the first place. The typist had transcribed the taped word as "Mick-a-lino," which he'd assumed was a WASP error in a wop environment. But was it possible that the typist had been correct, after all? *Had* Faviola said *Mick*-a-lino? Little *Mickey*? Was he making reference to a photograph taken at Disneyland when his son was . . . what? Michael could only guess because neither the caption nor the article itself gave a date. The kid, ears and all, looked to be about three or four.

The paper trail seemed suddenly overwhelming.

He went out into the kitchen for a glass of milk and a Famous Amos cookie, and then went back to the bedroom to stack the scrapbooks and call it a night.

It was close to eleven when they got back to her mother's house on the beach. Andrew parked the VW in the oval on the side of the house away from the ocean and then walked them to the front door. In the tall grass under the palms, there was the incessant sound of busy insects. It was a balmy night. Only the faintest breeze stirred in the palm fronds, rippling them with silver from the full moon above.

"Thank you for a wonderful night," he said.

"Thank *you*," Mollie said. "For saving my entire life."

Sarah extended her hand to him. "Thank you again," she said.

"For everything," Mollie said.

"I enjoyed every minute," he said.

"Good night," Sarah said, and released his hand.

"Have a good flight home," Mollie said, and reached up to kiss him on the cheek and then went hastily into the house. Sarah watched Andrew walk to his car. He started it, waved farewell, and backed out of the driveway.

Yolande was sitting in the kitchen, reading the newspaper and simultaneously listening to the news on the radio. Mollie had already gone upstairs.

"Any calls?" Sarah asked.

"No calls, *madame*," Yolande said. "Shall I leave this on?"

"No, thanks."

Yolande rose, snapped off the radio, said, "*Alors, à demain. Bonne nuit, madame.*"

"Good night, Yolande."

Yolande picked up her newspaper from the table and went into her room just off the kitchen, closing the door behind her. Sarah went upstairs to where Mollie was already in bed, waiting for her good-night kiss.

"He's cool," she said.

"Yes," Sarah said. "Good night, honey."

"Good night, Mom."

Sarah kissed her on the cheek, tucked the sheet up under her chin, and turned off the light. As she was starting out of the room, Mollie asked, "Do you think he liked me?"

"I think you were adorable," Sarah said.

"Yeah, but did *he* think so?"

"How could he not?" she said, and smiled. "Good night," she said again.

"He really is cool," Mollie murmured, beginning to drift off.

Downstairs, Yolande was already snoring gently. Sarah turned off the kitchen lights, opened the French doors in the living room, and stood looking silently at the ocean for several moments.

The scent of angel's-trumpet was overpowering.

She poured herself a somewhat hefty cognac, stepped out onto the deck, and wondered if she should call Michael. Her watch read eleven-fifteen, he was probably asleep by now. She took off her sandals and went down the steps onto the beach.

The waves whispered in against the sand.

The water was warm where it touched her naked feet.

This was a scene from a movie, she forgot which one, the woman in white standing at the water's edge with a brandy snifter in her right hand, the mild breeze riffling her blond hair, what was the name of that movie?

Out on the water, a cruise ship ablaze with light moved slowly through the darkness. She heard the distant sound of the ship's orchestra, visualized beautiful women in gossamer gowns drifting over a polished parquet floor. She wondered where the ship was headed, wondered why they always moved at night. A woman's lilting laughter rose to the stars, faded, vanished. The beach was utterly still. She watched the ship a moment longer, and then she finished the cognac, and looked up at the moon one last time, and went back into the house.

She was on the beach again at seven the next morning, eager for a long fast walk, wearing a brief lime-green bikini, her hair held with a matching band. She walked with her head bent, skirting the edge of the water like a sandpiper, the wavelets nudging the shore, the soft wind gently touching her hair. Last night had been a revelation in many respects, and she wanted nothing more than to be alone with her thoughts this morning.

She hadn't believed, before last night, that she could ever possibly be attracted to any man but her husband. Then again, before last night she'd never met a man like Andrew Farrell, whom she'd found altogether charming and delightful, and who'd been *wonderful* with Mollie, besides. There were times, in fact, when Sarah felt she was serving primarily as interlocutor-chaperone for Hero and Smitten Daughter. But whenever the spotlight veered to her, she'd . . . well . . . she'd actually *basked* in it, feeling, well, flattered by his attention and, well, complimented and . . . interested, actually.

She still didn't know whether he'd been deliberately reluctant to reveal anything about himself, or whether he was simply inordinately shy. She'd detected that whenever the conversation drifted toward the personal, he diverted it either to Mollie or to herself, seemingly fascinated by her daughter's prepubescent chatter or the everyday details of her own life. She guessed his age had contributed somewhat to these several awkward moments. He was, after all, only twenty-eight—one of the few facts he'd readily revealed about himself—but he seemed younger still, truly closer in spirit to Mollie than to a woman just this side of forty. Well, only thirty-*four*, sister, let's not exaggerate. Well, going on thirty-*five*, sister.

Twenty-eight was so very young.

In fact . . .

In fact, somewhere along around ten, ten-thirty last night, she'd begun wondering what possibly could have *possessed* her, asking a *boy* . . . well, actually an attractive young *man* . . . but nonetheless someone she didn't know at all, a *man* she didn't know at all, asking him to have *dinner* with her and her daughter, when a cocktail might have suff—

"Sarah?"

She turned sharply, startled by the voice behind her.

Andrew.

Here.

As if materializing from her thoughts.

"I'm sorry," he said. "I didn't mean to . . ."

"That's all right," she said. But her heart was pounding, startling her that way. "You surprised me, is all."

"I'm sorry."

"No, no."

"I should've coughed or something, let you know I was coming up behind . . ."

"That's okay, really."

He fell into step beside her. Barefooted, his trouser cuffs rolled up, he matched his strides to her smaller ones and began walking silently along with her. His hulking silence beside her magnified the sense of intrusion she felt, even though—and she realized this with an odd sense of surprise— she'd been thinking exclusively about him when he'd come up so suddenly behind her.

"I'm sorry I was so tongue-tied at dinner," he said.

She turned to look at him.

"Last night," he said.

"But you weren't," she said.

His eyes would not meet hers. His head was lowered, his gaze directed at the sand ahead of them. Up the beach, the wreck of a small dinghy on the sand gleamed blue in the sunshine.

"It's just . . ." he said, and hesitated, and then said, "Well, it doesn't matter. I just hope I didn't spoil your evening. Or Mollie's."

"Nothing could have spoiled Mollie's evening," she said.

"And yours?"

"I had a lovely time," she said.

"Well, I hope so," he said dubiously.

They were almost to the dinghy now. It lay skeletal and bleached, the sunlight tinting tattered gunwales and thwarts, the ocean gently lapping the damaged prow. The boat was just a mile from the house. She always clocked her morning walks on it. She turned back now, as she did every morning.

"It's exactly a mile," she said. "The boat."

"Uh-huh," he said.

"From the house," she said.

"Uh-huh," he said. "Do you like champagne?"

"Not particularly."

"Oh."

End of conversation.

"I left some on your doorstep," he said. "To make up for last night."

"You didn't have to . . ."

"I didn't know you hated champagne."

"Well, I don't *hate* it, I'm just not particularly *fond* of it."

"I'm on my way to the airport," he said, "I thought I'd just drop it off, I didn't expect to see you, it's so early. Then I spotted you walking, so I thought I'd . . . just say goodbye."

She said nothing. She could see the house up ahead, Yolande setting breakfast on the terrace.

"The reason I was so quiet last night . . ." he said.

"You weren't quiet at all," she said, and turned to look at him. His eyes were very blue in the sun.

"It's just . . . I've never met anyone as beautiful as you in my life."

"Well . . . thank you," she said. "That's very ki—" and suddenly he pulled her into his arms.

She thought Hey, *stop* it, and said out loud, "What the hell do you . . . ?" but never got the rest of the sentence past her lips because all at once his mouth was on hers. She pushed out against him, struggling in his embrace, his arms tight around her, his mouth on hers, trying to twist away from him, wondering if they could be seen from the house, the beach empty in the early morning sunlight. His tongue was in her mouth now, insinuating its presence, tangling her silenced words, *Please don't do this*, his cock hard against her, *please*, she could feel him through the flimsy bikini, his arms binding her to him, his mouth relentless, *please, please* . . .

And suddenly he released her.

"I'm sorry," he said. "Forgive me."

And turned and ran up the beach.

She saw him stopping at the end of the path beside the house, saw him picking up his shoes. He looked back toward her once more and then vanished around the side of the house.

Her lips burning, her thighs quivering, she heard his car starting and listened to the sound of its small engine fading in the distance.

The card on the bottle of Moët Chandon read:

Till next time,
Andrew

Michael found what he was looking for that morning, in an Italian-language newspaper called *Il Corriere della Sera*. The paper on his desk was yellowed and fraying; the date on it indicated that it was almost twenty-nine years old. Accompanying the article, in a plastic pocket fastened to the scrapbook page, was a typewritten English translation attributed to someone named Jenny Weinstein, more than likely a Bureau secretary.

Oddly, the article wasn't about *Anthony* Faviola—who was mentioned in it only once, and then as a rising young building contractor—but was instead about his father *Andrew*, the American-born son of Andreo Antonio Faviola and Marcella Donofrio Faviola, both immigrants from the town of Ruvo del Monte, Provincia di Potenza, Italy. Michael had no idea where this town might be. He continued reading.

The article celebrated two concurrent and virtually simultaneous events. The first of these was the fiftieth anniversary of the bakery Andrew Faviola had owned and operated on the same street in Coney Island ever since the death of his father some twelve years earlier. The second event, occurring three days after the bakery's anniversary, was the birth of Andrew's third grandchild, the first grandson presented to him by his son Anthony, "a rising young building contractor." The child had been named Andrew, after the subject of the article, his proud grandfather.

There was a picture of Andrew holding the infant namesake in his arms. It was summertime and the grandfather—fifty-two years old at the time, according to the article—was standing in his shirtsleeves before the plate-glass window of a shop called Marcella's Bakery. The baby was wearing a white unisex shift and little white booties. Even at that tender age, the kid's jug ears were clearly visible.

The article explained that the shop had been named by Andreo Faviola in honor of his wife, who—at the time the article was written—was eighty-four years old, "God bless her," Andrew told the reporter. This meant that Topolino was a great-grandson of the woman who . . .

Topolino?

Michael almost spilled his morning coffee.

. . . woman who sixty-five years earlier had made the long and arduous journey from a mountaintop village midway between Bari on the Adriatic and Naples on the Tyrrhenian. The elder Andrew . . .

. . . explained how his namesake had come by the nickname "Topolino." His mother still spoke broken English, although she'd been an American citizen for well on sixty years now, and when she saw the infant in the hospital for the first time, she turned to her son and said, in Italian, *"Ma sembra Topolino, vero? Con quelle orecchi così grande!"*

Which translated into English as "But he looks like Mickey Mouse, isn't that true? With those big ears!" The article went on to explain that Mickey Mouse was as popular in Italy as he was here in the United States, and that the old lady was using the name affectionately, since—as anyone could plainly see—the child was extraordinarily beautiful with the same blond hair and blue eyes as many of the region's mountain people.

Topolino, Michael thought.

Mickey Mouse.

Later Anglicized and bastardized to Mick-a-lino.

Lino.

What goes around comes around, he thought.

Poor but honest Italian immigrant comes to America around the turn of the century, opens a bakery shop which his native-born son, Andrew, inherits when he dies. Andrew in turn has a son named Anthony, who becomes "a rising young building contractor," and in turn sires two daughters and a son, subsequently named Andrew after his grandfather and nicknamed Topolino by his great-grandmother.

Andrew Faviola.

The "Lino" his father had chosen to succeed him if/ when he ever fell from power.

Andrew Faviola.

The student who'd made weekend visits from UCLA to Las Vegas, where he supervised his father's gambling operations when he wasn't being "a favorite of the town's chorus girls and a big roller at all of the casinos."

Andrew Faviola.

Who nowadays had to be consulted before a jackass gambler could be let off the hook.

Andrew Faviola.

Who was maybe running the whole damn show now that his father was locked away in Kansas.

It was nine A.M. on the thirtieth of December, two days before the new year. Michael picked up the phone and dialed his boss's extension.

2: JANUARY 11–FEBRUARY 17

He was waiting for her when she came out of the school.

It was a bitterly cold day, the sky overhead a dull gun-metal gray, a blustery wind sweeping ruthlessly eastward from the Hudson. It was only four in the afternoon, but it seemed as if dusk had already fallen.

Sarah pushed through the doors, pulling on her gloves, a red woolen hat yanked down over her ears, a matching muffler wound about her throat. She'd been back on the job for a week already, her tan was virtually gone. She normally walked a block east to the IRT station on Sixtieth and Lex, took the local uptown to Seventy-seventh, and then walked from there to the apartment on Eighty-first, altogether a fifteen-minute commute. She was starting for Lex now when he cut diagonally across the street toward her, popping up in front of her much as he had on the beach in St. Bart's.

"Hi," he said.

In the split second before she recognized him, she thought she was being accosted by one of New York's loonies. And then she realized who he was, and knew in that moment that his appearance here was not an accident, he had sought her out, he was here by design.

"What do you want?" she said.

"I have to talk to you."

"Please go away," she said.

"I want to apologize for . . ."

"There's no need to apologize, just go away, please, just leave me alone."

They started to cross Park Avenue, the light changing just as they reached the center island, where the wind seemed somehow fiercer. They waited in silence until the light changed again. He fell into step beside her, adjusting his longer strides to hers, and they began walking together toward Lexington Avenue.

"Do you know what movie she said that in?" he asked.

"No. *Who? What* movie? What are you talking about?"

"Garbo," he said.

"No, I don't. Listen, I'm on my way home, I'm a married woman, I have a daughter . . ."

"*Grand Hotel,*" he said. " 'I want to be alone.' "

"I *do* want to be alone," she said. "I don't know why you came here . . ."

"To apologize. Would you like a cup of coffee?"

"No. Goodbye, Mr. Farrell."

"Andrew," he said.

"Yes, Andrew, goodbye," she said, and started down the steps into the subway. He fell behind her for just an instant and then immediately caught up, falling in beside her again as she dug into her handbag for a token. She was out of tokens. She was starting for the change booth when he stepped into her path again.

"*Please* stop doing that!" she said.

"A cup of coffee. So I can explain."

"No."

"Please."

There was on his face the same plaintive look that had been on Mollie's the night they'd bought the Christmas tree. She was already shaking her head, no, no, *no,* but the look on his face was so forlorn, so very . . .

"Listen," she said, "I really . . ."

"Please," he said again. "I'm sorry for what I did that morning. I want to explain."

"There's nothing to explain. I accept your apology. It was nice seeing you again."

"You don't really mean that," he said.

"I really don't," she said, and stepped around him and up to the booth. The black woman behind the glass looked at her.

"Ten tokens, please," Sarah said, and took out her wallet and was reaching inside it when he said, "I've got it."

"What?" she said.

He slid a twenty under the glass panel.

"I'm paying for it, miss," she said at once, and slid a five and a ten under the panel.

"Take it from the twenty," he told the attendant.

"Who is paying here?" the woman said calmly.

"I am," they said simultaneously.

"You can't *both* be paying," she said, "and I'm busy here."

"She never lets me pay for anything," Andrew said, and grinned and retrieved the twenty.

Sarah picked up her change and the packet of tokens.

"Now I owe you a cup of coffee," he said.

"How do you figure that?" she asked.

She already knew she would allow him to buy her a cup of coffee.

"Well, *you* paid for the tokens, didn't you?" he said.

"The logic escapes me," she said.

"Is there a place nearby?" he asked.

There was a cluster of restaurants, coffee shops, and delis along Lexington Avenue near the subway station, but she did not want to take him to anyplace frequented by students from the school. She would wonder about that later. Wonder why she had chosen even then not to be seen in his company by any of her students. She walked him down to Second Avenue instead, where she told him she knew a little French place that served terrific croissants and wonderful coffee.

There was a sense of wintry coziness inside the shop, overcoats huddled on wall pegs just inside the enclosed entry, patrons in turtlenecks and tweeds, the aroma of strong coffee and good things baking, the paneled and bellied front window framing pedestrians hurrying past with their heads ducked against the ferocious wind.

They found a table near a giant copper espresso machine, and they both ordered *café filtre* and chocolate-filled croissants. He was wearing a blue flannel shirt, a gray tweed sports jacket, darker gray slacks. Sarah was wearing what she called her "schoolmarm threads": a moss-green sweater, a dark brown wool skirt, opaque green panty hose. Normally, she wore French-heeled shoes to work. Today, because of the rotten weather, she was wearing knee-high brown leather boots. She had taken off the red hat and stuffed it into the pocket of her coat. The red muffler was still draped around her neck. He'd been hatless to begin with. They sat on either side of a small scarred wooden table, blue-eyed and blue-eyed, blond hair and brown hair.

Later, she would tell him they made a good-looking couple.

And would wonder if she'd actually thought it on that first day together in New York.

"So let me explain," he said, and waited for her nod, and then said, "To begin with, I don't usually go around kissing married women."

"Okay," she said.

"I mean it. I'm usually very . . . careful that way."

"Uh-huh."

"That morning . . . I don't know . . . I just . . . I couldn't take my eyes off you the night before, and when . . ."

"Andrew," she said, and hesitated, and then said, "I don't want this, really. I'm not looking for it, I don't want it, I don't need it . . ."

"You want to be alone, I know."

"I'm not alone. I have a husband."

"I love you," he said.

"Oh, Jesus!" she said, and quickly glanced over her shoulder to see if anyone was sitting close enough to *hear* all this. "Andrew," she said, lowering her voice to a whisper, "I don't think you understand what I'm telling you. I'm *not* being coy, I'm not in any way trying to encourage . . ."

"I know."

"So cut it out, okay? Just *stop* it!"

There was a long silence.

Awkwardly, they sat across from each other.

The coffee and croissants arrived.

She sipped at the coffee. Cut into the croissant with a fork. The chocolate was rich and dark and delicious.

"Do you like teaching?" he asked.

"I love it."

"How'd it go today?"

"Fine."

"Good, I'm glad."

"How'd *your* day go?"

"Fine, thanks."

"I never did learn what you *do*."

"I'm a gangster," he said, and grinned.

"Sure," she said.

"Actually, I'm what you'd call an opportunity investor," he said, the grin giving way to the earnest look of someone very young trying to appear very serious and very grown-up. "I look for businesses that need an investment of time and money, and I nurture them along till they bring me a good return."

"What sort of businesses?"

"Import-export, shipping, real estate, construction, and so on. I'm into a lot of things."

"Sounds exciting."

"*You're* exciting," he said.

"Okay, I think it's time I went home," she said.

"Why?"

"Because you still don't under—"

"I'd love to kiss you," he said.

"Let's get a check," she said.

"Do we fight over this one, too?"

"No, you asked me."

"That's true. *May* I kiss you?"

"No."

"In that case," he said, and leaned across the table and kissed her full on the mouth.

She would later tell him that she became immediately wet the moment his lips touched hers again.

Now she stood abruptly.

"Goodbye, Andrew," she said, and left him sitting at the table while she went to the row of pegs and yanked her coat off the wall, and ran outside into the cold without putting it on and without looking back at him.

The two detectives initially assigned by Michael to the surveillance of Andrew Faviola met with him in his office on Tuesday morning, the twelfth of January. They'd been working the case for a week now, ever since Michael got back from the Caribbean, but there wasn't much to report.

Johnny Regan, the older of the two detectives, and the more experienced, sat in a chair alongside his young partner, Alex Lowndes. The men felt comfortable in this office, they'd been here many times before. Besides, the office encouraged casualness. When Michael was a teenager, his mother had engaged in a constant battle with him to keep his room from resembling a garbage dump. His office wasn't quite the mess his room had been; he was, after all, a grown man now. But an office told a great deal about the person who lived in it sometimes twelve out of every twenty-four hours, and Michael's bordered on the edge of neglect. This was not to say that it was either sloppy or untidy. Instead, there was a sense of . . . well . . . somewhat orderly clutter.

Stacks of transcripts and other legal documents rested on each of the three desks in the spacious room. Windows facing Centre Street covered one long wall, the area beneath them occupied by bound copies of New York's Penal Law, Criminal Law, and Criminal Procedure Law. A glassed cabinet held more legal volumes, together with framed photographs of Sarah and Mollie, and several blue peaked caps with the insignias or logos of various law enforcement agencies he'd worked with in the past. A mock, blue-enameled gold detective's shield—a gift from the DA's Office Squad after Michael had served as lead attorney on his first OCCA case—was hanging in a small bell jar. His framed B.S. degree from Duke hung on the wall above the cabinet, alongside his Juris Doctor degree from Columbia.

A television monitor with a VCR sitting on a shelf under it was in one corner of the room. Labeled videotapes from various surveillances were scattered on top of a table alongside the monitor. On that same table were a stacked amplifier and tape deck, together with a CD player. Labeled discs and tapes were fanned helter-skelter on the tabletop, together with Magic Markers and blank labels.

Hanging on the wall right-angled to the window wall, there were framed mug shots of the Lombardi Crew, six gangsters Michael had put away five years ago, when he first moved over to Organized Crime. Standing in the corner of the joining walls was a coatrack that held Michael's own beige Burberry trench coat and matching muffler, and the black raincoats both Regan and Lowndes had worn to work this morning. A black umbrella was lying on the floor near the coatrack; Michael had carried it to work with him two weeks ago.

"What we did," Regan was saying, "was run a routine check with Motor Vehicles. Guy lives in New York, chances are he's either a licensed driver or he owns a car."

Regan was puffing on a cigar. He looked like a fight manager. Brown trousers, a tan crew-neck sweater, little beer-barrel belly bulging above the waist. Always looked as if he needed a shave. He was left-handed, so he wore his shoulder holster strapped on the right side of his body.

"We got nothing at all in New York or Nassau County, so we hit Connecticut and Jersey. Nothing in Jersey, but Alex came up with something in Connecticut. Well, you tell him," Regan said, and turned to his partner.

Alex Lowndes looked mean as a pawnbroker's offer. Long and lank, with stringy dirty-blond hair and eyes that appeared gray although they were actually a pale blue, he sat in blue jeans and a black turtleneck sweater with a black leather jacket over it. There was a scar at the tail of his left eyebrow. He told people he'd got it in a knife fight with a crazed junkie. Actually, he'd had the scar since he was ten, when he fell down roller-skating and hit his head on the curb. Michael knew this because Lowndes had confided it to his partner, and Regan had passed the information on. The two men didn't get along. Everyone in the department knew that. It was amazing neither of them had asked for a new partner. Maybe this was because their arrest record was phenomenal.

"We got an Acura Legend coupe registered to an Andrew Faviola at 24 Cradle Rock Road, Stonington, Connecticut," Lowndes said.

"Terrific," Michael said sourly.

"Yeah, his father's house up there," Lowndes said.

"Where he don't live anymore," Regan said. "The old man."

"Where he *won't* live ever again," Lowndes said.

"What we figure, the *kid* doesn't live there, either," Regan said. "No sign of the Acura, anyway, the three nights we sat the house."

"When was this?"

"This past weekend. We figure you live in Connecticut, that's when you go home, right? For the weekend. Snow, trees, all that shit. But no sign of him."

"Has he got a driver's license?" Michael asked.

"I was coming to that," Regan said. "He *did* have one, but it got suspended after three consecutive speeding tickets. Far as we can tell, he doesn't have one now."

"How does he drive the Acura?"

"Maybe he doesn't. Maybe that's why he doesn't go visit his mama on weekends."

"What was the address on the license he had?"

"No luck there, Michael. It was a California license. From when he was in school out there. An address on Montana. It sounds like the Wild West, I know, but it's a street in L.A."

"Suspended in California?"

"Yes."

"When?"

"Eight years ago."

"What?"

"Yeah."

"He's been driving without a license all that time?"

"Looks that way."

"No application in New York for a new one?"

"No."

"Or Connecticut?"

"No."

"He's mob-connected," Lowndes said, "he can buy phony licenses a dime a dozen."

"What you're saying is we don't know where he lives yet."

"That's right."

"And if we don't know where to find him, we can't begin tailing him."

"Well, yeah."

"Have you checked for any parking violations?"

"I've got that call in now," Regan said, nodding. "If he's *driving* the Acura, he has to *park* it every now and then. And this is a guy with no respect for traffic laws . . ."

"Three speeding violations out there," Lowndes said.

"So he'll park the car wherever he feels like it."

"When did they say they'd get back?"

"You know those guys. They get thousands of scofflaws, what's the big deal?"

"Let's try 'em again now," Michael suggested.

Regan looked at his watch.

"Be a good time," he said, and went to the phone. "What's that extension again, Alex, you remember? At Parking Violations?"

"Three-two-oh," Lowndes said.

Regan dialed. Michael hit the speaker button. They listened to the phone ringing on the other end, once, twice, three times, again, again . . .

"Gone home already," Lowndes said.

"At four-thirty?" Regan said.

"Parking Violations, Cantori."

"Sergeant Henderson, please."

"Who's this?"

"Detective Regan, DA's Office Squad."

"Second."

Regan shrugged.

They waited.

"Henderson," a voice said.

"Sergeant, this is Detective Regan, I called you yesterday about this Acura we're trying to trace for the Organized Crime Unit? Connecticut plate on it?"

"Yeah?"

"I'm sitting here with the deputy unit chief, and he's wondering if you've made any progress on this."

There was a silence on the line.

"He's on the speaker now, in fact," Regan said.

"Hello, Sergeant," Michael said. "This is ADA Welles, how's it going?"

"We've been jammed here," Henderson said. "The holidays."

"I can imagine," Michael said. "And we hate to push you on this, but it's a matter of some urgency."

"They're *all* a matter of some urgency," Henderson said drily.

"I'm sure they are. But do you think you can kick up your computer, see if you've got anything on this particular car? We really would appreciate it."

"Give me the number there," Henderson said.

He called back in ten minutes.

"Blue 1991 Acura Legend coupe, Connecticut registration, vanity plate FAV-TWO, registered owner Andrew Faviola, address 24 Cradle Rock Road, Stonington, Connecticut."

"That's the car," Regan said.

"I've got fourteen parking violations since September of last year. What do you need?"

"Locations," Michael said.

"Four of them are outside a restaurant called La Luna on Fifty-eighth and Eighth."

Michael nodded.

"What about the other eight?"

"Various locations in Manhattan and Brooklyn."

"How are they listed?"

"By building."

"Where the car was parked?" Regan asked.

"Yeah, the address it was in front of."

"Any other repeaters?" Michael asked.

"What do you mean?"

"Any other places he parked more than once?"

"No, these are all different addresses."

"Any *streets* repeated?"

"Let me see."

There was a long silence.

"Yeah, we got three addresses on the same street."

"What street is that?" Michael asked.

"It's an *avenue,* actually."

"Which one?"

"Bowery. In Manhattan. But the addresses are pretty far apart."

"Can you let us have them, please?"

"What's your fax number?" Henderson said.

The apartment was above a tailor shop on Broome Street, just two blocks off Bowery. The tailor shop was on the ground floor of the building. The upper three stories had been remodeled as a triplex. From the outside, you saw a four-story brick tenement covered with the soot and grime of at least a century. On the inside, the apartment consisted of an entry and living room on the floor above the tailor shop, a kitchen and dining room on the second floor, and a bedroom on the third floor. There was a lot of expensive cabinetry and hardware in the apartment. Andrew's father had contracted the remodeling to one of his own construction companies, and they'd done a quality job because they'd realized exactly for whom they were working.

The building was a corner building. The entrance to the tailor shop was on Broome Street, but its large plate-glass windows wrapped around the corner to Mott Street as well. There was a wooden door painted blue on the Mott Street side of the building. The blue door had a Mott Street address on it, and a black mailbox with the name "Carter-Goldsmith Investments" lettered on it in gold was affixed to the jamb beside the door. Inside the door, there was a staircase that led to the first-floor entry of the apartment. There was one other entrance to the apartment. This was through the back of the tailor shop, where a door opened onto another staircase that led to the rear of the apartment's living room, adjacent to the wood-burning fireplace. The upstairs and downstairs doors to the apartment were fitted with identical deadbolt locks. Andrew was the only one who had a key that opened each lock.

He always parked his car wherever he could find a spot. The side streets in Little Italy and Chinatown were usually impossible, but he'd been lucky finding spaces on Bowery, where all the lighting and appliance stores were. He then walked the two, three, sometimes six blocks or more to the Broome Street tailor shop. The gilt lettering on both the Broome Street and Mott Street windows of the shop read:

LOUIS VACCARO
DRY CLEANING
FINE CUSTOM TAILORING
ALTERATIONS

A little bell over the door rang whenever anyone entered the shop. On this rainy, wet, and dismal Friday the fifteenth, the bell sounded particularly welcoming, a harbinger of the steamy embrace of the shop. As he entered, Andrew was greeted with the familiar sounds of the bell tinkling, and the pressing machine hissing in the back room, and the sewing machine humming. Louis sat working in the Broome Street window, squinting at a piece of cloth he was running under the feed dog, chewing on an unlit guinea stinker, his rimless glasses shoved up onto his forehead, his foot on the machine's treadle. To his left and deeper inside the shop was a double-tiered row of hangered garments awaiting pickup.

"Andrew, hello," he said, and rose immediately and put the stogie in a small ashtray near the machine's bobbin. Turning to Andrew, his arms wide, he said, *"Come vai?"*

"Good, thank you," Andrew said, and went to the old man and embraced him.

Louis was wearing a sleeveless sweater over a white shirt and trousers with a faint stripe. He had made the trousers himself. He had also made the sports jacket Andrew was wearing under an overcoat he'd had tailored at Chipp. Louis had picket-fence white hair, and he always looked a bit grizzled. Andrew guessed he shaved once or twice a week, and then under duress.

"I found a nice cloth for you," he said. "For a suit. You want to see it?"

"Not now, I'm expecting Uncle Rudy," Andrew said, and looked at his watch. "Send him right up when he gets here, okay?"

"Sure. What weather, huh?"

"Terrible," Andrew said.

"Is the jacket warm enough?"

"The jacket is warm enough," Andrew said, smiling and unbuttoning his coat. Opening it wide to show Louis, he said, "And beautiful, too."

"Yes, it is," Louis said modestly.

"I'll be upstairs."

"I'll send him up."

"How's Benny doing?"

"Ask him," Louis said, and shrugged.

His son was pressing in the back room.

"I hate this fuckin job," was the first thing he said.

"You're a good presser," Andrew said.

"Can't you get me something?" Benny said.

Tall and rake-thin, with his father's unruly hair—coal black as opposed to the old man's white—he, too, wore glasses, misted now by the steam rising from the pressing machine. He worked in a tank-top white undershirt and dark trousers. White socks and black shoes. He, too, needed a shave. Like father, like son, Andrew thought.

"I'll take anything you can find me," Benny said. "Con-

struction, the docks, anything, driving a truck, whatever.
I'm stronger than I look, Andrew, I mean it."

"I know you are. But . . ."

"I'm skinny, but I'm strong."

"I know that. But what would your father do without you?"

"It's just I hate pressing. I *hate* it."

"Does he know that?"

"I don't know."

"Talk to him. See what he says. If he agrees to let you
go, I may have something in the Fulton Market."

"Jesus, I *hate* fish," Benny said.

"Or something else, we'll see. But talk to him first."

"I can't even stand the *smell* of fish," Benny said.

"Talk to him," Andrew said, and walked back to the
door on the rear wall. Fastened to the jamb was a speaker
with a buzzer button under it. He fished out his keys and
unlocked the deadbolt. Flicking on the light switch in the
stairwell, he climbed to the apartment's first floor. The stairwell walls were painted white to match the back of the tailor
shop. The door to the apartment was also painted white on
this side. He unlocked the deadbolt on the upstairs door,
opened it, stepped into the apartment, and closed and locked
the door behind him, using the deadbolt's thumb latch. The
inside of the door was paneled in walnut, as was the rest of
the living room. He checked the thermostat, nodded when
he saw it was set for seventy degrees, and then sat down to
wait for his uncle.

In the newspaper office on the fifth floor of the school,
Luretta and Sarah were working on next week's issue of the
Greer Gazette, a name both of them despised. The clock on
the wall read eleven-forty. Sarah and the girl both had free
periods, and whatever they could accomplish now would
save time for the rest of the newspaper staff after classes
today. Luretta was better at headlines than most of the other
girls; she had a mind that cut instantly to the chase. The one

she was working on now was for a story that detailed the school's visit last week to the Matisse exhibit at MOMA. She'd tried two ideas on Sarah . . .

MISSES VISIT MASTERS

. . . and . . .

MISSES MEET MATISSE

. . . and then agreed with her when she suggested that the word "misses" sounded like what someone would expect at a school for girls somewhere in the Berkshires, but not here in the heart of New York, in a place full of sophisticated, smart . . .

"Gee, *thanks*," Luretta said, and flashed her wonderful smile.

Alone in the office, the two tossed around several new approaches, all of them rotten. The wind outside rattled the windowpanes, whistled and howled in a hairline crack where the window didn't quite meet the frame. It was Luretta who finally came up with the notion of telling what *impact* the exhibit had had on the girls; the story, after all, wasn't announcing a *future* outing, it was reporting on a *past* excursion.

"Well, what impact *did* it have?" Sarah asked.

"I personally found it awesome," Luretta said. "And I don't mean awesome as in Valley Girl, I mean goddamn *awesome*!"

"In what way?"

Get them to think, get them to explore, get them to . . .

"The way all his life he kept finding new ways of doing things," Luretta said. "Even when he was an old man, he was still saying, 'Look at me! I'm alive!' "

"Can you put that in a headline?"

"Wouldn't work," Luretta said.

They both fell silent.

Out of the blue, Luretta said, "Matisse Lives!"

"Good," Sarah said, and nodded.

"Cause he does, you know," Luretta said. "He still *lives,* that's the thing of it."

"Yes," Sarah said.

They worked silently for several minutes, each bent over their separate pasteups, the clock on the wall ticking, the wind rushing the window.

"I wish some of the kids where I live could see that show," Luretta said. "Make *them* want to live, too."

"Why can't they?"

"They're too busy *dyin,*" Luretta said.

Sarah looked up.

Their eyes met.

"Dope, I mean," Luretta said. "It's all over the streets up there. They make it so easy."

Sarah kept looking at her.

"No, not me," Luretta said. "You don't have to worry about that. I don't need that shit, excuse me."

"I'm glad," Sarah said.

"But it's tempting, I'll tell you that, Mrs. Welles. It *bein* there all the time. Easy to get, cheap as dirt. Makes you want to *try* it, you know? Everybody else up there is doin it, you say to yourself, 'Why not me? Why not go fly with all the others?' "

Sarah said nothing.

"But you know, you go see this work the man did, and you realize he didn't need crack to get high, did he? Matisse. He found all the high he needed right inside himself."

"Yes," Sarah said.

"Right in here," Luretta said, and tapped her clenched fist over her heart. "Right in here."

The bell sounded, shattering the silence.

"We got a lot done here, didn't we?" Luretta said.

"Yes, we did. Will you be back this afternoon?"

"Oh, sure."

"Look for you then."

"Matisse *Lives!*" Luretta said, grinning, and threw a black power salute as she went out the door.

The clock on the wall read twelve-ten.

Time for lunch.

Sarah didn't feel like the teachers' lunchroom today.

Despite the weather, she thought she might walk over to the coffee shop on Lex and Fif—

She thought suddenly of Andrew Farrell.

Of not wanting to take him to the coffee shop so close to the school.

Went instead . . .

The smell of strong coffee . . .

The taste of rich chocolate on her lips.

Andrew leaning over the table to kiss her.

Quickly, she put the thought of him out of her mind.

His uncle looked worse each time Andrew saw him.

He would always wonder if Uncle Rudy had turned down the job because he truly hadn't wanted it, or because he knew he had such a short time to live. He was next in line, everyone knew that. But cancer was in line ahead of him.

Best-kept secret in the family.

Never act from a position of weakness, his father had told him. Never let anyone know weakness is the reason for any decision. Always move through *strength*. Or make it *seem* that way.

Succeeding his father merely because his uncle was sick would have been taken by others as assuming control by default. Andrew did *not* have his uncle's seniority, was *not* a made man like his uncle, in fact had *none* of his uncle's experience or training. But when Rudy Faviola, moving through *strength,* said he did not want the job and named his nephew as rightful successor, the announcement had all the force of an irrefutable royal command.

Whether Andrew would in the long run be accepted was another matter. His own father had taken control of the Tortocello family by eliminating its leader. Andrew was well aware of this. He had read all the newspaper accounts of Ralph Tortocello's murder, and he knew the same thing could easily happen to him if someone disputed his assumption of power. He was hoping the Sino-Colombian deal would go a long way toward dispelling any such doubts. He and his uncle were here to discuss that today.

"Willie's been in touch with Moreno again," Rudy said. "I got to tell you, Andrew, he's shitting his pants down there, Willie. Moreno can do him in a minute and he knows it. He likes the Caribbean, he doesn't want to come back up north to live. But if this thing we're attempting doesn't work, then we have to yank him out of there or he's shark meat."

"I realize that."

"Moreno now has the message that he won't be able to do business anywhere in the U.S., he don't play ball with us. New York, Miami, New Orleans, Houston, San Diego, he's fucked wherever he tries to sell the shit cause our people will be knockin off dealers like they're rats in a sewer. The message'll be, you do business with Moreno, you have to answer to us. He don't particularly like being threatened, Andrew, but fuck him, we made him a good offer, he's playin hardball. He knows you're runnin this now, you weren't just an office boy went down there to do some fishin. He also knows you're your father's son, and there's no fuckin with Anthony Faviola *wherever* he may be, Kansas or wherever the fuck. He knows all this. What he's holdin out for I don't know."

"What do you *think* it might be?"

"A bigger slice. He knows we've got him by the balls, he can't deal with people who are scared *we'll* be comin after them, it's simple as that. He can shove his cocaine up his ass, he can't sell it to the people who put it on the streets. But he's not stupid. He knows he's letting us into his action in return for a third of what may turn out to be a tremendous market. But it ain't a true *market* yet, Andrew, it's what your father would call a *perceived* market, a *prospective* market. It's nothing *certain* yet, you follow?"

"Of course it isn't."

"Well, Moreno knows that, you think he's a fuckin dope? He's figurin I throw my fuckin coke in the pot, I may get a third of *nothing* in return. Which, in a way, he's right."

"He's got to be convinced otherwise, Uncle Rudy. This isn't pie in the sky here, this is a *cartel* taking shape. In time, his third'll be worth *millions* more than what he's putting up."

"Sure, in time," Rudy said. "Tell that to a fuckin spic with his dick in his hand."

"Well, as I see it, he's got no choice."

"Let me put Petey Bardo on this," Rudy said, "get him to work up some figures. In the long run, it might be worth giving this *jih-drool* a little more on his end, keep him aboard. There's no deal at *all* without his coke, you know."

"I know. But there's no deal without the Chinese, either, and they're beginning to get itchy. I can't wait *forever* for Moreno to see the light."

"Let me see what Petey thinks we can afford, okay?"

"What if Moreno turns it down?"

"Then we got to think of some other way to convince him, huh?"

"Mm," Andrew said.

The men were silent for a moment.

Andrew looked at his watch.

"You expecting somebody?" Rudy asked.

"One o'clock," Andrew said, nodding.

"Just a few more things I have to tell you."

"No hurry, I can make a call."

"The word's out all over that nothing's changed. Your father's partners are *your* partners, capeesh? Same deals every-where. Just in case somebody got it in his head, Hey, I'm on my own now Faviola's in the slammer. Wrong. One or two guys we still have to talk to, make sure they understand completely, but otherwise I don't see any trouble."

"Okay."

"One last thing. Some stupid fuck gambler in Queens stiffed Sal the Barber for fifteen grand plus the vig. Then he had the fuckin nerve to steal *another* five grand of cash he got for deliverin some coke for Frankie Palumbo. Frankie had a sitdown with Jimmy Angels, you know him?"

"No."

"Angelli, Jimmy Angelli, he owns a shitty restaurant in Forest Hills, he's a capo in the Colotti family. Anyway, his cousin's involved with this fuckin thief, and now Angelli's askin yet *another* favor."

"What was the *first* favor?"

"Lettin that asshole deliver the coke, for which he paid back Frankie by stealing five grand from him."

"Tell Frankie to take care of him," Andrew said. "So it won't happen again."

"I'll tell him."

"Anything else?"

"Nothing," Rudy said, "I'll leave you to your pleasure."

He rose, embraced his nephew, kissed him on both cheeks, said, "*Ciao*, Lino," and left the apartment through the door that led to the tailor shop downstairs.

The girl rang the doorbell on the Mott Street side of the building. The gold lettering on the black mailbox read "Carter-Goldsmith Investments." She wondered who Carter-Goldsmith was. He hadn't told her he was in the investment business. A voice came over the speaker set into the doorjamb.

"Who is it, please?"

His voice. Andrew's.

"Me," she said. "Oona."

"Come on up, Oona," he said.

A buzzer sounded. She turned the knob, opened the door, closed it again behind her. The buzzer kept sounding as she climbed the stairs, stopped when she was about midway up. The staircase was paneled with wood on either side. There was a lovely wood-paneled door at the top of the stairs. A small bell button in a brass circle was set in the doorjamb. She pressed the button. The door opened at once.

"Hi," she said.

"You made it," he said.

"I told you I would."

"Come in," he said.

Her name was Oona Halligan, she was an Irish girl from Brooklyn, he'd met her at a disco joint last night. Red hair and green eyes, Irish as they come, he loved fucking Irish girls.

She'd explained to him that she had a lot of time on her hands just now because she was looking for a new job while collecting unemployment. Her boss had fired her because she'd wanted to do a certain thing *her* way instead of *his* way, which she'd told him was a *stupid* way to do it. She guessed that wasn't a particularly clever move, huh? Telling her boss that *his* way was the dumb way, but live and learn. Anyway, she had a lot of time on her hands just now.

This was while they were sitting on a black leather banquette with music blaring from ten thousand speakers that had to be worth ten million dollars, Andrew with his hand on her knee, Oona with her short red skirt riding clear north to Canada. He'd casually mentioned that if she had so much time on her hands why didn't she stop by his apartment tomorrow afternoon sometime, say around one o'clock, they could listen to some music and he'd brew her some tea.

The tea always got them.

Made him sound like an English gentleman.

I just might, she'd said, arching an eyebrow. If I'm in the neighborhood.

You don't have to decide now, he'd said. I won't make any other plans, I'll be there all afternoon, I'll look for you around one.

Where *is* your apartment? she'd asked.

Actually, at the start of any relationship, he *preferred* matinees.

Most girls didn't like to pop into bed with you on the first date. You asked them to stop by the next day, that automatically made it a *second* date, and it made it daytime in the bargain which sounded very safe, especially if you were offering tea. Besides, if you *did* get a girl to go home with you at three, four o'clock in the morning, she'd almost certainly be there when you woke up not knowing who she was or how she'd *got* there. Afternoons, you played some soft music, you offered tea or hot chocolate or even booze if that's what the lady preferred, everything slow and easy, and then you took her upstairs later, fucked her brains out with the drapes drawn and daylight peeking around them. If the afternoon turned out to be a bummer, you cut her loose before dinner. If it went well, you asked her if she'd like to go out for something to eat, there were great Italian and Chinese restaurants in the neighborhood, and then you took her back here later, knowing her already, knowing that if she *did* spend the night it'd be a pleasurable experience and you wouldn't hate yourself when you woke up alongside a beast the next morning.

Irish girls turned him on.

He thought of an Irish girl as a religious little darling who'd suck your cock and then run to a priest in the morning to confess her sins and say penance at the altar. He particularly liked Irish redheads. A *real* Irish redhead could drive a person crazy, that wild carrot-colored hair on her head and between her legs. Loved to part that flaming thatch below, spread those innocent pink Irish-girl lips, lick her into an Irish frenzy that would later cost her a hundred Hail Marys and a thousand Our Fathers, not to mention a dozen or more Acts of Contrition. He hated the Catholic religion but he loved fucking religious Irish-Catholic girls.

He wondered all at once if Sarah Welles was Irish.

Secretly, she was happy this hadn't turned out to be another "family" weekend.

Today was Martin Luther King Day, the eighteenth of January, a school holiday in New York, which meant that Sarah and Mollie automatically had the day off. But the D.A.'s Office was closed today, too, and it looked as if this might turn into another long weekend like those the family had shared over Christmas and New Year's. Sarah felt strongly that King *should* have his own holiday—but not in January. By the time the third Monday in January came around each year, she'd had enough holiday to last a lifetime.

This year was different.

She would later wonder whether her life would have changed so completely if Mollie hadn't left for Sugarbush on Friday night to spend the long weekend skiing with a classmate named Winona Weingarten, whose parents owned a chalet up there; *or* if Michael hadn't decided to run downtown on Monday morning to spend "a few hours" working on this big mysterious case of his. She would recall that the moment he left the apartment at ten-thirty, she'd felt a delicious sense of aloneness, no daughter to care for, no husband to love, honor, and cherish, no students to nurture, just Sarah Fitch Welles, all by her lonesome on one of those magnificently balmy days January sometimes offered as solace to the dwellers of this otherwise wintry gray city.

She stepped smartly out of the building at a quarter to eleven, wearing jeans, ankle-high brown leather boots, a bulky wool turtleneck sweater, and a short woolen car coat— almost dressed too warmly, she realized at once. She said good morning to Luis, made an immediate left turn under the canopy, and began walking the two blocks to Madison

Avenue, where she planned to shop the windows and maybe
the stores as well. What the hell! Today was a holiday, and
she was gloriously alone.

A smoky-blue Acura was parked at the curb some three
doors up from her building. Andrew Farrell was half-sitting,
half-leaning on the fender of the car, his arms folded across
his chest, his head tilted up toward the sun. His eyes were
closed, he had not yet seen her. She was starting to turn away,
planning to walk back in the opposite direction, when—as
if sensing her nearness—he opened his eyes, and turned his
head, and looked directly at her.

Her heart was suddenly pounding.

She stood rooted to the sidewalk as he approached.

"Hi," he said.

No grin this time. Wearing his solemn, serious, grown-
up look.

"I've been waiting since eight o'clock," he said. "I was
afraid I'd miss you."

"How . . . how did you . . . what are you . . . oh, Jesus,
Andrew, what do you *want* from me?"

"Just you," he said.

In the car on the way downtown, he told her he remembered Mollie mentioning that they lived on East Eighty-first
Street, and whereas he didn't know her husband's first name
and didn't think a high school teacher would list herself under
her *own* name, he thought it *might* be possible that a twelve-
year-old girl could have her own telephone. So he'd checked
out the name Welles in the Manhattan directory and discovered that there were what appeared to be *hundreds* of them
spelled W-E-L-L-S, but not too many spelled W-E-L-L-*E*-
S. There were no Sarahs, as he'd surmised, and no Mollies,
either, but there *was* a listing for a "Welles MD," who—if it
wasn't a doctor—might just *possibly* be Mollie Doris or Mollie Diane or Mollie Dinah or even Mollie Dolly . . .

"It's Mollie Dare," Sarah said.

"Dare?"

"My mother's maiden name."

"Even so," he said, and shrugged.

As fate would have it, however, there wasn't an address following the MD Welles name, which he thought was maybe being overly cautious, hmmm? Even in this city? Using initials to confuse any obscene phone caller cruising the phone book, and then hiding the *address,* too?

"Made it very difficult for someone like me," he said.

But apparently not *too* difficult, she thought.

"When were you doing all this?" she asked.

"Late Friday afternoon."

"Why?"

"Because I had to see you again. And I didn't want to wait till tomorrow."

Knew today was a school holiday, she thought. Figured I'd be home today. Tracked me to . . .

"How *did* you find me?"

"Well, after I called the school . . ."

"You *what?*"

"I'm sorry, but I . . ."

"Are you *crazy?* You called the *school?* Let me out. Stop the car. Please, I want to get out."

"Please don't leave me again, okay?" he said.

She looked at him.

"Please," he said.

"What'd you tell them? Who'd you talk to?"

"I don't know, some woman in the office. Whoever it was that answered the phone. I told them we had a delivery for a Mrs. Sarah Welles . . ."

"Who's *we?*"

"Grace's Market."

"On Seventy-first and Third?"

"Yeah."

"How do you know Grace's . . . ?"

"Well, that's another story. Anyway, I told the woman

at the school that you'd given us an address on East Eighty-first, but we couldn't make out your handwriting and we didn't have a phone number for you. But Herman remembered your telling him you taught at Greer . . ."

"Herman?"

"I made up a name."

"Herman?"

"Yeah, which was why I was calling. Because if I could get the correct address on Eighty-first, we'd send the order right over because there was perishable fish involved."

"Perishable fish," Sarah repeated.

"Yes."

"So she gave you my address."

"No, she didn't."

"Good."

"Well."

"How *did* you get the address."

"I remembered something else Mollie said."

"What was that?"

"The only other time anyone came even *close* to saving her life was when Luis the doorman yanked her out of the way of a taxi."

"There must be a *hundred* doormen named Luis on East Eighty . . ."

"No, only three."

"Dear God, please save me," Sarah said, and began laughing.

"I went to every building that had . . ."

"A hundred *buildings,* then."

"No, I only went to the ones that had doormen. I told whoever was working the door . . ."

"When was *this?*"

"Saturday morning. What I said was that Mr. Welles had told me to ask for Luis. If there was no Luis, *adiós.* If there *was* a Luis, and if the guy on duty said, 'Who's Mr. *Welles?,' adiós* again. There was a doorman named Luis in a building near First, but no Welles. There was another Luis near Third, but again no Welles. *Your* building has a Luis *and* a Welles. I would have waited for you on Saturday, but I figured your husband might be home."

"He *should've* been home today, too."

"Then I'm lucky I caught you alone."

"Where are you taking me?" she asked.

"Are you hungry?"

"No."

"Would you like some tea?"

"No."

"A drink?"

"At eleven in the morning?"

"What *would* you like?"

She would never know what possessed her to say what she said next. Nor was she sorry when the words left her mouth.

"I'd like you to kiss me again," she said.

He kissed her at once.

Kissed her the moment she made her blatant suggestion, and then kept kissing her all the way downtown, every time he stopped for a traffic light. He drove the car like a maniac; either he was in a hurry to get wherever he was taking her, or else he was a habitual speeder. Whichever, he screeched to a stop whenever a light turned yellow, and then turned to her with the same alacrity and kissed her full on the mouth while the light remained red, which seemed a shorter while each time. She kept wishing there'd be more red lights, longer red lights, kept wishing he'd pull over to the curb and kiss her incessantly while all the traffic lights in the world flashed yellow and red and green. She kept telling herself this was crazy, she didn't know this man, who *was* this man she was kissing so hungrily?

She kept marveling, too, that she didn't feel any guilt at all. Well, maybe *any* married woman getting kissed at random traffic lights by a handsome young man six years her junior automatically put aside all thoughts of her husband toiling in the vineyards on a holiday, no less, maybe *most* married women about to be seduced . . .

She already knew she would go to bed with him.

. . . conveniently put aside any feelings of guilt when they were poised on the steamy edge of breaking a solemn covenant, maybe so.

Either that or she was an uncommon slut.

The name on the mailbox outside the door was Carter-Goldsmith Investments. Well, this was no surprise, he'd told her he was an opportunity investor, hadn't he? The surprise was that he'd taken her to his office, or so she supposed, and not to a hotel or a motel or wherever a twenty-eight-year-old man about to seduce a thirty-four-year-old woman might take her . . . where had Heather's sixteen construction workers taken her?

It was no surprise that he kissed her again the moment he closed and locked the outer door behind them. Pressed her against the door and kissed her more fiercely than he had on the beach in St. Bart's or in the French coffee shop on Second or in the Acura every time a light turned yellow, kissed her with his hands on her ass and his cock huge against her, oh Jesus, this was going to be something more than she'd bargained for, oh Jesus, she was doomed.

As she climbed the steps in the richly wood-paneled stairwell, Andrew behind her, she wished she were wearing a short tight skirt instead of the jeans, wished she'd had the foresight to have dressed in something more accessible, something that would make the impending, inevitable, and irrevocable act easier to accomplish. On the landing outside the door to what she still supposed was an office, he kissed her again and this time she moved in against him, the bulky car coat yet another obstacle to overcome, his hands inside the coat now, his hands on her sweatered breasts, she thought Oh Jesus and fiercely tilted her pelvis into him an instant before he broke away to unlock the door.

She scarcely saw the room. The room was a swirl of background impressions that served only as a setting for him, for Andrew, for what he was doing to her and about to do to her. This was not an office, she was certain of that, fireplace at the end of the room opposite the entrance door, he was slipping the coat off her shoulders, sofa facing the fireplace, he tossed the coat onto it, took her in his arms again, bookcases on the wall to the right, she wondered what he read, his lips found hers again, his hands were under the bulky woolen sweater now, on her back, she felt her breasts fall suddenly free, realized he had unclasped her bra, and stepped slightly back from him so that he could slide his hands under the sweater to find her naked nipples.

He took her hand in his, and led her swiftly to another wood-paneled staircase on the wall opposite the bookcases, climbing with her to the floor above where she glimpsed a kitchen and a dining room, and then to the floor above that, which was a bedroom at last, the one place in time she wanted to be with this man, the only place she'd wanted to be with him from the moment he'd kissed her on that morning beach in St. Bart's.

They both shed clothing as they moved toward the bed. He tossed his jacket wherever it landed, unbuttoned his shirt down the front and at the cuffs, took off that as well, and pulled her to him again, kissing her, her hands on his bare chest, his hands clutching her buttocks. Breathlessly, she broke away and sat in a chair facing a smaller fireplace than the one downstairs, took off the low boots and dropped them to the floor, stood again to pull the sweater over her head, draped it over the back of the chair, tossed the bra over that, unbuckled her belt and lowered her jeans, and stepped out of them and threw the jeans over the rest of her clothing, and turned to him wearing only white woolen socks and white cotton panties cut high on the leg.

He was naked.

Her eyes moved over his body, grazed his cock, boldly

lingered there. She wanted to touch him, suck him, take him inside her. She felt suddenly girlish standing there in the woolen socks and cotton panties, suddenly virginal though she was nothing such, suddenly so wet that she thought she would come in the next instant whether he touched her again or not.

She went to him still wearing the socks and panties.

He stood with his legs slightly parted, his arms opening to accept her. She moved into his embrace, felt at once the enormity of him between her legs, nudging the moist panties covering her crotch. They stood this way, joined but yet unjoined, for several seconds, her arms on his shoulders, his arms on her waist, she looking up into his eyes, his eyes coveting her mouth. He lowered his face to hers again and found her lips, and parted them with his tongue, gliding his tongue into her mouth, his hands reaching around her to claim her buttocks again. She rode his cock gently, her panties very wet now, rocking herself back and forth on him, her eyes closed, her mouth joined to his. He lifted her at last and carried her to the bed.

Lying beside him in his arms, she started to say, "I've never . . ."

"Shhh," he said, and kissed her again.

She thought she would faint. When finally he took his mouth from hers, she was sure her eyes were rolled back into her head. Gasping for breath, she tried to find the voice to tell him she'd never done anything like this before, never been unfaithful to her husband, never so much as even *thought* of . . .

He lowered his head to her breasts.

She clutched him to her passionately, twisting on the pillow, tossing her head and her hips as he licked first one nipple and then the other, fondling her breasts, yes, she thought, oh God yes. He suddenly clenched both breasts in his hands, bringing them together caught in his hands, the nipples almost touching, took both nipples in his mouth simultaneously, and sucked on them, and licked them, she was delirious, she had never in her life felt anything like, flicking them with his tongue, his fingers tightening on her as he worked her nipples relentlessly. She was going to come, oh Jesus she thought, don't make me come yet, just *fuck* me, damn it, put that *cock* in me, "Oh Jesus," she said aloud, and wondered if she'd remembered to take the pill this morning, and wondered if he had any dread disease she wouldn't care to catch, and breathlessly started to say, "Listen, you don't . . ." but his hand was between her legs now.

As deliberately as he'd worked her stiffened nipples, he now began to work the crotch of the saturated white panties, his hand moving mercilessly, stroking and caressing, oh God, she thought, you're going to make me, Jesus I *am* going to come. "Listen," she said, "you don't . . . you're not . . . you don't have anything I can *catch*, do . . . ?" and he said, "No, nothing," and she nodded in brisk relief and immediately rolled away from him, out of his arms and onto her back, raising her buttocks and hooking her thumbs into the waistband of her panties at the same time. She was yanking them down over her hips, when he said, "No, don't."

He gave her no time to register puzzlement. He clutched her hands by the wrists instead, her thumbs still hooked in the panties, and glided his body down the long length of hers, kissing her breasts again in passing, trailing a wet line between her ribs, licking her navel, kissing the fingertips of each hand captured in his, brushing his lips over the flat of her belly above the panties, and finally pressing them to the bulge of her cotton-covered crotch.

She felt the pressure of his mouth and chin on her pubic mound, knew he could feel how wet she was, how saturated the white panties were, how revealingly *soaked* she was, how drenched and dripping and *desperate* for him she was, and she thought For Christ's sake *fuck* me already, unwilling to say the words out loud, saying them over and again in her head like a mantra, fuck me, fuck me, *fuck* me, damn it! He's going to lose me, she thought, he's going to tease me right out of an orgasm, he's going to bring me there and strand me there, and it'll serve him right, the son of a bitch, kissing the insides of her upper thighs on either side of the panties now, licking the tender flesh there, moving the panties aside just the merest fraction of an inch to lick the soft secret skin close to her pubic patch, please, she thought, oh please, just *please,* bunching the panties in one hand so that they created a narrow thong covering only her slit, yanking up on the thong to capture the slit, working her clitoris with the cloth, slit and clit and cloth so thoroughly shamelessly *sodden* now, please for God's sake just . . .

And suddenly he grasped the panties in both hands, his fingers inside each leghole, and tore them wide open over her crotch, exposing her completely. She whispered, "Do it," as he lowered himself between her legs, "Yes, do it," easing himself down to where she was waiting open for him, "Yes, fuck me," entering her now, filling the wet aching void of her, "Oh Jesus," she said again, and wrapped her legs around him, and lifted herself to him, and said "Fuck me, *yes*" and realized she was still wearing the silly white socks. She felt herself cresting almost at once, dissolving moistly around him, felt his simultaneous explosion within her.

Later, as they lay spent and sweating beside each other, he murmured, "I love you, Sarah," and she thought Yes, that's me, and felt completely herself for the very first time in her life.

The guilt overtook her some ten minutes later.

He had kissed her gently on the nose and the cheeks and the forehead and then had eased himself out of her and out of bed, and was walking naked to the bathroom when suddenly she was shocked by the realization that this was a strange man with her, this was not *Michael* walking across the room with his ass white against a lingering suntan, this was a *stranger* who had just fucked her.

She almost got out of bed that very moment. Almost threw back the covers and dashed naked across the room to where her boots were on the floor and her jeans and sweater and bra were on the back of the chair. Her coat and her handbag were downstairs, but if she moved fast she could be dressed and out of here in a flash, disappearing from his life and reappearing in her own.

What time was it, anyway?

Was Michael already . . . ?

In sudden panic, she looked at her watch.

No, that couldn't be right.

Was it *really* only twenty to twelve?

Had they been here in the apartment for only *twenty* minutes?

Had what they'd done together taken only *twenty* minutes?

It had seemed like an eternity.

An ecstatic etern—

No, listen, she thought, are you out of your mind?

Get out of here. Get dressed and get the hell out of here before it's too late. That man in the bathroom is *not* your husband. He's a *boy* who momentarily turned your head, flattered you into thinking you were . . . you were . . . a . . . a passionate and desirable woman who . . . who . . .

God, I loved it, she thought.

Stop it, she thought. Don't even *think* it anymore. Just get dressed and get out. Go home to your loving husband who's been working all morning while you . . .

"Sarah?"

She did not turn to him at once.

He called her name again.

"Sarah?"

She turned. He was standing in the bathroom doorway. He had draped a towel around his waist. He looked very concerned. His serious little-boy look.

"Are you all right?" he asked.

"Yes," she said. "But I have to go."

"Okay," he said.

He did not move from the doorway. She felt suddenly embarrassed, not wanting to get out of bed naked, not wanting him to see her naked again. But she could not imagine clutching a sheet to her the way they did in the movies, she was not a dumb college girl, she was a thirty-four-year-old *mother,* God, what had she *done*? Without looking at him, she got out of bed, her back to him, still wearing the white socks and the torn panties, and went swiftly to the chair where the rest of her clothes were draped. She put on her bra first, covering her breasts, and then her sweater immediately afterward and was reaching for her jeans when he appeared suddenly behind her and wrapped his arms around her waist and pulled her in against him.

He was hard again.

She stood quite still, feeling all at once drained of all will, helpless to stop whatever was happening to her because the moment he touched her again, the moment his arms encircled her again, the moment he was there again with his cock hard against the torn cotton panties, she was instantly wet again.

She turned in his arms.

She looked up into his face.

He nodded.

She nodded, too.

For each of them, this was the true beginning.

Dominick Di Nobili's body was found in the trunk of an Oldsmobile Cutlass Supreme on Tuesday morning, the nineteenth day of January, in one of the parking lots at La Guardia Airport. There were two bullet holes in the back of his head, which—given Di Nobili's recent gambling and borrowing habits—almost certainly indicated a gangland-style slaying. The detectives assigned to protect him had allowed him out of their sight only because he'd begged for a lousy two minutes to go say hello to his girlfriend in Queens. He'd gone into her building and disappeared—until now.

On the afternoon of that same day, Regan and Lowndes located the blue Acura with the FAV-TWO vanity plate parked in front of a lighting-supply store near Kenmare and Bowery. There were no parking spaces anywhere near the car, so they double-parked their Ford Escort on the same side of the street, some half dozen cars behind the Acura. At about three o'clock, two cops riding Adam One from the Fifth Precinct pulled up alongside the Ford and asked to see a driver's license. Regan flashed his detective's shield. The officers nodded and rolled on.

At twenty minutes past four, a tall, hatless man with brown hair approached the Acura. He looked a lot like the picture Michael had Xeroxed from *People* magazine.

"Bingo," Regan said, and started the car.

Andrew Faviola, if that's who the man was, glanced at the windshield as if expecting a parking ticket—small wonder, given his history—and then unlocked the car on the driver's side and climbed in. The moment the Acura pulled away from the curb, Regan moved the Ford in behind it.

"Heading downtown," Lowndes said.

Which was a big surprise, Regan thought, since Bowery was a two-way thoroughfare and the Acura had been parked facing downtown.

"Probably going to Brooklyn," Lowndes said.

Another big surprise in that if the driver of the Acura made an immediate left, he'd be heading directly over the Williamsburg Bridge, or if he drove further downtown to Canal, he could take the Manhattan Bridge over the river, or yet further south, he could go over the Brooklyn Bridge, any of which would take him to Brooklyn, fuckin mastermind partner Regan had.

It was already starting to get dark at four-thirty. This city in January, you could have sunshine all day or you could

have a day like today which was gloomy all day long and
which got dark before you could take a deep breath. Street-
lights were on already, car headlights beginning to come on
as Regan nosed the Ford through the harsh gathering dusk,
sticking close behind the Acura, not wanting to lose Faviola
if in fact he decided to make the Delancey Street turn onto
the Williamsburg Bridge. Which is just what he did do.

"Told you," Lowndes said.

Fuckin genius.

The lights on all the bridges were on. You could look
up and down the East River and see this winter wonderland
of lights in both directions. Regan memorized the bridges on
the Lower East Side of Manhattan in ascending alphabetical
order. Brooklyn, Manhattan, Williamsburg. B, M, W. Like
the car. Further uptown, his alphabetical system started all
over again, but it still worked. Q and T for the Queensboro
and Triborough bridges. It worked on the West Side of Manhattan, too. Everything in ascending alphabetical order from
downtown to uptown. The Holland Tunnel, the Lincoln
Tunnel, and then the George Washington Bridge. H, L, and
W. If you had a system, everything in the world was simple.

They were on the Brooklyn-Queens elevated highway
now, the lights of apartment buildings and factories flickering
on sporadically as they moved into the fast-approaching
darkness, the Acura speeding into the night ahead of them.

"Probably heading for the LIE," Lowndes said.

Brilliant fuckin deduction, Regan thought sourly.

The Long Island Expressway was jammed with traffic
at this hour, the way it was every weekday all year round
and on weekends, too, during the summer months. Get a
snowstorm anytime during the winter, you could spend the
better part of your life trying to get home on the LIE.

"Lots of these wiseguys live on the Island," Lowndes
said.

Sighing heavily, Regan settled back for a long ride.

★   ★   ★

He could not stop thinking of her.

She had left him at two o'clock yesterday afternoon, making a phone call to her husband first, telling him she was in a phone booth at Saks, and would be heading home in a little while. He was not surprised by the speed and ease with which she'd learned to lie. He had earlier told her that he didn't go around making passes at married women, but that had been a lie, too. He didn't care if a woman was married or not, so long as she wasn't married to anyone in any of the families. That could lead to serious trouble, hitting on the wife of anyone connected.

Before she left, he asked her where he could reach her, and she told him he couldn't call her, she was a married woman, he had to understand that. He said, Okay, sure, nodding, shrugging, giving her a hurt little look, and then he wrote down both *his* numbers for her, the one on Mott and the one out on the Island. She'd promised to call. But if she didn't, he'd wait for her outside the school again, or her apartment building, he wasn't about to let this one get away from him.

They'd kissed each other deeply and hungrily just inside the door to the apartment, and then he'd walked her downstairs to the street door. Just before he unlocked the door to let her out, he'd said again, "I love you, Sarah." She'd said nothing in response, just reached up to touch his cheek, her eyes searching his face, and then she kissed him quickly and ducked out onto the sidewalk.

I love you.

He said those words a lot, he guessed, to a lot of different women. He'd even said them to Oona Halligan last Friday, Oona, I love you, the three cheapest words in the English language, I love you. He didn't suppose he loved Sarah Welles, but he sure loved fucking her.

Smiling, he glanced in the rearview mirror to see if there

were any highway cops behind him, and then picked up the speed a little, pushing it as far as he could in this heavy traffic. When at last he pulled into the driveway of the house in Great Neck, he didn't even notice the black Ford Escort that drove past the house as he hit the clicker and the garage door rolled up.

He was thinking that next time he saw her, he would *insist* on a number he could call. He didn't like her being in control this way.

The twenty-four-hour surveillance of Andrew Faviola began the moment Regan and Lowndes reported to Michael at home that afternoon. Sarah was in the kitchen preparing dinner when the telephone rang. Regan told Michael that they'd located an address for the suspect, and Michael said he would immediately assign some detectives to work through the night, but that he wanted them back on the job first thing tomorrow morning. Regan asked Michael how he planned to run this thing, the usual eight-hour shifts, or what? Because it was now close to six o'clock and him and Lowndes had been on the job since eight this morning, which meant they'd been sitting on their asses in an automobile for ten straight hours. If somebody came out there to relieve them by seven, say, then why couldn't a *third* team relieve tomorrow morning . . .

". . . instead of *us* again," Regan said. "This would give me and Alex till four tomorrow afternoon to pick up on Faviola again. That's what I'm suggesting."

Michael said he would prefer the second team relieving by seven, as Regan had suggested, but then have the *third* team come on at midnight, with Regan and Lowndes picking up the next morning at eight . . .

". . . because you're the two best people I have, and I want you on him during the daytime. And that'll put us on a regular eight-hour schedule. Eight to four, four to midnight, midnight to eight. With you and Alex working the day shift every day. Till we find out what the hell's going on here."

"Well, we were working the day shift *today,* too," Regan complained, "but now the *night* shift is half over, and we're almost into the fuckin *graveyard* shift, and we're *still* out here on Long Island. What I'm saying is I don't want this to happen every day of the week, Michael, I don't care if this guy is the boss of *all* bosses, you understand?"

"Well, I don't think that's what he is, but I can promise there won't be any more long days like this one. Unless you *choose* to make them longer."

What the fuck does that mean? Regan wondered.

"Okay, we're in a development called Ocean Estates," he said, "though there ain't no ocean I can see, up the street from 1124 Palm, that's the house he went in. Must be where he lives because he parked his car in the garage there. We're on the corner of Palm and Lotus, fuckin names here, you'd think it was Miami Beach. Tell the relieving team we're in a black Ford Escort. This is a busy place here, Michael, I don't know how we're going to sit this guy without one of the neighbors spotting us. Tell them to be careful."

"I will."

"Who do you plan on calling?"

"Harry Arnucci."

"Okay, we'll look for him."

At seven-thirty that night, Detectives/First Grade Harry Arnucci and Jerry Mandel relieved Regan and Lowndes, who were back on the job again at eight the next morning. At a little past ten A.M. that Wednesday, Andrew Faviola left the house and drove directly into Manhattan, where he parked the Acura in a space on Bowery again and then walked to a tailor shop on Broome Street, Regan and Lowndes following. He came out of the shop only once, to walk to a restaurant on Mulberry for lunch. He went back into the shop at two-thirty and was still inside there when Regan and Lowndes were relieved at four. During that time at least a dozen men in heavy overcoats went in and out of the shop, some of them staying inside there for hours.

No one was sitting the Mott Street side of the building. No one saw Sarah Welles ringing the bell set in the jamb beside the blue door at six-thirty that Wednesday night. No one saw her checking the street furtively and nervously as she waited for Andrew to let her in. Certainly no one saw her throwing herself into his arms and kissing him wildly the moment the door was closed and locked behind them.

This was the part he hated.

When they wanted to talk later. He sometimes felt they went to bed with you only so they'd be able to get into these long conversations afterward. That was the price they paid for being allowed to talk. She was no different from any of the others. A crazy woman while you were fucking her, and then all she wanted to do was talk. Full of questions. Only the second time they'd been to bed together, she wanted to know all about him. Wanted to *own* him was what it really got down to.

"Is this where you work?" she asked.

"Yes."

"It seems more like an apartment."

"No, there's a nice little office on the first floor."

"All I saw was a living room."

"There's an office behind it. And a conference room, too."

"Do you work here alone?"

"Most of the time."

"No secretary?"

"No. I don't need one. Most of my business is on the phone."

"Don't you write any *letters*?"

"Occasionally. I get help in sometimes. But rarely."

"Do you like working alone?"

"Yes."

"Are you here all day?"

"Usually."

"I had trouble getting through to you this morning."

"Yeah, it was a pretty busy morning."

Six hysterical phone calls from Frankie Palumbo, one after another. Frankie was worried that whacking that stupid fuck Di Nobili like Andrew had told him might cause the Colotti family to come back at him. Andrew had told him not to sweat it. The Colottis had only been doing a favor for Di Nobili and they were probably glad to have him off their backs. That was the first call. The second one, and the next three after that, were all about Jimmy Angels being a capo and this broad being his cousin, so how was Angels gonna feel now that his cousin's dumb boyfriend ended up in a fuckin trunk at La Guardia? Andrew kept telling Frankie that this was a favor the Colottis hadn't even *wanted* to do, and they'd been very upset when this thief stole money from the Faviola family, so don't worry about it, okay? The last call was Frankie asking if he thought maybe they should whack the broad, too, before she went yelling and screaming to her cousin again? Andrew said he didn't think that was such a good idea.

"Who's Carter-Goldsmith?" Sarah asked.

"Men who own the business," Andrew said. "They're partially retired now. I sort of run things for them."

This was a lie.

Two lies.

Three, in fact.

Nobody owned the business but Andrew, who not only "sort of" ran things but controlled them completely now that his father was no longer on the scene. Nor were "Carter" and "Goldsmith" partially retired, either. They were both very active capos in the Faviola family. Carter was Ralph Carbonaio, also known as Ralphie Carter and Ralphie the Red. Goldsmith was Carmine Orafo; the Goldsmith was a direct translation of his family name into English. Both men were listed respectively as president and secretary-treasurer of a perfectly legal investment corporation which—as Andrew had correctly informed Sarah—looked for businesses that needed an investment of time and money, and nurtured them along till they brought a good return.

These legitimate business interests, owned and operated by the Faviola family, included such diverse operations as restaurants (a favorite lawful enterprise), bars and taverns (another favorite), food distribution, real estate, garment manufacturing, photo-finishing, coffee bars (six in Seattle alone), travel agencies, motel chains, vending machines, garbage disposal, linen supply, and a score of retail shops that sold a wide variety of items including sporting goods, shoes, books and records, ladies' wear, and home appliances.

All of these legal businesses generated justifiable income, and these receipts were deposited in bank accounts all over the United States. Often, as was the case with several of the retail shops, there were branches in various states, and paper transfers of money were made on the books for goods shipped from one shop to another. It was next to impossible to monitor such legal business transactions. It was equally impossible to link any illicit activity to the recurring operating expenses paid by check from the various bank accounts of these businesses. A great many of the checks paid for salaries or services, however, went to criminals exchanging ill-gotten cash for discounted but laundered money.

Money as such is anonymous, which is why cash was the medium of exchange in most criminal transactions. But cash illegally gained was something of a curse, nice to *have* but essentially *useless* until it was converted into cash that seemed respectably earned. Money laundering was a crime that existed merely to make the fruits of *other* crimes usable. By funneling the proceeds of criminal activity through any number of legitimate businesses, cash obtained illicitly was magically transformed to cash that seemed earned through honest labor. Becoming unwanted partners in businesses that needed "an investment of time and money"—as Andrew had put it—often involved threatened or actual violence, yet another crime. But crime was the primary business of the Faviola family.

Andrew's father had been sent away forever on four murder counts, but it was open knowledge that the family was involved as well in narcotics and gambling and loan-sharking and money laundering and labor racketeering and possessing stolen goods and extortion and prostitution. Carter-Goldsmith had been created to generate a sheen of respectability for these covert criminal activities. Although Carbonaio and Orafo both lived in the Northeast—Carbonaio on Staten Island, Orafo in New Jersey—their legitimate business activities took them all over the United States, and they were gone more often than they were home. In the days when Anthony Faviola was in charge, they reported directly to him. Now they reported directly to Andrew.

And now Sarah Welles, lying cradled and naked in Andrew's arms as he began feeling the first faint stirrings of another erection, was asking him things like how many hours did he work every day, and didn't it get lonely working here all by himself . . .

"Well, I get reports from the field," he said. "People coming in all the time."

. . . and shouldn't an investment company have an office in the financial . . .

"Where are you supposed to be tonight?" he asked.

Bringing the conversation back to practical matters. If they were going to keep doing this—and that was certainly his intention—he didn't want her to get caught. All he needed was a dumb husband discovering . . .

"I'm at a teachers' meeting," she said.

"Where?"

"We're supposed to be having dinner together. Six of us. English teachers."

"Where?"

"I don't know, I didn't . . ."

"Think of a place before you go home. Think of it *now*, in fact."

"Well . . ."

He waited.

"Bice," she said.

"Where?"

"On Fifty-fourth off Fifth."

"Near the school," he said, and nodded in approval. He opened the nightstand drawer on his side of the bed, pulled out the Manhattan telephone directory, found the listing for Bice, and punched in the number.

"Hello," he said, "are you serving tonight? How late? Thank you very much." He put the phone back on its cradle, said, "Good choice. They serve till eleven-fifteen," and was about to take her in his arms again when she said, "What time is it, anyway?" and sat up immediately and looked at her watch. "Oh, Jesus," she said, "it's ten to *eight!*"

"I'll have a car run you home, don't worry," he said.

"Can you do that?"

"A phone call is all it takes."

"I still have to go," she said, and sat up.

"Half an hour," he said. "I'll call now, have you picked up at eight-thirty."

"That's not a half hour, that's forty minutes," she said.

"You'll be home by nine."

"That's late."

"Not if you met for dinner at six-thirty."

"Andrew . . ."

He had already picked up the receiver again.

"No, wait, please."

He waited. The dial tone hummed into the room.

"Please put the phone down. I have to talk to you."

He wondered what she thought they'd been doing *till* now. But he put the receiver back on the cradle. She sat with the sheet draped over her middle, knees up, breasts exposed.

She did not look at him when she spoke. She stared at her hands, instead, the fingers interlaced over her tented knees, the wide gold wedding band on her left hand.

"Getting here was very difficult tonight," she said.

"It's a long way, I know."

"I'm not talking about *distance*."

"Then . . . ?"

"I didn't like lying about where I'd been Monday, and I didn't like lying about where I was *going* to be tonight. It's difficult for me to lie, Andrew."

"I can understand that. I'm sorry. I'll call for the car right this . . ."

"It's just that urging me to *stay* when I have to leave only makes it necessary for me to . . . to . . . Don't you see, Andrew? If I'm late getting home . . . later than I *should* be . . . then I'll have to tell *another* lie about why I'm . . ."

"I'm sorry. You're right. I shouldn't have . . ."

"But that's not even the *point*. The point . . . Andrew," she said, and turned to him, "the point is I'm not sure I can . . . I can keep *on* lying this way," she said, and shook her head, and lowered her eyes and kept shaking her head over and over again. He took her chin in his hand. Turned her face toward his again. She looked up at him. Her eyes were beginning to mist.

"What are you saying?" he asked.

"I don't know what I'm saying."

"You're not saying . . . ?"

"I told you I don't *know* what I'm . . ."

"If this is just a matter of . . ."

"I'm lying to my husband, I'm lying to my daughter . . ."

"You've never told a lie before, huh?"

"I'm not that sort of person. I don't *lie* about things. I just don't."

"Never, huh?"

"Not to my husband."

"About *anything*?"

"Never anything important."

"Am *I* important?"

"That's got nothing to do with . . ."

"I asked you a question. Am *I* important?"

"Yes."

"Then lie about *me*," he said, and picked up the receiver again. He dialed a number, waited, said, "Billy? I'll need a car around eight-thirty. Uptown to Eighty-first and Lex. Don't be late."

He put the receiver down.

"Okay?" he said.

She was staring at her hands again, the wedding band on her hand.

"I'll send a car to get you next time," he said. "Make it easier for you. Someplace away from the school. Maybe on Fifty-seventh. That's a busy street."

"Who's Billy?" she asked.

"Man who drives for us."

"Women? Does he drive other women?"

"I do business with a lot of women. Yes, he drives other women."

"Because I wouldn't want him to think . . ."

"He's used to it. There's nothing to worry about."

Used to it, she thought.

"Maybe I'll take a taxi instead," she said.

"Fine, if that's what you'd prefer."

"Yes, I think so."

"Fine," he said, and picked up the receiver again, and dialed the same number again. "Billy?" he said. "Forget it," and hung up.

"Okay?" he asked.

"Yes," she said, and nodded. "I'd better get dressed."

"We have time yet."

"You're doing it again," she said. "I tell you I have to leave, and you . . ."

"I'm sorry. When will I see you again?"

"I'm not sure," she said, and got out of bed and went to where her clothes were draped over the chair.

"Next Wednesday night?"

"I don't know."

"Sarah," he said, "don't do this to me, okay? I love you, Sarah . . ."

"That's impossible," she said, "you can't, you don't. So please don't say it again."

"I mean it."

"I know you don't."

"I *do*."

She nodded, and sighed, and turned away from him. He watched as she began dressing in silence.

"Where can I call you?" he asked.

"You can't," she said.

"What time do you leave for work in the morning?"

"Seven-thirty."

"What time does your husband leave?"

"Sometime after that."

"When does he get home?"

"Six or thereabouts."

"And you?"

"Anytime between four-thirty and six. But my daughter's usually home by then. I'm never *alone*, Andrew, don't you see? This is impossible. I can't do this anymore. Really. I just can't. It's too . . ."

"Where do you have lunch?"

"The teachers' lunchroom."

"Is there a phone there?"

"A pay phone. But there are other teachers . . ."

"What time do you have lunch?"

"The fifth period."

"What time is that?"

"Twelve-thirty."

"I'll call you tomorrow. What's the phone number there?"

"I don't know. Anyway, don't call me."

"Then *you* call me. And you can read me the number off the phone. I want to be able to reach you whenever I want to."

She said nothing.

"Because I love you," he said.

She still said nothing.

"Do you love me?" he asked.

"Don't ask me that."

"I'm asking. Do you love me?"

"I haven't thought of anything but you since Monday," she said. She was buttoning her blouse. Her hands stopped. "There hasn't been anything but you on my mind since Monday. I think I'm going crazy," she said, and shook her head and finished buttoning the blouse, and sat in the chair, and reached for her pumps.

"I feel the same way," he said.

She stood up abruptly, smoothed her skirt, and walked to where she'd hung her coat in the closet.

"You haven't said it yet," he said.

"I have to leave," she said, and put on her coat.

"I'll get dressed," he said, "come find a cab for you."

"You don't have to do that," she said. "I'm a big girl now."

"But not big enough to lie for me, hmm?"

She did not answer him.

"Even though you love me," he said.

They looked at each other for a moment in silence, and then he nodded, and got out of bed and began dressing. They left the apartment together at a quarter past eight. Bowery was almost deserted at that hour, all the service stores closed, the street dark except for the streetlamps. It was bitterly cold. Vapor steamed up from the manhole covers. There wasn't a cab in sight. She was beginning to think she should have let Billy, whoever he was, drive her home. She was beginning to think she shouldn't have come here at *all*. She had already decided she would never see him again. If she got past lying to Michael when she got home tonight, she would never again—

A cab was coming up the avenue.

Andrew whistled for it.

Time was running out. She felt suddenly empty.

The cab stopped.

Andrew opened the back door for her.

"I'll call you tomorrow," he said.

"No, don't," she said.

"I'll find the number and I'll call you."

"I don't want you to," she said.

"I will," he said.

"Don't," she said, and pulled the door shut, and told the driver where to take her. She did not look back at Andrew as the cab pulled away from the curb.

Alonso Moreno was dressed for the equator. Andrew guessed no one had ever told him it got to be twelve degrees above zero here in New York City. The place Moreno had chosen for their meeting was a club on Sixteenth Street and Eighth Avenue. The band was playing Spanish music, and Moreno and Andrew were eating Spanish food. Moreno sat in a beige tropical-weight suit, a brightly colored floral print tie trailing down the front of his pearl-colored shirt. Hookers at the bar kept flashing wide smiles at him, but Moreno was too busy with his food. He ate the way Charles Laughton did in *Henry the Eighth*, which Andrew had once seen on late night television. Washed the food down with sangria he poured from the pitcher on the table. Two of his goons sat at a nearby table, keeping an eye on things. Moreno didn't want them in on the conversation, but he did want their presence to be felt.

"That was very brave, what you did that day," he told Andrew.

"I'm a good swimmer," Andrew said, brushing off the compliment.

"Still," Moreno said. "Sharks."

Andrew wanted to know what deal Moreno had come up with, never mind sharks. The orchestra was playing something that sounded very familiar, one of those Spanish songs you're sure you know, but can't remember the title or the lyrics. Moreno kept eating and drinking as if he were in a five-star restaurant instead of a dinky little club on Eighth Avenue, which his cartel probably owned. Andrew poured himself a glass of sangria. One of the hookers at the bar smiled at him and raised her glass to him. He raised his glass back.

This was Thursday night.

He had debated calling Sarah this afternoon, had gone so far as getting a number for the teachers' lunchroom from a woman in the main office who sounded like the one he'd tried to con earlier about the grocery delivery. He might have called at twelve-thirty, when Sarah had told him she'd be having lunch, but his uncle called five minutes earlier to tell him Moreno wanted a sitdown tonight, he suspected the man was ready with a counterproposal. They'd talked for about fifteen minutes, Uncle Rudy telling him these goddamn chemotherapy treatments were going to kill him quicker than the cancer would, the two of them arranging to meet tomorrow morning to discuss whatever Moreno had to say tonight.

So far Moreno hadn't said a word.

The hooker at the bar was a black girl wearing a blond wig. That was the only thing about her, the color of her hair, that reminded him of Sarah. He didn't know why he hadn't called her this afternoon. Maybe he was protecting himself. Married woman getting nervous, starting to feel guilty about lying to her husband, fuck her, there were plenty other fish in the sea. Or maybe he was intuitively playing her like the schoolteacher she was, letting her stew in her own juices for a day or two before he popped up again. He really didn't know. Or particularly care. He'd see how it worked out.

"So what's on your mind?" he asked Moreno.

"Well, first I have to tell you a story," Moreno said, and winked slyly, as if he was about to tell a dirty joke. "It's a story about a fox and a snake . . . Do you know they call me *La Culebra* in Spanish? That means The Snake."

"No, I didn't know that," Andrew said, lying.

"*Sí, La Culebra*. But this story isn't about me, this is an old Spanish tale that goes back centuries. I think the blonde there likes you. Shall I have her sent over?"

"Let me hear your story first," Andrew said.

"The story has to do with a sly fox and a wise snake. Did I tell you that this was a very young fox? If I forgot to tell you that, I'm sorry. This is a very young fox. Not that the snake is very old, either. It is just that the snake is more experienced than the fox. In years, they are not so far apart. How old are you, Andrew?"

"Twenty-eight."

"I'm eleven years older than you are. Thirty-nine. That's not very old, is it? But like the snake in the story, I'm very experienced. Not that the story is about me."

"I understand," Andrew said.

Get on with it, he thought.

"The fox, although very young, is very sly. And he thinks he can trick the snake into giving away all his eggs. Snakes lay eggs, did you know that, Andrew? In Spanish, the word 'snake' is feminine. Perhaps that's because snakes lay eggs, I'm not sure. *La culebra*. Even a male snake like the one in the story is called 'la' *culebra*. That's odd, don't you think?"

"Yes."

"That a snake, which so resembles the male sex organ, should be female in Spanish. Very odd."

"Mr. Moreno, this is a very interesting story so far . . ."

"Oh, it gets much more interesting. The sly young fox . . . did I tell you he was both sly and young? The sly young fox goes to the wise old snake and tells him that if he gives him all his eggs, he will make him rich for the rest of his life. Well, this is very tempting to the snake . . ."

"This is an old Spanish folk tale, huh?"

"Oh, yes, everyone knows it. *El Zorro y La Culebra*. A famous story."

"And the fox wants the snake's eggs, hmm?"

"That's the way the story goes, yes. In exchange for lifelong riches. The problem is the snake is already rich. And he knows that the fox is looking out only for his own . . . ."

"That's where the story veers off," Andrew said.

"Veers off? From what? This is only a story."

"I'm sure it is. In reality, we're offering you . . . ."

"The fox is very persistent, as I'm sure you can imagine. He is desperate to have those eggs. But the . . ."

"Not as desperate as you think," Andrew said.

"Perhaps not. But the snake knows one thing the fox doesn't. In this part of the forest, the fox is bigger than the snake, you see, and he thinks that size alone matters. He thinks he can swallow the snake in a single gulp. But the snake can outwit him in a minute."

"How?" Andrew asked.

"By eating the eggs himself."

He's threatening to dry up the supply of coke, Andrew thought. No coke, no deal with the Chinese.

"If the snake did that," he said, "he'd be poisoning no one but himself."

"Until the fox became hungry again. There will always be eggs. A deal can always be struck later."

"Is that the end of the story?"

"The beauty of the story is that the fox and the snake can write their own endings to it."

"Tell me how. In plain English."

"In plain English," Moreno said, "you're offering me something I already have for a share of something that may or may not become real."

"I'm offering you a third of a huge new market, here *and* abroad. The market is there, waiting to be exploited. All we have to do . . . ."

"Hear me out," Moreno said. "In plain English. There's no one to listen in this place. We can speak plainly here."

"Then speak plainly," Andrew said.

"Your deal, as I understand it, is this. We supply cocaine, the Chinese supply heroin. The two drugs are processed and combined by your people in Italy for distribution all over the United States and Europe. You envisage a three-way split."

"That's right."

"But you see, I already *have* a distribution setup in America and abroad. I don't *need* you or the Chinese to . . ."

"You don't have moon rock."

"I don't *need* moon rock, I have cocaine. Besides, moon rock is nothing new."

"Open borders *are*."

"We're *already* in Europe with cocaine. Open borders or not. Crack hasn't taken real hold yet, but Europe is always a little behind us. When the borders open . . ."

"When the borders open, moon rock'll be the thing of the future."

"Like it was the thing of the past, huh? Sprinkle a little heroin over a rock of crack, you've got moon rock. Nineteen eighty-eight, eighty-nine, they were already doing that. To level out the crack high."

"Sure," Andrew said. "And before that, you could get the same results with a speedball, shooting the mix in your arm. But this is the *nineties*! I'm trying to sell you the fucking *future*!"

Moreno looked at him.

"And, by the way," Andrew said, "while we're discussing the *future,* you might want to give some thought to your current cocaine clients."

"Oh? Why should I do that?"

"Because they may discover that doing business with you can get them killed."

"Fuck them," Moreno said, "I'll bring in my own people."

"In which case, we'd have to settle this in the streets."
Moreno looked at him again.

"We're stronger than you are," Andrew said. "And not
only in this part of the forest. We've been at it much longer."

"Bullshit. We have ties with Jamaican posses all over the
United . . ."

"We're not playing cowboys and Indians here, Jamaican
posses. Who gives a damn about those amateurs? You think
dreadlocks scare me? Are you a pro, or what the fuck are
you? I'm talking more money here than any of us has ever
seen in his life. Cocaine's *already* bringing four times as much
in Europe as it does here, and crack's only recent over there.
Crack can be *smoked,* Moreno, that's why it got so popular
here. People don't want to use needles, they're afraid of needles, they don't want to catch AIDS. And they don't want
their noses to fall off from snorting coke powder. They want
to *smoke*. Look at cigarettes. They make laws against them,
they raise the price on them, they put warnings on them,
people are still smoking them. All right, you want to know
why users are sprinkling heroin on their crack? Because it
prolongs the high. A crack hit lasts, what? Two, three minutes? And then you crash and you feel like shit. Instead, if
you spread heroin over the rock, and *then* fire it up, you get
a high that can last three *hours*."

"I already told you, chasing the dragon's nothing new,"
Moreno said. "Even before *crack* was on the scene, they were
mixing coke powder and heroin in aluminum foil, heating it
up, and sucking it in through a straw."

"And that's preferable to a rock half the size of a sugar
cube, huh? Which you can light up and smoke for a dollar a
hit? We bring in moon rock in huge quantities, the whole
fucking *country* will be smoking it. What am I offering you,
Moreno, a kick in the head? I'm offering you more money
than . . ."

"I still see risks."

"Believe me, there'll be *bigger* risks if you . . ."

"I mean *business* risks. There's no guarantee you can make any kind of dope popular. Moon rock's been around a long . . ."

"Not in quantity."

"Besides, a lot of crack users *prefer* mixing their own combinations. You can still get very good China White, seventy-five pure, ninety pure . . ."

"Sure, at a dime a bag. When you can get a crack hit for seventy-five *cents!*"

"I admit crack's selling cheap nowadays."

"We start moon rock at a dollar, once it takes off, the sky's the limit."

"*If* it takes off."

"If it doesn't, I'll give you my personal share of the deal, how's that?"

"You're that sure?"

"I'm that sure."

Moreno fell silent, thinking.

"The Italians supply the ships both ways?" he asked at last.

"Both ways."

"And do the processing?"

"Everything. Process it over there, handle the distribution for us in Europe, ship product to us for distribution in America. All you do is what you're already doing. Except you get a third of this huge market we'll be . . ."

"Make it sixty percent," Moreno said.

"That's ridiculous."

"That's the way I want it."

"There's no way I can get anyone to agree to that."

"Then there's no way we can deal. I'm sorry."

"I came here prepared to offer you . . ."

"Sixty percent of the total. You and the Chinese can share the other forty however you wish."

"As a token of good faith, I was willing to raise your share to forty instead of the third we offered. But . . ."

"I'd be losing money if I went lower than fifty-five."

"Forty-five and we've got a deal."

"Fifty. I can't go lower than that."

Andrew sighed heavily.

"Deal," he said, and the men shook hands.

"You're a wise old snake," Andrew said, and smiled.

"You're a sly young fox," Moreno said, and returned the smile.

Andrew had already decided to have him killed.

It was the last Wednesday in January.

The man approached her as she was leaving the school building. She had no idea how long he'd been waiting for her. She knew he was not one of New York's loonies because he addressed her by name.

"Mrs. Welles," he said. "I'm Billy. I was asked to pick you up."

It was four-ten.

She did not know why she got into the automobile. Andrew hadn't called last Thursday as he'd promised—or threatened—to do, but now there was a car and a presentable young man named Billy, who opened the back door for her and then closed it behind her and came around to the driver's side of the car. As he turned the ignition key, he said, "I've been waiting since three o'clock. I wasn't sure what time you'd get out."

She said nothing. Did not ask him who had sent the car, did not ask him where they were going, simply sat back against the leather seat and watched the city's darkness enveloping them as the car moved steadily downtown. The car was a Lincoln Continental, she could see the identifying logo on the dashboard panel. Oddly, she was thinking she would have to call Michael immediately, to tell him another teachers' meeting had been called and she wouldn't be home until eight-thirty, nine o'clock.

"You're pretty much the way you were described," Billy said.

She wondered how she'd been described.

She did not ask him.

He dropped her off some fifteen feet from the blue door on Mott Street. Around the corner, Detectives Regan and Lowndes were watching the tailor shop. They did not see Sarah as she entered the building.

She went into Andrew's arms at once.

Somehow this did not surprise her.

The touch of his hands was familiar. His hands cupping her face, his hands moving to her breasts, his hands sliding up under her sweater to unclasp her bra. She knew his lips far too well already, his lips on her face, on her mouth, on her nipples. He slid his hands under her skirt, bunched the skirt above her hips, his hands on her buttocks now, clasping her to him. She wished she'd worn sexier panties, but she hadn't expected the car, hadn't expected to see him ever again—or had she? He was on his knees now, his hands exploring the legholes of the panties, she did not want him tearing them open again, she started to say, "Please don't ruin . . ." but he was moving the nylon aside, exposing her blond pubic patch, parting her lips with his fingers and searching with his tongue until her sudden gasp told him he'd found her. Her back arched, her eyes closed, her hands clutching the bunched skirt above her hips, she stood before him helplessly trembling as he brought her to orgasm. In a near swoon she allowed him to carry her to the bed. He took off only her panties, sliding them down over her hips and her waist and the long length of her legs, and her ankles, and spread her to him still wearing her pumps and her skirt bunched above her waist, and her sweater raised to expose her breasts. She opened her legs wide to him, raised her hips, and guided him into her.

He moved against her slowly at first, sliding the full

length of him deep inside her, and then withdrawing until
her lips enfolded only the head of his cock, clinging there
precariously for the tick of a second, and then thrusting deep
into her again. She did not know how long he kept her on
the edge of screaming aloud, the deep penetration, the slow
withdrawal, the fear that she would lose him entirely, but
still enclosed, still there, still captured, and then the sudden
lunge again, the swift hard rush deep inside her, the near
orgasm each time his downward stroke battered her clitoris.
And then he began moving against her with a steadier
rhythm, and she joined the rhythm and urged it to a faster
pace, her legs around him, her ankles locked behind his back.
She found herself urging him with words as well, Yes, give
it to me, her skirt high on her waist, feeling vulnerable and
exposed because she was still dressed and he was fucking her
in spite of it, Yes, fuck me, she said, his mouth on her nipples, his hands fiercely clutching her ass, never in her life had
she, fuck me, never with Michael, never with the boy at
Duke, give it to me, fuck me, fuck me, fuck me.

At a little before five, she called Michael at his office and
was told by his secretary that he was down the hall with the
chief. Grateful that she could lie to Phyllis rather than to
Michael personally, she asked her to tell him that another
teachers' meeting had been called and since she wouldn't be
home until later this evening, could he please take Mollie to
the Italian restaurant on Third for dinner?

"And tell him I love him," she said.

Which she supposed she still meant.

Down the hall, Michael was reporting to Charles Scanlon, the Organized Crime Unit chief, on the progress being
made on the Andrew Faviola surveillance. Scanlon, as usual,
was puffing on a pipe and looking meditative. Michael was
of the secret opinion that Scanlon felt he was a reincarnation
of Sherlock Holmes. Why else the incessantly fired pipe and
the sweater with all the burn holes in it? If he didn't work

for the District Attorney's Office, Scanlon probably would have been shooting cocaine in emulation of his literary idol. Charlie, as he insisted all of his people call him, thought he had a deductive mind. Michael wasn't so sure about that. But he admired his immediate superior for his tenacity, his willingness to go head-to-head with the DA for any one of his people, and his true determination to rid this city of organized criminal activity. His obsession was similar in many respects to Georgie Giardino's, except that it was not ethnically motivated. He had asked Georgie to attend the late afternoon meeting because his knowledge of the Faviola family was impressive. Both men listened now as Michael told them what he thought was happening.

"I think the house in Great Neck is where he sleeps and that's all. None of the detectives tailing him reports anyone going in or out of that house but Andrew himself. The tailor shop is another matter."

"It's where again?"

Scanlon. Puffing on his pipe. Sitting behind his desk in room 671, behind the secured doors that sealed off all the unit's offices. A diminutive man with beetling black brows and a hooked nose. The nose could have been Basil Rathbone's when he was playing the master sleuth, but nothing else about him was even remotely Sherlockian. Michael himself had always felt the Holmes novels were badly written and not what he would call compelling in any way. Sue him.

"Broome Street," he said.

"Broome Street," Scanlon said, and nodded.

"Fifth Precinct," Georgie said.

He had come back from his trip to Vail and had listened all amazed while Michael reported his belief that the playboy son of Anthony Faviola was now running the show. He listened now in further amazement as Michael told them that Andrew Faviola was running things from a shitty little tailor shop on Broome Street.

"There's no question in my mind," Michael said. "He's

using the back of the tailor shop as a business office. We've had detectives go in there at all hours of the day to take in dry cleaning or to have alterations made, and none of them have ever seen him in the front of the shop. From what we can gather, there's a pressing machine in the back, you can catch a glimpse of it when Faviola or any of the others go back there. There's sort of a curtain on a rod that divides the front from the back. Vaccaro—that's the tailor's name, Louis Vaccaro—works at a sewing machine up front. Usually there are some cronies who drop in to smoke their stogies and shoot the breeze with him while he works. But they're neighborhood people, and we haven't identified any of them as wiseguys. They're just passing the time with their old goombah Louis. Who we don't think is mob-related, either."

"Who *is*?" Scanlon asked. "That you've seen going in there?"

"So far, we've been able to identify Rudy Faviola . . ."

"Anthony's brother," Georgie supplied.

"Used to be underboss," Scanlon said, and nodded. His pipe had gone out. It would probably go out a dozen times during the meeting. The ashtray on his desk was brimming with burnt wooden matches. Looking like Vesuvius on a bad day, Scanlon filled the office with a cloud of sweet-smelling smoke, puffing violently, intent on the flame of the match and the bowl of the pipe.

"Who else?" he asked.

"Petey Bardo."

"Consigliere," Scanlon said.

"Favors brown suits," Georgie said.

"*Used* to be consigliere, anyway," Scanlon said, "when Anthony was still boss."

"My guess is the hierarchy is still the same," Michael said, "except that Andrew's taken over for his father."

"Who else have you seen?"

"Capos from all over the city. We've been able to identify Gerry Lacizzare, Felix Danielli . . ."

"Heavy wood," Scanlon said.

"It gets heavier. Bobby Triani . . ."

"Rudy's son-in-law."

"Sal the Barber Bonifacio . . ."

"Guy who started it all," Georgie said.

"No, the guy who started it all is *dead*," Michael said.

"Dominus vobiscum," Georgie said in mock piety, and made the sign of the cross.

"Et cum spiritu tuo," Scanlon said by rote, and both men smiled in the conspiracy only lapsed Catholics shared.

"Fat Nickie Nicoletta, Frankie Palumbo . . ."

"Nice company the kid's keeping . . ."

"Joey Di Luca . . ."

"Enough already," Scanlon said.

"The way I figure it," Michael said, "we've got probable cause coming out of our ears."

"Oh, really?" Scanlon said. "Where? How do you *know* anything criminal is going down in that shop? They could be using it as a social club, a place to meet, have a cup of coffee, talk about who's cheating on his wife, what horse looks good in the fifth at Belmont, whatever, none of it criminal. Where's your p.c., Michael?"

"We've got Faviola and his brother on a wire, talking about the kid taking over when . . ."

"So let's say he did."

"So all at once he shows up at this tailor shop every day of the week . . ."

"Maybe he likes clothes."

". . . and he's visited there by ten thousand capos who are running operations like narcotics and loan-sharking and . . ."

"That doesn't mean that's what they *talk* about there."

"I think they're reporting to him, Charlie."

"Gut feelings don't add up to probable cause."

"Let's try it on a judge."

"I don't think it'll fly."

"It's worth a shot."

"Okay," Scanlon said, "write your affidavit, and I'll ask the Boss to make application for an eavesdropping warrant. We'll pick our judge, and hope for the best. Maybe we'll get lucky." He puffed on his pipe again, and then looked up and asked, "Who's sitting this week?"

She was wearing a black silk robe monogrammed in red with the letters *AF* over the breast pocket. She had rolled up the sleeves, and she was sitting in one of the living room easy chairs, her legs tucked under her. He had mixed drinks for both of them—a Scotch and soda for her, a Beefeater martini for himself. Like a cat getting used to new surroundings, Sarah had prowled first the upstairs bedroom and then the kitchen and dining room on the second floor, and lastly— while he mixed the drinks—the office and conference room behind the living room here on the entry level. From inside the living room, you couldn't tell there was an entrance door; the wall bearing the door merely looked like solid wood paneling. No doorknob, nothing to indicate the presence of a door. To open the door from the inside, you pushed on it, and a touch latch snapped it open to the walnut-paneled stairway leading to the street.

"Why isn't there a door on this side?" she asked.

"Architect thought it would look better."

"I guess it does," she said, appraising the wall again.

"Freshen that?" he asked.

"I'd better not," she said.

She felt comfortable in his robe. Rather like the way she'd felt wearing her father's shirts when she was a little girl. It was still only a bit past five-thirty, they had hours together yet.

"Why didn't you call me?" she asked.

"You told me not to."

"I didn't ask you to send a car, either."

"I thought I'd make it easier for you."

"I kept waiting for you to call. I kept visualizing one of the other teachers in the lunchroom picking up the phone and saying, 'It's for you, Sarah.' I kept imagining going to the phone, and saying 'Yes?' and then hearing your voice. I used to tremble just wondering what I would say when I heard your voice again."

"What'd you decide?"

"What do you mean?"

"To say. If I'd called."

"But you didn't."

"Because you told me not to."

"And you always do what I say, hmm?"

"Always."

"Since when?"

"Since now."

This both excited her and tempted her. She felt suddenly like giving him a command, tossing the robe aside, spreading herself to him, ordering him to kiss her everywhere again. There was something thrilling about being in his robe, too. Wearing something of his, possessing it if only for a little while, was like possessing Andrew himself.

"What *would* you have said?" he asked.

"I think I'd have said, 'Who's this, please?' "

"And when I said, 'You *know* who this is. When can I see you?' "

"I'd have said, 'Oh, yes, Dr. Cummings, I was going to call you later today. Do you have any free time on Wednesday?' "

"Is that your doctor's name?"

"No, I just made that up."

"*Cummings,* huh?"

"Yes," she said. And then, getting it, "Oh."

He was sitting on the sofa opposite her, wearing a robe not quite as luxuriant as the one she was wearing, a sort of cotton wrapper you might find at Bloomie's. His comment on her inadvertent pun recalled St. Bart's and his outrageous definition of "bimbo." Did he know how Freudian the Cummings pun had been? Well, of *course* he knew. Why else would he have mentioned it?

"Do you know the one about the Freudian slip?" she asked. "This man is with his psychiatrist and he tells him he made a terrible Freudian slip with his wife this morning. The doctor asks him what it was, and he says, I can't believe I made such a slip. The doctor says, Well, what was it? The man says, What I wanted to say was 'Please pass the toast, darling,' but I made this slip. Well, what *did* you say? the doctor asks. And the man answers, What I said was 'You fuckin *cunt*, you ruined my life!' "

Andrew's eyebrows went up in surprise for an instant, and then he burst out laughing. Watching the conflicting responses cross his face was amusing in itself. She began laughing as well.

"Did you ever see *That Championship Season*?" he asked, still laughing.

"No," she said, and wondered what that had to do with Dr. Cummings *or* Dr. Freud, for that matter.

"There's a line Paul Sorvino has. Do you know him? He's a wonderful actor. He was also in *GoodFellas,* did you see that one?"

"Are these movies?"

"Yes. Well, *That Championship Season* was a play first, but I didn't see it on the stage, I saw the movie. I don't go to see plays too often, do you?"

"Hardly ever," she said. She did not tell him that Michael felt most plays were simplistic.

"The other one was a book first. About the Mafia. But television stole the title—there was a show on television called *Wiseguy*—so they had to change it when they did the book as a movie. The movie was called *GoodFellas.* Paul Sorvino played a capo. He was very good. Very believable."

"A what?"

"A capo. That's some sort of lieutenant, I guess. I guess

the Mafia has all that kind of military crap. Like the army, I guess."

"Uh-huh."

She was wondering just how much she'd really shocked him with the word "cunt." She was also wondering if he was getting hard again. With Michael, you made love once, and that was it for the night. Or sometimes even the week. Andrew seemed to be perpetually ready. The idea that he was only twenty-eight was exciting to her. She felt as if she were bedding a seventeen year old. She also wondered if she'd get anything to eat tonight. Last Wednesday, she'd left here as ravenous as a bear. Dining out with the girls was fun except that you didn't get anything to eat. She was beginning to feel really very hungry again. She suddenly thought the Scotch might be getting to her; she'd already forgotten how they'd got to this part of their conversation.

"Anyway, the *other* picture was about a reunion of a basketball team. Robert Mitchum was in it, too, didn't you see it?"

"No."

"He played the coach."

She wondered if she could make him hard again without even touching him. Just sit here across from him and get him hard. She decided it might be worth a try.

"Anyway, Sorvino's talking to one of the other players about something, I forget what, and he says something like 'You know the only woman I ever loved? My mother. *Fuck* Freud!' "

She burst out laughing. Nodding in appreciation, Andrew began laughing, too. Their laughter trailed at last. He nodded again and sipped at his martini. She sipped at her Scotch and then shifted her position slightly on the couch, allowing the robe to fall partially open over her breasts.

"Is it possible we could send out for something to eat later?" she asked.

"Sure, are you hungry?"

"Well, later. Let's finish the drinks first," she said, and gestured with her glass.

"There are lots of good restaurants in the neighborhood," he said. "But I didn't think you'd want to go out."

"No, I don't think we should."

"I didn't think so."

"No," she said, and slipped her legs out from under her and then leaned over to put her glass on the coffee table. The robe opened wider over her breasts. She could feel his eyes on her. She pulled the robe closed, crossed her legs, leaned back.

"So how'd you describe me?" she asked.

He looked at her, puzzled.

"To Billy."

"Oh."

"The driver."

"I told him your name was Mrs. Welles, and I said you were a tall, beautiful blonde."

"Do you really think I'm tall?"

"Yes."

"How tall do you think I am?" she asked, and leaned over to retrieve her drink again, giving him a good long look at her naked breasts, and then sitting up again all oblivious and innocent.

"Five-ten," he said.

"I'm five-eight."

How're we doing under that robe? she wondered. That thing getting hard for me again?

"You look taller," he said.

"I give that impression," she said, and uncrossed her legs. "Did you *mean* the part about the beautiful blonde?"

"I meant it."

"What else did you say about me?"

"That's all I said."

"Did you describe my breasts to him?"

"No."

"Well, don't you *like* my breasts?" she asked.

"I love your breasts."

"Then why didn't you describe them to him?"

The thought of him describing her breasts to another man was making her wet again.

He said nothing.

"Did you think that might excite him?" she asked. "Describing my breasts?"

"It might have."

"Or my nipples?" she said, and opened the robe in a wide V over her breasts. "Do you like my nipples?"

"Yes."

"Can you see how hard they are?"

"Yes."

"Do you like my legs?" she said, and stretched them out in front of her, pointing the toes, pulling the robe up to her knees. "Did you describe my legs to him?"

"No."

"No, you *don't* like my legs?"

"I love your legs. No, I didn't describe them to him."

"Did you tell him I'm a natural blonde?" she said, and pulled the robe back and spread herself to him.

"Do you know what you're doing to me?" he asked.

"What am I doing to you?"

"What are you trying to do?"

"I'm trying to excite you."

"You're exciting me. You're the most exciting woman I've ever . . ."

"Get you hard again," she whispered.

"I am hard."

"Get you to put that big hard cock in me again."

"Yes," he said.

"*Now,*" she said. "Get you to fuck me again *now!*"

He rose and came to her. Her eyes flicked the hardness of him under the thin cotton robe. He unbelted the robe, let it fall open, reached out with his right hand to cup her chin.

His left hand brushed her hair behind her ear. His right thumb parted her lips.

"Yes," she said, "that, too."

She hated shopping on Saturday, she hated shopping with Mollie, and she hated shopping with Heather. The weather was rotten, too. It had been rotten ever since Thursday morning, when she'd awakened with thoughts of Andrew in her mind and sounds of Michael in the bathroom. She'd thought at once that she'd overslept, but instead he'd awakened early. It was snowing outside, she wondered if they'd declare a snow day. If so, she wondered if she should call Andrew, tell him she'd be there as soon as—but no, a snow day would give her daughter the day off, too. Anyway, the snow tapered by nine and ended by noon, leaving behind a slushy residue that froze solid that night when the temperature dropped to twenty-two degrees. For the past two days now, it had hovered just above the single-digit mark, fourteen degrees yesterday, twelve this morning.

Mollie wanted the new sneakers every other kid in school was wearing. Something about a disc instead of laces, who knew, who cared? Heather was looking for something that would make her look young and exciting again. Thirty-two years old, she wanted to look *young* again. Sarah felt as if she were merely along for the bumpy ride. They had already hit Bloomie's in vain, and were now trudging along a Fifth Avenue thronged with Japanese tourists and all blustery with winds that seemed raging directly from the Arctic. Sarah's cheeks were raw and cold, and her lips were chapped, and her nose was dripping and she was thinking she'd rather be reading a book on a miserable Saturday like this one. Or actually, she realized in an instant, what she'd *really* rather be doing was—

"Where does Uncle Doug live now?" Mollie asked.

"I don't know," Heather said.

"With the bimbo?" Mollie asked.

"I don't think he's seeing her anymore."

Sarah wondered if she herself could be considered a bimbo. Could a thirty-four-year-old mother be a bimbo?

"His lawyer probably advised him to quit the houghmagandy till we reach a settlement."

"What's houghmagandy?" Mollie asked.

"Hanky-panky," Heather said.

Sarah wondered if Mollie knew what hanky-panky meant. Then she wondered what Mollie would think if she knew her mother was engaged in hanky-panky with the man who'd saved her life not a month ago. But it wasn't really hanky-panky, it was—she didn't know *what* it was. She knew only that she couldn't stop thinking about him, couldn't stop hungering for him. She had never felt like this in her life. Even when she was head over heels in love with the Duke basketball player who'd taken her to bed—well, the backseat of his Mustang, actually—three weeks after she'd met him. Eighteen years old and thrilled by his every move. She'd told her roommate that Avery on a basket—that was his name, Avery Howell, six feet five inches tall, redheaded and freckle-faced—Avery on a basketball court was "poetry in motion." Direct quote. Eighteen-year-old Sarah Fitch, giddily in love. Even *that* was nothing compared to what she felt whenever she was with Andrew. But that wasn't *love*, was it? No, she knew exactly what it was. And that made her a bimbo, yes.

". . . question, Mom?"

"What? I'm sorry."

"Aunt Heather just asked you a question."

"My question *was*," Heather said, sounding more exasperated than the situation seemed to warrant, "should we go to that little omelette place on Sixty-first, or should we go further uptown to Coco Pazzo?"

"I vote Coco Pazzo," Mollie said.

"Too expensive," Sarah said.

"My treat," Heather said.

"Even so."

"Omelettes, then," Heather said, and sighed heavily.

"How come you always have the last word?" Mollie wanted to know.

"But I don't," Sarah said.

"Yes, you do, Mom. *I* want Coco Pazzo, Aunt *Heather* wants Coco . . ."

"They're always booked solid," Sarah said, "you have to call weeks ahead. Anyway, do you *really* want to walk all the way up there in this freezing . . . ?"

"Cabs, sweetie," Heather said, and winked at Mollie. "New invention. Yellow, motorized, all the rage."

"Sure, just try to get one in this weather," Sarah said.

"But suppose we *can* get one?" Mollie said.

"And suppose he's willing to drive us up to Seventy-fourth?" Heather said.

"And suppose we get there without crashing into a telephone pole or anything . . ."

"And suppose they *can* take us for lunch?"

"Would you *then* be willing to eat there?"

"Listen, I don't give a damn *where* we eat," Sarah said, suddenly annoyed. "Just stop ganging up on me, okay?"

"Wow!" Mollie said. "Where'd *that* come from?"

"We'll eat the fucking omelettes, okay?" Heather said.

"And watch your mouth when Mollie's around," Sarah snapped.

"Mom, I've *heard* the word before, really," Mollie said, and rolled her eyes.

"Fine, you've heard it, that doesn't mean your aunt has to use it every ten seconds."

"Use it every . . . ?"

"And bimbo and hanky-panky and whore gandy or *whatever* the hell else you . . ."

"Hey, listen . . ."

"Come on, Mom . . ."

"No, *you* listen! Every time the two of you get together, I become the . . ."

"Mom, what the hell's *wrong* with you?"

"Let's drop it, Mollie," Heather said.

"Right, let's *drop* it!" Sarah said.

They walked in silence past Saks and then St. Patrick's, Sarah fumingly aware that Heather and Mollie were exchanging puzzled glances. By the time they reached Tiffany's, her anger had dissipated, and she was beginning to wonder what had prompted her outburst.

"Okay, we'll go to Coco Pazzo," she said. "*If* they can take us."

"Yeah, well, I've changed my mind about treating," Heather said, deadpanned.

"Then *I'll* treat, damn it!" Mollie said.

They all laughed.

Sarah guessed everything was all right again.

The Tech Unit detective Michael had chosen was named Freddie Coulter. He had the long rangy look of an adolescent, with narrow hips, a thin face with high cheekbones and dark brown eyes, unruly black hair, and a black mustache that looked borrowed from a western gunslick. He was wearing jeans, a long-sleeved chambray shirt, and a blue denim vest. A .38 Detectives Special was holstered to his belt on the right-hand side of his waist. Coulter was a Detective/First attached to the District Attorney's Office Squad. He listened intently as Regan and Lowndes told him what he could expect at the tailor shop tonight.

"Today's Sunday, so the shop is closed," Lowndes said.

Jackass, Regan thought. Would they be sending him in if the place was open?

"There's no alarm," he said.

"The Mafia doesn't need alarms," Lowndes said.

"Anybody crazy enough to rob a Mafia joint deserves everything coming to him."

"You rob a Mafia joint, the next day you have four broken arms."

"That's *if* you return what you stole."

"No alarm," Lowndes said, "and a Mickey Mouse lock on the front door."

"What's the catch?" Coulter asked.

"The catch is there's only the one door going in and that's right on Broome Street."

"Any cops patrolling on foot?" Coulter asked.

"How's that gonna help you?"

"Shake a few doorknobs," Coulter said, and shrugged.

"Good idea," Michael said. "Can we suit him up?"

"You get caught inside in uniform, you're a dead man," Lowndes said.

"I don't plan to get caught," Coulter said, and smiled.

"They find a uniformed cop in there, next thing you know your relatives'll be sending flowers," Lowndes said.

"To a *funeral* home," Regan said.

"Don't worry about it," Coulter said.

He had a reputation for fearlessness which Regan personally found foolhardy. In this job, only a jackass took risks. You gave Regan a million bucks he wouldn't sneak in no fuckin Mafia joint wearing a police uniform and carrying bugging equipment. Far as Regan was concerned, Coulter was the dumbest fuck on the squad.

"This is the layout," he said, and began drawing a crude floor plan on a sheet of DAO stationery. Coulter watched as the tailor shop took shape. "The curtains going to the back are about here," Regan said, and drew a series of slash marks on the page. "They're on like metal rings . . ."

"You just shove them aside . . ."

"Right or left?" Coulter asked.

"To the left," Lowndes said. "In back, there's a pressing machine on the right and what looks like a table on the other wall."

"What kind of table?"

"We've never been back there," Regan said. "This is just what we were able to catch the times we been in the shop."

"Is there a phone back there?"

"Telephone company says there are *two* phones in the shop."

"One of them in the back room?"

"Is what we figure."

"What kind of warrant do we have?"

"Basic bug."

"No wiretap?"

"No. We already got an access line for you, by the way."

The access line was what they would need to activate the bug Coulter installed. As soon as they'd obtained their eavesdropping warrant, Regan had called New York Telephone to say he was with a security company that needed an access line in the terminal box behind the Broome Street address. This was standard operating procedure. A security company, an alarm company, a data communications company, anything of that sort. The billing addresses for the fictitious firms were separate mail drops maintained by the NYPD.

"Where's the terminal box?" Coulter asked.

"Out back on the rear wall of the building."

"That's the way they have them down there in Little Italy and Chinatown," Lowndes said. "Them old buildings."

On any hard-wire installation, Coulter connected his bug to the existing telephone line. The bug took the normal audio signal, raised it to a frequency much higher than could be heard, and using the phone line as an antenna, passed it on to the terminal box. Inside the box, Coulter would install a device known as a "slave," which would take the high-frequency signal, demodulate it, and bridge it electronically to the access line, where anyone listening would again hear it as a normal audio signal.

"Should be simple," Coulter said.

My ass, Regan thought.

The phone on Michael's desk rang. He picked up at once.

"ADA Welles," he said.

From where Sarah stood at the pay phone, she could see Mollie circling the rink, trying to do a series of linked pirouettes.

"How's it going?" she asked.

"Good," he said. "You having fun?"

"Mollie is. I hate skating. What time do you think you'll be home? It's Sunday, you know, I thought we could go to a movie. There's a good one playing on Eighty-sixth."

"What time does it go on?"

"We've already missed the two o'clock."

"When's the next one?"

"Four-fifteen."

"And the one after that?"

"I didn't even bother."

"What's it now?" Michael said.

"Three-ten."

"I'll try to wrap up here in ten minutes," he said, "be home no later than four."

"That's cutting it close."

"Best I can do."

"Chinese after the movie?"

"Yeah, good."

"Shall I reserve?"

"Be a good idea. Honey, let me go. Sooner I can . . ."

"Goodbye already," she said, and hung up.

She looked out over the rink to check on Mollie again, and then dialed "O" for operator, and then the area code and number Andrew had given her for his house on Long Island. When the operator came on, she did just what Andrew had instructed her to do.

"This is a collect call," she said.

"Thank you for using New York Telephone," the operator said.

Sarah waited.

The phone was ringing on the other end. Once, twice . . .

"Hello?"

His voice.

"I have a collect call for you, sir."

"Yes?"

"Miss, may I have your name, please?"

Miss, she thought.

"Sarah," she said.

"I'll accept," Andrew said.

"Go ahead, please."

"Hi," she said.

"Where are you?" he said.

"The Wollman Rink."

"Where's that?"

"Central Park. Are you from Mars?"

"Yes," he said. "I love you, do you know that?"

"Say it."

"I love you."

"Again."

"I love you."

"Say it in Martian."

"Meet me at the apartment and I'll fuck your brains
out."

"Is that Martian?"

"It's plain English."

"Basic English, I'd say."

"Can you meet me?"

"Andrew, it's Sunday!"

"So what?"

"You know I can't. You're not serious. *You* won't be
going there, will you?"

"Not unless you say you'll meet me."

"I can't."

"Are we set for Wednesday, then?"

"Yes."

"No problems?"

"None. What are you doing?"

"Watching television."

"Are you alone?"

"No, there are three Chinese girls with me."

"I'll break your head."

"What are you wearing?"

"Oh, I'm very sexy freezing here in the cold."

"What'll you wear Wednesday?"

"My teacher clothes."

"Do you plan to teach me something?"

"Maybe. I have to go. My daughter's skating over."

"Wednesday," he said. "Billy will be waiting."

"Outside the movie theater on Third and Fifty-ninth," she said. "Four o'clock."

"I love you," he said.

"Wednesday," she said, and hung up before *she* had to say it.

Mollie executed a smart stop near the fence, sending up a spray of ice flakes.

"Who was that?" she asked.

"Daddy," Sarah said.

In the bedroom of the Great Neck house, Andrew put the receiver back on its cradle and turned to the bathroom door. Redheaded Oona Halligan was standing there wearing high-heeled pumps and one of his pajama tops unbuttoned low over her breasts.

"Who was that?" she asked.

"My mother," he said, and opened his arms to her.

At eight o'clock that night, while Sarah and Michael and Mollie were coming out of a Chinese restaurant on Eightieth and Third, and while Andrew was *really* on the phone to his mother in Stonington, Connecticut, a uniformed police officer came up Broome Street, shaking doorknobs to make sure the shops lining the street were locked for the night. He tested doorknob after doorknob, rattling a knob, moving on, rattling yet another knob, until he came to the tailor shop on the corner of Broome and Mott, where he went through the same automatic routine before crossing the street. On the other side of the street, he went through the same ritual with the doors there, and then crossed over again and started back toward the tailor shop, checking both sides of the street as he approached the door. This time, there was a credit card in his left hand.

He took the doorknob in his right hand, made a swift pass at the doorjamb with the credit card, sliding it between jamb and spring bolt, and had the door open in exactly three seconds. In another two seconds, he was inside, the door locked again behind him. Two seconds after that, two men turned the corner from Mott Street and walked past the shop. By then, Freddie had brushed aside the hanging curtain and was in the back room. The two men took up a position in a dark doorway across the street. They were Freddie's backups.

He snapped on his penlight only long enough to find an electrical outlet. He plugged a quarter-watt night-light into it and then waited while his eyes adjusted to the scant illumination. A moving flashlight would have been unmistakable from outside the shop. The beat officers had been alerted that he'd be in here, but he didn't want one of the *paisans* passing by and noticing any flickering movement. From the outside, it would now appear as if someone had deliberately left a night-light burning, a not uncommon occurrence. He would work only by this light; he knew his tools well.

The back room was long and narrow.

You came through the curtains separating it from the front of the shop and immediately on the right, on one of the short walls, was a pressing machine. On the long wall opposite the curtains was the table above which Coulter had plugged in his light. There was a huge pair of cutting shears on the table, several cardboard patterns, a bolt of blue cloth, a heavy pressing iron. A calendar hung on the wall behind the table, just above the outlet. Its illustration showed a peasant girl in a scoop-neck blouse, grinning and holding a basket overflowing with ripe yellow grapes. The days in January had been methodically X'd out to date; today was the thirty-first, the end of the month.

There was a door to the left of the table. Doorknob on it, a deadbolt lock above it. The door was painted white, like the rest of the room. A speaker with a push button on it was set into the jamb on the right. Coulter moved to the door, rapped gently on it with his knuckles, testing. It did not give back the sound of another room behind it; he guessed it opened on a stairwell. There were no wires running around the jamb; the speaker had been wired from the other side of the wall.

There were several chairs pulled up to the long table. Coulter surmised the table served several purposes. Shove the chairs back when you wanted to cut a garment, pull them up again when you wanted to talk or eat. On the short wall opposite the pressing machine and right-angled into the wall with the door and the cutting table, there was a pay telephone. Coulter was in business.

When the batteries in a battery-powered transmitter gave out, they had to be replaced, and this meant having to go in all over again, doubling or trebling or even quadrupling the risk depending on the length of the surveillance. You wired a *person* with a battery-powered transmitter, but when you were bugging a *room*, you looked for your AC power source. A telephone of any kind gave you exactly what you needed.

Coulter guessed that any meetings taking place back here would be at the long table against the far wall. That was where the chairs were. He further guessed that any business-related calls were made from the pay phone on the wall. The eavesdropping warrant did not give them the right to install a wiretap, but using the phone's electrical power, he could install a bug that would pick up any conversation taking place in the room, including whatever was said into the phone on *this* end.

Coulter went to work.

He'd done jobs where the least-suspected installation was in plain sight. People felt comfortable in their own environments, they didn't go *looking* for anything unusual. Theory of "The Purloined Letter." Splice into the phone line, run your wire along the baseboard where it could be clearly seen, straight into a bug in your 42A block across the room. You could buy a 42A block in any store selling telephone accessories; it was just a simple two-by-three-inch ivory-colored receptacle with either a single or a double phone jack in it. A Brady bug fit neatly inside it. You fastened the block in plain sight, nobody ever noticed it or the bare-faced wire running to it. But according to Welles, there were some heavy wiseguys coming in and out of this place, and maybe they were a little smarter than your average Gabagootz Mafia bum.

Coulter took off the baseboard molding and tucked his wire behind that, leading it around to the door in the center of the room. He tacked the wire up one side of the door, and over it, and down the other side of it, where he tucked it behind the molding again. The wire surfaced again just under the table, where Coulter had fastened the 42A block with the Brady bug in it. He screwed the wire into that, tacked up the molding again, retrieved his tools and his night-light, checked the street before he went out, and pulled the door closed, making sure the spring latch clicked shut behind him.

As he attached the slave to the access line in the box hanging on the rear of the building, his two backups stood shivering across the yard from him, covering his foolhardy ass.

Mollie was preparing for bed. *Murder, She Wrote* had just gone off. Sarah snapped off the television set. Across the

room, Michael was reading the appeals brief Anthony Faviola's attorneys had filed on his behalf. Michael had called his
contact in the U.S. Attorney's Office . . .

"What's all this Faviola interest all of a sudden? First the
transcripts . . ."

"One of our people is thinking of writing a book."

. . . because he wanted to be sure he didn't make any
mistakes with Faviola's son. Any appeals loopholes the elder
mobster's shysters had found would help Michael when he
began sifting whatever the eavesdropping surveillance dis-
closed. He would not commit any technical errors. When he
was finished with this, father and son would be walking the
same exercise yard together for an hour after lunch every day
for the rest of their lives. He hoped.

The racketeering activity of which Faviola was con-
victed in this case consisted of the execution murders of George
Antonini, Carmine Gallitelli, John Panattoni, and Peter
Mugnoli at a restaurant on August 17, 1991. Shunting aside
the holding in U.S. v. Ianniello, *Faviola seeks to reverse his*
RICO convictions on the ground that committing or aiding
and abetting four murders cannot be a pattern if the murders
all occur at the same time and place. Faviola also distorts the
trial court's charge in an effort . . .

"Michael?"

He looked up.

"Are you going to be with that all night?" she asked.
"You worked all day today . . ."

"I'm sorry, honey," he said, and immediately closed the
brief and took off his glasses, and came to her and hugged
her close. "What would you like to do?" he asked. "Shall we
run around the corner for some cappuccino, leave Mollie
home alone, risk charges of . . ."

"I thought . . ."

"Or shall I go pick up a video?"

"Michael we just *saw* a movie. Can't we just sit and *talk*?
We've both been so busy lately . . ."

The deception, she thought. Share the blame. We've *both* been so busy.

"Good idea," he said. "Let's go kiss Mollie good night."

The deception. Ringing a variation on the familiar theme. Instead of the deceived husband asking, Is anything *wrong,* darling?, here was the unfaithful wife complaining of neglect while longing to be in her lover's arms tonight and every night, for the rest of her life. Her lover. The word echoed in her head, carrying with it lustful undertones contrary to the motherly act of tucking her daughter in.

"Mom?" Mollie said.

"Yes, honey."

"We had this dance, you know? On Friday? The older boys from Locksley came over? And there was this one boy I kind of liked. He kept staring at me, you know? This was in the gym?"

"Yes, darling."

"And I sort of kept staring back at him. Because he was so cute, you know. With blond hair like mine, but with very dark brown eyes. And I could tell he liked me."

"Um-huh."

"So . . . he came over. He walked all the way across the gym from where he was standing with some of his friends in their little blue Locksley jackets, and he stopped right in front of where me and Winona were sitting, and he asked me to dance."

"Um-huh."

"And I said no."

The room was silent for a moment.

"I don't know why I did that," Mollie said. "I really *wanted* to dance with him, and he was so cute and all, and he'd come all that way across the gym, but I said no. I sometimes think there's something wrong with me."

"No, there's nothing wrong with you, darling."

"I hope not. He was so embarrassed. I thought I would die, too, refusing him like that."

"Maybe you felt you couldn't handle it quite yet. Dancing with a strange boy. Someone older than you."

"Maybe," Mollie said, and fell silent again. "Winona got her period last week," she said at last.

"Did she?"

"Yeah. When do you think I'll get mine, Mom?"

"Soon enough."

"Winona says it's a nuisance."

"I suppose it is."

"But I wish I'd hurry up and get it."

"You will, darling," Sarah said.

"Winona's my best friend in the whole world," Mollie said.

"That's good, darl—"

"Except you, Mommy."

Sarah swiftly turned her head away.

"Mommy?" Mollie said.

"Yes, darling."

"Why are you crying?"

"Because I love you very much," Sarah said. She pulled the blanket to Mollie's chin and leaned over to kiss her on the forehead. "Good night, sweetheart," she said.

"I love you, too," Mollie said.

"I know."

"I wish I'd grow up one of these days," she said, and closed her eyes on a heavy sigh.

Sarah went back into the living room, where Michael was waiting for her.

The deception.

The goodwife, goodmother, goodteacher, telling Michael again that they'd decided to hold their teachers' meetings *every* Wednesday evening, careful not to use the word "night" with its heavier connotations . . .

"I hope you don't mind, Michael, we just feel . . ."

"Don't be silly," he said.

How easy to deceive him, she thought.

And how perfectly natural it seems.

Pouting a bit as she told him his work seemed more important that she did these days, what *was* he working on, anyway?

"Can't tell you," he said.

"Still a big secret, huh?"

"Very big."

"When *will* you tell me?"

"When it's nailed down."

"Meanwhile, you're gone at dawn every morning . . ."

"Objection, Your Honor."

"Six-thirty, then."

"Only one day last week."

"And you went to the office today."

"Important meeting."

"About what?"

"Putting in a bug."

"Where?"

"Secret."

"Why?"

"Secret."

"Tell me."

"Then it wouldn't be a secret anymore."

Secrets, she thought.

"Would you like to make love?" she asked.

"Yes," he said.

Whore, she thought.

"Although you're both experienced detectives . . ." Michael said.

Well, *one* of us is, Regan thought.

". . . who've investigated dozens of eavesdrop cases, I'm required by case law to brief you on the procedure to be followed in listening to any conversation originating in the back of that tailor shop."

They were in his office and this was early Monday morn-

ing, the first day of February. They were about to leave for
the apartment where they'd be monitoring the bug Coulter
had installed. Michael had read them the eavesdropping warrant, and was now about to give them the "minimization
lecture" they'd each heard ten thousand times before.

Well, *me*, anyway, Regan thought.

He told them first that the courts generally regarded an
eavesdrop warrant like any *other* search warrant authorizing
a limited search and seizure of evidence. The law made no
distinction between listening to, monitoring, or recording a
conversation.

"Whether a conversation is merely overheard, or *also*
recorded, makes no difference legally," Michael said. "Either
way, the conversation has been *seized*."

He went on to say that the warrant gave them authority
to intercept the conversations of the named subject—Andrew
Faviola—and various coconspirators, accomplices, and
agents also named in the warrant . . .

"The hoods you saw going in and out of the shop," he
said.

. . authority to intercept their conversations as they
relate to the crimes of loan-sharking, drug trafficking, and—
since the unfortunate waiter Dominick Di Nobili had been
found with two bullets in his head in the trunk of a car at La
Guardia Airport—murder as well.

"In short," he said "you're permitted to listen to any
conversation regarding these criminal activities, or for that
matter, any *other* criminal activity that might come up during
the course of the eavesdrop. What you *can't* listen to is any
privileged conversation."

A privileged conversation was defined as any conversation between the subject and his attorney, the subject and his
priest, the subject and his doctor, or the subject and his wife.
If Regan or Lowndes detected that Faviola was talking to
any of these people, they should immediately turn off their
recording equipment and stop listening.

Ho-hum, Regan thought.

"A conversation between the subject and his girlfriend isn't considered privileged," Michael said. "But the minute they start talking about anything *unrelated* to the criminal activities named in the warrant, you have to quit listening."

This did not preclude them from making occasional spot checks. For example, one moment the subject could be talking to his attorney about defending a suit that's been brought against him; this would be privileged communication. But five minutes later he could begin talking about whether or not the attorney wished to be present at a meeting in the Bronx where they'd be restructuring the narcotics distribution setup in the Four-One Precinct. Trafficking in narcotics had been mentioned in the warrant; this would clearly be a criminal conversation.

It was permissible, therefore, to listen even to a *privileged* conversation for a few seconds every minute or so. If during this brief spot check they intercepted evidence of any of the crimes named in the warrant, it was okay to keep listening and recording. But the penalty for listening to or recording anything *not* specifically authorized was that *everything* they heard might be suppressed.

"Be extremely careful," Michael said. "If you're in doubt, just turn off the equipment and stop listening."

In conclusion, he told them that the eavesdropping warrant had been obtained by the district attorney of New York County, and that he'd been appointed as the DA's agent to assure that the warrant was properly executed. The justice of the Supreme Court who'd issued the warrant had the right to require periodic reports about the progress of the investigation and the manner in which the warrant was being executed . . .

". . . and whenever he wants such reports," Michael said, "I'm the guy he'll turn to. The time may also come when a search warrant, or an additional *eavesdropping* warrant, or some other legal document or legal advice or legal decision is needed. I'm the one who'll have to do that, so I have to know what's going on. Please keep me informed, okay? Make sure I get copies of all the logs, tapes, and surveillance reports. I want to hear each and every tape as soon as it's duplicated. If anything seems to be breaking suddenly, call me. Here are my numbers, office and home. Post them in a conspicuous place at the plant. That's it," he said. "Good luck."

The phone numbers were posted on the wall above the telephone in an apartment on Grand Street, a block from the tailor shop. Regan and Lowndes had dialed the number of the access line, turning on the bug, and the line was now open. They could hear every conversation originating in the back room of the tailor shop as if they were sitting right there with the goombahs. Wearing earphones, adjusting and readjusting the volume controls, they learned almost instantly that the one *constant* player was someone named Benny, and they figured out quickly enough that he was the son of the owner and that he ran the pressing machine—at least for the time being. From one of the early conversations between Benny and his father that first Monday of the surveillance, they gathered that he might not be working there much longer.

"But I thought you *liked* working with me," the old man said.

Louis Vaccaro, owner of the shop. Regan and Lowndes knew what he looked like and sounded like because they'd been in and out of there at least a dozen times.

"I do like working with you, Pop . . ."

Benny Vaccaro, running the pressing machine. Steam hissing in the background as he spoke.

"It's just I don't like *pressing*. Andrew told me he could get me something on the docks. This was after . . ."

"You have to be careful, the docks."

"Yeah, I know. But I turned down the fish-market thing, I can't stand the *smell* of fish, Pop. Andrew said I could begin work right away, soon as I cleared it with you. I'd be making more money, Pop, and he said he'd see about some other little things I might be able to do for him, you know, special little things'd bring in even more money. I really want to do this, Pop."

"I thought you liked it here," the old man said.

"I do, Pop, I do. But, you know, just running this machine all the time . . ."

"When I first started this business, I used to do all my own pressing," Louis said. "The tailoring *and* the pressing, too."

"Well, that was the old days, Pop."

"The old days, yes."

"Andrew thinks he can help me make a better life for myself. Pop, I'm thirty-three years old, I can't spend the rest of my life behind a pressing machine."

The old man sighed forlornly.

"Okay, Pop?"

"Stay till I find somebody else."

"Well, how long will that be, Pop? Andrew says I can start next Monday. That's the eighth. Will you have somebody by then?"

"I'll ask Guido."

Guido was one of the old man's friends. He came into the back room of the shop on the first Tuesday of the surveillance and the two chatted over lunch. Regan and Lowndes figured they were eating because there were a lot of references to food and wine and a great many words mumbled around chewing and swallowing. The gist of the conversation was that Benny had been offered a better job and Louis would now need someone to run the pressing machine. Guido told him this was a great pity . . .

"*Che peccato, che peccato . . .*"

. . . but that he would look around and see if he could find someone.

"*È necessario che tenga la bocca chiusa,*" Louis said.

"*Sì, naturalmente,*" Guido said.

Since neither Guido nor Louis had been named in the

warrant, and since criminal activity did not seem to be the subject of the conversation, Regan and Lowndes turned off the equipment and stopped listening. Neither of them knew what the Italian meant. The sentences were translated by an Italian-speaking secretary in Michael's office on Wednesday morning as Louis saying, "It's necessary that he keeps his mouth shut," with Guido replying, "Yes, of course." Meaning, Michael supposed, that whoever ran the pressing machine would have to remain silent about the comings and goings in the back of the shop, a perfectly natural precaution. Suddenly, this, too, seemed like a criminal conversation.

The comings and goings started on Wednesday morning at ten o'clock, when Andrew Faviola himself arrived. Benny helpfully identified him for the digital recording equipment.

"Hey, Andrew, how you doing?"

"Good, Benny. Good."

Earphones on their heads, Regan and Lowndes listened. Benny was still at the pressing machine; apparently Louis hadn't yet found a satisfactory replacement. This was the first thing Benny complained about.

"I told my father I want to start working for you next Monday," he said, "but he's draggin his heels about finding somebody."

"I just spoke to him," Andrew said. "He thinks it'll be okay."

"Cause I'm really anxious to start, you know."

"It'll be okay, Benny. We're working on it."

"I hope so."

"Trust me."

"Go hide the silver," Regan said.

"*Trust* him," Lowndes said disdainfully.

"I'm expecting some people," Andrew said.

"Yeah, okay, I'll send them up."

"Send them *up*?" Regan said.

"Up *where*?" Lowndes said.

They heard his footsteps crossing the room. Over the hiss of steam from the pressing machine, they heard a scraping sound, and then a click, and then what sounded like a door opening and closing, and then only the hissing again.

The first of the people to arrive was Rudy Faviola.

"Hey, Rudy, how you doing?"

"Fine, Benny. My nephew here yet?"

"Yeah, he said to tell you to go on up."

Regan looked at Lowndes. Lowndes looked puzzled.

They heard footsteps crossing the room. Silence. Then another voice, sounding as if it were coming over a speaker. Andrew's voice?

"Yeah?"

"It's Uncle Rudy."

"Come on up."

A buzzer sounded. They heard what they recognized as the door again, opening and then closing with a firm thud. Then silence. In Coulter's report, he had mentioned a door with a deadbolt lock on it and a speaker set into the jamb beside it. They were already beginning to fear the worst.

The next person arrived at ten past ten. He was identified by Benny as "Mr. Bardo."

"Good morning, Mr. Bardo."

"Good morning, Benny."

"Petey Bardo," Regan said.

"The consigliere," Lowndes said, nodding.

No, the fuckin *Pope,* Regan thought. You jackass.

"They're upstairs," Benny said.

They listened carefully. Footsteps. Silence. Then:
"Yeah?"

The voice on the speaker again. Sounding very much like Andrew Faviola.

"It's Petey."

"Okay."

And the buzzer again. And the door opening and shut-
ting. And silence again. Upstairs was where they were
going. Downstairs was where Regan and Lowndes would
hear *shit*.

Sal the Barber arrived next.

"Sal," he said into the speaker, and was immediately
buzzed upstairs.

The fifth man to arrive that morning was introduced for
the record as Bobby.

"Hey, Bobby, how you doing?" Benny said.

"They here?"

"Upstairs."

Footsteps. The speaker voice again.

"Yeah?"

"Triani."

Thank you, Lowndes thought.

"Come up."

The door opening and closing. Silence again. At the
pressing machine, Benny Vaccaro began singing "I Left My
Heart in San Francisco."

The next two men arrived together. Before Benny could
greet them, one of them said, "Hello, Benny."

"Hey," Benny said, sounding surprised, as if he hadn't
heard them coming in. Regan and Lowndes listened to heavy
footsteps pounding across the room, heard the familiar voice
on the speaker again, "Yeah?" and then "Carmine and
Ralph," and then "Come on up," and the buzzer, and the
door opening and closing—welcome to the party. Ralph Carbonaio and Carmine Orafo were here, and everybody was
upstairs, and nobody was going to say a fucking thing down
here except Benny, who was singing again at the pressing
machine.

Regan took off his earphones.

In the conference room upstairs, they were planning the
murder of Alonso Moreno.

"This is not to teach *him* a lesson," Andrew said. "The lesson is for whoever *follows* him."

"I think we may be starting something we can't finish," Carbonaio said. He was called Ralphie the Red because he had red hair. He also had freckles all over his face, and years ago they used to call him Ralphie Irish till he broke a few heads. He had gained a little weight since then, and he sat now at the conference table in gray flannel slacks and a blue cashmere sports jacket with a gray V-neck sweater under it. He was due in Seattle tomorrow morning. He considered this business of having to take care of Moreno a nuisance. Better not to start something that could lead to complications. There were times when Ralphie considered himself a totally legitimate entrepreneur, all evidence to the contrary.

"If we *don't* start it, there's no Chinese deal," Rudy said. "The fuckin Chinks are tellin us shit or get off the pot. We gonna let this spic stand in the way of what could be billions?"

"Rudy's right," Sal the Barber said in his gruff, rumbling voice. "Fuck 'em. We do our own thing, fuck 'em."

"Easier to pay him, though," Triani said. "What he's askin."

Bobby Triani was married to Rudy's daughter, Ida, and as an intimate member of the family was fourth in the hierarchy of command. He was forty-two years old, a burly, brown-eyed, dark-haired chain-smoker who did not smoke when he was here in Andrew's apartment, office, whatever the fuck he called it. He resented not being able to smoke here. He felt he could think better when he smoked. He knew his father-in-law was dying of lung cancer, but he still thought smoking helped his thought processes. Whenever Bobby was with one of his little girlfriends, he smoked his fucking brains out. His father-in-law didn't know about the girlfriends. Bobby hoped he would die before he ever found out.

"We were prepared to give him forty-five as his end here in America," Andrew said. "He held out for fifty."

"Even so," Bobby said, and shrugged.

He was dressed more casually than any of the others, still sporting a tan he'd acquired in Miami, and wearing Ralph Lauren slacks and a purple Tommy Hilfiger sweater.

"Which, by the way, you agreed to," Petey said.

"*Fuck* what he agreed," Rudy said.

"Correct," Sal said. "Fuck 'em."

"Still," Ralphie said cautiously, "our word *should* mean something, no?"

"Not in this case," Orafo said.

Like Carbonaio, with whom he worked most closely in the organization, he was wearing a sports jacket and slacks, no sweater, dark tie on a white shirt. He was some sixty-odd years old, and went back a long way with Rudy and also with Anthony, who was now in prison. Carmine still believed in honor. They were *all* supposed to believe in honor. You gave a man your word, your word was your word. But the man Andrew now wanted killed was a man totally without honor. As he saw it, the rules did not apply here, even though Andrew had given Moreno his handshake.

"This would be a stickup in a dark alley," he said, "fifty percent of the take. The spic's out of his fuckin mind. Andrew's right. We dust him as a lesson to whoever's next in line. Then we go to them with the same deal, and they'll grab it in a minute."

"Still," Carbonaio said, and shrugged.

"I want to do it where he lives," Andrew said.

They all looked at him.

"Let them know they're not safe from us *wherever* they are. If we want to take them out, we can do it in a minute. They agree to our deal or we bury them one by one. That's what I want them to realize."

"Are you talking *Colombia*?" Bobby squeaked. His

throat got dry whenever he went too long without a smoke. He felt like killing *Andrew,* not letting him smoke, never mind the fuckin *spic.*

"Colombia, yes," Andrew said. "That's where he lives, that's where I want it done."

"I think he's still here in New York," Petey said.

"We could do it easier here, Lino," Rudy said reasonably.

"I know, Uncle Rudy, but we make a stronger point if we do it there."

"Do we have people there?" Carmine asked Ralphie.

"Everywhere," Ralphie assured him. "But I'll tell you, Andrew, this could backfire. We've got a lot of legitimate businesses in Miami, which is a stone's throw from where this man operates. It wouldn't be difficult for his people to find out *what* they are and *where* they are. We could be setting ourselves up for terrible trouble in the future."

"What kind of trouble?" Carmine asked. "What the fuck are you talkin' about, Ralph?"

"Murders, bombings, you name it. Moreno's people've killed *judges,* you think they're gonna draw the line at *us?*"

"The judges didn't go into Moreno's house and kill him in his own bed," Andrew said.

The men sitting at the conference table said nothing for several moments, each—with the exception of Rudy— wondering who would be the first to tell Andrew that this was an impossible thing he was proposing. Rudy didn't want to undermine his own nephew. He preferred the criticism to come from elsewhere. Besides, he wasn't sure this *couldn't* be done.

"Ahhh . . . how do we get *in* his house, Andrew?"

Petey Bardo. Wearing a brown suit, naturally. Brown tie, brown shoes. Mr. Brown.

"By offering someone a million in cash to get in there," Andrew said.

Which only made sense, Rudy thought, smiling.

★ ★ ★

At six o'clock that Wednesday night, while Johnny Regan and Alex Lowndes were reporting to Michael that a
heavy meeting had taken place at the tailor shop and they had
nothing of consequence to show for it, Sarah Welles was
buzzed through the door on Mott Street and hurried up the
steps to where Andrew was waiting for her. All of this past
week she'd thought of him in this place, sitting in one of
the big leather chairs in the living room, wearing his silk
monogrammed robe sashed at the waist, naked beneath it,
waiting for her.

She could not understand why the mere thought of
him aroused erotic thoughts she'd earlier entertained rarely
if ever. She knew that what she felt for him was not love—
how could it be, she hardly knew anything about him?—
but was instead what the Bible had called *lust* and what her
teenage students called a plain and simple *lech*. She didn't
know this man, yet she longed for him virtually twenty-
four hours a day. She longed for him now as she climbed
the stairs to the familiar door at the top, and saw the door
opening, and saw him standing in it wearing not a robe but
jeans and a sweater instead, and went into his arms, and
lifted her face to his, and drank from his lips and drowned
in his embrace.

"Meeting broke up at about twelve-thirty," Regan said.
"I went down for sandwiches," Lowndes said.
Jackass, Regan thought.
"All of them saying goodbye to Benny the presser," he
said. "Our guys watching the shop reported them filing out
one at a time, heading off in all directions. Except our main
man. He was in there all day long. Still there when we packed
it in at five."
"That's when the shop closes," Lowndes said. "Five
o'clock. Warrant gives us a nine-to-five. Which is when it
opens. Nine."

"Team's still outside watching the front door, though," Regan said. "They'll take Faviola home, put him to bed."

"What'd you mean by nothing of consequence?" Michael asked.

"They ain't talkin in that back room, Mike," Regan said. "Oh, sure, hello, goodbye, nice day, and so on. But where they're meeting is upstairs, wherever the fuck *that* may be."

"Freddie mentioned a door," Michael said. "Deadbolt lock on it, speaker off to the side."

"Yeah," Regan said, nodding. "Faviola buzzes them in, they go upstairs."

"Must be some kind of meeting room up there," Lowndes said. "There's windows across the front of the building, it could be a room up there."

"Freddie'll have to go in again," Michael said.

"When?"

"As soon as possible," he said, and stabbed a button on his phone. "We'll need another court order."

Apartment was too hot in the summer, too cold in the winter, never felt right in here. Luretta hated it here all the time. Summertime, with the windows open, you heard all the third-world noises out there, didn't even sound like you were living in America anymore. Wintertime, you closed everything up tight, keep out the cold, you got all these exotic cooking smells coming under the door, *other* kinds of foreign smells, too, she sometimes thought these people never took baths. The apartment was freezing cold already. They turned off the heat at eleven every night, and it was already eleven-fifteen.

Dusty had moved in with them three days ago.

Told Luretta's mother he wanted to be near her while his baby formed inside her. His exact words. "I wanns a'be near you, Haze, while mah baby forms in'sahd you." Fucking lying drug addict, all he wanted to be near was the welfare money her mother got for herself and the two children.

Luretta and her younger brother had two different fathers, neither of which either of them had ever had the pleasure of meeting. Hamilton Barnes was twelve years old, the baby of the family till now. Barnes was her mother's maiden name, which she chose to give her children 'stead of her boyfriends' names, thank you. Now Hazel Barnes was pregnant again, and her new junkie boyfriend had moved in, hooray. Seemed to always take up with junkies, Luretta couldn't figure why that was. Did she *need* needy people? Did she need men who couldn't take care of themselves?

"Fuck you lookin at?" Dusty asked.

She was on the way to the bathroom, wearing a cotton robe over a short nightgown, crossing through the kitchen to get to the hallway beyond. She shared a bedroom with Ham, did her homework in there, tried as much as she could to stay out of any parts of the house where Mr. Dusty Rogers might be sitting around shooting up.

"You hear me?" he asked.

When he wasn't doing dope, he was drinking booze. Matter of fact, he sometimes did both together. He'd cook his heroin, shoot it in his arm, then nod off for three, four hours sometimes, looking like he was dead sometimes, his chin on his chest that way, his eyes closed, sitting there in his stupor. She hated him like poison; her mother had taken him in over her protests.

She walked on by him now without saying a word to him.

He nodded in righteous agreement with whatever he'd been thinking about her, and poured himself another glassful of Thunderbird.

The kitchen divided the apartment into two uneven spaces. The bedroom she shared with Ham was on one side of it, to the left as you came in from the outside hall. To the right was a small living room, the bathroom, and her mother's bedroom. As she approached the bathroom, she could hear the television turned up loud in her mother's room down the hall. They never used the living room, because the only window in it opened on the air shaft, with a grimy brick wall opposite. If she and Ham ever wanted to watch TV, they had to ask her mother if they could come in. More times than not, Dusty was in there with her, lying on the bed in just his undershorts and his stupor. Luretta'd just as soon read a book, anyway.

You turned on the bathroom light, there was always a flurry of activity around the soap dish, where the roaches broke into a mad rush for cover. She wondered why roaches seemed to enjoy eating soap so much. Actually, she didn't mind them as much as she minded the rats. She was always afraid when she sat on the toilet bowl that a rat would come up and bite her. She always checked the water in the bowl before sitting down, making sure nothing was swimming around in there. She peed now, and then flushed the toilet and washed her hands and her face in preparation for bed.

She didn't bathe in the tub but every other night. Hot water ran out pretty fast in an apartment building this size, city didn't care *how* many tenants called to complain long as the landlord kept paying the taxes. Yes, miss, we'll see to it right away. Sure. Same as they saw to garbage collection, or snow removal, or electrical wires hanging from the hallway ceilings, you could get electrocuted just walking by. She brushed her teeth, rinsed, spat into the sink, put her brush back in the yellow plastic cup that was hers, alongside her mother's red one and Ham's blue one, dried her hands on her towel, and opened the bathroom door.

Dusty was standing in the hallway just outside.

"What takes you so long in there all the time?" he asked.

"Sorry," she said. "Didn't know you were waiting."

She started moving past him in the narrow hallway. In her mother's bedroom down the end of it, she could still hear the TV blaring. Somewhere outside the apartment, she could hear people arguing in one of the Middle Eastern languages, she didn't know which, the words harsh, the cadences strange.

"What's your hurry?" he said, and grinned.

"Out of my way," she said calmly.

But she was scared to death.

"Why, certainly," he said, and stepped aside, still grinning, and as she was starting to walk past, he grabbed a big piece of her ass and squeezed hard. She wriggled out of his grasp, scurried through the kitchen like a roach running from a suddenly blinding light, rushed into her bedroom, and closed the door behind her. There was no lock on the door.

Ham hadn't come in yet.

Twelve years old.

It's ten P.M. Do you know where your children are?

Except that it was already eleven-thirty.

She cleared the books spread on her bed, pulled back the covers, climbed in, and turned out the bedside light. The room was frigid. She pulled the blankets up under her nose and tried falling asleep, knowing there was no lock on the door, afraid Dusty would come into the room after her, afraid rats would scurry over the bed and gnaw at her face, afraid Ham wouldn't come home at all one of these nights, and they'd find him dead in the street the next morning.

At a little past midnight, she heard his key in the lock.

He tiptoed through the kitchen, came into the bedroom, undressed in the dark, and climbed into the bed across from hers. She did not let him know she was still awake. She did not ask him where he'd been or why he'd stayed out so long. In seven hours, she had to get up, and get ready for school. She hoped before then Dusty would die of a self-administered overdose.

★   ★   ★

It took exactly eleven days to get to Alonso Moreno.

The two men who'd agreed to do the job were both imported from Sicily. They spoke only broken English, but that didn't matter because they planned to present themselves as emissaries from Rome. To two skilled assassins like Luigi Di Bello and Giuseppe Fratangelo, Moreno meant nothing and Colombia meant less. For that matter, even Andrew Faviola was of little importance to them, even though the scheme they'd been hired to execute had been conceived by him. The only thing that had any meaning for them was the million dollars they would share when the job was done. Faviola had paid them ten percent on a pair of handshakes. Now all they had to do was earn the remaining nine hundred thousand.

It was common knowledge that Moreno had for years courted the Catholic Church in his native country. His constant traveling companions, in fact, were two priests respectively and respectably named the Reverends Julio Ortiz and Manuel García. These two clerics sat with Moreno on the board of directors of the charitable organization he'd founded for the elimination of slums in Bogotá, Medellín, and Cali. They appeared with him at rallies and benefits where they praised to the heavens all the wonderful things Moreno was doing for Colombia, forgetting to mention that the millions he distributed to the poor and the needy—*and* the Church— had been obtained by flooding the United States of America with cocaine. Andrew had read in *Time* magazine that Moreno had recently petitioned the Pope for a private audience. That was all he needed to know.

The papal stationery was provided by a forger in Rome, premised on a letter stolen from the Vatican mailbox.

The letter was typed on a Macintosh IIsi computer, in English, by an associate in Milan whose native language was Italian. It had all the authenticity of someone writing uncertainly in a second language:

Sr. Alonso Moreno
Rancho Palomar
Puerto Ospina
Putumayo, Colombia

Dear Sr. Moreno:

His Holiness has learned from your request for a private audience and
wishes to converse with you the availableness of several dates this
summer.

Please be advised that to the middle of February, will be coming to Puerto
Ospina on their way to Bogotá two holy fathers of the Franciscan Order
to consult with you. They are the friars Luigi Di Bello and Giuseppe
Fratangelo. It is the wish of His Holiness that you make them welcome.

Yours forever in Christ,

for His Holiness
Pope John Paul II

It had taken two days for the stationery to be copied and
printed and another two days for the letter to be typed and
posted from Rome. The letter was picked up at the local post
office by two of Moreno's men on the twelfth of February,
and driven to the Puerto Ospina ranch that same day in
one of Moreno's private Toyota Land Cruisers—what the
Colombian soldiers called *narcotoyotas*. The very next day,
the holy fathers Di Bello and Fratangelo arrived by dusty
jeep at the front gates of Moreno's riverside fortress on the
Equadorian border.

Each was wearing the long brown, hooded cassock of
the Franciscan order, roped at the waist. Each wore a black
wooden cross hanging from a silken black cord. Each wore

sandals on his otherwise bare feet. Under the cassocks, each carried a nine-millimeter Uzi manufactured in Israel and equipped with a silencer. In a mixture of broken English and Sicilian Italian, they produced a letter written in English, introducing themselves to two armed guards who spoke only Spanish.

One of the guards got on a walkie-talkie and said something in rapid-fire Spanish. The two Franciscan friars stood solemnly, piously, and patiently waiting. The riverfront was alive with the sound of insects. Father Di Bello slapped at a mosquito and mumbled a Sicilian curse neither of the guards understood. At last, someone drove down from the main house in a Mercedes-Benz. He read the letter of introduction slowly, clearly struggling with the English, and then his face brightened, and he bowed to each of the priests in turn, and said in an English as halting as their own, "Please to come. *Por favor*. Please, my sirs."

The grounds were sumptuous. Tropical flowers bloomed everywhere along the road as the Mercedes climbed higher and higher, away from the river. Fountains flowed. There were statues of nude women in all the gardens; the good fathers averted their eyes.

Moreno greeted them effusively, explaining in his very good English that he had no Italian, and that he hoped they could understand his poor English. Di Bello and Fratangelo nodded and beamed and told him in their hopelessly fractured English that they could only stay overnight, "Just'a for *la notte*, eh?"—although Moreno couldn't recall having invited them—because there was other church business they had in Bogotá. It might be good, therefore, if they discussed at once the dates available for Mr. Moreno's audience with His Holiness, which, they assured him, His Holiness was eagerly anticipating. Actually, what Di Bello said was, "He looks very much forward, eh?" Moreno was on the edge of wetting his pants.

He poured some California wine for the prelates and then

offered to show them through his mansion before dinner, an invitation they eagerly accepted because their instructions were to kill him in his bed, and to accomplish this, they had to know where he slept. He showed them his billiards room, and asked if they played, and he showed them his music room, with its grand piano (and asked if they played) and his Wurlitzer jukebox with its two hundred selections. He escorted them to a vast paneled dining room with a table that could have seated at least fifty guests, and he showed them his bar, and his living room decorated in furniture Fratangelo thought looked sumptuous but which some ungrateful guests had described—out of Moreno's earshot—as "cheap Miami shit" and he showed them the bedrooms where they'd be spending the night, and at last he showed them his own bedroom on the second floor of the house with a mirrored ceiling over the bed, and a rose-trellised balcony looking down the hillside to the river.

Over a splendid dinner served outdoors, Japanese lanterns lining the terrace and the paths winding down to the river, they discussed the dates that might be suitable—there were several in July and several more in August—and Moreno graciously submitted that whichever date was convenient to His Holiness would be more than convenient to him. Di Bello suggested that perhaps the beginning of July might be preferable . . .

"Not so hot like August, eh?" he said.

. . . and Moreno said the beginning of July would be fine. He poured more wine for the priests and they toasted the forthcoming audience, and Moreno casually mentioned that he was a heavy contributor to the Catholic Church here in his own land, and he would *love* to make an offering to the Church in Rome as well. Fratangelo tut-tutted this aside, and gave Di Bello a look of unmistakable surprise, which caused Moreno to believe he'd probably pulled a gaffe. He immediately added, "If His Holiness would not consider it unseemly," which neither Di Bello nor Fratangelo with their limited English understood. So they both merely nodded sagely and said that they had to get an early start tomorrow morning, so perhaps they all ought to call it a night.

At a minute past midnight, they left Di Bello's bedroom and went upstairs to the ballustraded corridor that ran past Moreno's bedroom. An armed guard was standing just outside the door. From the end of the corridor, firing with the silenced Uzi, Di Bello took out the guard with a single shot.

Inside the bedroom, Fratangelo pumped six equally silenced shots into Moreno's face. Then—as a token nod to the anniversary of a more famous Chicago slaying many years ago—Di Bello plucked a single red rose from the trellis outside and left it on Moreno's blood-soaked pillow.

The apartment was flooded with roses.

Valentine's Day had come and gone three days ago, but there were roses in the living room and roses in the kitchen and dining room and roses everywhere Sarah looked in the bedroom. Roses in vases on the nightstands flanking the bed and roses on the fireplace mantel and roses on the hearth and roses standing in vases under the bank of windows fronting Broome Street. Each bouquet carried a small white card:

Sarah,
I love you,
Andrew

She was beginning to believe him.

"I thought of sending a dozen on Sunday . . ."

"I'm glad you didn't."

"I hope this makes up for it."

"They're wonderful," she said.

"I got this for you, too," he said.

She knew it was lingerie even before she opened the gift-wrapped package from Bendel.

"Try it on," he said.

She went into the bathroom. There were roses in a vase on the countertop. She took off her clothes and then slipped the short white nightgown over her head. She was wearing red pumps. She felt like the devil's bride, the white gown scantily covering her, the high-heeled red shoes. She posed for him in the bedroom door, one hand over her head and resting on the jamb.

"Oh, yeah, I got this, too," he said, and handed her a tiny box.

She hoped against hope—but what else could it be? How on earth would she be able to explain . . . ?

"Open it," he said.

"Andrew . . ."

"Please," he said.

She undid the ribbon.

As she'd feared, there was a ring in the box. A ring with a slender black band and an oval black crown with some sort of signet.

"It's bronze," he said. "I bought it in an antiques shop on Madison Avenue."

"Andrew, it's . . . *beautiful!* But . . ."

"The figure is some kind of half-man, half-goat," he said.

"A satyr," she said, nodding. "But, Andrew, how can . . . ?"

"That's a bird he's holding. It's supposed to be Roman."

He slipped the ring onto the third finger of her right hand. Wearing the short white gown and the red shoes and the black ring on the hand opposite her gold wedding band, she felt truly like the devil's bride. She did not know how she could possibly wear the ring, it had to have cost a small fortune. She could not even imagine wearing it on a chain around her neck. Michael would surely question how it had come into her possession. But neither could she refuse it. He took her right hand in his. He brought the hand to his lips. He kissed her hand.

"I love you," he said.

"I love you, too," she said.

Lying beside him in bed, the black ring on her right hand, her left hand resting on his chest, her head on his shoulder, she tried again to understand how she could possibly *love* someone about whom she knew absolutely nothing. She supposed adolescents could fall instantly and madly in love with someone simply on the basis of looks and personality but that was only because there was so little *else* to know about a teenager. Didn't an adult have to *know* someone before she could love him? And yet, what other man had ever filled an entire apartment with roses for her? The only other man who'd ever bought her a ring was Michael. Her engagement ring, and then the wedding band she now wore on her left hand. Someone she did not know at all had filled her life with roses and slipped an ancient Roman ring onto her finger. Black, no less. She had never owned a black ring in her life. Before this evening, she hadn't even known that bronze *could* turn black.

I love you, too, she had told him.

And now she tried to learn who this man she loved was.

"Are your parents still alive?" she asked.

"Oh yes."

"Where do they live?"

"Well, my mother lives in Connecticut. My father's in Kansas."

"Are they separated."

"Sort of."

"What does your father do?"

"He used to be a building contractor."

"What does he do now?"

"He's retired."

"How old are they?"

"My father's fifty-two. My mother's fifty."

Only sixteen years older than I am, she thought.

"Where in Connecticut?"

"Stonington."

"Do you have any brothers or sisters?"

"Two sisters."

"Older or younger?"

"Older."

"I'll bet they spoiled you rotten."

"They did."

"Where'd you go to school?"

"Kent and UCLA."

"What'd you major in?"

"Business administration."

"When did you graduate?"

"I didn't. I got kicked out."

"What do you mean?"

"Well, suspended, I guess they called it."

"Why?"

"Drunk and disorderly."

"Be serious."

"I'm serious. I beat up four guys who poured spaghetti sauce in my bed."

"Why'd they do that?"

"I guess they thought it was funny. Anyway, I was already beginning to lose interest in school. I used to go up to Vegas a lot, gamble, fool around, you know. The two didn't mix."

"I've never been to Vegas."

"I'll take you there sometime."

"Why'd they separate? Your parents."

"Oh, I don't know. One of those things."

"Did your father want it? Or your mother?"

"Neither of them. It was something that just happened."

"My sister's going through a divorce right this minute."

"I know. Pretty woman."

"Yes."

"But not as pretty as you."

"Thank you."

She was silent for a long while. Then she said, "You shouldn't have bought me the ring, Andrew."

"I wanted to."

"How can I possibly wear it?"

"Wear it when you come here. I don't care about the rest of the time. Just wear it when you come here."

"All right."

"While you're here, I want you to take off the other ring. I want you to wear only my ring while you're here."

"All right. I'll find a place to hide it. I'd love to wear it all the time, it's so beautiful . . ."

"No, just when you're here," he said. His voice lowered. "Take off the other one now."

"All right."

She took off her wedding band and placed it on the nightstand alongside the telephone. She felt no guilt taking it off. She slipped it from her finger as though Michael no longer existed. Andrew kissed her finger where the ring had been.

"Now take my cock in your hand," he said. "The right hand. The hand with my ring."

"Here they go again," Regan whispered.

"Better turn it off," Lowndes suggested.

"Shhh," Regan said.

The bedroom bug was in the telephone on the nightstand alongside the bed. There were similar bugs in the kitchen counter phone on the second floor, and in the conference room phone on the first floor. New York Telephone had reported that there were three unpublished phones in the apartment above the tailor shop. Freddie Coulter had subpoenaed the phone company for the numbers, and then had subpoenaed again for cable-and-pair, terminal location, and pair-and-binding information. He'd put his access line in the same terminal that contained the target's phone lines, coming off the already existing B-P posts. Before entering the tailor shop again, he'd revisited the terminal box on the rear of the building, and shorted out all the phones, disabling them. It took him a total of nine minutes to bug all three phones.

But while he was in there, and just for good measure, he went to each room, found a wall with a good aural sweep, and unscrewed a 110-volt outlet from it. He then replaced each outlet with a one-watt radio transmitter. On the outside, this looked like any functioning wall outlet, which in fact it still was. Behind the faceplate, however, was the complicated circuit board that sent out the voice signal. Each transmitter had a range of some two to three blocks and required its own receiver. The devices were strictly emergency backups, and would be used only if, for one reason or another, the phones went out. In the bedroom, the fake outlet was on the wall close to the dresser. Freddie replugged a lamp into it, tried the lamp to make sure it still worked, and then started packing his tools.

The new application for a court order had this time cited reasonable suspicion as well as probable cause, and had requested both a wiretap and a pen register in addition to the bugs. The wiretap would enable them to listen to and record *both* ends of any telephone conversation. The pen register would print out only telephone numbers dialed from the premises, but it would also record the time and the duration of any call whatever, incoming or outgoing. All minimization requirements were still in effect. If Faviola's mother called to talk about her homemade lasagna, for example, the investigators would have to shut down at once.

Everything had been in place since Valentine's Day.

This was the first time Regan and Lowndes had heard a woman talking.

"Hold it tight," Faviola said.

"Yes," she said.

"Fuckin woman gives me a hard-on," Regan said.

"Better turn it off," Lowndes suggested.

"Can you see the ring moving up and down on your cock?" she said.

"Got to be a pro," Regan said.

"The black ring you gave me, moving up and down on your stiff cock?"

"Turn it off," Lowndes warned.

"I don't want you to come yet," she said.

"Then you'd better . . ."

"I want you to beg me to come."

"If you keep on . . ."

"No, no, not yet," she said.

"She's letting go of it, the cunt," Regan said.

"You're gonna blow the whole fuckin thing!" Lowndes shouted.

"So will she," Regan said, and laughed.

"For Christ's sake, Johnny, turn it off!"

"Let's see just how hard we can make you, all right?" she said. "Let's see what rubbing this ancient Roman ring on your cock can do, all right? My hand tight around you, the black ring rubbing against your stiff cock . . ."

"Must be a magic ring," Regan said.

"Johnny, *please!*"

"The satyr and the bird," she whispered.

"Jesus."

"Are you my satyr, Andrew?"

"Jesus, you're . . ."

"Am I your bird, Andrew? No no no, not yet, baby. Not till I want you to. Not till I say you can. Just keep looking at the ring. Just keep watching that black ring, Andrew. My hand tight on your cock and the ring moving . . ."

"Good enough," Regan said, and turned off the equipment.

3: MARCH 9–MAY 9

Mr. Handelmann's eyes narrowed the moment she showed him the ring. She hadn't gone to a neighborhood shop because she didn't want anyone who knew Michael to mention that his wife had come in asking questions about a ring. She'd settled on the Handelmann Brothers' shop on Sixty-third and Madison, close to the school, because she'd bought several pieces of jewelry from them in the past, most recently a pair of earrings for Heather's Christmas present. Andrew had told her the ring was Roman, but she wanted to know more about it. Where in the Roman Empire? When? She felt she had to know all this, just in *case* Michael stumbled across it and asked about it. She didn't think this could possibly happen. She'd buried it at the back of her lingerie drawer, under a pile of panties she never wore anymore. But *in* the event, she would tell him exactly what she'd just told Handelmann. She had bought the ring in an antiques shop in the Village and had paid seven hundred dollars for it. And then fill him in on the details she hoped to get today.

"Seven hundred, really?" Handelmann said, and reached into his sweater-vest pocket for a loupe. He was a man in his seventies, Sarah supposed, one of two brothers who'd been hurriedly shipped by their parents to London immediately after *Kristalnacht,* when any Jew in his right mind recognized what was about to happen in Austria and Germany.

They had spent their adolescent years in a hostel on Willesden Lane and had come to America at the end of the war, after they learned that both their parents had perished at Auschwitz. Of the two brothers, Sarah preferred dealing with Max, but he was on vacation today, and she was stuck with Avrum.

Loupe to his eye, he repeated, "Seven hundred, really?" and then fell silent as he turned the black ring this way and that, studying the band and the signet, and finally looking up at her and saying, "Mrs. Welles, you got quite a bargain."

"I did?" she said.

She'd been hoping he would tell her she'd paid too much. Seven hundred dollars was much more than she would ordinarily have spent on herself.

"Quite a bargain," he repeated, looking at the ring through the loupe again.

"How much do you think it's worth?" she asked.

"A Greek ring of this quality," he said, "at *least* . . ."

"I understood it to be Roman."

"No, it's Greek, at least second century B.C. And in mint condition. I'd say it's worth five to six thousand dollars."

Sarah was too startled to speak.

"But, Mrs. Welles, I have to tell you something," Handelmann said, and again the eyes narrowed. "I think this is a stolen ring."

"What?" she said.

"Stolen," he repeated, and handed the ring back to her as if it had suddenly turned molten in his hand. "I'm sure it's listed on the IFAR list I got just before . . ."

"The *what*?"

"IFAR," he repeated.

"What's that?" she asked.

"The International Foundation for Art Registry. They circulate a list of stolen art . . ."

"Art? It's just a . . ."

"Well, admittedly it's a minor piece. But some very important items were stolen as well."

"Stolen . . . *where*?" she said.

"From the Boston Museum of Fine Arts, just before Christmas," Handelmann said.

"Well, I'm sure this isn't the . . . the same ring. There must be hundreds of . . . of similar rings. I bought it from a *very* reputable . . ."

"Oh, yes, there are many similar rings," Handelmann said. "But not all of them show up on an IFAR list."

"What I'm saying . . ."

"Yes, it could have been another ring," Handelmann agreed. "Certainly."

"Because, you see, the shop I bought it from . . ."

"But these things often slip by," he said. "Stolen goods. They will sometimes work their way into otherwise reputable shops."

"Well . . . wouldn't they have the . . . the same list *you* have?"

"Not necessarily. We trade in antiquities. Which is why we subscribe to IFAR."

"I see."

"Yes," he said. "Would you like my advice, Mrs. Welles?"

"Well . . . yes. Please."

"You've already purchased what I believe to be a ring stolen from the Boston Museum of Fine Arts, which has reported the theft to IFAR and undoubtedly to the Boston police, with the result that the piece now appears on a list that goes out to subscribers all over the United States. You have several choices, as I see it," he said. "You can take it back to the shop where you bought it . . ."

"That's *exactly* what I'll do," she said.

". . . tell them you believe the ring to be stolen . . ."

"Yes."

". . . and ask them for your money back."

"Yes."

"Which they may or may not return. Especially once you inform them that the ring is a stolen one."

"I see."

"Yes. Or you can go to the police and tell them you believe you purchased a stolen ring, and turn the ring over to them. The police here, in New York. Not the Boston police, of course."

"That might be a good idea, too," she said, and sighed heavily.

"They'll give you a receipt for it, and they'll undoubtedly contact the Boston Museum, and that's the last you'll hear of it. Forget the seven hundred dollars you paid for it, that's gone the minute you turn the ring in. The police don't want to know from seven hundred dollars you paid for stolen goods. You'll be lucky they won't charge you with receiving."

Sarah sighed again.

"Or what *else* you can do," Handelmann said, and his eyes narrowed again, and she knew intuitively—even before his voice lowered—that he was about to suggest something at best immoral and at worst criminal. "What *else* you can do is keep the ring, forget I told you it was stolen—which, by the way, I may be wrong, you yourself pointed out there are many similar rings. Keep the ring, no one will ever know it appeared on some cockamamie list. You paid seven hundred dollars for it, did *you* know it was stolen?"

"Well, no, of course . . ."

"So forget about it," he said. "You never came in here, I never saw the ring, wear it in good health."

"Thank you," she said, and opened her bag and slipped the ring into her change purse. "Thank you," she said again, and went to the door and opened it. Outside, she blinked her eyes against a fierce wind that nearly swept her off her feet.

★ ★ ★

"Last time I was in this airport," Rudy said, "it was this shitty little thing with maybe two, three airlines coming in, you walked over to this little cinder-block baggage claim area. Now it's like any other airport in the world, *look* at the fuckin thing."

The Continental flight from Newark had landed in Sarasota at 1:45 P.M. Andrew and his uncle were carrying only the small bags they'd brought onto the plane with them, and were walking now through a glittery esplanade lined with shops. They had booked a pair of connecting rooms at the Hyatt; they planned to be here only overnight. As they'd been advised in New York, their driver was waiting for them just outside the baggage claim area, carrying a small sign that read FARRELL. He took the bags from them and carried them out to a white Cadillac sitting at the curb.

"Where's the fuckin bride?" Rudy said, and Andrew laughed as they got into the car.

"You brought some good weather with you," the driver said.

"Been raining or what?" Rudy asked.

"No, just a little chilly. Lots of wind, too."

"It's freezing cold up north," Andrew said.

"That's why I moved down here," the driver said.

"*How* chilly?" Rudy asked.

"Fifties during the day. Upper thirties, low forties at night."

So why the fuck'd you move here? Rudy wondered, but said nothing.

It took them some fifteen minutes to get to the Hyatt, where they registered respectively as Andrew and Rudy Farrell, and another ten minutes to get settled in their rooms. Andrew was already on the phone when Rudy came in through the connecting door.

". . . where we can talk privately," Andrew was saying. "Without any interruptions." He listened, said, "Um-huh," listened again, looked at his watch, said, "Fine, three o'clock, we'll be there," and hung up.

"Where?" Rudy said.

"They're sending a boat to the dock out back."

"What is it with these fuckin spics and their boats?" Rudy said, shaking his head. "I don't like boats. A boat, they can throw you to the fuckin sharks, nobody'll ever know it."

"I think we'll be okay," Andrew said. "They were going to pull anything, they wouldn't have asked for the sitdown to begin with."

"I don't trust spics as far as I can throw them," Rudy said. "They know we done Moreno, now they want to meet us on a fuckin *boat*. What for? So they can do *us*?"

"These are different guys, Uncle Rudy. They're as happy as we are that Moreno's dead."

"Still," Rudy said. "Years ago, you got on a plane, you carried a piece in your luggage. Nowadays, these fuckin terrorists, you got to go places naked."

Andrew looked at his watch again.

"Five minutes from now, you won't be so naked," he said.

At two-thirty sharp, the telephone rang. Andrew picked up.

"Mr. Farrell?" the voice asked.

"Yeah?"

"Got a package for you. Okay to come up?"

"What's your name?"

"Wilson."

"Come on up, Wilson," Andrew said, and hung up. "The guns," he said to his uncle.

"About fuckin time," Rudy said.

Wilson was a black man in his late thirties, carrying an attaché case with two Smith & Wesson .38-caliber pistols in it. He did not touch the guns, allowing Rudy and Andrew to remove them from the case themselves. Andrew figured he didn't want his prints on the pieces, just in case these dudes here were in Sarasota to dust somebody. When Andrew asked him how much they owed him, he said it had been taken care of already. Andrew wondered whether he expected a tip, but the man seemed to bear himself with such dignity and authority that he decided against it.

"Happy hunting," Wilson said, and walked out.

As promised, the tender from the boat came in at three o'clock sharp. The name of the boat was lettered in gold on the tender's transom: KATIENA. The same gold lettering marched across the big boat's transom, KATIENA, and beneath that her home port, FT. LAUDERDALE, FL. Rudy had told Andrew that nobody met on the east coast of Florida anymore. Too much dope shit in Miami, too much local, state, and federal heat all up and down the coast. Sarasota, Fort Meyers, even Naples were quiet little communities convenient to the Colombians and the New Yorkers as well. A person could sit down for a quiet chat in any one of those towns without anybody breaking down the door. Nonetheless, Rudy and Andrew had the thirty-eights tucked into their waistbands.

The man who greeted them as they climbed the ladder aboard was the ugliest person Andrew had ever seen in his life, his face a convoluted tangle of scars and welts that looked as if it might have been scarred by fire. He shook hands with both of them, and said in accented English, "I am Luis Hidalgo, I'm happy to see you." Apparently he'd already scoped them as they'd climbed the ladder. "You have no need for the weapons," he said. "Unless they make you feel more comfortable."

"They make us feel more comfortable," Rudy said.

"As suits you," Hidalgo said, and smiled thinly. "Something to drink?"

"Not for me," Rudy said.

"Thank you, no," Andrew said.

"Then come above, and we'll talk."

The boat was a huge fishing boat. They climbed up to the flying bridge and sat in the sunshine. Hidalgo was wearing chinos, black low-topped sneakers, and a black T-shirt. A gold chain with a thick crucifix on it hung from his neck and lay against the black shirt. Andrew and Rudy were both wearing lightweight gray slacks and navy-blue blazers, white shirts open at the throat.

"There's lemonade in the pitcher," Hidalgo said. "If you get thirsty."

"Thanks," Rudy said, and poured himself a glass.

"So," Hidalgo said, "it's interesting what happened to Moreno, no?"

"A terrible fuckin shame," Rudy said, and took a swallow of the lemonade.

"May he rest in peace," Hidalgo said, and smiled. When he smiled he looked even uglier. "But he leaves a tremendous vacuum, eh? Because he trained no one to take his place, do you see? For all intents and purposes, the organization is now finished, eh? *Se acabo.*"

"Which is why we're here," Andrew said.

"*Sí, desde luego,*" Hidalgo said. "But are you speaking to anyone else?"

"Just you," Rudy said.

"Good. Because the others may try to *achieve* supremacy, you see, may even *claim* supremacy, but there is really no one else who can fill the vacuum just now. *I'm* the one you must deal with. If you wish Colombian cocaine, that is."

Andrew said nothing.

Rudy sipped at his lemonade.

"You came to the right person, *señores,*" Hidalgo said, and smiled again.

Rudy was thinking he had a face could stop a fuckin clock.

"You understand the plan we have in mind, huh?" he said.

"It was explained to me, yes," Hidalgo said.

Willie Isetti had flown from the Caribbean to Bogotá to

discuss the preliminaries with one of Hidalgo's people. He
had reported back to New York that the climate appeared
favorable for a deal, his exact words. They were here to deal
now. Hidalgo knew they had taken out Moreno in his own
bed. His own fucking *bed*! They hoped this was impressive
to him. *They* were certainly impressed by it.

Cutting to the chase, Rudy said, "We offered Moreno
forty percent of the gross. Instead of a third all the way
around. This reduced us and the Chinks by something like
three and a third points each, *which* by the way we were both
willing to go along with . . ."

"Still are," Andrew said.

". . . because we recognize the existing market," Rudy
said, nodding. "What's right is right."

Hidalgo nodded, too.

"Moreno wanted sixty," Andrew said. "Which may be
why someone in his own organization had him eliminated."

"Mm, his own organization," Hidalgo said drily.

"Because they knew he was being fuckin ridiculous,"
Rudy said.

"*Ridículo, sí,*" Hidalgo agreed, nodding. "But still,
forty, you know," opening his hands wide, lifting his shoulders in a shrug, "seems low, when one considers the existing
market. As opposed to a market we merely *hope* to establish."

Son of a bitch is gonna stick to the sixty, Rudy thought.
We're gonna have to do *him* in his bed, too.

"I have to talk to others, you see," Hidalgo said, trying
to look put-upon, a mere salaried employee accountable to
the company's stockholders. "I have to *sell* this to others,
you see."

Bullshit, Andrew thought.

"Okay, what'll they buy?" he said. "These *others*. Just
remember what sixty bought Moreno."

Their eyes met.

Rudy wondered if his nephew wasn't pushing it too far
too fast.

"My people are not as ridiculous as *La Culebra* was," Hidalgo said at last.

"So what do you think they'll agree to? Your *people*."

His people, my ass, Rudy thought.

"Fifty, for sure," Hidalgo said.

"No way," Andrew said.

"*Quizá* forty-five. But *only* perhaps. I would have to talk to them very strenuously."

Bullshit, Andrew thought.

"Then talk to them very strenuously," he said. "We'll agree to forty-five, but that's as far as we'll go."

"*Bueno,* I'll call you this evening, after I . . ."

"Isn't there a fuckin *phone* on this boat?" Rudy asked. "A radio? Whatever?"

"*Sí, pero* . . ."

"Then call them now," Andrew said. "Your *people*." Stressing the word again. "Tell them you have a firm offer of forty-five, which you'd like to accept. That is, *if* you'd like to accept it."

Hidalgo hesitated a moment.

A grin cracked his ugly face.

"I don't think I will need to call them," he said. "I think you can take my word they will accept the forty-five."

He extended his hand.

Andrew took it, and they shook on the deal.

"I'll take that fuckin drink now," Rudy said.

"We figure he's out of town," Regan was saying.

The three men were eating in a diner off Canal Street. It was Michael's contention that most cops in this city would eventually die of heart attacks caused by smoking cigarettes and/or eating junk food. Despite the abundance of good, inexpensive restaurants in Chinatown and Little Italy, all of them relatively close to the DA's Office, Regan and Lowndes, cops to the marrow, had chosen a greasy spoon they much preferred.

Michael was eating a hamburger and french fries. He would have loved a beer, but he was drinking a Diet Pepsi instead. Regan and Lowndes were each eating hot pastrami sandwiches on rye. Lowndes kept dipping fries into the spilled mustard on the paper plate holding his sandwich. Regan kept frowning at this breach of etiquette. They were both drinking coffee.

The diner at twelve-thirty that Tuesday afternoon was packed with courthouse personnel, and clerks and secretaries and assistant DAs from the big building at One Hogan Place, and uniformed cops and detectives from the First Precinct and One Police Plaza, or for that matter *any* precinct in the city that had lost a man to testimony today. The noise level was somewhat high. This was good because they were talking about a surveillance presently known to just a handful of people.

"He's got maybe half a dozen girls he sees on a regular basis," Lowndes said. "He calls them, they call him. If he's not there, they leave messages on his machine and he calls them back."

"Two of them he sees more than the others," Regan said. "One of them is named Oona. The other one, we don't know her name yet, she just says 'Hi, it's me.' He knows who it is, he says 'Hi, come blow me.' "

"He doesn't *really* say that," Lowndes said, looking embarrassed and quickly picking up a fry and dipping up mustard with it.

"Close to it," Regan said. "This is unusual, you know, a person not identifying herself when she calls. In a room, a place that's bugged, you don't have people using names all the time. That's for books. A character saying, 'Well, Jack, I'll tell you,' and another character answering, 'Yes, Frank, please do.' So the person reading the book can tell the characters apart. But in real life, people don't use names except for emphasis. Like, 'I'm going to say this just once, Jimmy, so you better listen hard.' Emphasis, huh? That's because they *know* who's talking, they can *see* the person talking. It gets frustrating sometimes, listening to a bug. All these people *know* who's talking, but *we* don't. On the phone, it's different. A person usually says who's calling the minute the other person picks up. Unless she thinks she's the only broad in his life, in which case, 'Hi, it's me.' "

"Or unless she's married," Lowndes said, "and is looking over her shoulder."

"Yeah, that's a possibility, too."

"Anyway, we stop listening the minute it's any of the bimbos," Lowndes added.

Michael immediately figured they didn't.

He had checked their line sheets, and it showed them turning off the recording equipment the moment Faviola received any privileged calls or any calls clearly beyond the purlieus of the surveillance warrant. The times were listed for any and all to read, and Michael had no reason to doubt that they had indeed turned off the equipment at the times indicated, and then turned it on again for spot checks at the times subsequently listed. But did that mean they hadn't *already* listened a bit longer than they should have? Gee, we had to keep the machine on so we could make sure, you know? Cops were cops. Overhear some cheap hood in bed with his bimbo, chances were they'd keep listening longer than required by the minimization rules. Maybe he was wrong, but he was willing to bet six to five on it.

"Especially if it's Oona or the other one," Lowndes said. "Cause he's banging them on a regular basis."

"Oona is a broad named Oona Halligan," Regan said. "She left her number in Brooklyn, the phone company checked it out for us. That's also the number he calls back. We've also got numbers for five of the other broads, two in the Bronx, two in Manhattan, one in Great Neck, which is very nice of him, don't you think, also shtupping a local girl? Their names are . . ." he said, and reached into his jacket pocket for his notebook.

"And the winners are," Lowndes said, like a host at the Academy Awards.

"The winners are," Regan said, reading from his notebook, "Alice Reardon, Mary Jane O'Brien . . . he digs Irish chicks . . . Blanca Rodriguez . . ."

"Spics, too," Lowndes said.

"Angela Cannieri, who is the local talent from Great Neck, and another mick named Maggie Dooley. He fucks more Irish girls than I've ever fucked in my life, this kid."

"How about 'Hi, It's Me'?"

"Never leaves a number. Never says whether she's calling from home or from work. We can hear background traffic noises sometimes, we figure she's using phone booths on the street."

"Any idea where the booths are located?"

"Need a Trap-and-Trace for that," Regan said.

A wiretap surveillance did not normally record the telephone number of any incoming caller. This information required an additional court order specifying "reasonable suspicion" and requesting specific geographical locations, an expensive procedure usually followed in kidnap cases, where investigators were waiting for a ransom demand. Regan could not remember a single instance of the DA's Office requesting a Trap-and-Trace on a racketeering surveillance case.

"You *really* want to know where these booths are?" he asked Michael. "I mean, a Trap-and-Trace for some bimbo standin in the rain . . ."

"No, no," Michael said. "You don't have any reason to believe these women are related to the criminal activities listed in the court order, do you?"

"No, sir," Lowndes said at once. "Which is why we turn off the machine the minute we know who it is."

"Except this morning the one we got no name for says, 'Hi, it's me, I guess you're still in Florida, I'll try you tomorrow.' "

"Tomorrow's what?" Michael asked.

"The tenth. We figure he must've left early this morning. Leastways, that's when all the wiseguys stopped calling. They probably know he's out of town, so why bother? Today, it's just the bimbos been calling."

"Not *all* of them," Lowndes said. "Just Oona and the one we don't know."

"Oona," Regan said, and licked his lips. "I'd love to eat her pussy, a name like that. Grrrrr," he said, growling like a dog.

"Did *she* mention Florida?"

"Oona? No. I don't think he told her he was going away. What we think, the relationship with the other one is more important to him. From what we can pick up, anyway. Before we tune out."

"In the minute or so before we tune out," Lowndes added, and nodded.

"Did *any* of them mention the Florida trip on the phone?"

"Nobody," Regan said. "Well, Faviola told Bobby Triani he had to buy some oranges before he went up to see his mother next week, which when we tie it with what the bimbo said this morning, he had to be using a code word for Florida."

"Not Oona, the other one. The one who calls from the street."

"He told Petey Bardo the same thing, come to think of it."

"Yeah, the oranges," Lowndes said.

"He always wears brown, Petey Bardo," Regan said.

"Yeah, he likes brown," Lowndes said.

"Anyway, what do you want us to do about this harem he's got? You want us to put tails on 'em?"

"How do you figure they're important?"

"I don't."

"Does he talk mob shit with them?"

"Not so far."

"Until he does, we'd be wasting time." Michael thought for a moment, and then said, "*When* did she say she'd try him again?"

"Tomorrow."

"Do you think she *knows* he's coming back tomorrow? Or is she just trying him on the off chance?"

"Tomorrow's Wednesday," Regan said. "If he's back, you can bet your ass they'll be screwing their brains out again. That seems to be her regular night, Wednesday."

"Good," Michael said. "If he tells her *why* he was in Florida, and it just happens to be something criminal, stay on it. Otherwise . . ."

"Otherwise, we'll tune out," Lowndes said.

"Naturally," Regan said.

"God, I missed you."

"He's back," Regan said.

"I missed you, too," the woman said.

"You look great."

"You do, too."

"Hold me."

Silence.

"Kiss me."

"There they go," Lowndes said.

"God," she said.

"Grabbing a handful of cock," Regan said.

"God, I missed you."

"Must be an echo in the place," Regan said.

More silence.

Both detectives listened.

In a while, they heard the woman moaning, and they knew exactly what the pair of them were doing in that bedroom. They took off the earphones, turned off the equipment, and noted the time. Two minutes later, they listened again for some thirty seconds, ascertained that the two of them were still fucking, and tuned out again.

It wasn't the fucking itself they particularly enjoyed listening to, it was the things the woman *said* to Faviola when they *weren't* fucking. Or sometimes when she was coming, the things she shouted when she was coming. Compared to "Hi, It's Me," Oona Halligan was a novitiate nun. Oh, yes, at Faviola's urging Oona would sometimes politely ask him to keep fucking her, *Yes, please fuck me,* but never once did she construct a scenario comparable to those the other broad seemingly pulled out of thin air.

Oona was a redhead. They gathered this from little tidbits Faviola dropped about how Irish she looked with those masses of red hair, probably didn't know there were Irish girls with hair as black as his own, the dumb wop. The other one was unmistakably a blonde. This, too, they gathered from what was said in the bedroom, but mostly from *her* half of the conversation. She seemed to know he enjoyed her blondeness, seemed to realize it turned him on, so she kept mentioning it, *Do you like my being blond down here, too?,* wanting to know what effect her blondeness had on him, *Does it excite you to kiss my blond pussy?,* Faviola lapping it all up while simultaneously lapping *her,* from the sound of it. They imagined her as some kind of tall glacial beauty with blue eyes and long blond hair she tied around his cock, a fuckin nymphomaniac with great tits and legs, who Faviola worshipped like a naked blond goddess in a jungle movie, the dumb fuckin wop.

". . . told me it was stolen," she was saying.

They had just put on the earphones and turned on the machine for one of their periodic spot checks. If they heard anything related to a crime, they would continue listening and recording. If Blondie here started discussing the merits of sucking a big cock as opposed to a teeny-weeny little one, they would reluctantly turn off the machine, write down the

on and *off* times on the line sheet, and then wait another
minute or so before doing another spot check. Watching the
clock was painstaking and boring. So was listening—most
of the time.

"The ring," she said. "He told me it was stolen."

"Leave it on," Regan said. "She's talking about stolen
goods."

"He said it was stolen from the Boston Museum of Fine
Arts," she said.

"That's impossible," Faviola said. "I bought it
from . . ."

"That's what he told me. He has a list."

"Did he show you this list?"

"No, but . . ."

"Then how do you know . . . Look, it's impossible,
really. I bought it from a jeweler I've done business with for
years."

"Maybe you ought to take it back to him."

"Oh, you can bet on that," he said.

"I'll bet on that, too," Regan said.

"I also found out how much it cost, Andrew. I couldn't
possibly . . ."

"He shouldn't have told you how . . ."

". . . keep it, now that I know . . ."

". . . much it cost. The ring was a *gift*. Why'd you go
to him in the first place?"

"To find out where it had come from in Rome. You
told me it was Roman . . ."

"Yeah, that's what I understood."

"So I wanted to know where. The Roman Empire was
huge . . ."

"Yeah."

"It's Greek, as it turns out, the ring. The point is, I had
no idea it was so expensive, Andrew. Five thousand *dollars*?
Really, Andrew."

"Five . . ."

"I could *never* explain something that cost so much. Please return it, Andrew. Get your money back. Tell whoever you bought it from . . ."

"Well, sure, if the ring was stolen . . ."

"Yeah, yeah, tell us about the ring," Regan prompted.

"Where'd you buy it, anyway?"

"Good," Regan said.

"Guy on . . . uh . . . Forty-seventh Street."

"You should take it right back to him."

"I will. Trade it for something else. I *want* you to have a ring from me. To wear when you're here. So I'll know you're mine."

"You know I'm yours, anyway. When I'm here. I shouldn't have taken the ring home with me, that was too dangerous. But I wanted to keep looking at it. Because it was from you, and because seeing it on my hand, putting it on my finger whenever no one else was there, it reminded me of you. It's so beautiful, Andrew, it was so thoughtful of you to . . ."

"I'll get another one for you."

"That can't be traced this time," Regan said.

"But only to wear here," the woman said. "And nothing that expensive, please. I don't want you to spend that kind of . . ."

"I'll buy you some earrings, too. To wear when you're here."

"And some nipple clamps," Regan said.

Lowndes laughed. Regan laughed with him. They almost missed what she said next.

". . . there in Florida?"

"Shhhh," Regan warned.

"I had some business down there," Faviola said.

"So you told me. But how'd it go?"

"Fine."

"How was the weather?"

"Only so-so."

"I wish I could've been there with you."

"I didn't have much time for anything but meetings," he said. "Anyway, my uncle was with me."

"Rudy Faviola," Lowndes whispered.

Regan wondered why the jackass was whispering.

"Is he with the company, too?" she asked. "Your uncle?"

"Oh, *boy* is he," Regan said.

"Yes, he is," Faviola said.

"I thought . . . well, from what I understood, this wasn't a family business."

"It isn't."

"Like fun, it isn't," Regan said.

"You said the men who'd started it were semiretired . . ."

"That's right."

". . . and that you ran things for them."

"Well, I have *help,* you know. I mean, this isn't a one-man operation."

"I didn't think it was. The conference room down-stairs . . ."

"Uh-huh, for board meetings."

"The company car . . ."

"Uh-huh."

"Billy's a wonderful driver, by the way."

"Yeah, he's a good man."

"Are you planning to invest in Sarasota?"

"No, no. Well . . . uh . . . you remember my telling you we look for companies we can bring along till they become moneymakers?"

"Yes?"

"Well, this meeting was with a South American exporter who's interested in doing business with a Chinese firm. We're arranging a merger."

"Chin*ese*?"

"Yeah. We're bringing them together so there can be an exchange of products."

"What sort of products?"

"Rice and coffee."

"Ask a stupid question," she said.

"Rice and coffee, my ass," Regan said.

"How does *your* company fit in?"

"Well, I told you. We arranged the merger . . ."

"So?"

"So there's a fee for that. Naturally. Nobody does things for free, you know."

"A flat fee?"

"Sometimes. It depends on the deal. Our fee on this one is a share of the profits."

"You get a share of the profits just for bringing these two companies together?"

"In a manner of speaking, yes. The principals, yes."

"But a share of the *profits*?"

"It's not as easy as it sounds."

"How big a share?"

Faviola laughed.

"A pretty big share," he said.

"*How* big?"

He laughed again.

"Come on, tell me. How much?"

"How much what? How much do I love you?"

"That, too. But how much are you getting for a day's work . . ."

"I love you more than . . ."

". . . in Sara—"

". . . life itself."

There was a long silence.

At last, she said, "You don't."

"I do," he said.

Another silence.

Then, from the woman, "Mmmmm, yes. God, *yes*."

"Shit," Regan said.

Andrew Faviola was telling Sal the Barber that he wanted to know where that fucking ring had come from. Regan and Lowndes were listening. Faviola had moved fast; this was Friday, only two days after they'd first heard about the ring being a stolen one.

"You give nice presents, Sal," he was saying. "Next time tell me something's hot, and I won't . . ."

"Hey, Andrew, gimme a break, willya?" Sal said. "I didn't *know* the fuckin thing was hot."

"Hot? The fuckin Boston *Museum!*"

"The ring came my way, how was I supposed to know somebody lifted it in a fuckin museum?"

"How'd it come your way, Sal?"

"How do things come a person's way? I'll tell you the truth, I thought I was doin you a favor, Andrew, givin you a beautiful ring like this one. You got to admit it's a unusual ring, Andrew, ain't it? I never *seen* a ring all black like this one, did you?"

"Where'd you get it, Sal?"

"There's this shitty little crackhead named Richie Palermo used to do collections for me, this was maybe two, three years ago, before he got so hooked he don't know his own fuckin name. I wouldn't trust him to walk me across the street no more, but he gave me a fuckin sob story, so I lent him a grand, this was last month sometime. So naturally, the little fuck misses two payments, and when I find him he offers me the ring and a nine, I don't know where he got them. I tell him don't bother me with your fuckin problems, I'm not a fuckin fence. The nine . . ."

"Then you *knew* this was stolen goods, right?"

"No, no, did I say that? I was bargaining with him. Like makin him *think* I thought the shit was stolen. The nine was a good piece, but the ring looked rusty or something, you know what I mean, all black like that? What he owes me is still the grand, plus two weeks' interest at fifty bucks a week compounded. In short, he owes me eleven hundred and two dollars and fifty fuckin cents, the shitheel, for which he's offering me the ring and the Uzi in settlement of the whole thing. I tell him shove the ring up his ass, I'll take the nine for the two weeks' vig and he still owes me the grand. The ring looks like it came out of a Cracker Jack box, am I right? He tells me the ring is valuable, it's some kind of fuckin Roman antique, second century, third century, just like I told you when I gave it to you. He said you could tell it was Roman because of the satyr and the bird on it, what the fuck do I know?"

"It's Greek."

"Greek, okay, whatever. I tell him okay, I'll take the ring for the *next* week's vig, but he still owes me the grand. Which is where we left it. In other words, I got the gun for a hundred and change, and the ring for fifty. But it's a beautiful ring, Andrew, you got to admit that, once you get past it lookin rusty."

"In other words, you gave me a ring this fuckin Richie Palermo crackhead *stole* someplace . . ."

"Andrew, I didn't know it was stolen, I swear on my mother's eyes!"

". . . which my friend takes into a jewelry store to see which part of the Roman Empire it came from . . ."

"He said it was Roman, yeah."

". . . and it gets back to me that it's a *Greek* ring stolen from the Boston *Museum*. This *Jew* who owns the shop tells her it's a *stolen* ring, Sal. Which if the man wanted to cause *trouble,* he could've informed the *police,* Sal. The fuckin ring is on a *list,* Sal, capeesh? You almost brought the fuckin *cops* to my door with your fuckin rusty stolen *ring!*"

"I didn't know it was stolen."

"Did you ask him?"

"No, I didn't."

"Where did you think a crackhead got a Greek ring from the second fuckin century B.C. . . ."

"He said it was Roman."

". . . if he didn't *steal* the fuckin thing? Tell me that, Sal."

"I don't know where he got it. I didn't ask him where he got it. I didn't ask him where he got the gun, either."

"Where's the gun now?"

"Gone with the wind."

"Are they gonna trace *that* back, too?"

"Nobody's tracin nothin back, Andrew."

"How do you know that gun wasn't used in a fuckin murder someplace?"

"The gun is in some fuckin African country by now, don't worry about the gun."

"All I have to worry about is the ring, right?"

"You don't have to worry about the ring, either. There's no trouble here, Andrew, believe me. The gun's gone, and I'll take the ring off your hands. There's nothin to worry about, okay?"

"Just don't ever bring me anything else you know is *hot!*"

"I didn't know it was hot. But I'm sorry."

"You want to have stolen goods traced to you, fine. Just don't get me involved in it."

"I'm sorry, Andrew, I didn't know it was stolen."

"Here, take your fuckin ring back."

"Yeah, thanks. I'm sorry about this, I really am."

"You owe me five grand."

"What?"

"Five grand, Sal. For the ring."

"What do you mean?"

"That's what the ring's worth, five thousand bucks. That's what the Jew appraised it for, and that's what I want for it. For all the trouble you caused me."

"Hey, come on, Andrew, give me a . . ."

"Five grand, Sal. By tomorrow morning."

"Jeez, Andrew . . ."

"So I can buy a ring doesn't have a pedigree."

"I really didn't know the fuckin thing was . . ."

"Goodbye, Sal."

"Jesus."

The snow started on Saturday morning and did not end until Sunday sometime. Everyone was calling it "the storm of the century," though she seemed to recall heavier snowfalls when she was a child. She and Michael took Mollie to the park, and they sledded all afternoon and then had dinner at Fazio's on Seventy-eighth, one of the few places open for business that weekend. The streets, the sidewalks, the entire city looked clean and white. Tomorrow the snow would turn gray, she knew, and in the days after that a sooty black. But for now, the city was a wonderland, and she wished she could be sharing it with Andrew. She felt certain tomorrow would be declared a snow day. Could she possibly get away to meet him? Would Michael's office be open, or would *he* be home, too? When would the streets be cleared of snow? When would traffic start moving again? Would Andrew be able to send the car for her on Wednesday? If not, would the subways be running? She could not bear the thought of a blizzard preventing her from seeing him as usual this week.

When the phone rang on the Monday night following the weekend storm, Andrew knew at once that something was wrong. Oddly, the first thing he thought was *She told her husband.*

"Hello?" he said.

The digital clock on the nightstand beside the bed read 11:50 P.M. He was more than ever convinced that Sarah had broken under fire.

"Andrew?"

He recognized the voice at once. His cousin Ida. Uncle Rudy's daughter. Oh, Jesus, he thought.

"What is it?" he said.

"Honey," she said, "my father is dead."

"Oh, Jesus," he said out loud. "What do you mean? I thought . . ."

"Not from the cancer, Andrew. He died of a heart attack."

"Where are you?"

"At the hospital. The emergency room doctor told me two minutes ago. You're the first person I called," she said, and suddenly she was crying.

"Ida?" he said.

Sobbing uncontrollably now.

"Sweetie?" he said.

"Yes, Andrew. Yes."

Still sobbing. Her voice overwhelmed by tears.

"Where's Bobby?"

"Here with me."

"Put him on."

"Are you coming here, Andrew?"

"Yes. Put Bobby on."

Bobby Triani came on a moment later.

"Yeah," he said.

"What happened?"

"He went to bed right after supper, woke up around nine-thirty with first a pain in his arm and his shoulder, and then chest pains, and like he's burping, you know? Something's repeating on him. He called Ida, told her what was happening, but he figured it was something he ate. A little *acida*, you know? Anyway, Ida got worried, you know how she's been about him ever since her mother died. She tells me get dressed, we're going over his house. This is now around a quarter to ten. We went there, the pains are really serious now, he tells us it's like an elephant is standing on his chest. So I called the ambulance, and they took him straight to the emergency room. They were working on him for almost an hour, Andrew, but they couldn't do nothin, this stuff they gave him couldn't dissolve the clot, the strepto whatever they call it."

"How's Ida taking this?"

"Hard."

"Tell her I'll be right there."

"I will, Andrew."

"Tell me what hospital you're at."

He debated calling Billy at home, figured by the time he got to Great Neck with the Lincoln, he could already be on his way in the Acura. He was out of the house in ten minutes flat.

The Cross Island was empty at this hour of the night.

Snow was banked high on either side of the narrow cleared lanes. His headlights threw long bright tunnels into the darkness.

In many respects, he'd always been closer to Ida than he had to his own sisters. Angela was four when he was born, and Carol was two. A sort of twinship existed between them before he arrived on the scene, and although they lavished hugs and kisses and cuddly language on their cute little baby brother, he found it difficult to break into their cozy little gang when he was older and seeking true companionship.

Ida, on the other hand, was born two months after he was, and she was the one who became his constant playmate and confidante. Uncle Rudy and Aunt Concetta lived close by, and the two brothers and their families were constantly in each other's houses. On Sundays, too, the *entire* family gathered in the big old house on Long Island's North Shore, where Grandma and Grandpa had moved when they closed the bakery in Coney Island. Andrew's sisters secretly signed with their hands in the deaf language they'd learned from the encyclopedia, but Andrew didn't care because he had Ida.

Dark-haired, dark-eyed Ida, who resembled her father

more than she did her mother, with the same nose Andrew later saw on paintings made during the Italian Renaissance. Andrew was still a blond little boy at the time—his hair didn't begin turning first muddy and then chestnut brown till he was twelve or thirteen—but Uncle Rudy used to call them "Ike and Mike," and then invariably would add, "They look alike," though they didn't resemble each other at all. He was referring to their closeness, Andrew later realized.

He'd lost touch with Ida over the years.

As he sped through the night to where she now waited for him at the hospital, he remembered the time she broke his head with a pocketbook when they were both six and he'd been teasing her about something. Wham, she'd swung her little red leather bag at him, and the clasp hit him on the back of the head and drew blood.

She'd cried harder than he had.

Ike and Mike.

She used to tell him his ears were too big.

He used to tell her she had a big nose.

Eek, what a beak! Is that a nose or a hose?

She called him Mickey Mouse.

He called her Pinocchio.

He'd loved her to death.

He burst into sudden tears, and did not know for a moment whether he was crying for his dear Uncle Rudy or for all the dear dead Sundays he'd spent running around Grandma's house with his cousin Ida.

The front page of Tuesday morning's *Daily News* blurted out the story in a single hurried breath:

BOSS
HOOD
DROPS
DEAD

The *Post,* riven by internal problems, carried a headline that was equally blunt:

GODFATHER
DEAD

Sarah saw the headlines when she picked up the *Times* at the newsstand on the Seventy-seventh Street subway platform. On the ride downtown, she merely glanced at the Metro Section story about the death of some big-shot gangster who'd survived countless shootings only to die, ironically, of a heart attack. Which served him right, she thought, and turned the page.

When she got off the station at Sixtieth Street, she walked to the phone booth on the corner of Lex and dialed Andrew's number. Standing on a mound of snow as she leaned into the receiver, she heard his familiar voice telling her the office would be closed on Tuesday and Wednesday. She waited for the tone, said, "Hi, it's me. I hope nothing's wrong." Then she fished more change from her purse and dialed the number in Great Neck. There was no answer at all there.

The weekend's heavy snowfall was beginning to melt. The sun was shining brightly. Tomorrow was St. Patrick's Day, and spring would be here on Saturday. But she could only think she would not see Andrew this week.

Barney Levin called them at home that Wednesday evening, while she was making dinner.

"Happy St. Patrick's Day," he said. "Did you go march?"

"No," she said. "Did you?"

"I always march," he said. "With the gays," he added. "Have you got a minute?"

"If you want Michael, he isn't home yet."

"No, this is a question for you," he said. "I've got a couple of checks here written to a woman named Maria

Sanchez. Both of them for a hundred bucks even, one dated . . ."

"Yes, she's a cleaning woman. Comes in twice a week. I pay her fifty for the day."

"This something new, Sarah?"

"She started a few weeks ago. Why?"

"Did you withhold anything from those checks?"

"No. Was I supposed to?"

"Is she an illegal alien?"

"I have no idea."

"Then don't ask her. Pay her in cash from now on, and forget we ever had this conversation."

"Wouldn't that be breaking the law?" Sarah asked.

"Wouldn't *what* be breaking the law?"

"Come on, Barney. Michael's a DA. I can't do anything *criminal*."

"Then start deducting federal, state, and city withholding taxes, *plus* FICA. And make sure she's covered for workmen's comp, New York State unemployment insurance, and disability insurance, too. Either that, or fire her. Those are your choices."

"Thanks. I'm so happy you called."

"Who asked you to marry a DA?"

"Listen, Barney, while I have you . . ."

"Yeah?"

"What do you know about a company named Carter-Goldsmith Investments?"

"*What* company?"

"Carter-Goldsmith Investments."

"Are they on the Big Board?"

"I have no idea."

"What do you want to know about them?"

"Just how they're rated, what they do, who the principals are, that sort of thing."

"Thinking of investing with them?"

"Maybe."

"Let me ask around."

"Thanks. I'll call you from school tomorrow."

"Gee, can't you give me till midnight *tonight*?" Barney asked.

"Friday, then," she said. "Good night, Barney.

"Good night, Sarah. Say hello to Michael."

"I will."

Smiling, she put the phone back on the cradle.

While waiting for Andrew's return from *wherever* he was, she'd decided to write a little poem for him. She had already looked up "Andrew" in the name book she'd bought before Mollie was born, and had discovered the name was from the Greek and that it meant "manly, valiant, and coura- geous"—no surprise at all. The nicknames for Andrew were Andy, Tandy, Dandy, and Drew, which sounded like a vaudeville team, but which had given her a lot to work with.

The name Farrell was from the Celtic, and it meant "the valorous one"—how did these people *know* he'd once jumped into the sea to save her daughter? On the other hand, Farrell was a variant form of "Farrar," going all the way back to the Latin *ferrains,* which meant "a worker with iron," or, more simply, "a blacksmith."

She had already written the first stanza of her opus; now she wanted to do a second stanza that referred to his professional life. All by way of surprising him when he re- turned, whenever that might be.

As she checked the thermometer on the roast in the oven, she went over the first stanza again in her head:

> *Andy, and Dandy, and Tandy and Drew.*
> *Which is my love, and is my love true?*
> *Farrell the Valiant or Farrar the Iron,*
> *Which is my hero, and which one is mine?*
>
> *What to invest in this best of all men . . .*

. . . which was where she needed something about Carter-Goldsmith. She made a mental note to call Barney from the teachers' lunchroom on Friday, and wondered for perhaps the fiftieth time today when Andrew would be back.

On Thursday morning, the *Post* and the *News* both carried stories of the big gangland funeral, complete with photos of obvious hoodlums carrying the coffin of their fallen leader. There were more flowers in view than at the Brooklyn Botanical Gardens. What was *not* in view was the face of the third pallbearer on the right, blocked from sight by the ornate black coffin itself.

The *Times* covered the funeral in its Metro Section, giving it no photographs, and very little space. Mollie scanned the story as she rode the bus uptown to a Hundred and Tenth Street, where she would transfer to the crosstown bus that would take her to Hanover. Apparently, there was speculation and concern about who would take control of what was *now* called the Faviola family, but which had once been known as the Tortocello family. The *former* boss of the Faviola family, a man named Anthony Faviola, was now in jail and the most *recent* boss, his brother, Rudy, had died of a heart attack this past Monday night. So who was to succeed to the throne?

Ahhh, such an earth-shattering question, Mollie thought.

The article went on to say that law enforcement sources now believed that someone named Andrew Faviola, the nephew of the recently deceased dead gangster, would likely be heading for the maximum security prison in Leavenworth, Kansas, to consult with his incarcerated father, the aforementioned Anthony Faviola, about succession in the Faviola family, which name tickled Mollie because it reminded her of the Farkel family on the Nick at Nite *Laugh-In* reruns.

On the facing page there was a story about a big drug bust in the Washington Heights section of Manhattan. Undercover detectives from the Thirty-fourth Precinct had raided a supposed body repair shop where they'd recovered five hundred kilos of cocaine—according to the *Times,* this translated as eleven hundred pounds—and two and a half million dollars in cash. On the bottom of that same page, the *Times* ran a small item they obviously felt was related by subject matter if nothing else. A twenty-four-year-old man named Richard Palermo, described as a small-time drug runner, had been found dead in a basement room on Eighth Avenue. The two bullets in the back of his head led the police to believe this was a gangland slaying, more than likely drug-re—

The bus was pulling into the curb at her stop. Mollie grabbed for her bookbag and rushed to the exit door.

Standing in the bitter cold at the phone on the southeast corner of Sixtieth and Park, Sarah first dialed Andrew's Great Neck number, got no answer there, hung up, managed to retrieve her only quarter even though someone had fiddled with the return chute, and immediately tried the Mott Street office. She got his voice on the machine again.

"The office will be closed on Tuesday and Wednesday . . ."

But this was *Thursday* already.

"Please leave a message at the beep and I'll get back to you as soon as I can. Thank you."

But *when?* she wondered.

The beep sounded.

She said, "Hi, it's me. Where *are* you?"

Then she put the phone back on the hook and ran across Park and past Christ Church toward the school.

He had flown out on Wednesday night, after all of Uncle Rudy's friends, relatives, and associates had come by Ida's house to pay their respects following the funeral. Now, at ten o'clock on Thursday morning, he sat opposite his father in the visitors' room at Leavenworth. A thick glass panel was between them, a two-way microphone-speaker set into it.

"Everybody was there to pay their respects," Andrew said. "People from all over, Pop. Families from Chicago, Miami, St. Louis, in spite of the storm, they got there. Some of them I didn't even know."

His father nodded.

Andrew could sense the fury seething in him. Their attorney, Abraham Meyerson, had petitioned the warden to grant an overnight leave for Anthony Faviola to attend his only brother's funeral, but the request had been denied. The indignity of being kept here in a prison deliberately far from his friends, relatives, and business associates was now compounded by the fucking warden's refusal. Andrew's father sat on his side of the glass partition, his hands clenched on the countertop, his mouth set, his dark eyes glowering. He had lost weight in prison, and his complexion was pale, and his sideburns were turning gray. All at once, Andrew felt the same sense of sadness he'd felt when driving to the hospital on the night of his uncle's death.

"There were flowers, Pop, you'd've thought it was summertime, we had three cars of flowers following the hearse."

"Did anybody from the Colotti family show up?"

"Oh, yeah, they *all* came, sure, Pop. There was a tremendous snowstorm, you know, but it didn't stop anybody, they all came anyway. Jimmy Angelli, Mike Mangioni . . ."

"Mike the Jaw, huh?" his father said, and smiled. "I'm surprised. It was my brother *gave* him that jaw. This was when we were still kids. He was some fighter, my brother."

Andrew began reeling off the names of everyone he could recall who'd been at the church services or the funeral or at Ida's house later, but his father was staring into the distance beyond his shoulder now, his eyes appearing somewhat out of focus, remembering the brother they had buried only yesterday.

"The priest gave a nice elegy," Andrew said. "Father Nigro, do you know him?"

"Do I *know* him? He *baptized* you."

"This wasn't the boilerplate elegy they give when they don't know the dead person from a hole in the wall. Father Nigro *knew* Uncle Rudy, and he talked about him as a personal friend. It was very moving, Pop."

"I'm glad," his father said, and nodded.

There was a long silence.

Then he said, "They should've let me come."

"They should've, Pop."

"*Sfasciume,*" he said bitterly.

"Anyway," Andrew said, "I brought you some newspapers to look at. This is the *News,*" he said, and held the tabloid up to the glass to show his father the front page. "And this is the *Post,* it's a miracle they're still publishing with all the trouble they're having. Uncle Rudy got the front page there, too, and also a feature story inside. The *Times* had an obit and a story in the Metro Section. I'm leaving all these for you, they told me they'd send them to your cell. There'll probably be stories on the funeral, too. I'll send them to you when I get back. I asked Billy to hold them for me."

"Thanks," his father said.

"Who'd've thought a heart attack?" Andrew said. "The doctors were giving him six months, a year."

"Yeah."

"It's, you know, one of those things you can't figure."

"No, you can't figure something like that."

The two men fell silent again.

"How's everything else going?" his father said at last.

"Fine, Pop."

"The thing I was working on before I . . ."

He stopped talking, his anger virtually choking him. He was thinking again of the unfairness that had caused his present intolerable situation. He took in a deep breath, let it out, closed his eyes for a moment, opened them, and in a soft, controlled voice said, "Before they sent me here. My project. How's it coming along?"

"It's a done deal, Pop."

"Good."

There was satisfaction in his voice. Something he had conceived, something he had initiated, had come to fruition under his son's guidance. He nodded contentedly, and a tiny pleased smile touched his lips. Andrew figured this might be a good time to bring up the little matter of succession. Or was it too soon? Uncle Rudy just dead, just buried?

"Pop, I know this is a bad time, but . . ."

"I know what you're going to ask."

"What am I going to ask, Pop?"

"You're going to ask *who*."

"Yes."

"By rights, it should go to Petey Bardo."

"I know."

"Those brown suits," his father said, and shook his head and began chuckling. Andrew smiled. And waited.

"But Bobby has bigger balls," his father said.

"I know."

"So keep Petey where he is, and give Bobby the spot. Petey has a problem, tell him to talk to me about it."

"Okay, Pop."

"Don't you agree?"

"I do."

"Good," his father said, and fell silent again. After a while, he said, "I miss you, Lino."

"I miss you, too."

"Tell your mother I love her."

"I'll tell her."

"When you gonna find a nice girl, get married?"

"I don't know, Pop."

"Give me some grandchildren?"

"You've got grandchildren already, Pop."

"Not yours. Not my *son's* kids."

"Well, someday."

"You seeing somebody?"

"Few girls."

"Who?"

"Few girls, you don't know them, Pop."

"Anybody serious?"

"No," Andrew said. "Nobody serious."

The assigned coordinator of the detective team on the Faviola wiretap had duplicated Wednesday's audiotapes, line sheets, and pen register tapes, and had them delivered to Michael's office by eleven o'clock that Thursday morning. At four that afternoon, Michael called Georgie Giardino in his office down the hall and asked him to come by. Over coffee in cardboard containers, the two men tried once again to find a pattern to the calls coming in and going out of Faviola's office-apartment complex.

It had not surprised Michael that most of the calls Faviola made on Tuesday, the morning after his uncle died, were to known gangsters, informing them of the untimely demise and making certain they knew where the body could be viewed and where flowers should be sent. Georgie told Michael that at an Italian wake, it was usual for friends and relatives to drop little envelopes containing money into a box with a slot on its top, this presumably to defray the cost of funeral expenses. He did not think a multimillion-dollar enterprise like the Faviola family would either seek or accept such contributions, but who the hell knew?

"These guys are the cheapest bastards in the world," Georgie said. "Freddie Coulter told me the lock on that door leading upstairs from the tailor shop is the crummiest piece of shit he ever saw. What these guys do, they need a lock, they need an alarm, they remember that Joey Gabagootz's son went to a vocational high school and learned to be a mechanic or an electrician, so they'll call Joey and he'll send his kid over to rig an alarm or install a lock and they'll hand him twenty bucks, and tell him thanks, kid. What Freddie likes to do, whenever he finds one of these cheap alarms, he deliberately sets it off every time he leaves the premises. He goes in four, five times to do whatever he has to do, he sets it off as he's leaving each and every time. The target thinks Hey, what kind of job did Joey Gabagootz's son do here, the alarm's broken already? So he says the hell with it, and he doesn't turn it on anymore."

"Freddie does the same thing with a Medeco lock," Michael said.

"What do you mean? How can he set off a Medeco?"

"No, no, he gums it up. No one on earth can pick a Medeco and anyone who tells you he can is lying. When Freddie finds one, he squirts Krazy Glue in it."

"Oh, Jesus," Georgie said, and burst out laughing.

"The wiseguy sticks his key in, the lock won't work, he thinks it's because some *other* wiseguy's son installed it for ten bucks. So he figures the hell with it, it's broken, and he uses the other locks on the door instead."

"I love the way Freddie jerks these cheap bastards around," Georgie said, still laughing. "I'll bet they *did* expect those little cash envelopes in the box. And I'll bet Rudy's daughter didn't refuse them, either."

The original pen register tapes were about the same width as an adding machine tape, the printing on them a sort of violet blue. The Xerox copies were in black and white. The format was slightly different for a number dialed *out* of the apartment than it was for a caller dialing in. On any *outgoing* call, the tape showed the number of the phone being dialed, and then the time the call began, and the time the call ended, and the duration of the call. On an *incoming* call, the tape did not record the phone number of the caller, but in addition to the other information, it listed the number of rings before the target phone was picked up. On any wiretap surveillance, the detectives sitting the wire transferred the pen register information to their line sheets, and the phone company later supplied names and addresses for any outgoing-call numbers appearing on the tape. Most of the numbers Faviola called were familiar to Michael and Georgie by now, but they spot-checked the line sheets, anyway, to make sure they agreed with the pen register tapes and then, together, they listened to the audiotapes.

None of the wiseguys had called on Tuesday, the first day of the wake. Too busy kneeling before Rudy's coffin, Michael guessed. There was a call that day from a man named William Isetti, who said he was calling from St. Thomas. Whoever he was, he left a number with an 809 area code and asked that he be called back. He made no mention of Rudy Faviola's death.

Only one of Andy Boy's lady friends seemed to know.

The pen register and line sheet showed a call from a woman who identified herself as "Angela in Great Neck" at four o'clock on Tuesday afternoon, long after Faviola had left his office and turned on his machine. The audiotapes had her leaving a message saying she'd just heard about his uncle and wanted to tell him how sorry she was.

"The local talent," Georgie said.

"Mmm," Michael said.

There were several other calls from Faviola's parade of bimbos that Tuesday afternoon, all of them from familiar voices, all of them calling just to say hello and to wonder when they could get together again.

On Wednesday, "Hi, It's Me" called *four* times, never once leaving a return number. Her voice sounded breathy on the tapes. The last time, she sounded virtually frantic. That same day, Oona Halligan called three times from her new job in the Time-Life Building on Sixth Avenue, leaving a number and asking him to call when he got back to the office. Same message each time. "It's Oona, call me when you're back in the office." Oona sounded younger than "Hi, It's

Me." *Her* voice was somewhat breathy, too. Maybe women automatically affected the same sexy voice when they were on the phone with Andy Boy.

"Or maybe they're sisters," Georgie said.

"Be funny if he was banging sisters and neither of them knew about it," Michael said.

"Brooklyn girl," Georgie said. "Oona."

"I wonder where the other one lives," Michael said.

"Mystery woman."

"Calls from phone booths on the street."

"Never leaves a return number."

"Never."

"Got to be married."

"Maybe."

"Maybe to one of the *paisans*," Georgie said. "What was the name of that broad they all wanted to bang? On the trial tapes?"

"Teresa Danielli."

"Terry, yeah. Maybe it's her."

"Maybe."

"Who do you suppose Isetti is?"

"No idea."

"The Virgin Islands."

"Mmm."

"What's down there?"

"I don't know."

"Who do you think'll fill Rudy's spot?"

"Triani."

"You think so?"

"I feel positive."

"Bardo's in line."

"I still think it'll go to Triani. My guess is there'll be another meeting in Faviola's conference room sometime next week."

"Not Wednesday, though," Georgie said. "That's the *blonde's* day."

"Not Wednesday, no. But when*ever,* we'd better be listening hard."

"You think these line sheets are straight?" Georgie asked suddenly.

Michael was silent for a moment.

"No," he said at last.

"Me, neither," Georgie said. "I think Regan and Lowndes are listening longer than they need to."

"I think all *three* shifts are listening."

"Mike, that can . . ."

"I know. Time for another little talk. I'll tell you, Georgie, this better be strictly ABC, or they're off the case."

"Don't do it before the meeting, though. We can't afford a new team if anything big's going down."

"Not before the meeting," Michael said, and looked at his watch, and immediately picked up the receiver and dialed his home number. The phone rang once, twice . . .

"Hello?"

"Sarah, it's me. I know we're meeting the Learys for dinner, but is it up there or down here?"

"It's at Rinaldi's."

"Okay, I'll come home, then."

"It's for seven o'clock, Michael."

"Then I'd better get out of here."

"Don't be late, honey, you know them."

"I'll be home by six."

"No later. Please."

"I promise," he said.

Sarah put the receiver back on the cradle and wondered if she should try reaching Andrew again. Mollie was down the hall, watching something very noisy on television. If she used the phone in the bedroom, she felt certain she would not be overheard.

She considered it for another moment and then decided against it.

★ ★ ★

Richard Leary was an attorney who wrote amusing little
articles about lawyers and the law for any magazine that
would publish them. Michael suspected he had a closet desire
to be another Turow or Grisham. Richard told them now
that he was working on a piece about criminal conversation.

"What's that?" Sarah asked. "Talk among crooks?"

"Nope, it's a tort," Richard said.

"What's a tort?" his wife asked. "Some kind of Danish
pastry?"

Rosie knew damn well what a tort was; she'd been married to a lawyer for twenty years.

"A tort is, quote, any wrongful act, damage, or injury
done willfully, negligently, or in circumstances involving
strict liability, for which a civil suit can be brought, un-
quote."

"Except breach of promise," Michael said.

"As in a contract," Richard said, and nodded.

"I hate lawyer talk," Rosie said.

"Be that as it may," Richard said, "criminal conversation
is defined as defilement of the marriage bed . . ."

"Please," Rosie said, "not while I'm eating."

". . . *or* sexual intercourse," Richard went on, un-
daunted, "*or* a breaking down of the covenant of fidelity."

"He means fucking with a stranger," Rosie said, and
then immediately covered her mouth in feigned shock.

"I mean *adultery,*" Richard said, "considered in its aspect
of a civil injury to the husband, entitling him to damages."

"How about the *wife*?" Rosie said. "If the *husband's* playing around?"

"The tort applied only to debauching or seducing a
wife."

"So what else is new?" Rosie said, and shrugged.

"That's exactly the point of my article," Richard said.
"I think the issue still has relevance to the women's movement, even though the tort was abolished in 1935."

"You mean until then . . . ?"

"Until then, a husband could bring action against a man for criminal conversation, yes. For committing adultery with a man's wife."

"Funny name for fucking around," Rosie said. "Criminal conversation."

Sarah thought it was an entirely appropriate name.

Looking down at her plate, hearing Richard go on about the popularity of such suits in seventeenth-century England, where the tort was familiarly called "crim con," and where damages of from £10,000 to £20,000 were not uncommon, staring at the food on her plate, not daring to look up at Michael across the table, she thought Yes, criminal conversation is what I share in that bedroom with Andrew. We're a pair of thieves plundering a marriage, and the damage is far more severe than any court in the world can ever remedy.

"But *criminal* conversation?" Rosie asked, and turned to Sarah for support.

Yes, Sarah thought, *criminal* conversation.

Aloud she said, "It *does* sound odd."

The meeting took place on Tuesday morning, the twenty-third of March. Monitoring it with Lowndes in the room on Grand Street, Regan was still pissed off because Michael Welles had seen fit to read the minimization lecture to the entire surveillance team yet another time—with what you might call a veiled warning tacked onto the end of it.

"I know you all understand the importance of this case," he'd said, "and I think you understand, too, how serious a breach it would be if any one of us provoked suppression of the material we've been gathering so painstakingly. So I'd like to tell you one more time: when in doubt, shut down."

He'd also told them to pay strict attention during the days and weeks to come because the death of Rudy Faviola was sure to cause ripples. So here they were, three days after the beginning of spring, sitting in the middle of all those

ripples, listening to the broken noses discussing who was
going to take over The Accountant's position in the organization.

The mucky-mucks began arriving at two that afternoon.

Benny Vaccaro no longer pressed clothes in the back
of his father's shop. From conversations between him and
Andrew Faviola, earlier overheard and recorded, they knew
that he was now working on a pier on the West Side, probably off-loading false-bottom crates containing all sorts of
controlled substances. Or so they surmised. In none of the
conversations had anything illegal ever been mentioned.
They had tuned out the moment they'd realized Faviola was
offering the kid a seemingly honest job.

The new presser was someone named Mario.

They hadn't yet got his last name, but they figured he
had to be a cousin or nephew of a mob soldier, or the son of
someone a mob soldier knew, in any event a person who
could be trusted to witness the comings and goings of various
higher-ups without later discussing it with anyone.

"Hello, Mario."

"Hello, Mr. Triani."

Mario sounded younger than Benny. They figured him
to be sixteen or seventeen, a high school dropout working
his way up the echelons of organized crime, starting as a
presser who mistered and sirred all the big shots to death.

"Hello, Mr. Bardo."

"Hello, Mario."

Followed by the familiar voice on the speaker, Faviola
telling each of his *business* associates, the fuckin creeps, to
come on up, and then buzzing them in. By two-thirty, all of
them were assembled. Regan and Lowndes had counted an
even dozen of them, six more than had been present the last
time there'd been a meeting here, when all they had going
for them was the downstairs bug. *This* time if a flea farted
upstairs, they'd be hearing it and recording it.

The first order of business was to tell Faviola how sorry

they were about his uncle and to tell Triani how sorry they were about his father-in-law, who happened to be one and the same dead gangster. Sal the Barber led off with his condolences, and he was followed by Frankie Palumbo and Fat Nickie Nicoletta, who knew Rudy from the old days and who was one of the elderly thugs present who still called Andrew Faviola by his childhood nickname "Lino." On and on the ritual grief went, each and every wop hoodlum paying his respect to that poor, dear, departed fuck, Rudy "The Accountant" Faviola.

"Good riddance to bad rubbish," Regan said.

That out of the way, Faviola told the assembled mobsters that his uncle's death left a gap in the organization which he had discussed with his father when he went out to Leavenworth last week . . .

"So *that's* where he was," Lowndes whispered.

". . . and my father feels the way I do, we both agree on who should take Uncle Rudy's place, may he rest in peace."

"Amen," Regan said.

"Petey, I don't want you to get upset by this," Faviola said. "This has nothing to do with the very real value the family places on you . . ."

"I don't want it, anyway," Bardo said at once.

"It's simply that you're too valuable where you are," Faviola said.

"I told you I don't *want* it, Andrew!"

His voice rapping out angrily. He was no dope, Petey Bardo, and he'd undoubtedly guessed what was coming, and had prepared himself to get through this one with his dignity intact. But venting steam at little Andy Boy was one thing. Getting pissed off by a decision jointly arrived at by the Faviola *padre e figlio* was quite another thing.

"What you want matters to us, of course," Faviola said smoothly. "But what's best for the family matters even more. We need you where you are, Petey. And we need Bobby to

take over Uncle Rudy's responsibilities. That's the way we
think it'll work best."

The room went silent.

The words "underboss" and "consigliere" had never
once been mentioned. This could have been a meeting of the
board of any legitimate family-run business anywhere in the
world. The chairman had just announced a promotion.
Bobby Triani—Rudy Faviola's son-in-law and until this
moment a capo who'd been overseeing the family's stolen-
property operation—had just been promoted to the number-
two spot in the organization, where he would answer only
to Andrew Faviola. But apparently Faviola felt that the ruffled
feathers of Petey Bardo needed further smoothing.

"Petey," he said, "we can't afford to lose you where you
are."

"Look, I told you I . . ."

"Please. Hear me out. Please, Petey. If there are problems inside the family, you're the one who smoothes them.
Somebody wants a territory here, a territory there . . ."

Never once mentioning what *kind* of territory. Always
cognizant of the old Italian expression that said *"I muri hanno
orecchi."* The walls have ears. No suspicion whatever that the
place was bugged six ways from Sunday, but nonetheless no
one was saying anything that could be considered incriminating. Not yet, anyway.

". . . to you to make the case for each of the disputing
parties," Faviola was saying. "I don't know anyone who
can do it better. No one. Whenever a sitdown becomes necessary . . ."

Sitdown was criminal slang, but nothing you could take
to court.

". . . you're the one who tries to make peace between
the skippers . . ."

Another word for *capo*. Skipper. Or captain. So sue him.

". . . you're the one who has the experience, and the
patience, and the diplomacy to work things out to everyone's

satisfaction. There's no one we have who could fill your shoes if we moved you up a notch, Petey. But does this mean Bobby's going to take home a bigger piece of the pie because *technically* he's a step above you? I can promise you it won't, Petey. You have my word in front of every person in this room. I'm going to work out a proper compensation for you. I don't need to go into it now, but you have my promise. And when I say that *technically* Bobby's moving above you, I mean that. This is only *technically*. As far as I'm concerned, especially now with the new business that'll be coming our way . . ."

"What's this, what's this?" Regan said, and leaned closer to the equipment, even though he was wearing earphones.

". . . I'm going to need a three-way sharing of responsibility at the top. Three ways. This is a vast new challenge we're undertaking. My hope is that everything will be fully operational by the summer. To do that, we all have to work together, starting with the top, and continuing on down to the smallest member in the organization. Once we begin distributing the new product here in New York, I'm going to . . ."

"Dope," Lowndes whispered.

Regan nodded.

". . . support and cooperation of everyone here today. This can't work without you. It's too complicated and there are too many risks. But once it's in place, I promise there'll be plenty for all of us. I'm talking billions of dollars. For all of us to share."

"Fuck's he talking about?" Regan said.

"The Chinese have a saying, 'From each according to his ability, to each according to his needs.' We have the ability here right in this room . . ."

"Fuckin shitheads," Regan said.

". . . and we've got a lot of needy people in this room, too."

Laughter.

Lowndes shook his head.

"So what I'd like to do now is pour some wine all around . . . Sal, you want to open some of those bottles? Nickie? Can you lend a hand?"

The two detectives listened while the wine was being opened and poured. They could overhear several conversations at once now, chairs being shoved back, people moving about the room, and then finally the clinking of a utensil against a glass. Faviola began speaking again.

"I want to lift my glass first to my Uncle Rudy, who I loved to death and who I miss with all my heart. His fondest wish was to see this idea of my father's become a reality. He's not here to see it as it begins to take shape, but he was in on the meeting we had in Sarasota, and before he died, he was on the phone day and night with the people in Italy and with the Chinese. So he knows where he is in heaven that it's just a matter of time now, just a matter of getting all the nuts and bolts in place. Uncle Rudy, rest easy, this is about to *happen*, believe me."

"*Salute!*" someone shouted.

"*Salute!*" they all joined in.

"Next, I'd like to congratulate both Bobby *and* Petey, because in my eyes there've been *two* promotions today, and I plan to make that evident to Petey by way of compensation as you all heard me promise. Bobby, Petey, congratulations!"

"Thank you." From Triani, modestly.

"Thank you." From Bardo, skeptically.

It was almost four o'clock.

"There's a lot of work to be done in the weeks and months ahead," Faviola said. "I know I can count on you to get that work done. My father's keeping a close eye on this, this is his baby, he wants it done right. I want it done right, too. Don't let me down. That's it."

Before the men began filing out, they paid their individual respects to Andy Boy again by promising him he could count on them for their support and hard work. Fat Nickie

Nicoletta said, "You need any spic heads busted, Lino, they don't like our move, you let me know."

"I'll keep that in mind," Faviola said.

Sal Bonifacio said, "You hear about Richie Palermo?"

"Richie . . . ?"

"Palermo. This kid used to do some work for me? He was most recently in jewelry? You remember him?"

"Oh. Yeah. Right."

"He got killed in a shooting on Eighth Avenue," Sal said.

Faviola said nothing.

Regan and Lowndes were listening intently.

"A basement on Eighth Avenue," Sal said. "Two shots the back of his head. It was in the paper last week."

"I didn't see it," Faviola said.

"Yeah," Sal said. "A fuckin shame, hah?"

Regan and Lowndes lost the assorted hoods as they went down the stairs to the back room of the tailor shop, and then picked up their voices again once they were in the room saying their farewells to Mario. The new presser showered bouquets of sirs and misters on their royal asses as they filed out onto Broome Street where video cameras manned by two detectives in a second-floor window across the way recorded their separate departures for posterity.

Oona Halligan materialized out of thin air at seven-thirty that night. The two detectives who'd relieved Regan and Lowndes on the wiretap figured she'd been there all afternoon. Otherwise, since the tailor shop closed at five, how the hell had she got in?

Harry Arnucci was forty-eight years old, a bald and burly detective/first who'd worked Narcotics out of Manhattan North before his transfer to the DA's Office Squad. The one thing he knew about hoods was that as smart as they thought they were, they were basically very stupid. He kept sitting the wire waiting for Faviola to say the one dumb thing that would send him away for a hundred years. Sooner or later they all said the one dumb thing. The minute Faviola fucked up, the minute they arrested him and the parade of bums who marched in and out of his office up there over the tailor shop, the sooner Harry would make lieutenant.

His partner's name was Jerry Mandel, and he was shooting for lieutenant, too. He'd joined the police department over the protestations of a great-grandmother who could still remember when Irish cops were breaking Jewish heads on the Lower East Side. It was a fundamental principle of police work in this city that only an Irishman could rise above the rank of captain. Mandel wanted to prove this axiom false by becoming the first Jewish police commissioner in the city of New York. He was now only thirty-three years old, and was already a detective/second grade on the DAOS. Like Harry, he knew how important this case was, and was hoping it would result in an arrest that would almost certainly lead to a promotion.

Both men had felt insulted when Michael Welles gave them his little pitch about minimization this morning. They'd been keeping the line sheets scrupulously, turning off the equipment whenever Faviola was in bed with his Wednesday night bombshell. They knew what was riding on this wiretap, and they didn't need to be told again. They were, in fact, about to turn off the equipment when they heard the Halligan girl's voice out of the blue—where the hell had *she* come from? Must've been here all along, they figured, but then Faviola said, "Let me take your coat," and Oona said, "Thanks," and they realized she'd just come in, but *how*? There was a short silence, and then Oona murmured a long "Mmmmmmmm," which meant they were kissing. "Can I mix you a drink?" Faviola said, which meant they weren't in the bedroom, but were instead in the living room just above the tailor shop. Freddie Coulter had provided a rough diagram of all three floors, to assist them in visualizing movement from room to room. They were thinking now that maybe Faviola had gone down to let her in through the tailor shop, or maybe he'd given her a *key* to the tailor shop. In either event, the team running the video camera across the street would have picked her up coming in, if that's how she'd got in, end of mystery.

Mandel signaled to Arnucci to turn off the equipment. Arnucci nodded, and was reaching for the switch when the girl said, "Why is that door fake?"

"Architect thought it would look better that way," Faviola said.

"Hold it," Mandel said.

Arnucci nodded again.

"Makes it look just like the rest of the wall," Oona said.

"Well, that's the whole idea," Faviola said.

"I mean, no regular doorknob or anything. It looks like a *panel* there, instead of a door. Part of the walnut *paneling*."

"The architect didn't want to break the look of the wall."

"Yeah, but a staircase should lead to a *door,* not a *wall*."

"It *is* a door," Faviola said. "On the other side."

"Well, yes, I can *see* that."

"*With* a regular doorknob," he said.

"Not a knob that *turns,*" she said. "I never heard of a door with a knob you have to *pull* on to open the door."

"That's a touch latch," Faviola said. "From this side, you push on the panel. From the other side, you pull on the knob."

"Also, there's no lock on it," she said.

"There are *two* locks downstairs," he said.

"Even so," she said.

"How's your drink coming along?"

"Fine, thanks."

"Why don't we go upstairs?"

"Finish my drink first."

"Okay," he said, "take your time."

"Fine. Don't rush me."

"Nobody's rushing you," he said.

Edge to his voice. The cops figured she was beginning

to get on his nerves. Toying with her drink, wanting to know why a door was designed to look like part of the wall, when all he wanted to do was take her upstairs and boff her.

"Why didn't you let me know you were going out of town?" she asked.

Which they guessed was the reason for the stall. He hadn't informed her of his comings and goings, so now she . . .

"I didn't know I *had* to," he said.

The edge to his voice was a bit sharper now. They wondered if little Oona here knew this guy was a hoodlum who could order people *killed* if he wanted to. Few weeks ago, he'd complained about some dumb ring, and the crackhead who'd unloaded it on Sal the Barber ended up dead in a basement room. They wondered if she knew who she was playing games with here.

"You keep telling me you love me . . ." she said.

"I *do* love you," he said, which they guessed meant Finish your fuckin drink and let's go upstairs.

". . . but you're out of town for two days and you don't call me, and then you're back and I can't get in touch with you till Sunday."

"That's right," he said. "Do you have some problem with that?"

"Well, no, not what you'd call a problem . . ."

"Then what is it?"

"I just think, if you care for somebody, you're a little more considerate to her. I didn't even know you were *leaving*. You just all at once dis*appear,* and . . ."

"Lovers' quarrel," Mandel said, and reached for the OFF switch.

"Hold it a minute," Arnucci said.

". . . wondering if you got hit by a *car* or something."

"Harry," Mandel warned. "This is . . ."

"Shhh, shhh."

". . . important came up, and I needed advice from one of our officers."

"I'm not saying you shouldn't have *gone* wherever you went . . ."

"I went to Kansas."

"You're kidding me."

"No, I . . ."

"Wher*ever* you went, I'm saying you should have called me to tell me you were going. Or called me when you *got* there. Don't they have phones in Kansas? Where in Kansas *were* you, anyway?"

"That's none of your business," Faviola said.

There was a dead silence.

"Hey, listen," she said, "I don't have to . . ."

"That's right, you don't," he said.

"I mean . . . what do you *mean* it's none of my business? I'm telling you I missed you, I was worried about you, I was hoping you'd call and you tell me it's none of my *business*? What does *that* mean, it's none of my business?"

"It means do you want to leave right now, or do you want to come upstairs with me?"

There was a long silence.

"Well?"

"I thought . . ."

"Never mind what you thought. There's the stairway and there's the door. What do you say?"

There was another silence, lengthier this time.

"It isn't even a *regular* door," she said, and laughed a curious laugh that sounded almost like a sob.

"Make up your mind, Oona."

"I guess I . . . I'd like to go upstairs with you," she said.

Arnucci turned off the equipment and took off his earphones.

"There's another goddamn *entrance*!" he said.

Kirk Irving was telling them about a patient he'd had last week, a kid whose molar was growing out of his cheekbone. His wife, Rebecca, said she thought this was a particularly dis*gusting* subject to be discussing while they were eating. Kirk said he didn't think orthodontics was disgusting, and he reminded Rebecca that it was orthodontics that put the shoes on their daughter's feet.

"*One* of her feet, anyway," Rebecca said.

This by way of reminding him that she herself was a breadwinner, although in a more modest way; Rebecca worked as a publicist for a small publishing house in the Village. Kirk turned to Michael and began explaining the long and painstaking process of gradually moving the molar back down into the gum where it belonged. Seizing the opportunity, Rebecca caught Sarah's attention and began telling her how frustrating it was to have budget limitations that prohibited hi-tech author promotion like satellite tours. Sarah much preferred hearing about the difficulties of touring unknown novelists who wrote everything in first person present, but Kirk's deeper voice kept bullying through, and she found she was hearing more about orthodonture than she ever cared to learn in a lifetime.

When Kirk suddenly shifted the conversation to what *Michael* was working on, she turned to the men at once, hoping to hear something her husband had thus far been reluctant to reveal. But Michael simply shrugged and said, "Oh, the usual, good guys against the bad guys," and changed the subject at once, telling them he was thinking about renting a small villa in France this year for their three-week summer vacation. This was the first Sarah had heard about it. Normally, she would have leaped at the prospect. But now . . .

"Sarah, how *marvelous*!" Rebecca said, and turned to her at once. "Where? And when are you . . . ?"

"Not Provence, I hope," Kirk said, and rolled his eyes. "That guy's made a cottage industry of Provence, whatever his name is. I'll bet it's like Coney Island now."

"I was thinking of the area around St.-Jean-de-Luz,"

Michael said. "We went there on our honeymoon. I thought it might be fun taking Mollie there."

"Dash over the border to Pamplona for the running of the bulls," Kirk said, and held up his hands and shook them as if waving a cape.

"When would this be?" Rebecca asked.

"Well, I don't really *know*," Sarah said. "Actually, I was . . ."

"August sometime, I guess," Michael said. "That's when we usually . . ."

"I was planning . . ." Sarah said, and cut herself off when suddenly everyone seemed to turn to her. "I . . . I thought I might start on my doctorate this summer. This comes as a total . . ."

"Honey," Rebecca said, "*screw* the doctorate. Take France instead."

"It's just I . . ."

"Do you remember *Sunset Boulevard*?" Kirk asked. "The scene where Gloria Swanson takes him to buy a coat?"

"You didn't tell me you were going back to school," Michael said, sounding somewhat puzzled.

"You didn't tell me about *France*, either," Sarah said, and belatedly realized how sharp her voice had sounded.

"Where William Holden is trying to decide whether to take the cashmere or the vicuna?" Kirk said. "And this smarmy salesman with a mustache leans into the shot and says, 'If the *lady's* paying, take the vicuna.' "

"Take France," Rebecca said again, and nodded wisely.

"I suppose I can use the rest," Sarah said, recovering quickly. "France sounds wonderful to me right now."

"Quick study," Rebecca said, and winked at Michael.

"She's been working so hard," Michael said, and took her hand in his. "Leaves the house at seven each morning . . ."

"Well, that's the job," she said.

"But you *do* have summers off," Kirk said.

". . . doesn't get home till six most nights. That's when she . . ."

"With *pay*, no less."

". . . isn't at a teachers' meeting," Michael said.

"Well, that isn't too often," Sarah said.

"Every week," Michael said.

"I'd go on strike," Rebecca said.

"Not that often," Sarah said.

"Almost," Michael said.

"You're sure she hasn't got a boyfriend?" Kirk said, and winked.

"I *wish*," Sarah said, and waggled her eyebrows.

"Has he got a friend for me?" Rebecca asked.

"Maybe we can take him to France with us," Michael said, and everyone laughed.

"You bring the wine," Kirk said in a thick French accent, "and I'll bring Pierre."

"Lucky Pierre," Rebecca said, "always in the middle."

"Can you *get* a villa for such a short while?" Kirk asked.

"I think so. I think you can get them for a *week*, in fact."

"It's not called a villa in France," Rebecca said. "It's called a *château*."

"*Un château*," Kirk said.

"I thought that was a castle," Michael said.

"Same thing," Rebecca said.

"Want to come live in a castle with me?" Michael asked, and squeezed Sarah's hand again.

It was all she could do to keep from crying.

Luretta had to tell her. Couldn't wait till class was over so she could grab Mrs. Welles's ear and talk with her privately. Last-period class this Wednesday, the entire school running twenty minutes late because of the unexpected fire drill and assembly this morning, two things the kids at Greer could've done without on a nice sunny day like today, for a change.

"... no need to write the rest of the poem, am I right?" Sarah was saying. "It's all there in that first line, 'Oh, to be in England now that April's there.' By the way, if you want to test anyone who's ever studied English lit, just ask, 'What are the words that come after "Oh, to be in England"?' and nine times out of ten, you'll get 'Now that *spring* is there.' But the words are 'Now that *April's* there,' and all the longing, all the passion, all the sweet sorrow of that beautiful month, is right there in that first line. As a matter of fact, the rest of the poem is something of a letdown, isn't it? Ab? Read us the first few lines aloud, would you?"

Abigail Simms, a lanky fourteen year old with straight blond hair trailing halfway down her back, cleared her throat and read, " 'Oh, to be in England now that April's there, and whoever wakes in England sees, some morning, unaware, That the lowest boughs and the brushwood sheaf Round the elm-tree bole are in tiny leaf . . .' "

"Hold it right there, Ab, thank you. Now, to how many of you does that business about the lowest bough and the brushwood sheaf conjure *any* images of April at all? Browning should have quit while he was winning, right?"

The class watched her warily, suspecting a trap. She had a way of doing that, Luretta knew, leading them down the garden, letting them think one thing, while all the time she was teaching them something just the opposite. But no, this time she really *did* seem to be sharing her disappointment. She just hoped the class would hurry up and be over so she could tell her what was happening at home, Dusty hitting on her all the time, her mother looking the other way.

" '. . . and after April,' " she was quoting, " 'when May follows, and the whitethroat builds, and all the swallows!' Okay, we all live in the big bad city, we don't see too many whitethroats or swallows or buttercups waking anew at noontide. But do any of you find those images *evocative*? Do any of you even know what a whitethroat *is*? Or a chaffinch? 'While the chaffinch sings on the orchard bough.' Sally? What's a chaffinch?"

Sally Hawkins, looking like a chaffinch herself, whatever that was, tall and spindly with stringy brown hair and bulging brown eyes, a true chaffinch if ever Luretta saw one.

"Some kind of bird," Sally said. "I guess."

"Any idea what it looks like?"

"No."

"Is it blue? Yellow? Red? Any idea?"

"No."

"Well, isn't it important for a poet to give us images we can *visualize*? How about a melon-flower? Anyone here know what a melon-flower looks like? Alyce? Any idea?"

"It's something like a squash, I guess."

Alyce Goldstein. Cute little girl with dark hair and darker eyes, burdened with the "y" in her name because her mother thought it was more stylish.

" 'Far brighter than this gaudy melon-flower!' That's the last line of the poem. Where is he, anyway? Browning? The poem is titled 'Home Thoughts, from Abroad.' So where is he? Is the melon-flower where he happens to be at the time? Or does it grow in England?"

"It must be where he is."

Jenny Larson, thick glasses, freckles all over her face, shy as a butterfly.

"And where's that?"

"Probably Italy."

"What makes you say Italy?"

"The melon-flower makes it sound like Italy. I don't know why. It just *sounds* like Italy."

"Also he wrote 'My Last Duchess,' " Amy Fiske said, "and that was about Italy, wasn't it?"

"Well, he also wrote 'Soliloquy of the Spanish Cloister,'

so how do we know this isn't Spain? If we know nothing at all about a melon-flower . . ."

Luretta found Browning a total bore, even when Mrs. Welles was teaching him. Yesterday, she'd read them the T. S. Eliot poem that began with the words "April is the cruellest month," and those five words had said more to her than all the words Browning had ever . . .

The bell rang.

"Nuts!" Sarah said.

Luretta clutched her books to her chest, ran to the front of the classroom, took a deep breath, and said, "Mrs. Welles, I have to . . .

"Honey, can it wait till tomorrow?" Sarah said. "I've got to get out of here."

She was gone almost before the words left her mouth, snapping her attaché case shut, snatching her handbag out of the bottom drawer of the desk, grabbing her topcoat out of the closet near the door, and waving a brief farewell to Luretta as she ran out.

Luretta supposed it would have to wait till tomorrow.

She ran the three blocks from Sixtieth to Fifty-seventh, sure Billy would be gone by now, knowing she would first have to call Andrew, tell him she was on the way, and then try to catch a rush-hour taxi. But miracle of miracles, the car was still there, waiting for her at the curb outside Dunhill's, where it waited for her every Wednesday at four-ten, four-fifteen, except that today it was closer to four-*thirty* because of the assembly and the fire drill.

The poem she'd written was in her handbag.

She hadn't seen Andrew in two weeks. She could not wait to be alone with him. She yanked open the back door, slid onto the black leather seat, pulled the door closed behind her, caught her breath, and said, "I thought you'd be gone, Billy, thank you for . . ."

"My orders are to wait till the cows come home," Billy said, and turned the ignition key.

"That doesn't sound like him."

"Ma'am?"

"Mr. Farrell," she said. "Till the cows come home."

"Mr. Farrell, huh?" Billy said.

His eyes met hers in the rearview mirror.

There was a faint smile on his mouth.

"Well, those weren't his *exact* words," he said. "Mr. Farrell." Still smiling. "What he said is I should wait for however long it takes. I just wait, and that's it."

"Does that go for *everyone* you drive?"

"No, ma'am, it doesn't."

He had turned the car onto Park Avenue now, heading downtown. The traffic was heavy. She was beginning to think the assembly and fire drill would cost her a lot more than the twenty minutes they'd added to the school day.

"How long do you wait for *other* people?" she asked.

"Depends. If it's the airport, I wait till the plane gets in, however long it takes."

"Do you pick up many people at the airport?"

"Oh sure."

"What if it isn't the airport?"

"Twenty minutes, half an hour. I call in, ask if . . ." He hesitated and then said, "Ask if Mr. *Farrell* wants me to wait longer or what I should do. Whatever he wants me to do, I do. He's the boss."

She wanted to ask him if he drove many other *women*. Wanted to ask if his instructions were to wait for as long as it took with any other women but herself. She did not ask. She settled back against the soft black leather, instead, losing herself in the steady drone of the traffic, closing her eyes, lulled almost to sleep until Billy tooted the horn at another car, jolting her immediately back to her senses.

"Where are we?" she asked.

"Brooklyn, he wants me to bring you to the Buona

Sera," Billy said, and paused, and grinned into the rearview mirror again. "Mr. Farrell."

"The what?"

"Buona Sera. It's a restaurant."

"A rest—?"

"Very good one, in fact. Right around the corner, in fact."

"A restaurant? I can't . . ."

She was suddenly panicked. A *restaurant*? Was he crazy? Even in Brooklyn, was he *crazy*?

"It's very nice," Billy said, "you'll like it."

He was pulling the car up to the curb in front of what looked like the sort of cheap little Italian joint you passed in Queens on the way to Kennedy if there was traffic and you got off the parkway and took the backstreets. Green awning out front, plastic stained-glass windows in the two entrance doors, big ornate metal door pulls that were supposed to look like bronze, a frayed red carpet stretching under the awning, from the curb to the entrance doors. Billy was out of the car already, coming around it now, opening the back door for her. She would not get out of the car, this was ridiculous. Why had he . . . ?

Andrew suddenly came through one of the twin entrance doors, stepping out onto the sidewalk, walking swiftly toward the curb.

"Hi," he said.

"Andrew, what . . . ?"

"Time we broke out," he said, and grinned.

The moment they were seated, Andrew reached across the table to take her hands. Both hands. He was making no effort to hide. This both frightened her and thrilled her.

"I have things to tell you," he said.

"Couldn't you have said them in . . . ?"

"I wanted to be with you in public."

"Why?"

"To show you off."

"Andrew . . ."

"To show everyone how beautiful you are. To show everyone how much I love you."

"This is very dangerous," she whispered.

"I don't care."

"I know we're in Brooklyn . . ."

"That's why I chose it."

"But even so . . ."

"Don't worry."

"I do worry."

"Let me tell you what . . ."

"Can we please *not* hold hands?"

"I *want* to hold your hands."

"I want to hold yours, too. But . . ."

"Then don't worry about it."

"Andrew, suppose someone . . . ?"

"What would you like to drink?" he asked, and signaled to the proprietor, who came sidling obsequiously over to the table, wringing his hands, big grin on his wide round face. They were sitting at a small corner table where a candle burned in a Chianti bottle on a red-and-white-checked table-cloth. The proprietor wasn't quite Henry Armetta in the old black-and-white movies she'd seen on television, but he ran a close second. Hovering over the table, wringing his hands in joy, he seemed to be daring them *not* to be in love. From speakers discreetly hidden only God knew where, operatic arias suffused the room, audible enough to be heard, soft enough to sound as if they were drifting from open leaded windows above the Grand Canal. The place was relatively crowded for a Wednesday night. There was the pleasant hum of conversation, the clink of silver on china, the smell of good food wafting from the kitchen.

"*Sì, signor faviola,*" he said grandly, which she guessed was Italian for "Yes, favored sir" or "Yes, favorite gentleman," or something of the sort, *favola, faviola,* whatever. A solemnly attentive look on his face now, his hands still pressed together, he lowered his voice and gravely said, *"Mi dica."*

"Sarah? What would you like?"

"Johnnie Walker Black on the rocks," she said, "a splash."

"Beefeater martini on the rocks for me," Andrew said, "with a couple of olives. Or three or four, Carlo. If you can spare them."

"Signore, per lei ci sono mille *olive, non si preoccupi,"* he said, and went swiftly toward the bar.

"Do you understand Italian?" she asked.

"A little."

"Have you ever been there?"

"No. Are you reading my mind?"

"What do you mean?"

"That's part of what I have to tell you."

Carlo was back.

"Bene, signor faviola," he said. *"Ecco a lei un* Johnnie Black, *con una spuzzatina de seltz, e un* Beefeater martini *con ghiaccio e molte, molte olive. Alla sua salute, signore, e alla sua, signorina,"* he said, and bowed from the waist, and backed away from the table.

"Even *I* understood the *signorina* part," she said.

"He thinks you're seventeen."

"Ho-ho-ho."

He raised his glass, held it suspended. "Here's to you and to me," he said. "Together. Forever."

She said nothing. He extended his glass across the table. They clinked glasses. Still, she said nothing. She sipped at the Scotch. He watched her across the table.

"Does that scare you?" he said.

"Yes."

"Why?"

"You know why."

"I've been doing a lot of thinking this past little while," he said. "About you. About us." He took another sip of the drink, fished an olive from the glass, popped it into his mouth, chewed it, swallowed it. She had the feeling he was stalling for time. At last he said, "Sarah, you know I'm single, you know I've been seeing other girls . . ."

She *hadn't* known that.

The admission hit her like a bullet between the eyes. *What* girls? *Girls?* Seventeen year olds like those the unctuous Carlo had conjured with his flattering *signorina?* How many seventeen-year-old *girls* had the "favored sir" brought here? She realized he was still talking, realized she had stopped listening the moment he'd . . .

". . . until I was out there in Kansas, a million miles away, in the middle of nowhere. I began really thinking out there. About you. About just what you meant to me. I couldn't shake it. Even when I got back, it was with me. Thinking about you all the time. Trying to figure out what you meant to me, what we meant to each other. It was like having a fever and not being able to think straight, and all at once the fever breaks, and you're okay, you can think clearly again. What finally happened, I said to myself Who *needs* these other girls? Who's the only person I really *want* to see, the only person I want to *be* with, the only person I *love?* And the answer was you, you're that person. You're the only person I want to be with from now on, from today on, this minute on, till the end of my life. That's why I brought you here tonight, so I could tell you in public, right out in the open. I love you, I want to be with you forever."

"What girls?" she asked.

"Well . . . is that all you have to say?"

"Yes. What girls?"

"Well . . . there was someone named Oona I was seeing,

but that's over with now. And there was a girl named Angela I knew from Great Neck, but I've already told her . . ."

Sarah was still conjuring Oona. Great name for a cooze, Oona. Great name for a seventeen-year-old Irish *cooze* he'd probably been screwing in the very same bed he . . .

"Did you take them there?" she said. "These girls?" she said. "To the apartment?" she said. "To . . . to . . . our . . ."

"Yes," he said.

"Andrew, Andrew, how could . . . ?"

"But I'm telling you that's *finished*. It's done with, it's *over*. Do you understand what I'm saying? I thought you'd be happy. I thought . . ."

"Happy? You're *screwing,*" she said, and then immediately lowered her voice, and repeated in a whisper, "you're *screwing* I don't know how many young girls, and I'm supposed to be . . ."

"Was," he said. "Not anymore."

"How many?" she said.

"Two hundred and forty," he said, and grinned.

"Very funny, you bastard."

"I'm trying to tell you . . ."

"How many?"

"Half a dozen, maybe."

"You sound like my goddamn *sister!*"

"What?"

"Half a . . . !"

"Sarah, I'm *single!* Before I met you, I was . . ."

"Go to hell," she said, furious now.

She picked up her glass, drained it.

"I want another one of these," she said.

He signaled to Carlo.

"Another round," he told him.

"Sì, signor faviola," Carlo said, and scurried off again.

"Favored sir, my *ass,*" she mumbled.

"What?"

"Nothing."

"You gonna stay angry all night, or what?"

"Yes."

"Okay, fine."

They sat in silence until the fresh drinks came. Carlo went through his presentation routine yet another time, and then said, *"Alla sua salute, signore, signorina,"* and backed away from the table again.

"Some *signorina,"* she said, and pulled a face, and lifted her drink and took a heavy pull at it.

"I'm leaving for Italy next week," he said.

"Good," she said.

"I want you to come with me," he said.

"Take Oona," she said. "Take the whole dirty dozen."

"*Half* a dozen."

"Who's counting?"

"I can't understand you, you know that?"

"Gee," she said.

"I tell you I'm never gonna see any other woman but you in my entire . . ."

"*Girls,* you said. *Girls.* And, gee, is that what you were saying? I thought you were confessing to multiple forni—"

"You *know* it's what I was saying. And now I'm asking you to come to Italy with me."

"And the answer is no."

"Why?"

"Because I don't like being part of a harem. Besides, there's this little matter of my being married, hmmm?"

"It wasn't a harem. And anyway, I told you six times already, that's over and *done* with."

"How old are they?"

"*Were.*"

"*Were,* are, this isn't an English class."

"Why do you want to know?"

"So I can cry myself to sleep tonight," she said, and suddenly began weeping.

"Honey, please," he said, and reached across the table for her hands again. She pulled them away. "Sarah," he said, "I love you."

"Sure," she said, and lowered her head, still crying, shaking her head, looking down at the checked tablecloth, shaking her head.

"I want you to come to Italy with me."

"No."

Shaking her head, sobbing.

"I want you to marry me."

"No."

Still shaking her head, still staring at the . . .

It registered.

She looked up and said, "What?"

"I want you to divorce your husband and marry me."

She began shaking her head again.

"That's what I want," he said.

"No," she said.

Shaking her head, her eyes glistening with tears.

"Yes," he said.

"No, Andrew, please, you know I can't . . ."

"I love you," he said.

"Andrew . . ."

"I want you forever."

"Andrew, you don't know me at all."

"I know you fine."

"All you know is making love to me."

"That, too."

"I'm six years *older* than you are!"

"Who's counting?"

"I'm not one of your little *girls*."

"I don't *have* any little girls."

"I *do*. I have a twelve-year-old *daughter,* Andrew, re-member?"

"We'll discuss that in Italy."

"I can't go to Italy with you."

"Yes, you can," he said. "Are you hungry? Shall I get some menus?"

"Do you realize this is the first time we've even been in *public* together? And you want me to go to *Italy?*"

"Wrong."

"Wrong?"

"We had dinner in public in St. Bart's. And we also had coffee and croissants in that little place on Second Avenue."

"That was all before."

"Yes. That was all before. Chocolate croissants. The day we had our first fight."

"That wasn't a fight," she said. "I simply got up and left."

"Because I kissed you."

"Yes."

"I'm going to kiss you now," he said. "Don't leave."

He leaned over the table and kissed her the way he had that afternoon long ago, the taste of the chocolate on his lips, the weather raging outside.

"Are we finished fighting?" he asked.

"I think so."

"Good, will you marry me?"

"I know you're not serious," she said. "We'd better eat."

"How can I convince you?"

"Tell me all their names."

"Why?"

"I told you. So I can cry myself to sleep."

"*Don't* start crying again. *Please!*"

"I'm not. I won't. I want to know because . . . because then I can exorcise them."

"Exercise them? How? Walk them around the block on a leash?"

"*Exorcise,*" she said. "Like you do with the devil."

"Oh, *exorcise,*" he said, and grinned. "Now I get it. You mean *purge* them."

"Don't be such a wiseguy," she said. "Yes, *purge* them. Get them out of my system."

"The way I got them out of mine."

"Sure," she said skeptically.

"But I had you to help me," he said.

"Their names, please."

"You sound like a cop," he said.

"Their names."

In a rush, as if he were reciting one name and not half a dozen of them, he said, "Mary Jane, Oona, Alice, Angela, Blanca, Maggie, that's it. Carlo!" he called. "Could we see some menus, please?"

"*Sì, signor faviola, immediatamente!*"

"What's that he keeps saying?" she asked.

"What do you mean?"

"*Favola? Faviola?* Something like that. What does it mean?"

"I have no idea."

"I thought you understood Italian."

"Just a little."

"Where'd you learn it?"

"At Kent. Why'd you call me a wiseguy just then?"

"Because you were being so smart."

"I thought it might have had something to do with the movie I was telling you about."

"What movie?"

"That time."

"I don't know what you mean."

"Then forget it," he said.

"So," Carlo said, appearing at the table with the menus. "I will explain to you the specials tonight?"

"Please," Andrew said.

She listened as Carlo reeled off the specials in Italian, immediately translating each one into English. She watched Andrew all the while. Watched him listening. What were those names again? How could she exorcise all those girls if she couldn't even remember their names? And suddenly she realized they'd already *been* exorcised.

"So," Carlo said, "I give you a few moments, *signor faviola, signorina,* please take your time."

Bowing again, he backed away from the table like a ship leaving port.

"He just said it again," Sarah said.

"Yes, I heard him," Andrew said. "What sounds good to you?"

It wasn't until Billy dropped her off on Lex and Eighty-third later that night that she realized she'd forgotten to read him her poem.

The detectives were telling Michael that even if they *could* get a court order for the surveillance of the newly discovered entrance on Mott Street, they couldn't see anyplace they could do the job.

"Because what it is," Regan was saying, "there's this restaurant-supply place on the northeast corner there, opposite that blue door . . ."

"Mailbox says Carter-Goldsmith Investments," Lowndes said.

"Check it," Michael said. "Find out if it's a corporation, a partnership, who the principals . . ."

"Already working it," Regan said.

"Good."

"The thing I'm saying," he went on, hating it whenever anyone interrupted him, "is there's windows upstairs facing that Mott Street entrance, but the restaurant-supply people *own* the whole building, and *use* the whole building, so there's no place we can put in a camera, even if we *did* get a court order, which the court might find excessive, by the way, seeing we've *already* got one right around the corner."

"It's worth a try," Michael said. "We don't know *who* goes in that other entrance. It might be . . ."

"We figure the bimbos," Lowndes said.

"If that's all, it's not worth the trouble. But if we're getting people who for some reason or other don't want to be seen going through the tailor shop . . ."

"Yeah, that's possible," Regan agreed dubiously.

"So why can't you plant a truck on the street?" Michael asked. "We won't need an order for that."

"Mike, I'll tell you," Regan said, "this ain't Greenwich, Connecticut down there, a bunch of rich assholes can't tell spinach from crabgrass. This is Little Italy. We put a truck across the street from that blue door, we paint it like a bakery truck or a telephone company truck or a Con Ed truck or whatever we want to call it, the whole neighborhood's gonna know in ten seconds flat there's cops in that truck taking pictures of what's going on across the street."

"Mmmm," Michael said.

"Now so far, we got a good thing going here. We got the whole place bugged, and we've got a camera on the front door of the tailor shop gives us movies of every cheap hood going in and out of the place. The camera picks them up going in, the bugs upstairs pick up whatever they're saying, it's a sweet setup. We also got a wiretap in place, we know everybody he calls, and we can dope out most of the people who call him. We're gathering lots of information, Mike. What I'm saying is we put in a truck, the truck gets made, we might blow the whole surveillance. Is what I'm saying."

"Yeah," Michael said, and sighed heavily.

It was peculiar.

In America, if you stopped any native-born son or daughter whose ancestors had long ago immigrated from Ireland or Italy or Puerto Rico or Serbia, and you asked them what nationality they were, they did not say they were American. They said they were Irish, Italian, Puerto Rican, Serbian, Hungarian, Chinese, Japanese, Albanian, whatever the hell, but they never said they were American. Jews called themselves *Jewish* wherever their ancestors had come from. The only people who called themselves *Americans* were WASPs. You never heard a WASP say he was anything but American. Oh, yes, he might make reference every now and then to his illustrious mixed British-Scottish heritage, but he would never tell you he was British or Scottish because he simply wasn't; he was *American,* by God.

Andrew and almost everyone else he knew had been born in America. He'd never met his grandparents' parents who'd come over from Christ knew where in Italy, and the occasional ancient relatives who still spoke broken English were promptly dismissed as "greaseballs" by his mother, who insisted with every other breath—but why did she *have* to?—that she was "American." He was American, too, even though if anyone asked him what he *was,* he answered automatically, "I'm Italian." But this was merely a handy means of reference, this meant only that somewhere way back in a distant past of chariots and togas and arenas and laurel leaves, some relatives he'd never known had sailed for America to become citizens here. Even if he *said* he was Italian, he *knew* he was really American, and everyone else knew it, too. Anyway, that's what they taught him in elementary school and in junior high; he was American, the same way Grandma and Grandpa and his father and his Uncle Rudy and his Aunt Concetta and his cousin Ida were American.

Sure.

It wasn't until he got to Kent up there in woodsy waspy wealthy Connecticut that he met a *different* sort of American for the first time. Until then, he hadn't known so many blue-eyed blonds even *existed.* Kids with names that didn't end in vowels. Kids with last names like Armstrong and Harper and Wellington. Kids with first names like Martin and Bruce and Christopher and Howard. Well, so what? His own blond hair had turned a little muddy, true, but his eyes were still blue, weren't they? And his first name wasn't Angelo or Luigi, it was *Andrew,* wasn't it? Which should have made him as American as all the other blue-eyed kids with names like Roger, Keith, Alexander, or Reid. But it seemed there was a catch. It seemed that his *family* name was Faviola—oh yeah, right, the *Italian* kid playing quarterback.

Somehow—and he didn't know *quite* how—but *somehow* the American dream they'd taught him in elementary and junior high had been denied his grandparents and his parents, which was why he guessed his mother insisted so vociferously and so frequently that she was American. And now that same dream was being denied *him* as well. Somehow, in this place where he'd been born, in this land of the free and home of the brave, in this his country, in this his America, he had become something *less* than American. Somehow he had become just what he'd said he was all along—but, hey, folks, I was just explaining my *roots,* you know?—somehow he had become, and would always remain, merely *Italian.* And whereas he didn't know who the *real* Americans were, he knew for damn sure he wasn't one of them. Moreover, he knew they would never allow him to *become* one of them. So he said Fuck it, and went gambling in Las Vegas where Italians like himself were running the casinos.

Now, *this* was the peculiar part.

Here in Milan . . .

What *they* called *Milano* . . .

Sitting at a little outdoor bar . . .

What *they* called *una barra* . . .

Talking to a man his mother instantly would have labeled a greaseball, he felt American for the first time in his life. Here he was not an Italian. Here he was an American. The man he was *talking* to was Italian. He thought it odd that he'd had to come all the way here to find out he was American. He wondered if the moment he got back home again he would begin feeling not *quite* American.

The man was smoking what his mother called a "guinea stinker." His name was Giustino Manfredi. He did not look as important as he really was. Wearing rumpled black trousers that seemed a trifle long for him, and a white dress shirt open at the throat and rolled up at the sleeves, and a little black vest, he reminded Andrew of Louis the tailor, except that he didn't have white hair. Manfredi's hair was black and straight, and parted in the middle. He kept puffing on the little thin cigar, sending up clouds of smoke that drifted out over the square.

This was ten o'clock in the morning on a beautiful sunny day during the last week of April. The little bar was virtually empty at this hour of the morning, and besides, Manfredi had chosen a table at the extreme far end of the outdoor space, under the canopy close to the bank next door, which he suggested with a laugh he would not mind robbing one day. Manfredi lived in Palermo, but he had chosen Milan as the city for their meeting, explaining in his broken English that for the moment it was *extremely* difficult for businessmen to conduct any sort of business in Sicily. It was not much better in Milan, for that matter, but here you could at least sit and talk about financial matters without the *carabinieri* rushing in with machine guns.

Both men were drinking espresso served to them by a young man who seemed more intent on impressing a buxom German girl sitting under the other end of the canopy than he was in serving a man who could order him dropped into the fucking Adriatic tomorrow morning with an anvil around his neck. Manfredi seemed not to mind. He knew he wasn't well known in Milan, which was why he'd chosen the location to begin with. He alternately puffed on the cheap cigar or waved it grandly in the air when he spoke, a man supremely confident of himself, secure in the knowledge that what they were discussing would net him millions and millions of dollars, which in turn would allow him to continue dressing like a ragpicker and smoking cheap little cigars.

The more he spoke, the more Andrew felt like an American.

The man's English was atrocious.

At one point, Andrew burst out laughing, and then—when he realized Manfredi was about to take offense—immediately explained why the comment had been so comical.

Manfredi had been explaining that the goods could move freely in or out of any number of Italian seaports . . .

"*Ma non la Sicilia,* eh? Too difficult now Sicilia. Other ports, *naturalmente.* We have much ports, Italia . . ."

Andrew was thinking his mother should be here listening to this greaseball . . .

. . . explaining now that most ports in Italy were *available* to them for their purposes, which translated as *controlled* by them, which he would not say aloud either in Italian or in his impoverished English, and then uttering the words that caused Andrew to explode in laughter.

"We come in, we do what to do, eh? And then we just pass away."

The laughter burst from Andrew's mouth like a cannon shot. Manfredi was so startled he almost dropped his foul-smelling cigar. Rearing back as if fired upon, his eyes and his mouth opening wide in surprise, he realized in an instant that he was being *laughed* at, and he was on the narrow edge of displaying some fine Sicilian rage when Andrew quickly said, "Let me explain, Signor Manfredi," and then managed to control himself long enough to define the American euphemism. The definition immediately tickled the Sicilian's funny bone, causing *him* to burst into laughter as well, which allowed Andrew to join him before he busted.

"Pass away, *Dio mio,*" Manfredi said, drying his eyes, still laughing. He signaled to the waiter for refills, but the waiter was now staring into the German girl's blouse and impressing her with his command of English, greater than Manfredi's to be sure, but nothing to write home about,

either. The girl seemed overwhelmed by the pimply kid's
Italian charm. Andrew felt more and more American.

Manfredi was telling him that all next week he would
show him the various ports . . .

"Better more than one port, eh?"

. . . that would be off-loading the product from the
East . . .

Refusing to say either "China" or "Asia" . . .

. . . which should be arriving in Italy sometime late in
May. He was hoping the *southern* product . . .

Refusing to say either "Colombian" or "South American" . . .

. . . would be arriving in Italy at about the same time so
that they could begin their work here.

The way this came out in his hopeless English was,
"They come Italia, the ship, we lift one, two, *immediatamente* . . ."

And we just pass away, Andrew thought, and almost
burst out laughing again.

That night, long after he and Manfredi had parted company, Andrew walked the streets of Milan and tried to find
something in common with these elegantly dressed men and
beautiful women who moved by on the soft spring night
trailing hushed foreign voices behind them. Even the Italian
they spoke seemed different from the language he'd heard
when infrequent visitors from distant provinces in Italy
dropped by smoking stogies as foul as Manfredi's and stink-
ing up his mother's drapes. Her face said I'm American, what
are you doing in my house?

These people were foreigners to him.

This country was alien and strange to him.

He recognized in Italy a place of beauty and grace, a
gentle land of soft light and rolling hills, but nowhere could
he find any real connection to himself, nowhere could he
discover those much touted "roots" Americans were incessantly seeking all over the world. He wondered again why

anyone born in America should have to seek his roots elsewhere. That was the irony of it. Americans swarming all
over the globe searching for identities denied them in their
native land.

He bought a *gelato* on a cone at a stand in one of the
arcades, and was stepping out onto the ancient cobblestoned
street again when he almost collided with a tall man whose
eyes were as blue as his own.

"Mi scusi, signore, mi scusi," the man said.

"Sorry, my fault," Andrew said.

They did a little sidestepping jig around each other, each
apologetic and smiling, and as the man rejoined his compan-
ion, Andrew heard him softly explain, *"Americano."*

Yes, he thought.

The girls were sweaty and tall and the boys were sweaty
and short. This was a fact of life when you were twelve and
had just done forty minutes of gymnastics in Morningside
Park. Mollie and her best friend, Winona Weingarten, called
the seventh-grade boys "Munchkins"—sometimes, and cru-
elly, even when they were within earshot. Boys and girls alike
were wearing the blue-shorts, blue-sweatshirt gym uniform
with the white Hanover crest over the left breast. Mollie was
wearing the sneakers she'd finally found the day she and
her mother and Aunt Heather had gone shopping together.
Winona was wearing identical sneakers. The seventh-grade
boys called the girls "Tweedledum and Tweedledee," in re-
taliation for the Munchkin label and also because they did
look very much alike, both of them tall and slender with long
blond hair tucked now under identical billed caps, and also
because they talked some kind of dumb secret language only
the two of them understood.

The girls were straggling a bit behind the other kids,
talking that language now. The language was called "Frankendrac," named for Frankenstein and Dracula because it was
supposed to sound like a Baltic mix of German and Slavic

even though it was an entirely new language with a vocabulary the girls had invented themselves when they'd first met
at Hanover at the age of five. The girls would not have
revealed the structure of their language even if threatened
with torture or rape. The rapid-fire mélange sounded like
gibberish to anyone else, but made total sense to both of
them. At Hanover, you had to study two foreign languages;
Frankendrac was their third. Enjoying the bright sunshine on
this last Friday in April, the first *truly* glorious spring day
they'd had so far, the girls ambled behind the others, chatting
like a pair of foreigners in their native tongue.

This was not a day for physical exertion—which they
both deplored, anyway, *despite* Miss Margolin's total *obsession*
with fitness, fitness, fitness. Nor was it a day for contemplat-
ing a return to the classroom after half an hour of jumping
up and down. What they both would have *preferred* doing was
walking up to Rosa's on a Hundred-Tenth and Amsterdam,
buying some sweets, and then strolling along lazily while
they savored every luscious bite. Instead, there'd be a mad
scramble in the locker room to change out of gym uniform
and back into the *de rigueur* pleated watch skirt and white
blouse before rushing off to their next class, which happened
to be French, and much easier than the language they'd invented.

Empty crack vials lay strewn along the sides of the park
path.

"They look like those little perfume samples they give
away," Mollie said in Frankendrac.

And to her utter astonishment, Winona said, "*Ich kenner-
nit vetter trienner gitt.*"

Which translated into English meant "I can't wait to try
it."

She had been counting the days since he'd left for Italy,
counting the days till his return, and she wondered now what
her response would be if Andrew again suggested, sometime

in the future, that she accompany him on a trip someplace. She could not have gone *this* time, in any event; she was a teacher and the last week in April was not a school holiday. The *first* week in April might have been another story. Passover started at sundown on Monday, and then Good Friday fell in the same week, followed by Easter Sunday—she might have been able to make a good case for taking off those extra few days in the middle of the week. A good case with the *school,* anyway. What she would have told Michael was quite another matter. But the very *idea* of a week alone with . . .

". . . know what it is in a minute," Michael said.

"Uh-huh," she said, and realized she hadn't been listening to him, hadn't heard a word of what he'd been saying for the past two or three minutes.

"So I'm thinking of a hot dog wagon instead," he said, as if that would explain it all.

"Uh-huh."

They were finishing their coffee and dessert. Mollie was crosstown with her friend Winona for the weekend. Andrew was in Genoa. Tomorrow he would be in Naples. And the day after that . . .

". . . with the striped umbrellas, you know? Sabrett, whatever. Have Freddie Coulter rig it with a video camera, none of the locals'll think it's a detective selling knishes and pretzels down there. What do you think?"

"Down where?" she said.

"That I *can't* tell you," he said.

"This is some kind of surveillance, right?"

"Yes. The case I'm working."

"Which you still can't . . ."

"Can't, sorry."

"But you *can* tell me you're thinking of putting a camera in a hot dog wagon."

"Yeah. Well, one of those carts, you know?"

"Sounds like James Bond," she said.

"Half the things Freddie rigs *are* James Bond."

"Why do you have to rig something so elaborate?"

"Because there isn't a facility we can use in the building across the street."

"Then I think it's a good idea," she said, and nodded. "*If* Freddie thinks it'll work."

"And *if* you can find a detective with dirt under his fingernails," Sarah said.

"So he'll look like a *real* hot dog seller," Michael said, and they both burst out laughing.

Michael suddenly reached across the table and took her hand in his.

"What?" she said, surprised.

"I don't know," he said, and shrugged.

But he did not let go of her hand.

The lights were out and they were speaking Frankendrac. Winona was saying she thought it was all a conspiracy that their parents and teachers had cooked up to keep them from having a good time. She was saying she couldn't see anything wrong with using drugs, and she couldn't wait to be old enough to try them.

This from Winona Weingarten, her very best friend in the entire world, who had an IQ of 156, and who spoke Frankendrac like a native.

"*Miekin bro stahgatten smekker pot venner hich har twofer tin,*" Winona said.

Which translated loosely as "My brother started smoking pot when he was twelve."

In English, Mollie whispered, "That was another time and place, Win."

"*Zer* lingen*tok!*" Winona warned.

Mollie immediately switched to their secret tongue, telling Winona she could *not* for Christ's sake compare her brother growing up in 1972 with what was happening today, when all these dangerous drugs were on the market . . .

"That's what they said about LSD, too," Winona said

in the language. "My brother tried LSD, do you see him running around like some sort of crazed freak?"

"Crack is insidious," Mollie said, having a tough time translating "insidious" because it wasn't a word in the secret vocabulary, but Winona seemed to catch the improvisation, because she immediately replied in letter-perfect Frankendrac, "No more lethal than pot, my dear."

"You're so eager to *try* something," Mollie said in English, and before Winona could shoot her another warning glare, immediately said, "*Tryker zin* blow*den jobber.*"

Both girls burst out laughing.

In bed that night, Sarah found the courage to explore what she hadn't been able to at dinner.

Michael had been reading, and she knew from the heavy-lidded look of his eyes and his deeper breathing that he was about ready to doze off.

Out of the blue, she said, "Would you be terribly upset if I went off for a few days with the girls?"

"Mollie and Winona?" he asked.

She'd started off on the wrong foot. She *never* called women "girls." She'd done so now only because she was nervous and the cliché had come so readily to mind, a night out with "the girls," a few days off with "the girls." She quickly said, "I meant the other teachers. *Some* of us. We were thinking we might get away for a weekend this summer . . ."

"A *weekend*?" he said.

"Or during the week, to discuss the fall curric—"

"When did this job get so *serious* all of a sudden?"

"Well, it's always been *serious,* Michael, you know that."

"Well, yeah, but *Jesus,* Sarah . . ."

"We thought we'd keep contact over the summer . . ."

"You've never done that before."

"Well, I know, but . . ."

"Eight years now at Greer . . ."

"Yes, but . . ."

"All of a sudden, *meetings* every week . . ."

"Well, that's the whole . . ."

"All of a sudden, a few days *off* with the *girls* . . ."

"That's the whole idea, Michael. We're trying to make this a more coordinated teaching effort. If we can get input from each other on a regular basis . . ."

"We're going to *France* this summer, remember?"

"Well, this wouldn't be *then*, Michael."

"When *would* it be?"

"We haven't set any dates yet. Three of us are married, we wanted to discuss it with our husbands first."

"Weekends are out of the question," he said.

"With all the weekends *you've* been working, I would have thought . . ."

"This is an unusual case."

"It would seem so."

"And I've worked weekends before."

"Yes."

"In the past."

"Yes. So it's okay for *you* to work weekends . . ."

"Going away with the *girls* isn't *working,* Sarah!"

"Oh, isn't it?"

"Where would you be going?"

"I have no idea. We haven't taken it that far yet. I *told* you, Michael. Jane and Edie are married, too. They have to discuss it with their husbands. We're talking two or three *days* here, for Christ's sake, not two months in the country!"

"You said a weekend."

"Or a few days *during* the week, I said. I didn't know this would be so upsetting to you, Michael."

"It's not upsetting."

"You sound upset. Look, forget it, I'll tell them I can't . . ."

"Sure, make *me* the heavy, right?"

"Michael, what's *wrong* with you?"

"The other husbands'll say, 'Sure, darling, go to *Tokyo* for a *month*, that's fine with me.' It'll just be Michael the *Shmuck* who makes a big fuss."

"It's not that important," she said. "Forget it. I'll tell . . ."

"No, no, it's fine with me. Just let me know in . . ."

"I wouldn't think of . . ."

". . . advance, so I can send out for some Chinese food."

She wondered if she should accept graciously, or back out while she still had the chance. Her heart was pounding. She hadn't even *suggested* to Andrew that she might be able to get away for a few days, but now it seemed almost too easy, and Michael's final if reluctant compliance made her feel manipulative and cheap. Tell him no, she thought. Tell him it was a stupid idea. Do it now, this minute. But the thought of driving up to New England someplace, finding a quiet little inn, spending two or three days there with Andrew . . .

"It's just that I'll miss you," Michael said, and kissed her on the cheek and then reached up to turn out the light.

In the dark, her eyes wide open, Sarah wondered what she'd become. She did not fall asleep for a long, long time.

At nine o'clock on the balmy spring evening of May fourth, the telephone in the Welles apartment rang, and Michael picked up after the second ring.

"Hello?" he said.

There was a click on the line.

"Hello?" he said again.

Nothing.

He looked at the receiver, annoyed, and then hung up.

"Who is it, darling?" Sarah called.

"Nobody there," Michael said.

She knew at once that the call was from Andrew. He was back.

She kept reading. The words made no sense to her. They swarmed over the page. She had to get out of here, had to

get to a telephone. But not too soon after the call. Give it
time, she thought, and read again the same paragraph for the
third time. At twenty past nine, she said, "Do you feel like
some frozen yogurt?"

"Not really," Michael said.

"I think I'll go down for some, would you mind?"

"I think there's some in the freezer."

"I want the soft kind," she said, and got up and marked
her place in the book, taking plenty of time, closing the book,
setting it down on the coffee table, all of this feeling like slow
motion to her, wanting to race out of the apartment, find the
nearest phone booth, walking to the entry hall to the same
slow-motion beat, "Can I bring one back for you?"

"No, thanks, hon."

Hoping he wouldn't suddenly change his mind and tell
her he'd like to come along, picking up her bag from the hall
table, opening it in slow motion, and then opening her purse
to make sure she had quarters because otherwise she'd have
to go to the laundry jar in the kitchen cabinet and steal some
quarters, but there were three quarters in the purse, together
with a handful of nickels and dimes, she was all right. She
snapped the purse closed with a click that sounded like a
cannon shot, and put it back in her bag, and slung the bag
on her shoulder, and said, "I'll be back in a few minutes."

"Maybe I . . ."

No, please, she thought, *don't!*

". . . will have one," he said. "The no-fat Dutch chocolate, on a sugar cone. If they have it. Otherwise whatever
they've got."

"In no-fat, you mean?"

"Yeah."

"Okay. See you in a bit."

Casually. No further talk. Just get *out* of here. Reaching
for the doorknob. Opening the door. Stepping out into the
hall. Pulling the door shut behind her. The click of the lock.
Forcing herself to walk slowly, slowly, slowly down the hall

to the elevator, and pressing the button for the elevator, and hearing it clattering up the shaft, the door sliding open, stepping into the car, pushing the black button with the white *L* stamped onto it, the door sliding shut again, and the elevator starting its descent.

She did not feel safe until she reached the coffee shop on Seventy-eighth and Lex.

"Hi," she said, "it's me."

"Sarah! God, I missed you!"

"You're back."

"I'm back. You knew it was me calling . . ."

"Yes."

"Where are you?"

"Downstairs. I made an excuse to get out."

"Are we okay for tomorrow?"

"Yes."

"Billy'll be there. Same time."

"Yes."

"I can't wait."

"Neither can I. I wish I were there with you right this minute."

"So do I."

"I love you, Andrew."

"I love you, too, Sarah."

"Tomorrow," she said.

"Tomorrow," he said.

There was a click on the line.

The pen register recorded the duration of the conversation as twenty-three seconds. Sitting the wire in the apartment on Grand Street, Detective/First Grade Jerry Mandel picked up the clipboard with the line sheets on it and recorded the caller's name as Sarah.

At that very moment, a block away, Detective/First Grade Freddie Coulter, wearing Con Ed coveralls and a Con

Ed hard hat, was unscrewing the plate from the street pole on the corner of Mott and Broome. He had installed a video camera with a pinhole lens in the hot dog cart that would be in place on the corner tomorrow. Now he needed his power source.

Power was always the main consideration. You either supplied your own power or you *stole* your power. In this instance, either a boat battery or a car battery inside the cart would have been sufficient, but sooner or later it would have needed replacement. He preferred stealing his power from Con Ed. He tapped into the pole now, fitted his cable with a male plug that would fit into the female outlet he'd already installed in the cart, and then screwed back onto the base a new panel notched to accommodate the cable running from inside the pole.

Hiding the cable with a tented wedge of wood painted in yellow and black stripes to look official, Coulter packed his tools and walked away from his handiwork, secure in the knowledge that tomorrow morning at ten, the hot dog cart would be here on the corner, ready to take pictures of anyone who went through that blue door across the street.

By four-thirty P.M. that Wednesday, the fifth day of May, Detective/Third Grade Gregory Annunziato of the District Attorney's Office Squad was beginning to think the plant was a lousy idea. He'd sold a lot of hot dogs since ten this morning, true enough, but selling hot dogs wasn't taking pictures of wiseguys.

Annunziato was wearing a plaid sports shirt and corduroy trousers and a white, mustard-smeared apron that effectively hid the .38 Detectives Special in a clamshell holster on his belt. He had curly black hair and dark brown eyes and a lot of his customers asked him if he was Italian. When he said he was—although he'd been born in Brooklyn—they invariably broke into Italian, which he spoke only sparingly, telling him how good his hot dogs and knishes were and expressing gratitude for the presence of the cart on this otherwise dismal corner. Annunziato kept his eye on the blue door across the street.

At four forty-three P.M., a black Lincoln Town Car pulled up on the same side of the street as the cart, some fifteen, twenty feet ahead of it, and a good-looking blond woman wearing a gray suit and carrying an attaché case and a gray leather shoulder bag got out of the car, leaned back in to say something to the driver, and then closed the door behind her. As she began walking diagonally across the street toward the blue door, Annunziato hit the remote button that started his video camera.

Her back to the camera, the woman went to the shadowed door and rang the bell.

She leaned in close to the speaker to say something.

Annunziato heard a buzzer sound across the street, unlatching the door.

As the woman went in and closed the door behind her, the tape digitally recorded the time and date as MAY 05–16:43:57.

She didn't get to read him the poem she'd composed until that afternoon. She took it out of her handbag, and sitting naked in the center of the bed, feeling very much like a child reciting for an expectant parent, she began.

"Andy, and Dandy, and Tandy and Drew.
Which is my love, and is my love true?
Farrell the Valiant or Farrar the Iron,
Which is my hero, and which one is mine?

"Carter and Goldsmith, now who might they be?
Nothing on AMEX or NYSE.
Phantom investors, they . . ."

"What does *that* mean?" he asked sharply.

"Well, we couldn't find . . ."

"Couldn't *find*?"

"Yes, we . . ."

"We?"

"My accountant. I asked him . . ."

"You *what*?"

"I asked him to run a check on Carter-Goldsmith. So I could use the information in the poem. But there wasn't anything, so I . . ."

"Why'd you do that?"

"For the poem."

"Asked someone to check CGI?"

"Yes, but . . ."

"And he found nothing, huh?"

"It's not listed on any of the ex—"

"That's because it's privately owned. You shouldn't have checked on me."

"I wasn't. I . . ."

"Never mind. Let me hear the rest of the poem."

"No."

"Let me hear it."

"I don't want to now."

"Fine."

"Fine," she said.

She sat stunned by his outburst, trying to understand what had provoked it, suddenly sensitive to her own nakedness, feeling exposed and vulnerable, somehow betrayed, utterly bewildered, and hurt, and close to tears. They were silent for what seemed a very long time. Then, wishing to retaliate, hoping to cause in him the same hurt twisting inside her, she said, "I'm going away this summer."

His scowl changed at once to the familiar hurt and petulant little-boy look. Good, she thought.

"When?" he asked at once.

"I think he said August."

Enjoying his discomfort. He would miss her. His face said he would miss her. But the scowl returned almost at once.

"You think *who* said? Your accountant?"

"My husband. That's when he usually takes his vacation."

"For how long?"

"Three weeks."

"What am *I* supposed to do during that time?"

The petulant look again. His changing emotions immediately flashing on his face.

"You can always call one of your teenagers," she said, and shrugged. Sitting upright. Arms at her sides supporting her, elbows locked.

"*You're* my teenager," he said.

"Oh sure."

"I hate these rich lawyers who can pick up and go at the drop of a hat."

"He's not a rich lawyer."

"No? All of *my* lawyers are rich."

"*All* of them? How many do you have?"

"Three."

"Well, my husband earns eighty-five thousand a year."

Deliberately using the word "husband." Still wanting revenge for the way he'd pounced on her over a silly damn . . .

"Good reason to leave him."

"What makes you think I'd ever do that?"

"Well . . ." he said, and shrugged.

Still sulking. Good, she thought. Lying naked on the bed beside her, looking limp and forlorn and gorgeous and utterly adorable. Casually, with the edge of her right hand, she brushed at an imaginary something on her left breast.

"What if I told you I may be able to get away for a few days?" she asked. Brows slightly raised.

"What do you mean?"

"With you."

Turning to face him.

"You're kidding. When?"

His expression changing again at once. The eyes brightening with expectation.

"It would have to be in July sometime. During the middle of the week sometime. A Tuesday, Wednesday . . ."

"You're *kidding*!"

"I've already asked him."

Lowering her eyes like a nun. Breasts beckoning, eyes averted.

"And he said okay?"

"Well . . . reluctantly."

"But no fuss?"

"A slight fuss."

"If you were married to me . . ."

"But I'm not."

". . . and you told *me* you were going away for a few days . . ."

"I'm not saying he *liked* the idea."

"But he agreed to let you go."

"Yes."

"Don't ever try that with me."

"Oh? No? What would you do?"

"I'd kill him."

"Oh sure."

"I'd find out his name, and I'd kill him."

"Sure."

"Try me. Do you know how much *I* make in a year?"

"I don't care how much you make."

Still annoyed that she'd brought up her husband again. Good. Stay annoyed, she thought.

"I never heard of a lawyer who makes only eighty-five a year," he said.

"He works for the city. That's what they pay."

"Eighty-five a year."

"Yes. Well, actually a bit more."

"How much more?"

"Two hundred and fifty dollars."

"Why would someone go to law school for however many years, pass the bar exam, go to all that trouble, and then settle for a job that pays so little?"

"He doesn't consider it *settling*. He finds it challenging."

"Oh, yes, it must be *very* challenging."

"It is."

"Bringing suit against landlords who don't turn on the *heat* when they're supposed to . . ."

"October fifteenth," she said. "That's the date you have to turn on the heat."

"How do you know that?"

"When we were first married, we had an apartment that was *freeeeeeezing* cold. We called the Ombudsman's Office . . ."

"How'd you know to do that?"

"My husband researched the law, found out the mandatory date for . . ."

"I *hate* it when you talk about him. All the things he *does* or *doesn't* do in his crumby little job that pays . . ."

"Getting the heat turned on had nothing to do with his job."

"Where will you be going?"

"France. St.-Jean-de-Luz."

"Where's that?"

"Near the Spanish border. We went there on our honeymoon."

"Terrific."

"Andrew, this won't be any kind of *romantic* trip. Mollie's going with us."

He was silent for several moments.

Then he said, "I'll miss you."

"I'm not gone yet," she said, and suddenly wanted to take him in her arms again, stroke him, pet him, adore him.

"How's *this* thing doing?" she asked.

"There she goes again," Regan said.

"Leave it on a few more seconds," Lowndes said.

"Looks like it might need a little help," she whispered.

"Looks that way, doesn't it?"

"Mmmmm," she said.

"Gobbling it again," Regan said.

Tomorrow was Mother's Day, and—with the exception of Heather's estranged husband—the family would be gathering to celebrate at the Fitch apartment on Seventieth and Park. Sarah's parents had returned from St. Bart's on the third. Tomorrow would be the ninth. She had spent a lazy Saturday with Michael and Mollie and now, at fifteen minutes before midnight, she was ready to read herself to sleep. But Michael was waiting for her when she came out of the bathroom in her nightgown.

"Something I want to talk to you about," he said. "Come on down the hall."

She followed him down the corridor, past Mollie's room, her daughter already asleep. Silently, they went past the loudly ticking grandfather clock standing against the wall, a gift from Michael's mother, and then into the den at the far end. The room was small, a sofa on one wall, a French lieutenant's bed on another, an audio/video center on the third wall, and windows overlooking Eighty-first Street on the fourth wall. Michael closed the door behind him. The walls in the prewar apartment were thickly plastered, making each room virtually soundproof. She wondered why he was whispering.

"This case I've been on?" he said.

She nodded.

"I think I can tell you a little about it now."

She wondered why he had chosen to tell her at just this moment, close to midnight, when she was exhausted and wanted nothing more than to lose herself in *Vogue* before she drifted off to sleep. Family gatherings at her parents' apartment were never quite stress-free. She'd been looking forward to a good night's sleep in preparation. But no, Michael was telling her how they'd been conducting this surveillance since the beginning of the year . . .

"The son of a Mafia boss the U.S. Attorney put away for good. We're certain he's running the mob now, we've just been waiting to get enough for an OCCA conviction. To do that, we've got to show a pattern of racketeering activity. Problem is we haven't got anything *concrete* as yet. We know he's linked to narcotics and loan-sharking, but we can't prove it from what he or anyone else has said. We also think he may have ordered a hit or two, but again, no proof. The reason I'm telling you all this . . ." Michael said.

Yes, why *are* you telling me all this? she wondered.

". . . is that I think we've found a way to get to him."

"Well, good," she said.

"I got hold of all this stuff on Thursday morning," he said, and went to the tape deck in the cabinet on the wall. She noticed that the power was already on. "Here, listen," he said, and hit the PLAY button.

At first she thought she was living a nightmare.

"October fifteenth," a woman's voice said. "That's the date you have to turn on the heat."

"How do you know that?"

A man's voice.

"When we were first married, we had an apartment that was *freeeeeeezing* cold. We called the Ombudsman's Office . . ."

"How'd you know to do that?"

"My husband researched the law," the woman's voice said. *Her* voice said.

". . . found out the mandatory date for . . ."

"I *hate* it when you talk about him," the man's voice said.

Andrew's voice said.

She thought her heart would stop.

"All the things he *does* or *doesn't* do in his crumby little job that pays . . ."

"Getting the heat turned on had nothing to do with his job."

"Where will you be going?"

"France. St.-Jean-de-Luz."

"Where's that?"

"Near the Spanish border. We went there on our honeymoon."

"Terrific."

"Andrew, this won't be any kind of *romantic* trip. Mollie's going with us."

There was a long silence.

"I'll miss you."

Andrew's voice again.

"I'm not gone yet. How's *this* thing doing?" Her voice changing to a whisper now. "Looks like it might need a little help."

"Looks that way, doesn't it?"

"Mmmmm."

Another long silence.

She did not know where to look. She would not meet Michael's eyes. Was it possible he hadn't recognized the voice on the tape? Was it possible he didn't realize that the woman performing . . . ?

"You ever do this to your husband?"

"Yes, all the time."

"You don't."

"I do. Every night of the week."

"You're lying."

"I'm lying."

"Jesus, what you *do* to me!"

"Whose *cock* is this?"

"Yours."

"*Mine,* yes. And I'm going to suck it till you scream."

"Sarah . . ."

"I want to see you explode! Give it to me!"

"Oh God, Sarah!"

"Yes. Yes. Yes. *Yes!*"

And another long silence.

Michael snapped off the machine.

"We think we know who she is," he said, and moved to the VCR. Again, the power was already on, a cassette was already in place; Michael simply pressed the PLAY button.

From the right-hand side of the screen, Sarah saw herself moving into the frame . . .

He knows, she thought.

. . . crossing hurriedly to the blue door on Mott, her back to the camera . . .

Oh God, he knows.

. . . and then pressing the bell button under the Carter-Goldsmith Investments nameplate, back still to the camera . . .

There was no way that any objective viewer could say for certain that the blonde leaning into the speaker in that shadowed doorway, her face partially hidden, was Sarah Welles. No way that any stranger could possibly identify her as the woman announcing herself beside that blue door. The picture simply wasn't that good.

But as she watched herself reaching for the doorknob the instant the buzzer sounded, watched herself breathlessly letting herself in, she knew that anyone who *knew* her would recognize her in an instant. Michael knew her. Knew the clothes she was wearing, knew the way she moved, the way she walked, knew every nuance. Even with her back to the camera . . .

The door closing behind her now.

The camera lingering on just the door now.

Outside in the hall, the big clock tolled midnight.

"Happy Mother's Day," Michael said bitterly.

4: MAY 10–JUNE 2

Mollie complained that she didn't need a baby-sitter, and besides why were they going *out* on a Monday night? Mollie was twelve years old, and twelve in the city of New York was considered grown-up, at Hanover Prep, anyway. Michael told her there were lots of bad guys out there, and he would feel happier with Mrs. Henderson in attendance. Secretly, Mollie felt Mrs. Henderson would be the first to pick up her skirts and run out the door if a bad guy came climbing through the window. Michael gently told her they wouldn't be long.

"But why are you going out on a *Monday?*" Mollie whined like a twelve-year-old grown-up.

Walking beside him on the street now, people everywhere around them, Sarah felt he might kill her. He had left the apartment immediately after their confrontation on Saturday night; she suspected he had spent the night in his office. His anger now was monumental. He walked as if propelled by an inner fury, his jaw set, his eyes refusing to meet hers, his gaze, his head, his entire body, thrusting into the night like a dagger. In a voice she scarcely knew, cold and distant and barely audible, he said, "This man represents everything I hate. Everything I've devoted my life to destroying, this man rep—"

"Yes, Michael, I know that."

"Don't give me that damn im*patient* . . ."

"I didn't know what he was."

"Would it have made a difference?"

She was silent for several seconds.

Then she said, "I don't know."

He turned to her at once, as if to strike her, his fist clenched, his arm coming up. She stopped dead on the sidewalk, flinching away from him, saw his contorted face and the anger seething in his eyes a moment before he withdrew his hand, trembling. They were on Lexington Avenue, it was a mild night, the sidewalks were crowded; she felt certain he would have hit her otherwise. He began walking again, faster now. She debated running away from him, back to the apartment. She was afraid to do that, afraid he might chase her, grab her, punch her, she didn't know *what* he might do. She no longer knew this man. Her husband. This man.

"I'd *kill* him if it were legal," he said, his voice quivering with the effort to regain control of himself. "I'll settle for putting him in jail, and getting you out of my life forever."

On Saturday night, he'd told her they'd been conducting a surveillance since the beginning of the year . . .

The son of a Mafia boss the U.S. Attorney put away for good. We're certain he's running the mob now, we've just been waiting to get enough for an OCCA conviction.

Andrew. He'd been talking about Andrew. Andrew was the target of his investigation, Andrew was the son of a Mafia boss in prison, Andrew was himself a gangster.

We know he's linked to narcotics and loan-sharking, but we can't prove it from what he or anyone else has said. We also think he may have ordered a hit or two, but again, no proof . . .

She had lain awake all that night, wondering if this was true, knowing it was true, they had tapes. Wanting to call Andrew, wanting to ask him, Is this *true*, can this be *true*? But of course it was true.

"This is the deal," Michael said. "Plain and simple." His voice had suddenly changed. It sounded clipped, cold, detached, professional. "If you get me what I need, Mollie never finds out about you. We divorce, we share custody, we live our separate lives. If you *don't* cooperate . . ."

"I'm not one of your criminals," she said.

"If you *don't* cooperate, I'll play those tapes in divorce court, you'll be declared an unfit mother . . ."

"You wouldn't do that," she said.

". . . you'll be denied custody . . ."

"Listen," she said, "don't . . ."

". . . and you'll never see Mollie a—"

". . . threaten me."

She was suddenly shaking. My daughter? she thought. You're threatening me with the loss of my *daughter*? My *Mollie*, you son of a bitch? What sort of man . . . ?

"This is what I want," he said. "You . . ."

"Don't offer me any *deals*!" she said. "I'm *not* a criminal!"

"Aren't you?" he asked.

And, of course, she was. Moreover, she had made the criminal's unforgivable error. She had been caught. He had her cold.

"I don't care how you do this," he said, "and I wouldn't presume to advise you. That's entirely your business." From the way he said those words, so slowly and carefully, she knew at once that he was somehow covering himself, a skilled lawyer protecting himself against some future allegation that might come his way. "*My* business is putting Faviola in jail," he said. "I want you to get him to talk, that's all." She noticed again that he did not suggest—not even by innuendo—*how* she should get him to talk. It was as if, for the record at least, he was wiping out all knowledge of her infidelity, completely forgetting that she'd already made love to this man, and dismissing the possibility, for the record at least, that in order to elicit *further* information, she might have to make love to him again. Even here in the open air, where no one could possibly overhear them, he was unwilling to mention that sex was in fact the basic element in this transaction, unwilling even to suggest that in order to encourage conversation about criminal matters, Sarah would have to engage in criminal conversation of quite another sort. There had to be a reason for this, and she wondered what it was. "Get him to describe everything in detail," Michael was saying now. "Get him to describe all the *wonderful* things he's involved in."

"I don't know if I can do that," she said.

"Oh, I think you can do it, Sarah." Spitting out her name as if it were something vile on his tongue. "I think you'd *better* do it, Sarah. Unless you want your daughter to learn what kind of woman you are."

"Don't *threaten* me!" she said again, louder this time, and turned to him with her fists clenched, ready to *kill* him if he told her one more time that he would use Mollie to . . .

"Oh?" he said, and raised an eyebrow.

They stood rooted to the sidewalk, both of them silent and staring, people rushing by heedless in this city of strangers, Sarah trembling, Michael looking down at her the way he must have looked at countless criminals in his office, a smug, superior look on his face, knowing he had her, knowing she was trapped. A faint angry smile flickered momentarily on his mouth and in his eyes. Then he turned away and began walking again, secure in the knowledge that she would follow him. Defeated, she fell into step beside him, trying to match his longer strides, struggling to keep up.

He told her exactly the sort of information he wanted her to elicit from her boyfriend. He kept calling Andrew her "boyfriend." Each time he used the word it made whatever she'd shared with him sound shoddy and cheap. Her boyfriend. Was that all it came down to in the end? Was Andrew merely a boyfriend? And was she now to do whatever her husband asked of her in order to keep the cheap and shoddy, sordid and shameful truth from her daughter? She was wondering what sort of man could even make such a threat. For that matter, what sort of man would never *once* suggest that perhaps this marriage might still *work*. Not even to *suggest* it? Not even to say I love you, Sarah, I'll forgive you, help me do this thing and I'll forgive you? No. The opposite instead. Help me do this thing or I'll . . .

It suddenly occurred to her that the detectives had heard everything he'd heard, seen everything he'd seen. Even if she agreed to do what he wanted, the detectives already *knew*; her daughter would still be vulnerable to . . .

"The detectives," she said.

"What about them?"

"They know. They heard the tapes . . ."

"They don't know who you are. There are millions of Sarahs in this city."

"Didn't they see the video?"

"All they saw was an unidentifiable blonde going in. And they already *knew* Faviola's whore was a blonde."

"Please," she said.

"Lovely person you turned out to be," he said. "You must be very proud of yourself."

"State of the art," Bobby Triani was saying. "The phones do everything but vacuum the floor. Thanks," he said to the waitress, and looked her over as she left the table. Top to bottom. Didn't miss a thing she was showing, and she was showing a lot.

It was late Tuesday afternoon, the eleventh of May, a bright sunny day. They were sitting at a sidewalk table outside a little *pasticceria* on Mulberry Street, eating cannoli and drinking cappuccino. Bobby had suggested the place. Andrew suspected he'd been here before. He also suspected he'd returned because of the waitress. He wondered if he should give his underboss a friendly little warning. Keep your eyes off the legs and the tits, Bobby, and keep your hands in your pockets.

"Lenny's kid put the phones in for me," Bobby was saying, his eyes moving to the espresso machine, where the waitress was now filling several small cups. "Lenny Campagnia?"

"Yeah?"

"His kid works for AT&T, he gets a break on the equipment, you know?" Bobby said, and winked. "You want me to send him around the office?"

"What for?" Andrew said.

"Fix your phones," Bobby said, still ogling the waitress.

"There's nothing wrong with my phones," Andrew said.

"Put in new ones," Bobby said, and shrugged. "You'd be surprised, the stuff these phones can do nowadays. He gets a good break on the equipment," Bobby said, and winked again. "Anyway, the office, it's a business expense, am I right? I had him go to La Luna, you know? On Fifty-eighth? He put in new phones every place, the kitchen, the front near the cash register, the table where Sal the Barber sits in back, the office, all over the restaurant. Sal gave him a coupla hundred bucks and this crummy black ring he says came from Rome when there were emperors there. I ought to send him around, Andrew, check out the place, see what he can do for you."

"I like the phones I have now," Andrew said.

Bobby signaled to the waitress. She came to the table at once.

"Can I get another cappuccino here?" he asked, smiling.

"Certainly, sir."

"Andrew? Another cappuccino?"

"I'm fine, thanks."

"Just one, then," the waitress said.

"What's your name, miss?" Bobby asked. "So I don't have to keep yelling, 'Hey, you!' all the time."

"Bunny," she said.

"Bunny. That's a nice name, Bunny. Is that your real name, or did you make it up?"

"Well, my real name's Bernice," she said.

"Bernice," he said, weighing the name gravely. "Is that Jewish, Bunny?"

"No, I'm Italian," she said.

"Cause I always thought Bernice was a Jewish name."

"Well, I don't know," Bunny said. "Both my parents are Italian, and they named me Bernice. So I guess it's Italian, too."

"Bunny, tell me something. How old are you?"

"Twenty-two," she said.

"I woulda said nineteen," Bobby said.

"Oh, well, thank you."

"Tell me, Bunny, do you live down here in Little Italy?"

"No, I live in Brooklyn."

"What's your *last* name, Bunny?"

"Tataglia."

"Really?" Bobby said. "That's a nice name. Bunny Tataglia. Very nice."

"Well," she said, and shrugged.

"Bunny Tataglia in Brooklyn," Bobby said, nodding.

"Mm-huh," she said.

"I'm Bobby Triani," he said, and extended his hand.

"Nice to meet you, Bobby," she said, and took his hand. He was wearing a big diamond pinkie ring. Bunny looked at the ring as they shook hands. "I'd better get that cappuccino," she said at last, and let go of his hand and went swiveling away on her black high heels, in her little black flounced skirt and white scoop-neck peasant blouse.

"Don't call her," Andrew said.

"What?"

"I said, 'Don't call her.' "

"What?" Bobby said. "What?"

"You cheat on my cousin, I'll break your fuckin head," Andrew said. "*Capeesh?*"

"Hey, come on, Andrew."

"Enough said."

"I mean, what kind of person do you . . . ?"

"Enough *said*, Bobby."

Bobby shook his head and tried to look hurt and amazed. When Bunny brought his cappuccino, he didn't even glance at her. She went off looking *really* hurt and amazed.

"So you want me to send him around or not?" Bobby asked. "Lenny's kid. Take a look at your phones."

The pay phone on the tailor shop wall was an antique with a rotary dial. Whether or not Mr. Faviola decided to go along with a new communications system, Sonny Campagnia would suggest that he contact New York Telephone and ask them to replace the unit with new equipment. That's if he was thinking of adding the tailor shop phones to whatever he did upstairs, *if* he decided to do anything.

Mr. Faviola had told him he'd be here at one o'clock to unlock the door and take him upstairs for a look at the system he now had. It was now a quarter past, and he still wasn't here, and the old guy who owned the tailor shop had asked Sonny three times already if he wanted a cup of coffee or anything, but Sonny had seen how filthy the cups looked, and each time he'd said, No, thanks, really.

It was while he was checking out the wall phone that he made his first discovery. What it was, a wire had been dropped from the phone to the baseboard, disappearing into it. Sonny followed the baseboard around the room, trying to figure out where the wire was leading, and saw that it came out of the baseboard alongside a door, where it was tacked up the wall and over the doorjamb molding, and then down the wall again into the baseboard, where it finally surfaced under a long table. The wire ran up from the baseboard into a 42A block that didn't have any phone plugged into it. Sonny was on his hands and knees, wondering about this, when Andrew walked in.

"Sorry I'm late," he said. "I wasn't thinking of putting any new phones in the tailor shop, if that's why you're . . ."

"No, I was just wondering about this wire, that's all," Sonny said, getting up and dusting off the knees of his trousers.

Andrew was already unlocking the door that led upstairs. He had no particular interest in changing all the goddamn phones in the place, except that Lenny Campagnia was a well-respected capo, and letting his kid install a new system would be a favor to him. He just hoped looking over the place wouldn't take too much time. Sarah would be here sometime after four, as usual.

"This won't take too much time, will it?" he asked.

"No, no. I just want to see what you've got, maybe take a look outside, at the terminal box."

"What's that?" Andrew asked.

"Where the lines come in."

"Just so it doesn't take too long. I have to drive up to Connecticut this afternoon."

"No, it shouldn't take too long, Mr. Faviola."

Sonny looked at all the phones on every floor upstairs, commenting that this was really very old equipment, Stone Age stuff, you know, and suggesting that he could install a state-of-the-art system, at very little cost, that would make Andrew's life much simpler. Andrew told him he didn't want his telephone service interrupted while all this was going on—*if* he decided to go ahead with it—because the telephone was very important to him, he did a lot of business on the telephone. Sonny assured him that once he'd designed a system for him, the actual installation would be a very simple thing, and he could promise that at least one phone would be completely functional all the while he was working inside the building and out. He told Andrew he'd like to take a look at the terminal box now, which he guessed would be on the rear wall of the building, or perhaps on a pole outside.

The box was, in fact, on the rear wall of the building. Sonny opened it and began studying the various wires inside

it, and that was when he found the slave Freddie Coulter had
installed there on the last day of January.

The first thing Michael thought was that Sarah had told
him.

Regan was saying that all at once everything went dead.

"We're listening to Faviola talking to some guy about
putting in a new phone system, and the guy says he's going
out back, take a look at the terminal box, and next thing you
know, everything goes dead. I figured you ought to know
about it right away."

The bitch *told* him, Michael thought.

"So what do we do now?" Regan asked. "We turned on
the backup receivers the minute everything quit, but so far
we haven't heard a thing."

"You think they found the backups, too?"

"Who knows? These guys, the minute they find *one* bug,
they go around tiptoeing with their fingers to their mouth."

"I'll talk to Freddie Coulter," Michael said. "He may
have to go in again."

"What do we do meanwhile?" Regan asked. "Pack it in,
or what?"

"Stay with it," Michael said. "The backups may still be
working."

There was activity everywhere around them on Canal
Street, tourists strolling, residents shopping, Chinamen
hawking fish in baskets, souvenir sellers waving lacquered
bowls and paper lanterns to the three men as they came up
the street. Spring was truly here at last, and the air was
virtually balmy. Andrew was walking in the middle. Petey
was on his left, Bobby on his right. Petey was wearing
brown. A brown suit, brown shoes, a maize-colored shirt, a
brown tie. He walked with his hands behind his back, the
thumbs linked. The expression on his face was extremely
grave. Bobby, on the other hand, looked as though someone

had just hit him with a baseball bat. He kept shaking his head in disbelief.

"Which other rooms?" he asked.

"The kitchen, the phone on the counter there," Andrew said. "And the one upstairs in the bedroom. On the night-stand alongside the bed."

"They *all* have bugs in them?"

"Yeah, what Sonny called 'Brady bugs,' I'll show you what they look like when we get back to the office. There was one downstairs under the cutting table, too. In the tailor shop."

"Is the *pay* phone bugged, too?" Bobby asked. "The one in the shop?"

Andrew wondered who he'd been calling from that phone.

"I don't think so. But the bug under the table could pick up anything in the room."

"How long has this shit been in place?" Petey asked.

"Sonny didn't know. This thing he found out back, in the terminal box, is something called a 'slave.' It takes the signal from the bug, does something to it, sends it out again to whoever's listening."

"Who do you think's listening?" Petey said.

"Who the fuck knows?" Andrew said.

"That meeting about Moreno . . ."

"Yeah."

"In the conference room? We were talking some pretty heavy stuff there," Bobby said.

"How about when Rudy died?" Petey said. "When we were discussing the whole damn . . ."

"I know."

"This is very serious."

"I'm tryin'a think what *else* we talked about," Bobby said. "On the phone. In the conference room. You mind if I smoke?" he asked, and without waiting for Andrew's answer, pulled a package of Camels from his breast pocket, tapped a cigarette loose, popped it into his mouth, and flipped open his lighter. Andrew didn't object. They were outdoors, and this was serious business.

"Anyway," he said, "Sonny yanked out the slave and all the bugs, so nothing's operational anymore."

"How'd they get in there, is what I'd like to know."

"You let any people in there could've done this thing?" Bobby asked.

"You crazy?"

"Well, who's been up there, for example?"

He was puffing frantically on the cigarette now, clouds of gray smoke trailing behind them as they walked. A little girl in a pale blue dress, running by with a boy younger than she was, stopped dead in the middle of the sidewalk, pointed her finger at Bobby, and squealed, "You're gonna get cancer!"

"Get lost," Bobby said.

"Cancer, cancer," the little girl chanted, and ran off with the younger boy, who gigglingly picked up the chant, "Cancer, cancer, cancer, cancer . . ."

"Fucking brats," Bobby said.

"What about the bedroom phone?" Petey asked.

"I told you."

"Ever talk business on it?"

"Not that I can think of."

"The kitchen phone?"

"Most of the business is on the phone in the conference room."

"You ever talk business with any of your *girlfriends*?" Bobby asked.

"No."

"You may have said something you didn't realize," Bobby said, and shrugged, and stamped out his cigarette, and immediately lighted another one.

"I didn't tell anyone anything, don't worry about that,"

Andrew said. "I'm more worried about the phone in the fucking *conference* room!"

"Andrew, who *are* these girls?" Petey asked solemnly and gently, sounding very much like a priest in a confession box.

"Why do you want to know?"

"Cause somebody put a hundred fuckin *bugs* in," Bobby said.

"None of these girls put . . ."

"How do you know one of them ain't a cop?" Bobby said, puffing furiously again.

"I know none of them are cops."

"For Christ's sake, none of them are cops," Petey said. "Would Andrew be dating a fuckin *cop*?"

"You sure of that?" Bobby asked.

"Yes, I'm sure," Andrew said.

"Because, Andrew, I mean no disrespect," Bobby said, recognizing he was treading dangerous ground here. "But if the place got bugged once, it can get bugged again. Your father's in *jail* because there was a bug in a place he never thought there could be one."

Andrew listened.

"Tell us who these girls are, we'll ask around," Bobby said. "Quiet, no fuss. We'll just ask around. See who's who and what's what, okay? No disrespect intended."

"None taken," Andrew said. "But I don't want anybody asking around. I'll do my own asking."

"I meant no disrespect," Bobby said.

"I told you none was taken."

"We were talking murder that day," Petey said softly.

"I know that."

"We were talkin about killing that fuckin *spic*!" Bobby said.

"This is very serious," Petey said again.

"He was killed in a foreign country by two foreigners

we never heard of," Andrew said. "We've got nothing to do with it."

"You ordered the hit," Petey said gently.

"I'm not worried about it."

"Well, I'm not a lawyer," Petey said, "but when those cocksuckers get hold of anything we say in private, they have ways of makin a fuckin federal case of it. Literally."

"They put together three felonies," Bobby said, "we're . . ."

"Two and a mis," Petey said.

"We're lookin at twenty-five for openers."

"We don't know what they have," Andrew said. "The bugs could've gone in *yesterday*, for all we know."

"Or they could've been in there forever, for all we know," Petey said.

"They could be makin their case right this fuckin minute," Bobby said.

The men fell silent. They walked in the sunshine on a bright spring day, each separately wishing those bugs had never been installed, each separately wondering what they'd said while someone somewhere out there was listening. They were silent until they reached Broome Street. As they turned the corner, Bobby said, "You think they flipped that fuckin Benny, used to press clothes? Or that new kid, whatever his name is?"

"Mario," Petey said.

"I don't think they flipped any pants pressers," Andrew said.

"Then how'd they get in there to do all that?" Bobby said.

"Bugs all over the place," Petey said. "How'd they get in?"

"You didn't give a *key* to any of these broads, did you?" Bobby asked.

"No," Andrew said.

"Cause they had to've got in some way."

"They have ways of gettin in," Petey said. "They're bigger thieves than *thieves*."

"Be easier with a key, though."

"I didn't give anyone a key."

"Be funny one of them was a cop, wouldn't it?" Bobby said.

"Yeah, very," Petey said drily.

"Throw her down a fuckin sewer," Bobby said, and looked across the street. "Anybody want a hot dog?" he asked.

On Wednesday morning, Michael advised her to keep her usual Wednesday afternoon tryst with Faviola. If it was true that she hadn't told him about the existence of the backup listening devices . . .

"It's true," she said.

"I hope so. Otherwise . . ."

"Don't threaten me again," she warned.

"I own you," Michael said.

She was here now. Owned. Apprehensive at first. Frightened. Expectant. Certain she would be repelled by this man she now knew was a gangster. But lying here in his arms, he did not seem to be a gangster. He seemed only to be Andrew. And she wondered again what kind of woman she was.

Unless you want your daughter to learn what kind of woman you are.

Michael's words.

What kind of woman?

I'm not cut out for this role, she thought.

I wasn't meant to be an informer, the garment doesn't quite fit me. Lying here in his arms, I want to shout my treachery aloud. What will I do if he ever starts telling me he's *murdered* someone? Or *ordered* someone's murder, like father, like son, I've had a dozen men killed, didn't you know, Sarah? Will I scream No, don't tell me, it's a trap, I'm a trap, don't say anything, don't trust me, don't love me, I'm an informer! Will I try to save him from himself and from me?

"What's wrong?" he asked.

"I'm afraid people are still listening to us," she said. She was whispering.

"Nobody's listening," he said. "Not anymore. I told you. We ripped everything out."

Both of them whispering now.

Get him to talk, she thought. Get him to talk or lose my daughter.

"But who would *do* such a thing?" she said. "If a person's not involved in criminal activity . . ."

"I'm not."

"Well, of course, you're not. So why would anyone want to put a bug in here?"

Get him to talk.

"A lot of business is conducted in this building," he said, "on the phones in this building. We have competitors. I wouldn't be surprised if any one of them was ruthless enough to do something like this."

"Then this is just a business thing, is that right?"

"Strictly business, yes."

"It has nothing to do with . . . well, when you think of bugs, you think of police. Or spies."

"Business spies, yes."

"But not the police."

"No," he said, "not the police," and looked at her intently for a moment. "My associates are very concerned about this," he said. "About how anyone could have got in here to bug the place."

"Your associates," she said.

"Yes."

"Carter and Goldsmith?"

"Well, the people I work with. They think someone must have got hold of a key somehow. Someone I know *personally*. Got hold of a key and turned it over to whoever got in here to bug the place. That's what my associates think."

She realized all at once that he was accusing her. *She* was the personal someone who'd somehow stolen a key and delivered it to her husband's detectives so they could later listen to her making love to him. The irony was so delicious, she almost burst out laughing. He was watching her intently again, waiting for some kind of answer. Well, she thought, how would Sarah Welles, the innocent schoolteacher, respond to such a bizarre notion? Never mind the Sarah who's here as a spy. How would *I* myself react if the man I love accused me of working with his competitors?

She swung her legs over the side of the bed and began walking to where her clothes were draped over the back of the easy chair. She was reaching for her panties when he said, "What are you doing?"

"Getting dressed."

"Why?"

"Because I don't like being told . . ."

"I'm trying to *protect* you!"

"Oh?" she said, and yanked up her panties and let the elastic go with an angry *thwack*. "And here I thought you were suggesting that I unlocked the door for whoever came in here to bug your phones," she said, and reached for her bra.

"I'm only repeating what was said to me."

"By whom?"

"One of my business associates."

"Who?"

"Never mind who. He suggested . . ."

"What? That I stole a key?"

"That *somebody* might have, not necessarily . . ."

"Anyway, how do they know about me, these people?" she asked, reaching behind her to clasp the bra. "Did you *tell* them about me?"

"They know I have girlfriends."

"Oh? Is it still plural? Still more than . . . ?"

"They know I used to see a lot of girls. All they suggested was that *one* of them . . ."

"Not me, pal."

". . . might have . . ."

"Try one of your . . ."

". . . got hold of . . ."

". . . teenagers!"

". . . my *keys*, which you have to admit is a . . ."

"No, it's *not* a possibility! Not as it concerns me," she said angrily, and stepped into her skirt, and pulled it to her waist and was fastening it when he came to her and took her by the shoulders.

"Get away from me!" she said.

"I don't want anybody hurting you."

"You're hurting me right this minute!"

"I'm sorry, but you have to hear what I'm saying."

"Let go of me."

"Only if you promise to listen."

"Just *let* . . ."

"All right, all *right*," he said sharply, and released her. She reached immediately for her blouse.

"Listen to me," he said.

"I'm listening," she said.

But she was putting on the blouse.

"They suggested two things. One . . ."

"They? I thought this was only *one* of your associates. Is it more than one? Do they *all* think I stole your keys and . . . ?"

"It's just this one person."

"Who?"

"It doesn't matter who."

"I'd like to know who my accuser is, if you don't mind. You owe me at least . . ."

"Bobby, all right? His name is Bobby."

"Bobby what?"

"Just Bobby, okay? He said maybe somebody I know is working for one of our competitors."

"You tell Bobby I'm not working with any of your competitors. Is that what you think, too, Andrew? That I'm some kind of company *spy*?"

"I don't know what to think."

"Well, you tell Bobby he doesn't have to worry about me anymore. Because the minute I walk out that door, you won't be seeing me again."

He looked at her for a long moment.

"You do that," he said, "and Bobby'll know he was right."

She was slinging her shoulder bag. She turned to him, clearly puzzled, her eyes squinted, her brow furrowed.

"We find the bugs," he said, "and next thing you know, you're walking out on me. Bobby'll say that sounds very suspicious."

"Really?" she said, and walked to him, and stood very close to him. "Then maybe you ought to tell Bobby just *why* I'm walking out," she said, "whoever Bobby may be. The *first* thing you can tell him, in fact, is that you don't trust me enough to tell me his last name, if he *has* a last name. And you can . . ."

"Triani," he said, "all right? Bobby Triani."

"Thanks," she said, "but you're a little late. You can tell him next," she said, "that you don't trust me enough to believe I come here every damn Wednesday because I love you and want to be with you and not because I'm hanging bugs all over the place. You can tell him, too," she said, "that I'm walking out because I didn't hear what I wanted to hear from you, I didn't hear a single word of apology for getting me *involved* in your damn corporate maneuverings. I didn't once hear you say, 'Gee, I'm sorry that strangers were listening to everything you said to me, all those things you said to me, complete strangers hearing all those things. I'm sorry you landed in the middle of all this, whatever it is, I'm really *sorry* about that, because I love you to death and I wouldn't want you hurt for anything in the world.' You can tell Bobby Triani *that's* why I'm walking out," she said. "Because you never once told me you're sorry you got me *into* this whole damn *mess*!"

She realized all at once that she was not acting. This was not the Sarah Welles who was "owned" by the district attorney. This was the Sarah Welles who'd lost her heart to a gangster, a mobster, a hoodlum, a bum. And she was talking about something quite other than business spying. She stood motionless, looking at him, tears streaming down her face.

"I know you had nothing to do with this," he said, and took her in his arms.

"Serve you right if I did," she said, sobbing.

From where Regan and Lowndes sat listening in the room on Grand Street, they heard only her muffled sobs now, and figured she was weeping into his shoulder. But they had heard and recorded all of the earlier conversation as well, because whoever had yanked out the Bradys and the slave had missed at least the one-watt transmitter Freddie Coulter had installed as a wall receptacle last February.

Heather looked as if she were already flying. Her new haircut was swept back and away from her face to give an appearance of windblown flight. In exactly forty minutes, she would be boarding the plane to the Dominican Republic, where she would get her overnight divorce before flying back to New York the day after tomorrow. She was in constant motion already, though, tapping her fingers on the tabletop, jiggling her foot, spasmodically sipping at the gin-tonic she'd ordered.

"I wish you were coming with me," she told Sarah.

The sisters sat in a small lounge near the security gate. There weren't many people flying to the Caribbean this time of year. Most of the passengers moving through the X-ray machines looked like natives going home.

"I keep asking myself why *I'm* the one doing this," Heather said. "Why isn't *Doug* going down for the divorce? He's the one who wants to marry Miss Felicity Twit in such a hurry, isn't he? He's the one yearning to be so goddamn *free* of me. But on the other hand, there's something fitting about my being the one who does the actual *thing*, who gets the actual papers signed and sealed down there. *I'm* the aggrieved party, do you see, Sarah?"

"Yes," Sarah said, and wondered if she should tell her sister about Andrew and the awful situ—

"I don't want people thinking *Doug's* the one leaving *me* because of something *I* did," Heather said. "*He's* the son of a bitch who broke the contract, the covenant, whatever. He's the one who fouled the marriage bed, Sarah, not me. If *he* went down to Santo Domingo, people would think I'm so reluctant to *give* him the damn divorce, he's got to run down there *himself* to get it. Am I making any sense to you?"

"Yes, I understand completely," Sarah said.

Everywhere around them urgent messages erupted from hidden speakers, announcing arrivals and delays, boardings and departures. Sarah wondered if on a Sunday like this one, she would soon be sitting in this lounge again, sipping drinks with her sister, who'd be seeing *her* off instead. Or would Michael, as the injured party, be the one to fly south for the divorce?

The injured party.

She wondered who, after all was said and done, would truly be the injured party.

She could think of no one but Mollie.

". . . laughing at me," Heather was saying. "That's the one thing I couldn't stand. She's so *young*, you know, that's the thing of it. I wouldn't have minded so much if he'd chosen someone closer to his own age. But nineteen? Jesus!

Well, she's twenty now," Heather said, and sighed deeply. "Twenty to my thirty-two, where's the competition? Closing fast on thirty-three, in fact. You don't know how lucky you are, Sarah."

"Heather," she said, and paused, and then said, "There's something I ought to tell you."

Heather looked at her over the rim of her glass.

"Michael and I . . ."

"No, please don't," Heather said. "That's all I need right now. Please, Sarah, no."

"All right," Sarah said, and picked up her own drink, and looked away because she was afraid she might burst into tears. Heather kept staring at her across the small round table.

"What is it?" she asked at last.

"I don't want to burden you."

"You've already burdened me. What is it?"

"Trouble."

"What kind of trouble? Tell me."

Sarah told her.

Heather listened intently, one eye on the clock. The airline announcements riddled Sarah's recitation, making it difficult for her to complete a single sentence without being interrupted by what sounded like bulletins from the front. Heather finished her drink. She did not ask for another one. She listened wide-eyed to what Sarah was saying, her face expressionless, only the eyes revealing a mixture of horror and disbelief. A final-boarding announcement exploded like a mortar shell, but Sarah was finished now. She sat looking down at the wedding band on her left hand.

"When did this start?" Heather asked.

"St. Bart's."

"Not the handsome kid under the angel's-trumpet?"

Sarah nodded.

"What do you plan to do?"

"I don't know yet."

"Does Michael suspect?"

She had left a few salient points out of her story. She had neglected to mention, for example, that Andrew Faviola was a criminal and that Michael hoped to put him behind bars. She had also left out the part about the eavesdropping warrant. She had not told her sister that every word she and Andrew uttered in that third-floor bedroom was recorded by detectives. Telling her sister she was having an affair had been bombshell enough. Heather still looked as though she'd walked into a wall.

"I don't think he knows," Sarah said. "Yet."

"Do you plan to tell him?"

"I don't know."

"Sarah, this kid's asked you to *marry* him! You've got to decide one way or . . ."

"He's not a kid. He's twenty-eight."

"Just a bit older than Felicity Twit," Heather said, and grimaced. "Do you *love* him?"

Sarah hesitated for what seemed a very long time.

Then she said, "Yes."

The loudspeaker erupted again, announcing the boarding of American's flight five eighty-eight to Santo Domingo. Heather picked up her carry-on.

"I'll get this," Sarah said, and took the check from the table.

"You know where I'm staying," Heather said, and leaned over to kiss her on the cheek. "If you want to talk, call me."

"Okay, honey. Be careful."

"Wish me luck," Heather said, and gently touched Sarah's face, and slung the carry-on over her shoulder, and went swiftly toward the security gate.

Sarah watched as she put her bag onto the moving belt and then stepped through the detector frame. She remembered suddenly a playhouse she and her sister had built of branches and twigs when they were respectively eight and six years old.

"It has no door, Sarah," Heather had complained.

Her sister stepped through the doorless frame now, moving toward her bag on the other end of the belt, slinging the bag again, and then stepping out briskly into her future.

Sarah watched her until she was out of sight down the long corridor.

A river ran through the property upon which Anthony Faviola had built his sprawling Connecticut estate. There were trout in the river, but Tessie Faviola would not allow anyone to fish for them. That was because she personally fed the fish every day, and she felt it would be unfair to first throw bread in the water for them and then bait a hook and take advantage of their tameness. Tessie also felt it was unfair that her birthday always followed so closely after Mother's Day. It meant that unless they were reminded, some people might forget a gift on one or the other of the two reasons to celebrate her existence. Petey Bardo's personal opinion, Tessie was a tyrant. *All* fuckin mothers were tyrants, you wanted to know, his own included.

It was still chilly on this third Sunday in May, so Petey was wearing a brown woolen sweater over his brown swimming trunks. Bobby Triani, sitting beside him on the dock, dangling his feet in the very cold water, was wearing a snug blue swimsuit and a white mesh shirt, his muscles bulging. Bobby was smoking. Petey had quit smoking three years ago, when he'd suffered a mild heart attack. He still believed the reason he'd been passed over for underboss was the fuckin heart attack. Rudy drops dead of a heart attack, they're gonna fill his shoes with somebody *else* has heart trouble? No way. Instead, they gave it to Bobby here, who didn't know his ass from his elbow about the business, except where it came to stolen property.

Petey found it difficult to be near people who smoked, but he said nothing about it now because there were more important things to discuss with the fuckin underboss. The women were all up at the house, cooking, running after the kids. Andrew was up there, too, bullshitting more with his cousin than with his own two sisters, as usual. Ike and Mike, they look alike. Petey sat shivering in bathing trunks and a woolen sweater, and thinking the only good thing about a fuckin brook, you knew it wasn't bugged.

"I think it's dangerous the way Andrew's treating this so lightly," he said. "It's one thing he found the bugs and yanked them out. It's another how it could've happened."

Bobby nodded.

"I don't mean any disrespect to him . . ."

"Yeah, yeah," Bobby said, and waved this aside with the hand holding the cigarette.

"But I really think we *should* find out who these broads are he's boffin. What I'm worried about," he said, glancing at the fish darting below, "is that they got in there once, they can get in again. We got heavy stuff comin down the pike *very* soon, Bobby. Even if we change where we meet, if one of Andrew's girls is workin for them, those cocksuckers'll follow us wherever we go."

"Yeah," Bobby said.

"They got somebody in there boffin Andrew, they can put bugs in wherever we go, hear everything we're saying."

"They ain't allowed to do that, are they?" Bobby asked.

"Do what?"

"Let a cop sleep with somebody? I'll bet there's a rule about that. About an undercover sleepin with somebody. It's the same as a vice cop takes off his clothes in front of a hooker, the bust goes out the window."

"Who says it has to be a cop?"

"I thought you said an undercover."

"No, I said who*ever* he's boffin. It could be somebody they flipped," Petey said. "A hooker, a junkie, somebody they got the whole nine yards on, she'll go down on the Pope, they ask her to."

"Yeah, that's possible."

"She's in there workin for them, they'll be under our skin forever," Petey said.

"You know," Bobby said, "I *told* him we should ask around . . ."

"I know you did."

"Find out what's what."

"I know."

"He said forget it, he'd do his own askin."

"I know."

"He's the fuckin boss," Bobby said, and shrugged.

The men sat in silence on the riverbank. Trout splashed in the water. From far above them, the children's voices came rolling down the sloping lawn. Petey dipped one foot in the water. It was freezing cold. This wasn't even the end of May; summer was a long way off.

"The other hand," he said, "sometimes you gotta do things are for the boss's own good."

The garage where Billy Lametta kept the company car was on Delancey Street, over near the East River. Bobby found him there the very next day, in his shirtsleeves, the sleeves rolled up, polishing the Lincoln, a cigarette dangling from his mouth as he worked. Bobby admired people who still had the courage to smoke.

"Hey, Billy," he said, lighting up a cigarette himself. "How's it goin?"

"Okay, Mr. Triani," Billy said. "How was your weekend?"

"Very nice," Bobby said. "We went to the country."

"Great day for the country."

"Beautiful," Bobby said.

"So what brings you down here?"

"Few things I wanted to talk to you about," Bobby said.

The polishing cloth hesitated for just an instant. Billy was wondering what he'd done wrong to rate a visit from the underboss.

"Always glad to see you," he said, and resumed running the cloth over the shiny black metal of the Lincoln. But he had begun sweating.

"First," Bobby said, "I know this ain't Christmas, but you been doin a good job, and there's nothin wrong with a little bonus in May, is there?"

He reached into his jacket pocket and took from it a fat roll of bills fastened with a rubber band. The outside bill was a C-note. Billy could see that at once.

"Gee, hey, that's nice of you, Mr. Triani," he said, "but Mr. Faviola takes good care of me, you don't have to worry."

"Get yourself a new suit, whatever," Bobby said, and nudged him with the roll of bills.

"No, really, I wouldn't want Mr. Faviola to think . . ."

"I'll tell him about it, don't worry. Here," he said. "Take it. It's two thousand bucks."

Billy's eyes widened.

"Take it," Bobby said.

Billy hesitated.

"Go on, take it," Bobby said, and tucked it into Billy's shirt pocket.

"Well . . . thanks, Mr. Triani, I appreciate it."

"Hey," Bobby said, and grinned expansively.

Billy was wondering what he wanted from him. He kept polishing the car. The garage was a place where a lot of so-called black cars were kept. These were either Caddies or Lincoln Continentals like the one Billy was polishing, but they were mostly owned by limo companies instead of privately. The difference between the black cars and the stretch limos was that the limos cost thirty-five an hour to hire whereas the smaller cars cost only twenty-eight. Billy was salaried, more or less; he received a legitimate check from Carter-Goldsmith Investments every two weeks. In addition, Faviola slipped him a coupla hundred bucks whenever the mood struck him. Triani had just stuffed a month's salary into his shirt pocket.

"Been using the car much?" Bobby asked.

So that was it. Triani thought Billy had been using the company car for his own pleasure. But then why had he slipped him the two K?

"Yeah, well, you know," he said, "Mr. Faviola's a busy man."

"What I want to ask you, Billy . . ."

Here it comes, Billy thought.

"You been driving many girls in the car?"

"Hey, no, Mr. Triani," Billy said at once, "I never use the car on my own. This is a company car, I wouldn't dream of . . ."

"For Mr. Faviola, I mean," Bobby said, and winked.

Billy looked at him.

"You drive girls for him?" Bobby asked, and winked again.

"Well, yeah, every now and then. Not too many nowadays, though. Nowadays, he's got like a steady."

"You know the names of these girls?"

"Well . . . yeah. I guess."

Billy still didn't know where this was going. Was Triani asking to be fixed up with one of these girls? Was *that* what the two thou was for? Billy waited.

"You know their addresses, too?" Bobby asked.

"Yeah, I wrote them in my book. Cause they were regulars I used to pick up and drop off all the time. Nowadays, though, like I said, there's only the . . ."

"I want all their names and addresses," Bobby said.

"I don't know all their home addresses."

"The ones you know."

"Cause some of them, I only picked up after work."

"Give me the ones you know."

"The work addresses, too?"

"Yes."

"Well . . . I better get a piece of paper from the office."

Billy dropped the polishing cloth on the hood of the car

and walked to a corner of the garage where there was a small, glassed-in office. The driver of a long white stretch that looked like a wedding limo tooted his horn and came rolling in. Bobby watched a short Spanish guy in a chauffeur's uniform get out of the stretch and saunter toward the men's room. When Billy came back, he was carrying a pencil and a lined yellow pad.

"Okay, let's see now," he said, and went to where his jacket was draped over a railing and took a black notebook from it. Thumbing through the book, he casually asked, "Why do you need this, Mr. Triani?"

Bobby looked at him.

Billy simply turned away, avoiding Triani's gaze, leaned over the hood of the car, and kept leafing through the pages. "There's this redhead he used to see all the time," he said. "On my block, she's the winner." He was still thinking Triani was looking to lay one of these girls. "She lives in Brooklyn, but she works here in the city, in the Time-Life Building," he said, and wrote the name *Oona Halligan* and then both addresses. "There's also this girl in Great Neck," he said, "her name is Angela Cannieri, she's got black hair and tits out to here," and wrote down a single address for her. Bobby watched as he copied more names and addresses onto the yellow pad, Maggie Dooley and Alice Reardon, both living and working in Manhattan, Mary Jane O'Brien and Blanca Rodriguez, with home addresses in the Bronx and work addresses in Manhattan, and "the only one he's been seeing lately," Billy said, and wrote the name *Mrs. Welles* on the pad, and then her address on Eighty-first Street.

"What's her first name?" Bobby asked.

"I don't know. That's all he gave me."

"Mrs. Welles."

"Yeah."

"Where does she work?"

"I don't know. I usually pick her up somewhere around Fifty-seventh, Fifty-ninth, the neighborhood there."

"You think she works someplace around there?"

"I'll tell you the truth, I don't know. I never pick her up at the Eighty-first Street address no more, that was only the first time. I usually drop her off someplace in the neighborhood there. I pick her up midtown, drop her off uptown. She's married, is what I guess it is."

"Mm," Bobby said. "Who's this Angela Cannieri in Great Neck? Tony Cannieri's daughter?"

"I don't ask those kind of questions," Billy said.

"I'll bet it's Tony's daughter," Bobby said. "He's fuckin a spic, too, huh? Rodriguez. That's a spic, ain't it?"

"Well, I told you, Mr. Triani, all I do is pick 'em up and drop 'em off. I don't ask questions whose daughters they are or whether they're spics or Chinese."

"One of them is *Chinese*?" Bobby asked, surprised, scanning the list of names again.

"No, no, I'm just saying."

"You got phone numbers, too?" Bobby asked. "For these girls?"

There it is, Billy thought. Just what I figured.

"No, sir," he said, "I don't. But maybe Mr. Faviola can help you there."

Bobby looked at him again.

"I don't want Mr. Faviola to know you gave me these names, capeesh?" he said. He reached into his pocket and took out another roll of banded bills, smaller this time. "It might piss him off at you, he found out," Bobby said, and tucked the roll into the shirt pocket with the other one. "You want to drive me home now?" he asked, and grinned like a shark.

Up here on the roof, Luretta could see the George Washington Bridge spanning the river, see the lights on the Jersey cliffs, see clouds scudding by on a stiff breeze. She sometimes thought the roof up here was the safest place in all Washington Heights. Wasn't safe in the streets, wasn't safe in the apartment, wasn't safe anywhere but here on the roof. Night like tonight, quiet night like tonight, she could stand here near the parapet and look out over the river if she liked, or else move to the other side of the roof and look down at the lights of the cars moving by on the streets below. Up here she was queen of her own kingdom and she could do whatever she felt like doing.

You went to the movies, you saw men in tuxedos and women in long shimmering gowns, they'd be standing on a terrace someplace in midtown Manhattan, looking out at all the glittering lights of the city, sipping martinis in long-stemmed glasses. Here on the roof, Luretta sipped Diet Pepsi from a can, and looked out at the lights on the Jersey side, but she knew that someplace in New York there really *were* people like the ones in the movies, most of them white. Only time she'd ever seen *black* people in tuxedos and gowns was when her cousin Albert got married. Luretta had worn a pretty dress her mother'd made for her, this was before she'd started taking up with the Hundred Neediest, dragging in any junkie who'd share her bed and call her darling.

She knew her mother was doing crack.

Suspected it a month ago, learned it for sure this past Tuesday, when she found an empty vial in the bathroom. Knew it wasn't Dusty's because Dusty was on heroin, Dusty wouldn't bother himself with something cost only seventy-five cents a rock, oh no, Dusty was a *big* man hooked on the *big* stuff. So here was her mother with a baby five months gone inside her, sleeping with a junkie and smoking crack that'd hook the baby, too, sure as shit. So what was Luretta supposed to do?

Up here on the roof, she had no worries.

Up here, she could feel the cool breeze touching her cheek.

Could look out over her kingdom.

Smile a little.

Little enough to smile about, these days.

A tugboat was moving up the river. Chugging along, moving under the bridge, lights strung like diamonds in the sky.

The door to the roof opened.

"Thought you might be up here!"

His voice came like a cannon shot, exploding on the stillness of the night, spilling diamonds from the sky. Startled, she dropped the can of soda. It fell to the roof at her feet, rolled away trailing syrup. She started to move from the parapet, attempting a flanking maneuver, trying to pass him and get to the metal door behind him. But he recognized what she was trying to do, and moved diagonally to intercept her, so that she was still standing with her back to the roof's edge, the low parapet behind her.

"You mama wants you," he said.

"What for?"

"Needs you t'pick up suppin f'her."

Stepping closer to her. Forcing her to move a few steps back again, closer to the parapet at the roof's edge.

"Pick up what?"

Her heart pounding.

"Suppin she needs."

A step closer to her.

She could smell alcohol on his breath.

"What you got under that dress, girl?" he said.

"Get out of my way," she said.

"Sweet li'l tiddies under that dress?" he said, and reached for her.

She shoved out at him instinctively, wanting only to push him out of her way, wanting only to get past him to the stairs. In her dream world, in her twinkling magic kingdom up here on the roof, he reacted by sidestepping at once—which he did—doing a sort of twisted little dance step that took him out of her way, but sent him spiraling toward the edge of the roof instead. In her dream world, here in her glittering magic realm where men in tuxedos sipped martinis with women in long shimmering gowns, he lost his balance, flailed at the air, looked startled, and then went over. One moment he was there, silhouetted against the lights of the bridge and the Jersey shore, and the next he was gone.

In her dream world, he didn't make a sound as he fell.

No long trailing scream like in the movies.

Nothing.

It was as if he'd magically disappeared.

But that was in her dream world.

In real life, he recovered his balance at once and came at her snarling, ripping the front of her dress before she could break away, clawing at her breasts like a wild animal. She hit him with her clenched fists, and screamed, and tore free of his grasp at last, and went running down to the street, without stopping at the apartment to see what her mother needed, because she suspected that what she needed was crack.

In the street, walking on this balmy springtime night humming with voices, covering her torn dress with her spread hands, she began sobbing gently.

Detective/First Grade Randolph J. Rollins liked dealing with these people. He didn't consider it *working* for these people, he considered it *dealing* with them. He knew cops in his precinct who were looking the other way when it came to serious crimes like dope. Rollins had never in his life taken a nickel for squaring a dope rap. These people he dealt with knew better than ever to ask him to square any kind of criminal offense, even a parking ticket. But when they came to him with something like this, find out if any of these broads are police informants, Rollins was happy to flash the tin in pursuit of the gold, which in this instance was exactly six thousand dollars.

Rollins knew it was next to impossible to flip anyone who wasn't in deep shit to begin with. No one was going to become an informer unless you had something on him that could send him to jail for a long, long time. Better to sleep with the enemy than to sleep behind bars, no? So he ran a computer check to see if any of the women on the list had ever run into the law in any serious way. The only person with a felony arrest, and a subsequent suspended sentence, was a person named Oona Halligan, who turned out to be an absolutely gorgeous twentysomething redhead. He fell into step beside her as she came out of the Time-Life Building at ten minutes past five P.M. on the eighteenth of May, and showed his shield and said, "Good evening, I'm Detective Rollins, I wonder if I can ask you a few questions."

The girl looked at him in surprise and then said, "How do you know who I am?"

Rollins explained that the super at her building in Brooklyn had pointed her out to him this morning, but he hadn't wanted to approach her just then because he knew she was on her way to work, and he thought this might be a more convenient time. She still looked a bit puzzled, probably wondering how he'd learned where she worked, the super didn't know that, but he jumped in before she could question him further, and told her they were investigating a burglary in the building next door to hers, and he wanted to know if she'd seen anything or heard anything suspicious on the night of May fourteenth, this past Friday night, which she hadn't, but which was all part of the bullshit. He then got down to brass tacks.

"Miss Halligan," he said, "please forgive me for asking all these questions, but I have to fill out a report—in triplicate, no less," he said, and rolled his eyes, "and I do need the answers."

Oona had a cocktail date all the way downtown with a multimillionaire stockbroker, to hear him tell it, and she didn't want to waste any more time here with a fat-assed detective investigating a dumb burglary in the building next door, of which there were probably hundreds in her neighborhood.

She said, "Well, if you make it fast, because I have a date."

Which didn't surprise him, her looks.

"Miss Halligan," he said, "can you tell me what sort of work you do?"

"I'm a receptionist with a firm called Blue Banana Cosmetics."

"Really?" he said.

The name of the company amused him. Blue Banana Cosmetics.

"Yes," she said, and looked at her watch.

"How long have you been working here?" he asked.

"Since March," she said.

"And before that?"

"I worked for an accounting firm."

"Named?"

"Haskins, Heller and Fein."

"Where?"

"Here in the city."

"How long did you work for them?"

"Six months. I got fired because I told the boss his way of doing something was stupid. Or dumb, I guess I actually said," she said, and looked at her watch again.

"Ever been arrested?" he asked.

"Never."

"Sure? I can check."

"Hey, what is this?" she said.

"Routine investigation," he said. "Not even a minor violation? Speeding? Parking in a no-parking . . ."

"I've had traffic tickets, yes."

"Any DUI violations?"

"No. What?"

"Driving under the . . ."

"Oh. No. Never."

"Nothing serious, then?"

"Nothing."

"I can check," he said again.

"Okay," she said, and sighed heavily. "I was arrested when I was sixteen for possession of an ounce of a controlled substance. Marijuana. I got off with an ACD because it was a first offense and I was only sixteen and it was only an ounce. Okay?"

"Ever work for the police?" he asked.

"No. What?"

"Any strings attached to that ACD?"

An ACD was an Adjournment in Contemplation of Dismissal. Rollins knew there'd have been no strings attached to it. This was a bullshit violation they were discussing.

"I don't know what you're suggesting," Oona said. "I told you. This was just a lousy ounce of . . ."

"Were any deals offered?"

He knew no deals would have been offered.

"Of *course* not! For an ounce of marijuana?"

"Ever go in anywhere wearing a wire?"

"What?"

"Miss Halligan, I'm a police officer. If you were ever an informant for the department, the information is safe with me."

"What?" she said.

"Were you? An informant? Ever?"

"I thought this was about a burglary next . . ."

"It is," he said. "But we have reason to believe a member of the force may be involved," he said, lying. "I'm telling you this in strictest confidence."

Oona blinked.

Gorgeous green eyes wide open now.

"I knew about the adjournment," Rollins said, lying.

She kept staring at him.

"You've never done any work for the police, is that right?"

"Never."

"Wouldn't know any bent cops, would you?"

"I don't know any cops at *all*. I don't even remember the names of the ones who *arrested* me."

"In that case, thank you, Miss Halligan, sorry to have bothered you."

"Not at all," she said, and looked at him, still baffled, and then looked at her watch again, and hurried off toward the subway kiosk on the corner.

He figured she was clean.

Rollins didn't get to the end of his list until that Friday, the twenty-first of May. He showed his shield to the doorman of the building on Eighty-first Street, asked him what his name was . . .

"Luis," the doorman said.

. . . and then told him that everything they said in the next few minutes was to be held in strictest confidence, did he understand that? This was an ongoing police investigation, and he was not to reveal this visit to anyone, was that clear?

Luis almost wet his pants.

His sister was an illegal alien from the Philippines.

He nodded and assured Rollins that he would not tell a soul the police had been here.

Rollins went inside and looked at the mailboxes, jotting down several names at random. He came back out again and started asking questions about the various nameplates in the boxes, really wanting to know only about the nameplate for 12C, which read M. WELLES. He tossed in a few red herrings to keep Luis off base, and then he said, "How about Welles? Know who's in apartment 12C?"

"Oh, yes," Luis said. "Mr. and Mrs. Welles and their daughter."

"What's her first name?"

"Mollie," Luis said.

"Mrs. Mollie Welles?"

"No, no, tha's dee *daughter*," Luis said.

"What's the mother's first name," Rollins asked, closing in for the kill.

"I don' know," Luis said.

"How about the husband? Know his name?"

"Michael," Luis said. "Michael Welles."

And clear out of the blue, he added, "He worrs for the DA's Office."

"What it is," Rollins was explaining to them, "he's the deputy chief DA in the Organized Crime Unit."

In the rearview mirror, Petey exchanged glances with Bobby.

The three men were driving through Queens in Petey's car, which he knew was not bugged because he had it checked by a mechanic every Friday. He'd had it checked yesterday, and he knew it was clean. He almost wished it *was* bugged, this kind of information. Andrew Faviola fucking a DA's wife, this was information he'd *love* them to hear downtown. Rollins was sitting on the front seat beside him. Bobby Triani was in back. The car was a new Cadillac Seville with dual air bags and a telephone. It was a gift from a person for whom Petey had done a favor, like having somebody break his wife's boyfriend's legs. Rollins had one arm draped over the back of the seat. He kept turning his attention from Bobby to Petey and back again.

"I checked the minute this spic doorman told me where he worked. Turns out he investigated and tried a very big case five years ago, put away the whole Lombardi Crew, six of them altogether. They're still doing OCCA time."

"*What's* his name again?" Bobby asked.

"Welles. Michael Welles."

"Michael Welles," Petey said.

"Yeah."

"The Lombardi Crew."

"Yeah."

"So it's possible," Bobby said.

Rollins knew better than to ask what was possible.

"That she could be the one," Petey supplied.

Rollins still said nothing.

"You're sure she's this guy's wife, huh?" Bobby said. "The one done the Lombardi Crew?"

"Positive."

"What's her name?"

"I still don't have it."

Bobby sighed.

Petey sighed, too, and nodded to Bobby in the rearview mirror.

Bobby began peeling off hundred-dollar bills.

"Thanks, Randy," he said, "you done a good job."

Rollins liked dealing with these people.

They gave good weight for the pound, and they always paid cash on the barrelhead.

"I hear you're serious about some girl," Ida said.

She looked a lot like her father, with Rudy's strong nose and ink-black hair. Andrew could never be with her without thinking of the little girl she'd once been. The Sunday visits to Grandma's house. Roller-skating with her on the sidewalk outside. Watching television together in the room Grandma had that looked as if it had come straight from Italy on a boat carrying olive oil, a small, warm, cozy room with red velvet drapes and big heavy furniture and ornately framed pictures of mustachioed men in stiff white collars and cuffs.

Whenever he came to Ida's house on a Sunday, Andrew spent most of the time there with her. Bobby he could see any day of the week. In fact, he sometimes saw Bobby more days of the week than he could stand. Ida he saw once every couple of months, if he was lucky.

"So who is she?" she asked.

She was at the stove, tasting the tomato sauce bubbling in a pot. She wasn't such a terrific cook, Ida. She hadn't been a great stickball player, either, but that hadn't stopped her from trying. She was wearing a plastic apron over the blue dress she'd worn to church this morning. The apron had the words PLEASE DON'T KISS THE COOK printed on it.

"Where'd you hear that?" he said.

"Your father wrote to me," she said, and shrugged. "He said when you went out there, you mentioned some girl. He told me he thinks it's serious. You and this girl."

"No, I never said anything like that, Ide."

Ida wouldn't let it go.

"You can tell me, come on," she said.

"I'm telling you there isn't anybody," Andrew said, but he grinned like a schoolboy.

"Your father said it sounded serious."

"He heard me wrong, Ida. I told him there was nobody serious. I mean it," he said, and grinned again.

"Would you tell me if there was?" she asked, and lifted the wooden spoon from the pot and brought it to her lips, tasting the sauce.

"Sure, I would," he said.

"Or is there a problem?" she asked.

"What kind of problem?"

"I don't know. She could be somebody's daughter, for example . . ."

"No, no."

"Like I heard, you know, you were dating Tony Cannieri's daughter, which I have to tell you isn't such a good idea, Andrew, messing with somebody's daughter who's respected like Tony is."

"I stopped seeing her, Ide."

"Good. That was a wise decision," she said, and began stirring the sauce again. "I hope it's not somebody's *wife* you're serious about."

"I told you I'm not serious about anyone," he said, and grinned again.

"Yeah, yeah, come on, this is me."

"I'm telling you, Ide."

"Cause that could be *really* dangerous, somebody's wife."

"It's not anybody's wife you would know," Andrew said.

"Then she's married?" Ida asked at once, and looked up straight into his face.

"Ida," he said, putting on the serious little-boy look she knew so well, "I really can't talk about this right now."

"She's married, hmh?"

"Yes."

"But not to anybody it would be like a problem, hmh? You wouldn't be dishonoring anyone in the . . ."

"No, Ida, how could I do that?"

"Listen, you dated Tony's daughter, who knows *what* you could do?"

"It's not anybody's wife like that."

"Then what's the problem?"

"Who said there's a problem?"

"Well, you're so secretive about her . . ."

"I told you, Ida, she's married. I can't go blabbing all over town about her."

"Of course not," Ida said. "But this isn't all over town, Andrew, this is me. Ida. Remember me, honey? Your cousin Ida? Remember?"

"No, who are you?" Andrew said, and smiled.

Ida returned the smile.

"Is she married to anyone *else* could be a problem?" she asked, still smiling.

"I don't know what you mean."

"I don't know. Someone who could be a *problem*."

"Like what kind of problem?"

"I don't know. You're the one being so secretive, I figure there's got to be some kind of problem."

"She's married to a lawyer, there's no problem," he said.

"What kind of lawyer?"

"I don't know. He works for the city."

"Doing what?"

"I don't know."

"What's his name?"

"I don't know his name, tell you the truth."

"Well, what's *her* name?"

"Come on, Ida."

"What's the big *secret*? All I'm asking you is her name."

"I'm not ready to tell you that, Ida."

"When will you be ready?"

"When I know."

"When you know what?"

"Whether she'll marry me."

"Did you ask her already?"

"I asked her."

"So what's taking her so long to decide?"

"Well . . . she's got a daughter, Ide. It isn't easy."

"How old? The daughter?"

"Twelve."

"You're ready to take on a twelve-year-old kid, Andrew?"

"Yeah. I am, Ida."

"And this isn't serious, huh?"

"It's very serious."

"Then you better discuss it with some other people before you make a final decision," Ida said.

"Why?"

"Bringing someone into the family? It should be discussed with Petey. And with Bobby. They should know about this. If you really decide to marry her."

"That's what I'm hoping, Ida."

"Then you have to sit down and talk to them about it. That's what Bobby did when he wanted to marry me. He talked not only to my father but to *your* father, too. *And* to Petey. It isn't as if you have no obligations, Andrew. This has to be discussed, you understand what I'm saying?"

"Well, I'll see."

"What's the problem?" Ida said.

"No problem."

"I think there's a problem," she said, and nodded wisely.

"I'm telling you no."

"Then sit down with them."

"When I'm ready."

"I think you'd better do it *now*. Before she says yes and surprises you."

"I hope to God she does, Ida."

"I hope so, too," Ida said, and lifted another spoonful of sauce from the pot, and tasted it, and said, "But talk to your people first, hmh? Get their opinions. Show them the proper respect. You're a very important man, Andrew. This has to be dealt with in the proper manner. Sit down with them. Talk to them," she said, and tasted the sauce again.

"Well, I'll see," he said.

"Does this need salt?" she asked, and extended the wooden spoon to him.

In bed with her husband that same Sunday night, Ida said, "I don't think he's hiding anything from you."

"What'd he say about the husband?" Bobby asked.

"Only that he's a lawyer."

"That's all? What *kind* of lawyer?"

"He doesn't know. All he knows is the guy works for the city."

"He doesn't know the guy's a *DA*?"

"I don't think he knows," Ida said.

"Is he protecting her, or what?"

"I don't think so. I told you a hundred times already I don't think he *knows*. Now go to sleep."

"Because *if* he knows . . ."

"Mm-hmh."

". . . and he's not *telling* anybody about it . . ."

"Mm-hmh."

". . . that could be serious."

"Yeah."

"That could be *very* serious," Bobby said. "I wish you coulda got him to open up more."

"I did all I could," Ida said, and rolled over. "Go to sleep," she said. "Tomorrow's another day."

The baby-sitter was in the living room at the other end of the apartment, watching the Sunday night movie on TV. Mollie and Winona were in Winona's room, next door to her brother's room, which he still used whenever he and his wife came home to visit. Max's bedroom was cool, with a full-length poster of Tina Turner tacked up on the ceiling over the bed, and pennants for all the major league baseball clubs and NFL football teams on the walls, and a Mason jar full of pennies alongside a model of the *Kitty Hawk* on his dresser. Winona had found his marijuana stash on the top shelf of his closet, in a metal box containing fishing tackle.

Winona was rolling a joint now.

She kept spilling marijuana flakes all over the bed.

"I don't think we should be doing this," Mollie said.

"I think we should be doing it," Winona said firmly. "Don't be so chickenshit, Moll."

"How do you know it's still good? How long has it been in the closet?"

"It doesn't go stale," Winona said. "In fact, it gets better with age."

"Who told you that?"

"It's a known fact. Anyway, this isn't *old* pot. Max smokes every time he comes home."

"Doesn't it stink up the whole house?" Mollie asked.

"He opens the windows. There," Winona said, and triumphantly held up a messily rolled but nonetheless reasonable facsimile of a cigarette.

"Suppose what's-her-name comes in?"

"Fat Henrietta? She won't come in. She never comes in. She thinks my mother pays her to come watch television."

Winona began rolling a second joint. Mollie watched her intently.

"So what do you think I should do?" she asked.

"Smoke it and shut up," Winona said.

"I mean about France."

"Did they tell you for sure the trip's off?"

"Yeah. He said he had too much work to do, and my mother starts going for her doctorate soon as school lets out."

"Which is when?"

"The tenth. Same as us. I told them we'd been planning this whole thing about our two families being in Paris at the same time, because you're going to the Riviera in July, which is when *we* were *supposed* to be going to St.-Jean, and you and I were so excited about *being* there together, the two of us in *Paris* . . ."

"True," Winona said, her head bent studiously over her task.

". . . and now they tell me we're not going. I told my father that was cruel and unusual punishment, and he knew it."

"What'd he say?"

"He said we weren't going away this summer, and that was that. And he threatened to send me to camp if I didn't get off it."

"Camp!" Winona said. "Jesus!"

"Yeah. So what do you think I should do?"

"Cool it for a while. Maybe it's a phase they're going through."

"They're going through *something*, all right," Mollie said, and rolled her eyes.

"There," Winona said, "practice makes perfect. This one is yours, Moll."

Twenty minutes later, both girls were stoned out of their minds. They had smoked the joints down till they'd almost burned their fingertips, and had then opened the roaches and sprinkled the remaining pot out the window, rolling the papers into tiny balls and flicking those out, too. The windows were still wide open to the traffic below, and the girls lay side by side on Winona's bed, wearing only panties, talking loudly and giggling every ten or twenty seconds.

Mollie wanted to know if this was really the first time Winona had tried this. Somehow the question struck her funny, so she burst out laughing. Winona assured her that she would never do anything for the first time unless it was with her very best friend in the entire world. Both girls began giggling at this fresh witticism.

"Except play with my buzzer," Winona said.

Since the word "buzzer" was in itself hysterically funny, the girls began giggling all over again. Winona said she'd done *that* for the first time without Mollie, played with her buzzer, that is. Mollie wanted to know what a *buzzer* was and how you played with it. Winona told her you had to *find* it first. She herself had found hers quite by accident in February, up in Vermont, while she was leaning against the washing machine downstairs off the kitchen, doing all her socks and thermal underwear and turtlenecks from the week's skiing. The machine kept vibrating against her and all at once she realized something was, well, *buzzing* down there in her jeans. So she pressed a little harder against the machine to make the buzzing a little stronger. Mollie found all this hysterically funny, the idea of somebody having a *buzzer* in her jeans.

Winona went on to say that in the bathtub later that night, while she was washing herself down there, she began to feel that same buzz again, though not as strong as it had been when she was doing her laundry. So she searched around with her fingers to see if she could find what was causing this very peculiar, very pleasant sensation, and she discovered this little, well, *buzzer* between her legs—"*meine kleine friggin buzzerei*," she said in Frankendrac.

"Sometimes I do it to music," she said, and sat up, and

climbed over Mollie, and padded to the bookcase. Mollie watched as she put a digital disc on the machine, turned the volume up loud, and then came back to the bed. She climbed over Mollie again, lay back down on her side of the bed, and slipped her hand into her panties. "Just do what I do," she said. "It's fun."

Five minutes later, Mollie was masturbating for the first time to the stereo beat of Michael Jackson's "Wanna Be Startin' Somethin'," both girls giggling at the wonder of it all. Sixteen-year-old Henrietta in the living room up the hall, watching her movie blithely unaware, thought they sounded like they always did, dumb and going on thirteen.

"How do you know this?" Andrew said.

"We asked around," Petey said.

"*Who* asked around?"

"We had a detective check on her."

"A private eye?"

"No, a real cop. A tin shield. Somebody we got in our pocket."

"You checked on her without first asking me?" Andrew said.

"We were trying to protect you, Andrew," he said. "If this was something you didn't know, we had to find out. For your own protection."

"What's his name? The husband?"

"Michael Welles. He put away the Lombardi Crew five years ago."

"You're positive about all this?"

"Pos—"

"Because if you're making a mistake . . ."

"No mistake, Andrew."

"Causing me trouble over a mistake . . ."

"Andrew, I swear on my mother's eyes, this is the truth. I personally phoned the DA's Office, asked for Michael Welles, it went right through."

"Who answered the phone?"

"He did himself. 'ADA Welles' is how he answers."

"Then how do you know he's a unit chief?"

"Cause that's who I asked for on the phone, Deputy Unit Chief Michael Welles. Anyway, Andrew, whether he's a chief or just an Indian, who gives a shit? He's a DA who works in the Organized Crime Unit. For me, that's enough."

Andrew was silent for several moments.

Then he said, "What do you expect me to do about this?"

"That's entirely up to you," Petey said. "I know what I would do. Because you see, Andrew, he may be the one put in the bugs, her husband. And she may be working for him, Andrew, I hate to tell you this. She may be a snitch, Andrew. She may be a rat."

"So what would you do?"

"I think you know what I would do, Andrew."

As the last class broke on Wednesday afternoon, Luretta came up to Sarah's desk and handed her a long white envelope.

"Mrs. Welles," she said gravely, "if you get a chance, I'd appreciate it if you read this sometime."

"I'd be happy to," Sarah said. "What is it?"

"Well," Luretta said, and ducked her head.

She had never been a shy girl. Sarah looked at her.

"What is it, Luretta?" she asked again.

"Jus' something. There's my phone number on it, case you feel like calling me."

Sarah studied her, puzzled.

"Is something wrong?" she asked.

"No, no. Well . . . jus' read it, okay? When you can," she said, and ran swiftly out of the room.

Sarah put the envelope in her attaché case.

★ ★ ★

The sun was blinding as she walked southward on Park Avenue, wearing sunglasses, hurrying toward Dunhill's where Andrew's blue Acura was parked in front of the store. She said nothing as she got into the car.

"Hi," Andrew said, and smiled.

"This is dangerous," she said, and tossed the attaché case into the backseat. "Could we please get moving?"

Andrew started the car at once, heading directly crosstown, toward the river. Billy usually began driving immediately downtown on Park, but she knew Andrew was taking her to dinner tonight. When he'd told her about it on the phone, she'd wondered immediately if he'd discovered the still operative bugs in the Mott Street building. They were on the East River Drive now, heading uptown toward the Bruckner Expressway.

"Where are we going?" she asked.

Edge to her voice, still nervous.

"I know a nice little place in Connecticut," he said.

"Connecticut? Andrew, I haven't got that much time, you know I can't . . ."

"Well, I think you may have time," he said.

She did not take off the sunglasses, even though the sun was no longer blinding her. She sat quite still in the seat beside him, her bag in her lap, her hands over it, Andrew darkly silent behind the wheel.

He was wondering if she was wired.

He knew the car wasn't bugged. He had taken it to the garage where they kept the Lincoln and had asked Billy to put it on a lift and check it top to bottom, inside and out. The car was clean. Whatever he and Sarah Welles said in this car today would not get back downtown to her husband in Organized Crime. Unless she herself was wired.

"I know who your husband is," he said.

She said nothing.

"His name is Michael Welles, he's deputy chief of the DA's Organized Crime Unit."

Still, she said nothing. Her heart was pounding. He knew about Michael, it was senseless to lie. But if she told the truth . . .

"Your husband who makes eighty-five a year for putting away people like me."

"I don't know what you mean."

"I think you know what I mean," he said.

He did not turn to look at her. He kept his hands on the wheel and his eyes on the road. They were passing through a section of the Bronx that used to be Italian but was now Latino. The small, joined, two-family row houses reminded him of the homes his father sometimes took him to when he was small, to visit this or that soldier in the organization, "Keep up the morale," he told Andrew. The older men would smoke their guinea stinkers and pat Andrew on the head, and tell him, "Hey, you getta so big, Lino."

"Was it your husband who had the place bugged?" he asked.

Still not looking at her. Eyes on the road.

"I told you I don't know what you . . . ."

"Sarah, you're in serious trouble. If you know who I am, you know what I can do. I suggest you start telling me the truth."

"All right," she said.

"*Was* it your husband?"

"Yes."

"Very nice. He uses his own wife to . . ."

"No," she said. "That's not true, Andrew."

"No? Then how . . . ?"

"I didn't know about the bugs. He found out about us *through* the bugs."

"But now he knows."

"Yes."

"And you're still seeing me. Which means Sonny missed

something, the place is *still* bugged. Otherwise, why would your husband . . . ?"

"Yes, the place is still bugged."

"How long have you known about me?"

"Since Mother's Day."

"You know since May sometime, and you keep seeing me. So what do you mean no? You *are* . . ."

"I see you because . . ."

"You *are* working for him, leading me on . . ."

"I see you because I love you."

"Bullshit. You're getting me to talk . . ."

"No . . ."

"Yes, you're an informer, you're here to send me to *jail!*"

"I had no choice," she said.

She was thinking he would kill her. She had seen movies where people like him took informers to the country for a nice little ride. In his eyes, she was an informer.

"Yes, you had a choice," he said. "You could have told me. You could have . . ."

"I'm telling you now."

"Only because I already *know!*"

"I was going to tell you, anyway."

She wondered if this was true.

He was wondering the same thing.

"Do you realize I can have you killed in a minute?" he said.

Which meant he *himself* was not about to kill her. But this didn't exclude the possibility that he was driving her to a nice little place he knew in Connecticut, where two happy goons would be waiting with garrotes and chain saws.

"I don't think you'll do that," she said.

"In a *minute!*" he said, and took his right hand from the wheel, and snapped his fingers for emphasis, still not looking at her, his eyes on the road. "A goddamn *informer*? A fucking *rat*? You know what we do with rats?"

He said nothing for the longest while, searching for a spot where he could turn off Bruckner onto a side street. He found one some three minutes later, pulled off the road, drove past a gas station pumping diesel for trucks, and then turned onto a sunny street with scrawny trees and small whitewashed houses. He drove along until he came to an empty corner lot with a Cyclone fence around it. There were junked cars heaped high in the lot. There was razor wire on top of the fence. Not a soul was in sight. He cut the engine. The sun-washed street was still except for the sound of cars and trucks rushing past in the distance. He turned from the wheel.

"Are you wired?" he asked.

"No."

She was still wearing the sunglasses. He couldn't see her eyes.

"Take off the glasses," he said.

She took off the glasses. Reached into her handbag. Put the glasses into their case.

"Look at me," he said.

She turned to look at him.

Blue eyes wide in that gorgeous face.

"Tell me again. Are you wired?"

"I'm not wired, Andrew."

"Open your blouse," he said.

She obeyed immediately, unbuttoning her blouse to expose her bra. He felt inside the bra, ran his fingers around and under her breasts, ran his hands over her back and her ribs and her belly and her buttocks, reached under her skirt to touch her thighs and her pubic mound. These were not a lover's hands.

"Empty your handbag," he said.

She looked at him stonily for a moment, and then she picked up her bag and turned it over, dumping its contents on the seat between them. She buttoned her blouse while he began rummaging through the items on the seat. The sunglass case, her wallet, her house keys, a package of chewing gum, her Filofax, a tube of lipstick, a comb, a hairbrush, a package of Kleenex, a paperback copy of *Howard's End*, some loose change. He flipped through the pages of the book to make sure it hadn't been hollowed out. He opened the Filofax to make certain nothing was buried in its pages. He turned the bag upside down, shook it, felt inside it with his hands. He found nothing even remotely resembling a recording device.

"All right," he said at last, and turned away from her and started the car. As he drove back toward Bruckner, she put everything back in the bag, item by item, silently, slowly, deliberately, angrily. When they were on the highway again, she said, "Well, *that* was a nice little indignity."

"Listen," he said, "it's *your* husband who's the fucking DA, not *mine*!"

"Are you satisfied now?"

"Yes."

"That I'm not wired?"

"Yes."

"That I'm here only because I *want* to be here?"

"Yes."

"Then slow down," she said. "I don't want to die in a car crash!"

He glanced swiftly into the rearview mirror, nodded, and eased up on the pedal.

"I didn't realize I was going so fast."

"You drive like a maniac," she said.

They rode in silence for what must have been ten, fifteen minutes. At last he said, "Does he know you're with me today?"

"Yes. He wants me to keep this going. Until he has everything he needs."

"How much does he already know?"

"I'm not sure."

"What did you mean when you said you had no choice?"

"My daughter."

"What's she got to . . . ?"

"He threatened to take her away from me."

"Would he do that?"

"I don't know. I don't know him anymore. He has a video of me going in, he has . . ."

"A video! Jesus, what *else* have they . . . ?"

"They've been watching the door on Mott Street," she said. "They have pictures of anyone who goes in or out."

This had to be the truth. She wasn't wired. She was telling him the absolute truth.

"He showed me the video," she said. "He also has tapes of everything you and I said together. He played them for me."

"Who else?"

"Did he play them for? I guess the people he . . ."

"No, who else has he got on *tape*?"

"I don't know. He's going for an OCCA. Do you know what that is?"

"Yes, I know what that is."

"He threatened to use the tape in a divorce action if I didn't do what he asked."

Andrew nodded.

He was silent for several moments.

Then he said, "They want me to have you killed. They know about your husband, they think you may have . . ."

"How'd they find out?"

"They put a detective on you."

"A private de—?"

"NYPD. Tin. Somebody we own. They already knew about you and me, I don't know how they found out."

"Billy," she said at once.

"Maybe," he said, and nodded. "They think you're an informer. A rat. And informers have to be taught a lesson. So nobody else will even *think* of informing."

"Informers have to be *killed*, is that what you mean?"

"Yes," he said. "Informers have to be killed."

"Even well-connected informers?" she asked.

"Especially well-connected ones," he said.

"I'm not talking about my husband. Not *that* connection."

He turned to look at her, puzzled.

"I'm talking about *you*," she said.

Trucks were speeding by on either side of them.

"What do you mean?" he said.

"You asked me to marry you," she said.

A huge eight-wheeler rushed past on their left, raising dust, scaring them both.

"Did you mean it?" she asked.

"I meant it," he said.

"Then, yes," she said.

She came out of the bathroom naked, her bag slung over her shoulder. She carried the bag to the dresser near the four-poster bed, and went to him at once.

There was for her—as there was whenever she was with him—the same sense of urgency and need. She went into his arms like a wanton, immediately abandoning herself to the same passion she'd known from the very first time they'd made love. Even knowing who he was and what he represented, she was nonetheless helplessly, hopelessly enamored. He was her love, and she loved him still.

The inn was on the edge of a narrow river with a small waterfall. Swans glided on the still, pondlike expanse of water before the falls, just under their second-story window. As they lay naked in embrace on the four-poster bed, they could hear the tumbling water below.

He was brimming with questions, bursting with plans, bubbling with excitement, babbling as steadily as the rippling river outside. When would she tell her husband, how soon could she get the divorce? Would he consent to it? Could she move out meantime? What about her daughter?

Ah yes, what *about* my daughter? she thought.

"I know she likes me," he said, "but . . ."

"She adores you," Sarah said.

"But this is different, this is a divorce, this would be a new father coming into the picture . . ."

"It'll be difficult, I know."

"I'll take good care of her, Sarah."

"I know you will."

"And you, too. No one will ever harm you while I'm around."

"I know," she said.

"You'll have to meet everybody," he said. "Well, not *everybody*, just the people who matter. Actually, it gets down to two people who have to know, Bobby Triani and Petey Bardo, they're second and third in command—I make it sound like an army, but it isn't that at all."

"Do you need their approval?" she asked. "Is that it? To marry me?"

"No, hell no, I don't need *anybody's* approval to do anything. This is like a courtesy, Sarah, a way of showing respect for the people you work with. When I told you I was in the investment business, I wasn't lying, that's what we are in a sense, investors looking to make a profit, the same as any other investors. Bobby is immediately under me in the organization, and Petey comes after him. Everything funnels through us, the profits, and we decide how they'll be distributed, which percentage goes to which person, whatever position he may hold in the organization . . ."

And now, perhaps because hiding the truth about himself had become an intolerable burden over all these months, now the truth that had been dammed within him burst free, rushing over the dam and through the dam, destroying the dam itself and the silence it had forced, words tumbling free in a torrent as swift as the running river outside. And as he spoke she thought she'd never loved him so much as she did now, when he was telling her the truth about himself at last, revealing himself completely at last, trusting her, revealing all at last.

". . . mostly a cash business, so most of our distributions are in cash. In fact, one of our big problems is getting *rid* of money. I don't mean throwing it in the streets, I mean giving it respectability, do you understand what I'm saying? I guess you realize the reason my place was bugged isn't because what I do is *legal*. You asked me if I was involved in anything criminal, and I told you no, because in my mind a criminal is somebody who kills somebody else or who sticks up somebody else or who hurts somebody else in a serious way, none of which things I've ever personally done. I suppose in your husband's eyes—and maybe in yours, too, for all I know, I don't know—doing things like making it easy for people to gamble or to borrow money or to indulge in pleasures they seek of their own accord, these things may seem *criminal* to him, which would mean that anybody involved in these things would automatically become someone involved in so-called criminal activity. But my father and my uncle and me, too—I have to admit I feel the same way—think of this *activity* as providing services that people want and need. Petey, Bobby, we all feel the same way. Sal the Barber, these are all people you'll meet someday, Ralphie Carbonaio, he's the Carter in Carter-Goldsmith Investments, Carmine Orafo, he's the Goldsmith, it actually means that in Italian, Orafo, *all* of them, we're all in this business together to provide services *which*, by the way, in different times of history and in different places all around the world, would have been considered *legal*.

"You won't have to worry about the business, my mother never worried about it, still doesn't, you'll be meeting her, too, so she can give you her Good Housekeeping Seal of Approval, huh? I'm not expecting a problem with her, she'll fall in love with you the minute she sees you, why wouldn't she? I have to tell you, though, it isn't going to be easy, expecting these guys to open their hearts to someone who's got a history like yours, your marriage I'm talking about. There's what you might call a natural animosity there. It's a matter of mind-set, Sarah. Guys who are used to believing that loan-sharking isn't such a terrible thing, these guys aren't going to understand why I would want to marry a woman whose ex thinks otherwise. Sal the Barber, for example, who's the man who gave me that ring, remember? The black ring? The one your jeweler said was stolen? He's a decent, hardworking man, you'll see when you meet him, though he sounds like a roughneck—well, look at the beautiful ring he came up with. That's not the kind of thing someone without sensitivity could find beautiful, is it? Sal didn't know it was stolen, either, by the way. The guy who passed it to him is sorry he ever did, believe me—if he can still be sorry about anything, which I promise you he can't.

"So there might at first be *Hey*, what's Andrew doing, bringing this woman around, what kind of craziness is *this*? But you'll get to know them, they'll get to know you, and before you know it, everything'll be fine. Especially since later this month they're all going to come into a lot of money, everybody all the way down the line, when this new venture of ours goes into operation. Everybody's going to be *very* happy, believe me, when the profits begin rolling in and we start distributing those profits all the way down the line. All these people are going to be looking very affectionately on *anything* I do. I don't think any of them are going to find fault with you in any way, I promise you. I think each and every one of them will show you the proper respect."

"What new venture is this?" she asked.

"Well," he said, "I don't know how you feel about dope, Sarah, I'm sure there are people who would like to lock up anybody caught smoking even a joint. But there are millions of people all over the world who smoke marijuana on a daily basis, and there are millions of others—I'm not talking about hopheads or junkies now, I'm talking about legislators and lawyers and criminologists and judges and social workers, people like that—these people believe that the best thing that could happen is for narcotics to be legalized. I'm not taking a stand one way or the other. I'm only saying there are millions of people who depend upon drug use to get themselves through the day, and it might be a bigger crime to *deny* these people the support they need to live their lives in some kind of peace. I'm not even talking about marijuana. I'm talking about hard drugs like cocaine or heroin, yes, there are people who believe these drugs are less dangerous in the long view than either alcohol or cigarettes. I never heard of a cocaine addict dying of cirrhosis of the liver or lung cancer, did you? And, by the way, I'm not even sure there's any proof that *crack* cocaine is addictive. Cocaine you can smoke, you know? Crack cocaine. Or even heroin you can smoke, which is this new thing we're bringing in, a combination of cocaine and heroin, what's called 'moon rock.' Do you remember when I went down to Florida with my uncle?"

"Yes?"

"It was to talk to this man named Luis Hidalgo, who took over the Putumayo Cartel after Alonso Moreno met with a terrible, ahem, accident. What we're doing . . . Do you remember when I asked you to go to Italy with me? That was to meet with the man who's handling distribution on the Continent. It's a three-way setup, you see, what you might call a triangle. Hidalgo provides the Colombian product, which we ship to various ports in Italy. Meanwhile, Manfredi is taking delivery of the Chinese product. We process it right there in Italy, and turn it around as moon rock . . ."

On and on he went, the words gushing from his mouth, trapped too long, pouring forth excitedly now, directed toward Sarah where she sat cross-legged on the four-poster bed, listening intently, and then moving past her to where her bag sat on the dresser near the bed.

A reel-to-reel NAGRA tape recorder was hidden under a Velcro flap at the bottom of that bag. A wire from the recorder had been sewn into the lining and fed up into the bag's strap, where the microphone showed only as what appeared to be one of a pair of black rivets fastening strap to bag. Sarah had turned on the machine while she was in the bathroom. It was now capable of recording four hours of conversation before the tape ran out.

". . . Stonington some Sunday," Andrew was saying. "I'll ask my mother to invite Ida and the kids, you'll love Ida, she's my cousin, we've been best friends from the day she was born. I used to call her Pinocchio, because she has my uncle Rudy's nose, and she used to call me Mickey Mouse, because I had big ears when I was a kid. I was nick-named 'Topolino,' in fact, which means Mickey Mouse in Italian, because of the ears. Well, 'Lino,' it got abbreviated to. My mother still calls me Lino every now and then, can you imagine? Lino? The house in Stonington . . ."

The two men met on Memorial Day in the rectory of the Church of the Holy Redemption on Flatbush Avenue in Brooklyn, where a priest named Father Daniel frequently extended hospitality and privacy to men of their persuasion in exchange for contributions to his perpetual building fund. In the cloistered silence of the rectory, with sunlight streaming through the leaded windows, and music floating from the church outside where someone practiced in the organ loft, Bobby Triani and Petey Bardo discussed this serious problem they now seemed to have.

"You think he's gonna take care of this?" Bobby asked.

"I don't think so," Petey said.

"So what do we do? This is a complicated thing."

"Not that complicated."

"Should we talk to some of the others?"

"I don't think so. I'd rather line up some people. Move ahead on this before it gets out of hand."

"I worry about doing that," Bobby said. "Some of these old wops who knew his father . . . I don't know, Petey."

"You got a better suggestion?"

"I'm saying there's still these old guys around who knew him when he was a kid with big ears."

"Yeah, and now he's a kid with a big mouth."

"Petey, let's be fair. We don't know for sure he told her anything."

"If he's fuckin her, he's tellin her," Petey said.

"Yeah," Bobby said, and sighed heavily. "Still. To the older guys, he's still Lino, you know what I mean? I think we oughta ask them first. Don't you?"

Petey was thinking the *first* mistake Andrew had made was appointing this jackass his underboss.

"Petey? Don't you think we should call a meeting, get their advice?"

"No."

"At least ask Fat Nickie what he thinks."

"No."

"Because . . ."

"What I see here," Petey said, "is a pussy-whipped snot-nose who couldn't keep it zipped and who's gonna get us *all* in trouble, that's what I see. I won't go over your head on this, Bobby, you know I won't . . ."

"I appreciate that."

"But I'd like t'line up some people."

"They won't like it, the older ones."

"Fuck them *and* him," Petey said.

Lino, Michael thought.

What goes around comes around.

It was now a quarter to midnight on the hot Tuesday night immediately following the holiday, and he was sitting in a car opposite Andrew Faviola's house in Great Neck, waiting for him to come home. Resting on the seat beside him was a tape player containing a copy of the reel-to-reel Sarah had recorded last Wednesday. Despite a waterfall and a river in the background, the fidelity of the tape was exceptionally high. Michael now had close to three hours of conversation that linked Faviola and his goombahs to enough criminal activity to bring racketeering charges against almost all of them. In a breathless, virtually nonstop monologue, Faviola had attested to the family's involvement in virtually every crime defined in the section on criminal enterprise. You named it, the family was involved in it—from A to Z.

Arson, Assault, Bribery, Burglary, Coercion, Criminal Contempt, Criminal Mischief, Criminal Possession of Stolen Property, False Written Statements, Forgery, Gambling . . .

He told Sarah he'd administered and enforced his father's gambling operation in Las Vegas throughout the two and a half years he'd attended UCLA, and that he'd personally transmitted orders from his father to two contract hitters who'd cursorily eliminated a heavy gambler who was "into the family for a hundred thousand and change . . ."

Grand Larceny, Hindering Prosecution, Homicide . . .

The way he'd casually admitted to ordering the murder of the Queens gambler who'd set this whole thing in motion was typical of the abandon he'd felt while talking to Sarah: "I told Frankie Palumbo to take care of him . . . so it wouldn't happen again. Frankie's the capo this jerk stole the money from. It was supposed to be a cash pickup, he stole five grand from the bundle."

As offhandedly as that.

Insurance Fraud, Kidnapping, Narcotics . . .

And here he went into vast detail about a three-way Colombian-Italian-Chinese operation that would imminently flood the streets of New York with moon rock. "The ships are already on their way from Italy," he'd said. "We'll be off-loading and distributing sometime in June . . ."

Perjury, Promoting Prostitution, Robbery, Usury . . .

Which was loan-sharking and which he described as one of the mainstays of their operation; the others, of course, were gambling, and narcotics, and labor racketeering, and receiving and distributing stolen goods. He described in detail the profitable loan-sharking operation run by Sal the Barber, who—he did not fail to mention—had himself broken many a head in his time, and who had ordered the murder of a punk named Richie Palermo . . .

"Do you remember the ring I gave you? The one that turned out to be stolen? I brought this to Sal's attention, and the kid turned up dead in a basement room in Washington Heights. You have to maintain control over these lower-level people, or they'll do something dangerous or stupid that can turn against you, and then the law will swarm all over you."

Weapons . . .

Not only the criminal possession of what amounted to an arsenal but involvement in a vast arms trade that included the manufacture, transport, disposition, and *defacement* of weapons—as in converting a semiautomatic into an illegal *fully* automatic rifle.

Well, no Z.

And, to his credit, Faviola had not admitted to anyone in the family ever having committed rape.

But everything else was there. The crimes, in many cases the names of the people who'd committed those crimes, in other instances the places and dates of commission, more than enough to bring charges and seek indictments. In two hours and fifty-three minutes of almost continuous babble, apparently driven by a need to impress Sarah with his acumen, cunning, power, and stealth, Faviola had let out all the stops, and had been rewarded afterward with . . .

Michael had turned off the tape the moment they began making love.

He detested them both.

The problem he still had, however, was the same one he'd had all along, except that the moment Sarah had actually gone in wired, she'd technically become an "informant" instead of the unknown "subject" she'd been on the previous tapes. He could not now call Sarah to testify without revealing her identity. He could not get this tape admitted in evidence unless Sarah swore under oath that she'd *been* there at the Rockledge Inn in Norwalk, Connecticut, while the conversation was taking place . . .

That this was a complete and accurate tape of the conversation . . .

That the man she'd been conversing with was Andrew Faviola . . .

And that the conversation had taken place on such and such a date . . .

At such and such a time . . .

And so on and so forth, if it please Your Honor.

His unwillingness to call her had nothing to do with his promise to her. He had given her his word of honor that if she delivered the goods, he would never reveal to Mollie or anyone else what kind of woman she was. That was the deal he'd made. Upon more circumspect reflection, however, he felt he'd be justified in telling Mollie all about her mother's infidelity; she was, after all, a mature child who deserved to know exactly *why* her parents were divorcing. In truth, then, he was ready to throw Sarah to the sharks provided the sharks didn't then turn on *him*.

He felt he'd adequately protected himself against any due-process challenges that might have stemmed from deliberately sending Sarah in to exchange sex for information. "Outrageous government conduct," as defined in *U.S. v. Cuervelo*—where federal courts warned government investigators against using sex as a means of gathering evidence— had been very much on his mind when he'd presented her with her marching orders. He further knew that no sane defense attorney would ever claim he had been the one who'd initiated or encouraged a love affair between his wife and Faviola. Sarah had started that all on her own, thanks, before the eavesdropping surveillance had begun.

Besides, it was unthinkable that the DA would even *allow* him to prosecute this case. Were that to happen—and it couldn't, it was simply an impossibility—the defense would enjoy an unprecedented feeding frenzy, portraying him as a man with an overly vindictive motive, a man with too much personal interest in the case, a man who was *not* in that courtroom to see simple justice done . . .

"I ask you, ladies and gentlemen of the jury, to consider just what kind of man this district attorney is. I ask you to ask *yourselves* what kind of man would use his own *wife* as an informant, would send his own *wife* into another man's embrace, would listen to his own *wife* making love to another man, just so long as she betrayed her lover, just so long as she played the role of Delilah to my client's unsuspecting Samson. I ask you to consider the *moral* values of this district attorney who's so very *eager* to put my client behind bars that he'd sacrifice his own wife to the cause. I ask you to consider whether the evidence he's offered here in this courtroom is not evidence procured by a *zealot* and not a man even remotely interested in the even hand of justice. I ask you to consider . . ."

No.

Even if the case miraculously survived a due-process challenge under Cuervelo standards, he himself would never be allowed to try it. In fact, given the circumstances—the close personal relationship of a key informant to someone in the District Attorney's Office—*whoever* tried it was in severe danger of losing it. The trick was to nail Faviola without *ever* going to trial. Toward that end . . .

A car was turning the corner. A blue Acura. Michael waited until it pulled into the driveway, its headlights illuminating a beige-colored garage door that immediately began opening. He was already crossing the street as Faviola drove the Acura into the garage. The tape player was in his right hand. He was waiting in the driveway when Faviola got out of the Acura, walked to the door-closing button, hit it, and then stopped dead in his tracks when he realized he wasn't alone. The closing door almost got him. He ducked to avoid it, and then clenched his fists as if expecting immediate trouble.

"Who is it?" he said.

"ADA Welles," Michael said.

He had expected a boy. The pictures in *People* showed a handsome college kid, and the voice he'd heard on far too many tapes had sounded very young. But the person sitting opposite him now was a man. Handsome, yes, and bearing himself with the sort of casual ease only the very young can bring off, but there was maturity in those knowing blue eyes and the smirking set of his mouth. Seeing him in person at last, sitting here with him, a cold dark fury began seething inside Michael. The realization that his wife's seducer had been knowledgeable and mature, a cunning son of a bitch who'd understood all along the consequences of his actions, was almost too much to contain. Michael wanted to kill him. It was all he could do to keep from leaping up and grabbing him by the throat. Strangle the bastard where he sat, listen to him choking and gasping for breath, eyes rolling back in his head, drop him still and gray and lifeless to the thick carpet underfoot.

The two men sat opposite each other on brocaded chairs in a lavishly furnished living room illuminated only by a tassel-shaded lamp on a marble-topped table. Michael was wearing what he called his prosecutor threads, blue suit, white shirt, dark tie, dark socks, black shoes. He was here on business. Andrew was wearing tan summer slacks and a blue double-breasted blazer, blue tasseled loafers, a pristine white shirt open at the throat. He kept watching Michael in what appeared to be enduring surprise. He did not offer Michael a drink. Michael would have refused one, anyway. He was here to play a tape. He was here to cut a deal with the man who'd stolen his wife.

They sat in relative darkness as the tape unreeled.

When it ended, Andrew rose and went to the bar and poured a drink for himself. He still did not offer one to Michael, who, in any case, *still* would have refused it.

"So?" he said.

"So you're going," Michael said. "And you're taking a lot of people with you."

"Then what are you doing here?"

"I want to talk a deal."

"Why? You've got your fucking tape . . ."

"A gold mine, in fact."

"Where'd she have the wire?"

"What difference does it make?"

"None, I guess," Andrew said, and shrugged.

His question suddenly took on new meaning. They'd made love in that room in Connecticut. She'd been naked, he'd been inside her. So where had the wire been? A perfectly natural question. Where had she hidden the wire? Images conjured by the earlier tapes suddenly flashed on the screen of Michael's mind.

Let's see just how hard we can make you, all right? Let's see what rubbing this ancient Roman ring on your cock can do, all right? My hand tight around you, the black ring rubbing against your stiff cock . . .

Again, Michael wanted to kill him.

"This is my offer," he said. "You walk in and plead, or I bring down all of you."

"Plead to what?"

"Two counts of murder, an agreed twenty-five to life on each. Consecutive."

"Don't be ridiculous."

The satyr and the bird. Are you my satyr, Andrew? Am I your bird, Andrew? No no no, not yet, baby. Not till I want you to. Not till I say you can. Just keep looking at the ring. Just keep watching that black ring, Andrew. My hand tight on your cock and the ring moving . . .

Kill them both.

"If I go public with the Connecticut tape," he said, "you're a dead man. Your own people will learn you told all their business to a woman, they'll get to you wherever you are. Even if you're denied bail, they'll reach you in jail. On the other hand, if you plead, I forget I ever heard this tape . . ."

"Who *else* has heard it?"

"Just me."

"Who else *knows* about it?"

"Just Sarah."

"Nobody in law enforcement?"

"Nobody."

"How about the detectives working the case?"

"I said nobody."

"Why should I believe you?"

"Because I'm telling you."

"I'm supposed to believe a man who's ready to suppress evidence . . ."

"It isn't evidence *yet*. It's evidence only when it's *admitted* as evidence. Right now, it's just a man and a woman talking on tape."

Andrew was listening.

"To introduce this tape," he said, "I've got to call Sarah. I can't try this case without her testimony. The minute I reveal the existence of the tape, I have to . . ."

"There are other tapes."

"No one knows who she is on those tapes."

"You do."

You ever do this to your husband?

Yes, all the time.

You don't.

I do. Every night of the week.

You're lying.

I'm lying.

Jesus, what you do to me!

"No one will ask me who she is."

"How do you know that?"

"Because her identity is a nonissue. On those tapes, she's merely a subject. We don't *have* to know who she is. Those tapes can be introduced through the detectives who conducted the surveillance."

"But you, *personally*, know who she is."

"That's irrelevant," Michael said.

Whose cock *is this?*

Yours.

Mine, yes. And I'm going to suck it till you scream.

Sarah . . .

I want to see you explode! Give it to me!

Oh God, Sarah!

Yes. Yes. Yes. Yes!

"She said you've also got her on videotape."

"She's unrecognizable."

"What you're saying . . ."

"What I'm saying is I'll only have to call her if I introduce the Connecticut tape. She went in wired for it, that makes her an informant. But I won't have to introduce *anything* if there's no trial. You plead to the two counts . . ."

"What's in this for you? If you can put us *all* away, why are you willing to settle for me alone?"

"I don't want to hurt my daughter. If I call Sarah, the whole thing comes out."

"It's a little late to be thinking about that, isn't it?"

"It's a little late for all of us," Michael said softly.

The room went suddenly still.

"I'm willing to give up the better case just so Mollie . . . just so my daughter doesn't get hurt," Michael said.

"There's another reason, though, isn't there?"

"No."

"I don't believe you."

"There's nothing else. You plead to the two counts, I make a small presentation, we get our indictment, and you accept the agreed twenty-five to life. Nobody will know this tape ever existed. Not my daughter, not your *paisans*. What do you say?"

"I'll plead to just the one count. And I do the time in a federal prison."

"No. You go to Attica."

"Then we don't have a deal."

"You want me to use Sarah, is that it?"

"You've *already* used her."

The room went silent again.

"I'll plead to one count," Andrew said, "or you take it to trial. Once the jury hears you turned your own wife into a whore, I may even walk."

"It was my understanding that you loved her," Michael said.

Andrew said nothing.

"I didn't think you'd want this to happen to her," he said.

Andrew still said nothing.

"Well," Michael said, "think about it," and rose ponderously, and walked to the door.

Andrew sat alone in the living room, listening to the sound of the car starting outside, listening to it disappear on the night.

He could not fall asleep.

He lay upstairs in the big bed in the master bedroom of the house, going over every word of the conversation he'd had with Sarah's husband, debating over and over again the only viable course of action that seemed open to him.

He would have her killed, of course.

First because she'd betrayed him yet another time . . .

But she had done it for her daughter.

Fuck her daughter, he thought angrily. She double-crossed *me*, she came in wearing a wire, this wasn't a spur-of-the-moment thing, this was something that required *planning*, this was something she did to me *personally*! Told her husband we wouldn't be going to the bugged apartment this Wednesday, we'd be going out instead to a delightful little restaurant someplace. Oh, really, darling? Well, no problem. Here's a tape recorder to stuff up your kazoo.

Have her killed, of course.

Call Sal the Barber.

Sallie, baby, remember what happened to that runner in Washington Heights, the one who stiffed you with a stolen black ring? Well, I have something similar that needs taking care of.

Immediately.

Call him right now, nail her tomorrow morning on the way to school.

Now!

Do it!

He hadn't looked at all like what Andrew had imagined.

Eighty-five grand a year, he'd expected a wimp.

A nice-looking guy, actually. Controlling himself, Andrew could see that. His hands shaking. Wanting to kill him, he supposed, well sure. Fucking the man's wife, of *course* he'd want to . . .

But I love her, he thought.

Never mind that, call Sal.

She has to go.

Because without her, there's no case. He admitted himself that he can't get that Connecticut tape in without calling her as a witness. And if he had enough on the *other* tapes, he wouldn't have come here trying to deal. *Whatever* he's got, it isn't enough without the Connecticut tape, and without her he can't get the tape in. So, it's simple really. When you think of it, it's really very . . .

But I love her.

He stared up at the ceiling and wondered how she could have done this to him, coming in wired, telling him she wanted to marry him, was she serious about that, had she at least meant *that*? Did she know how he was aching inside right this minute just *thinking* she may have been lying to him about that, too? Just so he would open up, just so she could get him talking for the wire?

He'd have to call Sal.

What time was it, anyway? Two, three o'clock? Sal would be asleep, it could wait till morning. Catch her as she came out of school tomorrow, catch her as she . . .

Tomorrow was Wednesday.

She'd be expecting Billy to pick her up on Fifty-seventh, as usual. Or had her husband told her he'd be coming here with a deal tonight? I shouldn't be too long, darling, I just want to play this incriminating tape for your lovely boy-friend. Ta-ta, don't wait up.

Well, come on, he wasn't like that at all.

Tall, good-looking guy, you could sense a kind of . . . I don't know . . . strength about him. Something strong about him. The way he sat there, looking me dead in the eye. Except when . . . whenever he mentioned Sarah, his lip began quivering. Well, his wife.

But you know, Andrew thought, I didn't want to *hurt* you, mister, I mean that. For what it's worth, I mean that. I didn't even *know* you. You weren't even a part of the scheme, the equation. It was just Sarah and me. You had nothing to do with any of it. So . . .

You know.

I hope you didn't come here thinking you'd find some kind of . . . bum.

Some kind of cheap . . .

Wop.

I love her, you see.

Oh, Jesus, how could this have . . . ?

I mean . . .

I wanted her to meet Ida. Ida, I was gonna say, this is her. This is the woman I was telling you about, isn't she beautiful, Ida? I love her to death, Ida, we're gonna get married.

Why did she have to *do* this? How the fuck could she

have *done* this to me? To us? Come in *wired*? How could she have *done* such a thing?

Well, the daughter.

You love someone, you do whatever's necessary to protect that person. You really *love* someone with all your heart, you can't let that person be destroyed. You can't do that.

It was my understanding that you loved her.

The stiff way he'd said those words, as if they were very hard to get past his lips. As if he would choke on them.

It was my understanding that you loved her.

Yes, Andrew thought, that's true, Counselor, your understanding is entirely correct, I *do* love her, Counselor, but if you think I'm going to cop to murder one . . .

I didn't think you'd want this to happen to her.

. . . and spend twenty-five to life in a state pen just so you won't put her on the stand and embarrass your fucking daughter . . .

I didn't think you'd want this to happen to her.

"I don't," he said aloud.

It was my understanding that you loved her.

"I do love her," he said aloud.

He lay in bed for a long while, silent and thoughtful and troubled.

At last, he snapped on the bedside lamp and opened the drawer in the nightstand. He found the number in his directory and swiftly dialed it.

Billy drove her to the Buona Sera, the Brooklyn restaurant where first they'd dined in public . . .

Wrong

Wrong?

We had dinner in public in St. Bart's. And we also had coffee and croissants in that little place on Second Avenue.

That was all before.

Yes. That was all before. Chocolate croissants. The day we had our first fight.

That wasn't a fight. I simply got up and left.
Because I kissed you.
Yes.
I'm going to kiss you now. Don't leave.
He kissed her the moment she was at the table.
"You look beautiful," he said.
"So do you," she said.
She was wearing a blue suit, a white blouse with a stock tie, and patent blue pumps. He was wearing a blue suit, a white shirt, a rep tie, and black shoes.
"We match," he said.
"We do," she said.
He took her hands in his. The way he had that first time they were here. When she'd been so terribly afraid they'd be seen.
"We have to talk," he said. "But let's order drinks first."
"What about?"
"The future. Our future."
The unctuous proprietor came over, wringing his hands, smiling like Henry Armetta.
"Sì, signor Faviola," he said. *"Mi dica."*
They went through the drink-ordering ritual yet another time. She was thinking There *is* no future to talk about. When the drinks arrived, Andrew lifted his glass and said, "To you."
"To you," she said, and lifted her glass.
"To us," Andrew said, and clinked his glass against hers.
They drank.
"Ahhh," he said.
"Ahhh," she said.
He put down his glass. He took her hands again.
"When I called last night . . ."
"I thought you were crazy."
"Why? He knows. There's nothing to worry about anymore."
"Four in the morning?"
"Do you still sleep with him?"

"No."

"Good. I called because I was going to tell you all this on the phone. But I thought . . ."

"All what?"

"I heard the Connecticut tape."

She almost pulled her hands back from his. They tightened on hers. His hands would not let her go, his eyes would not let her go. He's going to kill me, she thought. He's taken me here so that someone will kill me.

"I think I know why you did it . . ." he said.

"Andrew, you have to understand . . ."

"I wish you hadn't, but I . . ."

"Mollie," she said.

"I know."

"I had to."

"I know."

"But . . . the *tape*? You heard the *tape*?"

"Your husband came to see me."

"What? When?"

"Last night. He offered me a deal."

"Andrew, what are you saying?"

"I plead, he sends me away, we keep you out of it."

"Plead?"

"Guilty. To two counts of murder one. I refused. I think he'll agree to a single count. If he does, I'll take it."

"What do you mean, you'll keep me out of it?"

"No one will ever know. No one will ever hear any of the tapes."

She nodded.

He kept holding her hands, looking across the table at her. She turned away from his steady gaze.

"I feel rotten," she said. "I feel as if I'm *personally* sending you to prison."

"No." He shook his head. "Sarah," he said, "I still want to marry you."

She looked into his eyes.

"I don't know how long I'll be away," he said.

She squeezed his hands hard.

". . . but I've got good lawyers, and maybe we can pull some strings here and there. I'm hoping to get out . . ."

"Andrew," she said, "please don't break my heart this way."

"I love you, Sarah," he said.

"Oh, I love you, too, Andrew. Oh my darling, darling, darling, I love you so very much."

"Then tell me you'll . . ."

Petey Bardo's goons came in the front door.

They moved like automatons, right hands inside their jackets, fingers wrapped around the nine-millimeter Uzis under the jackets, legs propelling them speedily toward the rear of the restaurant. "Excuse me, sirs, do you . . . ?" a waiter started to say, but they shouldered him aside and continued their swift, steady glide to the table on the right in the rear of the place. The man at the table had spotted them, he was already beginning to stand up. The woman stood up, too, puzzled, her hand in his, and turned to look where he was looking as he started to pull her away from the table. The gunman in the lead fired four rounds into the man's face. He fell over backward against the wall, his chair falling over, the gunman pumping round after round into him. The woman was screaming. She held onto his hand as he went over and backward, screaming, screaming all the while.

The second gunman fired seven rounds into her face and her chest, and left her slumped against the blood-spattered wall as he and the other one ran down the hall and into the kitchen and out a back door into the alley.

5: JUNE 2–JUNE 9

The owner of the Ristorante Buona Sera was a seventy-three-year-old man named Carlo Gianetti, who had migrated from Puglia some fifty years ago, but who still spoke English with a marked Italian accent. He told reporters he had no idea who the slain man was. When informed that he was almost certainly a known gangster named Andrew Faviola, he shrugged and said he didn't know this, but he hoped someone would by the way pay for the damages to his place.

He did not know who the dead woman was, either, and he had no idea whether they'd come in together or not. When one of the reporters suggested that the woman had possibly come there to *dine* with the murdered man, Gianetti said he supposed they might have been there for dinner, though five-fifteen was a little early to be eating; normally, they didn't start serving till six. In any event, he was sorry this had happened here in his restaurant.

The cashier told them that the man had come in first, and was waiting for the woman when she came in. A black town car had dropped her off at the curb, but the cashier hadn't noticed the license plate. It seemed to her she'd seen these two before, though, seemed to remember them coming here some months back, she couldn't remember exactly when, and sitting at that same table.

The investigating detectives tossed the dead woman and

found in her handbag a current New York State driver's license that gave her name as Sarah Welles. A laminated ID card with her picture on it stated that Sarah Fitch Welles was a member of the teaching staff of the Greer Academy on East Sixtieth Street in Manhattan.

They did not learn until later that day that she was the wife of an assistant district attorney.

The *New York Post* headlined it **DEADLY IRONY**.

The inside story raised more questions than anyone in the District Attorney's Office was willing to answer "at this point in time," as Chief Charles Scanlon of the Organized Crime Unit was quoted as saying. There was no question but that Sarah Fitch Welles was the wife of the unit's *deputy* chief, a man named Michael Welles, who was responsible for sending away the Lombardi Crew, which before his successful investigation and prosecution had been a powerful arm of the selfsame Faviola family run by the murdered hoodlum. Apparently, Mr. and Mrs. Welles had planned to meet at the restaurant for an early dinner. She'd arrived before him, and was caught in the deadly hail of bullets as she passed Faviola's table on her way back from the ladies' room.

The *Post* asked why the reservations book showed no listing for a party of two in the name of Welles. The *Post* asked why the cashier seemed certain the two murder victims had been sitting at the same table. The *Post* asked why one of the waiters thought he'd seen the murder victims holding hands and in deep conversation shortly before the gunmen came in. The *Post* asked why one of the busboys thought he'd seen Faviola trying to yank the woman away from the table as the two assassins approached. The *Post* asked whether the District Attorney's Office was in the habit of sending town cars to pick up and drop off the wives of salaried employees.

In the coverage of Sarah's funeral two days later, a good

photograph of Luretta Barnes appeared on the front page of the *Times*'s Metro Section. It showed her coming out of the funeral home, weeping. The caption under it read: **GRIEVING STUDENT LEAVES CHAPEL**.

Up where Luretta lived, nobody read the *Times*.

The meeting had been called for the Monday following the sumptuous funeral given Andrew Faviola. Bobby Triani called the meeting, and it was held in a place they all knew to be absolutely clear of any eavesdropping devices. This was the notorious Club Sorrento on Elizabeth Street, which was so full of bugs you'd have thought it was a mattress.

The two detectives assigned to the wiretap were working under a re-up court order granting permission to listen for yet another thirty days. They did not know the voices of all the wiseguys gathered here, so they listened very carefully for mention of identifying names.

Bobby Triani, they knew.

"This is a terrible thing that has happened here to the family," he said, "the loss of this great man, especially in a time of increased activity and prosperity."

"He sounds like a fuckin *banker*," one of the detectives said.

"Shhh," the other one said.

"I want to promise each and every one of you here today," Triani said, "that we won't rest till we find out who did this, and till this murder is revenged. Not only to prove this won't happen again while *I'm* around, but also out of respect to the man who was killed."

"May he rest in peace," someone said.

"The minute we find out . . ." Triani said, and there was a sound that resembled *zzsstt*. The detectives figured he was running his finger across his throat like a razor, indicating what would be done to the assassins the moment their identity was known. Too bad you couldn't show an unseen, unheard gesture in court.

"As you know," he said, abruptly switching gears, "the stuff arrived from Italy a week ago," never once mentioning *what* stuff, even though the club was as sacred as the Vatican when it came to anybody listening, "and is already being distributed to our various people throughout the city. In short, Anthony Faviola's plan is in motion. The stuff is here and will be hitting the streets any day now. Our hope is to retail it for a dollar, attract new customers that way. Very soon, thanks to Anthony, and thanks to Andrew, too, who made sure the original plan got the legs it needed, there'll be more money pouring in than we know what to do with. This will require new thinking, new ideas. I'm hoping this new leadership will be able to come up with plans that will be acceptable to all of us. Me, Petey Bardo as my second, and Sal Bonifacio under him. I think you all know . . ."

There was a round of applause.

"Thank you," a new voice said.

"*Grazie mille,*" another new voice said.

"Okay, okay," Triani said. "Thank you, okay. I think you all know what kind of experience these two men have had, and what kind of people they are. I want you to know . . ."

"Yeah, they're fuckin *hoodlums,*" one of the detectives said.

". . . first order of . . ."

"Shhhh."

". . . business will be to find the two bastards who did this murder. I promise you we will not *rest* till our honor's been . . ."

"Bullshit," one of the detectives said.

"Shhh," the other one said, and grinned. "Pay a little respect here, huh?"

Mollie could not understand how the man who'd saved her life last December happened to be in that same restaurant where her mother was killed last Wednesday. Six months since they'd seen him, and all at once he pops up in the same restaurant where catastrophe is about to happen. This was *some* odd coincidence, it seemed to her, something she'd have surely asked her mother about, if only her mother were still alive.

She could not believe all the things the newspapers were saying about Andrew, whose name it now turned out wasn't really *Farrell*, but was instead *Faviola*. How could the person they'd had *dinner* with shortly after Christmas last year be the leader of a powerful crime family, a person the newspapers were calling the "Boss," as if he were Bruce Springsteen? The *Boss* having an early dinner in a little Italian restaurant in Brooklyn, where coincidentally, mind you, her mother and father were *also* meeting for dinner. Small wonder that all the newspapers were just *full* of speculation and innuendo as to what the ADA's beautiful young blond wife was really doing in that place last Wednesday.

What the newspapers did not know was that Sarah Fitch Welles—they kept adding her maiden name, as if she were Hillary Rodham Clinton—had met Andrew Faviola six months earlier. Only *Mollie* knew this. Well, her father knew it, too, but in a slightly different way; they had told him all about Andrew *Farrell*, the nice young man who'd saved her life. So what the hell was her mother doing in that restaurant with him last Wednesday?

Well, *with* him, who says she was actually *with* him?

Her father insisted he'd been on the way to meet her there, so Mollie had to believe the restaurant employees were mistaken about her mother sitting there with a gangster, holding hands with a gangster, in deep conversation with a . . .

Was Andrew *really* a gangster?

That was his picture in all the papers, unmistakably his picture.

The Boss.

Who the DA's Office was saying had been sitting there alone when her mother accidentally walked past his table into a "deadly fusillade," as the *Daily News* called it. But wouldn't her mother have *recognized* Andrew on the way to the ladies' room? Wouldn't she have yelled "*Andrew!* How nice to *see* you again! Do you remember saving Mollie's life, do you remember saving my darling daughter's life?" Wouldn't she have *recognized* him, for Christ's sake? *I* would have recognized him in a minute.

Mom, she thought, Mommy, she thought, what were you doing in that restaurant last Wednesday?

She thought maybe she should ask her father if he really had been on his way to meet her when this thing happened. When her mother got murdered last Wednesday. Instead, she asked him if all the stuff they were saying about this Andrew Faviola person was true.

Her father said, "Yes, Mollie, it's all true."

So she didn't tell him Andrew Faviola was the same Andrew Farrell who'd once saved her life a long time ago, when she was just a kid.

Michael found the pages while he was going through Sarah's effects. He found them in an envelope in her attaché case, along with several other papers she'd been carrying home from school last Wednesday.

The pages were typewritten, double-spaced on good bond paper.

They had been written by someone named Luretta Barnes, whom Michael recalled Sarah mentioning every now and then, one of her best students, wasn't she?

Typed onto the first page was the title *What I Will Do This Summer.*

Sitting on the French lieutenant's bed in the den where first he'd played the incriminating tapes for Sarah, the grandfather clock ticking noisily down the hall, he thought at first that this was an assignment Sarah had given the kids. But he knew her well enough . . .

Had *thought* he'd known her well enough . . .

Had once, long ago, thought he'd known Sarah better than any woman on earth . . .

Still . . .

Knowing her . . .

. . . this *did* seem a somewhat simplistic assignment to have given any of her classes, even the youngest ones. So he had to assume the student, this Luretta Barnes, had come up with the title herself and was using it to put spin on all the "What I Did *Last* Summer" papers she'd been forced to write ever since kindergarten.

Her intent became immediately apparent the moment Michael began reading:

What I will do this summer . . .

When school lets out . . .

What I will do . . .

I think I'll watch the clockers and the dealers and the dopers doing their dance of death on this block in hell where I live, and I'll hope to stay alive.

What I will do this summer . . .

I think I'll dodge the bullets of the dealers firing nines from their sleek deadly drive-by machines, and I'll leap over pools of blood on my way to church each Sunday, where I'll pray to stay alive.

What I will do this summer . . .

I think I'll stare at infants in withdrawal in their cribs and I'll curse their junkie moms and the pricks who sold them death, but I'll plan to stay alive.

What I will do this summer . . .

I'll keep running from the man who's trying to rape me where I live in hell and I'll pray to God every day he dies of an overdose before he succeeds because I don't know if I have the strength to stay alive even though I plan to.

At least until the fall.

Because in the fall ...

In the fall, I'll move from here to another world where there's a beautiful woman I would like to be someday.

In the fall, I'll go back to her and become alive again.

Until next summer, at least.

What I will do *next* summer, I think, I'll start counting the days and weeks and months till autumn.

And ... if I can survive hell one more time ...

I'll go back to my school and my teacher.

Michael was suddenly sobbing. Alone on the cast iron bed, he wept uncontrollably, until at last he was able to catch his breath again. Drying his eyes, still clutching the pages in his hand, he went to find his daughter in the empty apartment.

Luretta kept wondering if Mrs. Welles had ever got around to reading those pages she'd given her. She guessed maybe she hadn't. Probably planned to read them sooner or later, maybe after she got home from dinner with her husband one night, walked instead into something worse than any drive-by.

Up here where Luretta lived, the drive-bys were a common thing, you learned to live with them, same as you learned to live with a junkie chasing after you all the time, trying to get in your pants, she'd kill him next time. She had sworn that in church on Sunday, she would kill him the next time he came at her. Mrs. Welles had taught her April was the cruellest month, but she'd been wrong. *June* was really the month that got you. June was when you had to face it, girl.

> Let us go then, you and I,
> When the evening is spread out against the sky.

Luretta walked through this evening spread against the sky, seeing this place where she lived with laser-beam eyes. White-hot laser cutting through the jiveass dealers on every corner, pushing their six-bit hits off of crack pipes. White-hot eyes burning through hookers no older than herself strutting like movie stars in high heels and silk, selling blowjobs to cruising motorists for twenty bucks a throw. Her ears tuned out the incessant word *fuck* that rang on the air like a one-note call-and-response. Her ears closed to the screaming police sirens, and the screaming fire engines, and the rapping of the automatic pistols, and the rage everywhere, the white-hot rage reduced to cold dead ashes by her white-hot eyes and her indifferent ears. She wished to be Eliot's hyacinth girl, her arms full, her hair wet, speechless, neither living nor dead, looking into the heart of light, the silence. He had written of a heap of broken images where the sun beat. He had written of a cry of fear in a handful of dust. Walking alone and breathing deeply of a night turned suddenly gentle by the first flush hint of summer, Luretta wished with all her heart that Sarah Fitch Welles was still alive to show her what roots might clutch, what branches grow out of this stony rubbish.

On the ninth day of June, the day before Hanover Prep and most of the other private schools in the city were scheduled to close for the summer, Winona Weingarten took the M-11 bus uptown from where she lived on Seventy-fifth and West End, and then walked through Morningside Park on her way to the old stone building behind the cathedral.

It was a beautiful day, the kind New York City was often blessed with in early summer, the sky a piercing blue,

the air crisp and clear. Winona was wearing the school uniform with the short pleated skirt and the white blouse and
blue jacket with the crest over the pocket.

"Hey, kid," the voice called.

She turned to look.

A black man was sitting on one of the park benches.

"Wanna try suppin *new*," he said, "fly you to the
moon?"

"No, *thanks*," Winona said.

"Coss you on'y a dollah," the man said, and flashed a
wide entreating grin.

Winona shook her head and hurried past.

But her heart was pounding.

And she wondered if he'd be there again tomorrow.